MUFFIN MAN

BRANDON WHITINGTON

Also by Brad Whittington

Novels

Welcome to Fred

Living with Fred

Escape from Fred

Non-fiction

What Would Jesus Drink?
What the Bible Really Says About Alcohol

BRAD WHITTINGTON

MUFFIN MAN

{ A NOVEL }

WUNDERFOOL

W/P

PRESS

ISBN: 978-1-937274-14-6

Published by Wunderfool Press
Austin, Texas

Dewey Decimal Classification: F
Subject Heading: Fiction / Mystery & Detective / General

CONTENTS

What they're saying about Whittington

Whittington spins an enjoyable literary story and is definitely a novelist to watch. –Publisher's Weekly

Brad Whittington is an artist with a pen.
–Ethan C. McDonald, DancingWord.com

It is always a joy to find a new writer who knows what he's doing.
–Rick Lewis, Logos Bookstore

Whittington is a welcome new voice in the world of fiction.
–Cindy Crosby, author of *By Willoway Brook*

Who can resist a story of someone else's alienated youth if that someone else is as talented as Brad Whittington?
–JT Conroe, author of *The Blue Hotel*

The pacing, humor, honesty, and believable characters made me turn page after page in rapid succession until there were none.
–T Leigh

Brad Whittington paints some of the best word pictures I've seen.
–Cammi Ellis

What they're saying about Muffin Man

Brad Whittington is not only back, he's at his best. I haven't been this excited about a new fictional detective since Martin Walker's *Bruno, Chief of Police*. Have no doubt: *Muffin Man* delivers!
–J. Mark Bertrand, author of *Back on Murder* and *Pattern of Wounds*

I love the way Brad Whittington writes. Smooth and snappy as jazz. Whittington has baked up a winner in Muffin Man. With dry wit, poignant humanity, and a setting as rich as Texas earth, Whittington proves his flair for storytelling once again.
A great book.
–Tosca Lee, NY Times bestselling author of *Demon: A Memoir*, *Havah: The Story of Eve*, and *The Books of Mortals* series

For Jeremy,

Who sat not in the seat of the scoffers
but delighted in the muffin
from the beginning

Selah

Doubt thou the stars are fire;
Doubt that the sun doth move;
Doubt truth to be a liar;
But never doubt I love.
- Polonius, *Hamlet*

DAY 1: TUESDAY

At 1:32 p.m. on Tuesday, Sheriff John Lawson was unexpectedly seduced into a battle to the death.

It was more of a siege, really.

On one side, the long and painful death of his body. On the other, the long and painful death of his soul. And in the middle, a sheet of butcher paper.

On the butcher paper, Stella's beef ribs. Three in number. Three, the number of completeness.

Three ribs, three states of matter, three blind mice, three dimensions, three stooges, three musketeers, three-legged stools, three-cornered hats, three days in the belly of the great fish, three days in the grave, three knocks on the ceiling if you want me. But most of all, three ribs.

At least once a week John walked through Stella's door at one-thirty to savor the beef ribs and contemplate the divine unity of the universe.

The event that had transformed his normally idyllic lunch into a skirmish of second guessing was his morning doctor's appointment, the one where he got the test results. Doc had called his glucose numbers prediabetic, but he wasn't tentative about the cholesterol numbers. Off the charts was the most charitable phrase he uttered as he shoved a wad of prescriptions in John's hand.

John had left the medical plaza on autopilot. He was through the line at Stella's and planted at the table before he connected the numbers on the paper in his pocket with the items on the butcher paper.

He could eat the ribs and tap a nail into his coffin, or he could walk away, pick up a salad at Flo's, and drive a spike into his soul.

John could understand it if he had a dunlap gut, but he was long and lean and always had been, no matter what he ate. How could he have a three-alarm cholesterol count?

He toyed with the side dishes, working his way obliquely to the ribs, like a ranch hand indifferently approaching a skittish colt. No sauce, just meat. The black pepper on them teased his nostrils. Then he heard his call sign from the radio on his belt.

Everybody knew not to interrupt him on his lunch break, especially at Stella's. He set down a forkful of coleslaw and thumbed his radio.

"What's up, Sam?"

"Sorry, boss. I thought you should take this one. It's Cook Brothers."

"Picketers getting out of hand?"

"They stormed the warehouse and barricaded theirselves in the storeroom."

John frowned and thought about this an extra second. "Pastor Jackson?"

"No, he's not on site. It's two of his people."

He looked at the ribs. "Hostages?"

"No, sir. They're in there by theirselves."

"Weapons? Injuries?"

"No, sir."

He considered finishing lunch first, but decided against it. You don't rush your way through forbidden fruit. You savor every illicit second. "On my way. Have Lovejoy meet me there."

"10-4. Sorry."

John surveyed the virginal plains of his lunch. Three untouched beef ribs lying parallel at an angle, half a cup of coleslaw, a small pyramid of fried okra, and the hollow circles of a few slices of red onion. Arrayed on the shiny side of a scrap of butcher paper, it looked like barbecue hieroglyphics.

He could probably encase it in Lucite and sell it to the Museum of Modern Art in New York City for half his annual salary. But wasting good barbecue is a crime in Texas.

John stood, pushed his grey felt Stetson on his head, and levered his lanky legs over the picnic-table bench. He carried his provisions between the rows of picnic tables, past other diners possibly experiencing existential crises of their own, or not.

The proprietor perched on a barstool behind the counter. John set down his lunch with an apologetic sigh. "I'm sorry, Stella. Could you bag this for me?"

Stella was a short wiry black woman who had terrorized three hulking boys all the way to pro football and beyond. She shook her head as she transferred the okra to a cardboard take-out box. "You got to take time for the things that matter, Sheriff Lawson."

"Yes, ma'am. That's why I'm saving them for later."

Stella's face relaxed slightly, from censure to concern. She slid off the stool, carried the coleslaw to the line and topped it off. Then she put it all in a paper bag with the Stella's Kitchen logo on it.

"Stella, it's a testament to your cooking that they're almost as good cold. Right, Jessie?"

Jessie replied without looking up from slicing brisket. "I heard that."

Stella pushed the bag across the counter. "You be careful, wherever you're rushing off to, Sheriff. There are evil men out there, lovers of darkness who hate the light for fear that their deeds will be exposed."

"I heard that," John said, wondering how it applied to the church folk barricaded in the Cook Brothers Construction storage room.

Jessie stopped slicing, glanced up at John and smiled. Stella swiveled on her stool. Jessie put his head back down and resumed slicing the brisket.

John walked out of the dim cool of Stella's Kitchen into the full heat of a Texas August afternoon. He was in his shirtsleeves and tie, his black suit jacket on a hanger behind the driver's seat, but he felt like he was rolled in an electric blanket in a convection oven inside a sealed boxcar on the train to hell. Even the dust of the dirt parking lot was too beat to kick up much of a fuss.

He climbed into the cab of a dusty brown pickup with a sheriff's department logo on the door. A patina of sweat had already formed on his brow. He set the bag in the passenger seat, started the engine, and cranked the AC to MAX.

As John waited to turn onto the highway, Deputy Lovejoy sped past in a cruiser, lights flashing and siren wailing. Lovejoy was barely out of the academy, so new the shine hadn't worn off yet. He'd calm down once he figured out that small-town football and small-town law enforcement didn't have that much in common. John learned early on that the job was less about testosterone and brute force and more about vigilance and the well-placed word.

Lovejoy would learn, eventually. Maybe. If not, John would suggest that greater career opportunities awaited him in San Antonio or Austin. But he'd give him a few years first.

John pulled out of the gravel lot onto the two-lane blacktop and proceeded at the speed limit without lights or siren. The church folk locked in the storeroom would keep. He wondered if he knew them.

Like its neighbors in south central Texas, Bolero County had a population under 10,000. As a result, John originally knew all one hundred or so members in the sleepy little Hill Country church. But then Pastor Jackson arrived. He took his title as fisher of men seriously. He got a radio show and Sunday morning TV slot and began reeling them in from the bluffs and arroyos of south Texas. Within a few years he had enough people and cash to hire Cook Brothers to build a megachurch with a 2,000-seat auditorium. John didn't even know a tenth of the members anymore.

Here on the edge of the Edwards Plateau, people tended to spread out. Farm-to-ranch and farm-to-market roads snaked through the rugged landscape, flanked by oak and mountain cedar and thick undergrowth, sometimes rising and falling and twisting between limestone outcroppings and dry creek beds, and at other times straightening out on a bare mesa blanketed with prairie grass and dotted with cactus, agave, mesquite, and granite lumps, affording arresting southwest vistas of the south Texas plains.

In more recent years, developers had snatched up the high ground and carved it into oversized build-to-suit lots inside gated communities where mainly outsiders lived bunched up, like folks in San Antonio or Laredo.

Like Jim Battles. John spotted a *Battles for Sheriff* campaign sign on the side of the road. It was an election year and for the first time since he took the job from his ex-father-in-law in a brutal campaign, John had an opponent.

Last year Battles, a police chief from the Dallas-Fort Worth metroplex, had retired after twenty years on the force and come down to Bolero. He evidently saw the job of county sheriff as a diverting pastime for his twilight years. John suspected Judge Gibson put him up to it.

He forced his eyes away from the sign. His gaze fell on the bag of ribs and he thought how good they would taste after he dealt with the church folk.

He wasn't far from the Cook Brothers compound. He tried to remember the layout inside the warehouse. The offices were up front, of course, built out years ago in paneling, indoor-outdoor carpet, and acoustic ceiling tiles. If he remembered correctly, the storeroom was behind the offices, out in the open space of the warehouse, which meant the protesters didn't have to go through the offices to get to it. They could have come in through the warehouse door.

The cell phone rang over the noise of the AC. He picked up the phone.

"Hey, Mom."

"Honey, is this a bad time?"

"Not for the next ten minutes."

"I wanted to tell you . . ." Her voice faded out, temporarily replaced by the sound of rustling paper, the Austin *Statesman* she had delivered daily. "You have to hear this. It says right here, 'Expect big changes in your relationships, both personal and professional. It's a very liberating time.'"

"I thought my sign changed."

"Oh, honey, you're definitely a Libra. You couldn't possibly be a Virgo. Not the way you eat."

John pulled a newspaper from between the seats and dropped it over the bag of ribs. He mocked the daily horoscope reading, but sometimes she scared him.

"This horoscope," Mom said. "I think it's a sign."

John waited, but was met with silence. He finally said, "Of what?"

"You'll never guess who is here."

"At the shop?"

"It's my day off. I'm at home. And Rusty is here with me."

It took a few milliseconds to register.

"What's he doing here?" The sun-drenched highway seemed to recede to a pinpoint an infinity away, like the truck was speeding in reverse. The washed-out blue of the summer sky bleached to a pale gray. John blinked his eyes and shook his head.

Mom's voice came over the phone as if from a long distance. "He's come back."

"Where has he been? What does he want?" Dread mixed with adrenaline in a nauseating cocktail.

"Want? Nothing. He's just back, back with his family where he belongs."

John felt his heart rate double. "Mom, he can't move in!" He realized he was shouting and took a few deep breaths to bring his pulse down.

"Honey, I should have read you this first. 'Old misunderstandings with friends or family may resurface, especially if you feel taken for granted. Don't let the past sabotage the future.' That was my horoscope this morning. And while I was eating lunch, I read your father's horoscope. 'It's a time to look objectively at your relationships. This can be a fruitful period in which to learn what you truly value.' And then the doorbell rang and there he was."

This was quintessential Mom. Take in every stray. Donate to every charity. Support every freeloader. Forgive every offense. But this was beyond even her most extravagant indulgence.

"No, Mom," John said with a forced calm. "After twenty years he's not going to waltz back in like nothing happened."

"Now, John, remember the Lord's Prayer. Forgive us as we forgive others. You want your sins to be forgiven, don't you?"

"I'll take my chances." Forgive the man who drained the bank account and disappeared, forcing her to take a job at the beauty shop to avoid foreclosure?

"People change, John."

"Do they? Ask him if he's on his medication."

"Here, dear, I'll let you talk to him."

"No, Mom! Don't put him on the phone! I don't want to—"

Rusty's voice came over the line. "Hello, son."

Even after twenty years, that maddening tone still had the power to infuriate John, Rusty's calm conviction that despite the obvious facts, any conflict or unrest originated somewhere else, anywhere else but with him or his actions.

"I told her . . . Why are you here?"

"How have you been, John? Deborah tells me you're the sheriff, now. When did Weiss retire?"

Sheriff Weiss didn't retire. It was a long story and probably none of it would have happened if Rusty had not abandoned them twenty-four years earlier. But John had no intention of encouraging a conversation.

"Don't bother to unpack your suitcase. I'll be there in a few minutes."

John ended the call and tossed the phone against the bag of ribs. He looked down and realized he was driving twenty miles over the speed limit. He jerked his foot off the accelerator, placed his hands on the wheel at ten and two, checked his mirrors, and took several deep breaths.

The Cook Brothers sign loomed into view. He braked and took the turn into the gravel parking lot too fast. A crowd of picketers turned to see him fishtail in. He probably looked like Lovejoy scurrying to a crime scene.

The truck came to a noisy stop in the gravel yard in a cloud of dust next to a bus that had *Abundant Life Tabernacle* emblazoned on the side. In smaller letters below it, *I came that you may have life, and have it more abundantly.* He grabbed his hat and jacket, jumped out and slammed the door, noting with annoyance that a KHIL-TV news truck from San Antonio was parked on the other side of the bus. He pulled on his suit jacket, hoping to trap some of the cool of the truck cab against his skin, but before he had taken three steps, he felt himself sweating.

Cook Brothers owned dozens of equipment yards, scattered from Austin to Brownsville and Del Rio to Port Arthur. It faced the highway, bordered by woods on the other three sides. A gravel driveway led to a gravel parking lot and twenty or so acres fenced with chain-link topped with barbed wire. The yard held rows of front-end loaders, forklifts, cherry pickers, welding rigs, and a large warehouse in the front right corner.

The warehouse held equipment and material that couldn't be left out and the offices, which were at the front. Between the office doors and the parking lot, a landscaped garden with cement benches encircled two flagpoles where the US and Texas flags hung limp and dispirited in the humid afternoon. Pastor Jackson stood near the flagpoles, talking to the news crew.

John ignored them and walked past the office door toward the church folk crowded in front of the gate to the yard, thankful that the jacket would hide the sweat. They seemed defeated by the heat, their protest signs hanging from their hands like coal shovels. He pushed through the gauntlet to the Cook Brothers security guard, Billy Swallow, a local boy about the same age as Lovejoy. He held an axe handle. Sweat dripped from his chin.

John nodded. "Hey, Billy."

Billy nodded back.

The motorized gate was partially knocked off its track. A heavy chain had been looped through it to the fence. John looked around at the docile crowd. He recognized some of them, members in good standing at the Abundant Life Tabernacle. A few nodded a greeting, but said nothing. He looked back to Billy.

"These folks been giving you some trouble?"

Billy slapped the axe handle into the palm of his hand. "Not anymore. But two of them broke through here and got inside before I could stop them."

He pointed the axe handle at the warehouse doors, twenty feet tall and pulled open about ten feet. A voice boomed from the darkness within. "Come out with your hands up!"

John looked a question at Billy.

"Oh, that's Tyler, I mean Deputy Lovejoy. He told me to come out here and make sure nobody else got through the gate."

"Where are they? The two that got in?"

"The storeroom. They barricaded the door."

"Do we know who it is?"

Billy shook his head.

John turned to the church folks. "Anybody know who it was that broke in?"

They were a dispirited lot. The excitement of the break-in had faded and the heat had taken over.

A blonde girl caught his eye. Her sign read, "The 1st Commandment is Not a Suggestion." She dragged it behind her back and John saw that the other side said, "The 1st Amendment is Not a Suggestion." It had a certain symmetry to it, John conceded.

He turned to the man standing next to her, Dr. Ellis, who had done his root canal last year. Ellis held a "Stop Religious Persecution" sign loosely at his side.

John considered this sign a bit over the top, but not out of line with Pastor Jackson's polarizing views. To John's mind, if the members had worried less about persecution and more about fire-code compliance, they would still have a church building.

John suspected that Ellis would have trouble sleeping tonight, if not from a guilty conscience, then from the sunburned scalp glaring from beneath his comb-over.

"Dr. Ellis, do you know who it was that broke through the fence?"

Ellis stepped forward, eager to help. "No. We didn't really see them. We were picketing by the front door and he," Ellis pointed his sign at Billy, "came out and said we had to leave or they would call you."

John looked at the other sweaty and mostly sunburned church folks. They nodded. He looked at Billy, who confirmed the statement with a shrug. He turned back to Ellis.

"And then?"

Ellis licked his lips and glanced at his cohorts. "We held hands in a circle around the flagpoles and started praying," he said and stood defiantly, breathing heavily through his nose.

John turned to Billy. "And?"

Billy's expression implied a fraternal circle that excluded mere civilians. "I was preparing to take appropriate measures when I heard the noise at the gate. That's how they got the jump on me. This bunch created a distraction." He pointed the axe handle at the chastened protesters and then slapped it into his palm, again.

"I think we can dispense with that." John nodded at the axe handle.

"Sir?" Billy said, a hint of betrayal in his voice.

"You have it under control. Why don't you just set that inside the fence? It'll be handy if they start any trouble."

Billy's hesitation betrayed his doubts as to the wisdom of this advice. John smiled at him. Billy hefted the axe handle wistfully, then slipped it through the gap and rested it against the fence.

John turned back to Ellis. "Is anyone missing from your group?"

Ellis scanned the faces of his conspirators in civil disobedience. The other protesters did the same. Some nodded, some shook their heads, some looked away. Ellis turned back to John.

"I don't think so."

John could see that nailing down a complete list of the protestors was about as likely as stacking marbles on a basketball.

"I need your contact information so I can get a statement from you later, and then I think it's best if you all go home."

There was a murmur from the church folk. Dr. Ellis stepped up.

"We have a right to protest. This is a lawful assembly."

"You do have a right to protest on public property. You'll have to take it off the Cook Brothers property to the right of way along the road."

There was a long moment as the church folk looked to Dr. Ellis, who seemed reluctant to resign the campaign. He turned to John, who gazed back steadily. Ellis glanced at Billy, who responded with the most intimidating glare in his arsenal.

"And you'll need to move the bus, too," John added.

The standoff held for another ten seconds. John checked his watch as if anticipating some official deadline after which he would round them up and cart them off to jail.

Ellis addressed the group. "Okay, let's go." The protesters began to shuffle off, dragging their signs behind them.

"Wait," John called out to them.

They stopped and looked back, confused.

John glanced at Billy. "Go get a pad and a pen."

Billy trotted off to the office.

John turned back to the protestors. "I have to go inside and sort this out, but there's no need for you all to wait out here in the sun. Give Billy your contact information and I'll get statements from you later."

They grumbled, complaining about the heat, although up to now they had been happy to fry for Jesus. But they stayed.

John crossed the gravel parking lot toward the office entrance where a TV reporter interviewed Pastor Jackson under the flags. John frowned. On the radio, Sam had said Jackson wasn't here. Jackson must have gotten the word from his flock and conveniently brought a news crew along when he came.

If Jackson wasn't here when the incident happened, there was no need to talk to him, yet, which was fine with John, since the pastor's line of reasoning tended to be as straight as the Frio River, and about as clear as well.

John skirted past talk about the founding fathers coming to this country to escape this kind of religious intolerance. John didn't wait around to hear how Jackson connected the dots between persecution and his church burning down without crossing the line to libel. Jackson had previously claimed that Cook Brothers intentionally installed a faulty fire suppression system because of a Hidden Agenda to Destroy the Church. Jackson frequently spoke in capitals, and it had taken the threat of a libel suit from Cook to tone down the rhetoric.

John stepped into the comparative dim chill of the office. He wanted to get through to the warehouse before he acclimated to the air conditioning. Once you were in the heat, it was best to stay there until you could quit it altogether.

Nadine looked up and smiled."Thank God you're here, Sheriff." Her drawl was so dense it could seine for minnows. She dabbed at her nose with a tissue.

Like many office dwellers in Texas, Nadine wore a sweater during the summer. Businesses tended to over-refrigerate their offices, creating more than one case of summer sniffles, particularly for women who liked to go shopping, due to the systemic shock of extreme temperature change while popping in and out of stores and coffee shops and theaters.

"Hey, Nadine," John said.

The office was built in the late sixties and left in pristine condition, like the bedroom of a Vietnam soldier that never returned. Mass-produced prints of bucolic scenes hung on paneled walls, mixed with a series of dust-encrusted mounted fish, primarily big-mouth bass, probably caught in Medina Lake. Fluorescent light fixtures dotted the drop-tile ceiling. Orange plastic furniture and vintage copies of *Field and Stream* were available for the comfort of visitors.

In the wall on the left, a gigantic pane of glass revealed the work processes of Bert Masters, the manager. Inside the fishbowl, Bert was on the phone and apparently not very happy about it.

Without glancing at Bert, Nadine pressed an intercom button with an overly manicured but stubby finger. John heard her voice echo from ceiling speakers in multiple rooms. "Bert, Sheriff Lawson is here."

"No need to bother Bert. I'll find Deputy Lovejoy." John stepped toward the hall. "Is he back this way?"

"No trouble. Bert said he wanted to talk to you, first."

From his office, Bert looked up, held up a finger, and stood. He bent over the desk, gradually leaning his head toward the base of the phone, still talking and still holding up a finger.

Nadine leaned forward, thumped her elbows on the desk, dropped her chin in her hands, and sighed loudly. Although short and dumpy, with a backhoe-operator husband and two kids in high school, Nadine had not allowed life to tame her. She wore a snazzy blouse and skirt, like she was going out for dinner and a show in Branson. Her sweater wasn't some frumpy beige cardigan she kept on the back of her chair in off hours, but a slinky black wrap filigreed with silver thread, something John's ex-wife would have worn.

Nadine looked up at John without moving her head, like a coquettish basset hound hoping for a slice of cheese. "Sheriff, this business has got on my last nerve. Darlene's got cheerleader camp coming up, I have to cart Scooter around to job interviews, those folks are out here picketing every day, and now this. I'm fit to be tied."

John watched Bert. By now he was leaning so far over while holding the phone to his head that it looked like he was ironing his ear. But he still held one finger aloft, indicating that his freedom from this torture was imminent.

John turned back to Nadine. "Did you see the incident?"

Nadine snorted. "I don't have time for that. I was filing invoices. There was a bunch of shouting and running and banging around. Then it got real quiet, if you don't count Billy yelling, 'You come out of there right now!' Then Deputy Lovejoy showed up and took over the yelling."

"John, come on in." Bert stood at the door of his office, holding it open.

John nodded to Nadine and followed Bert into his office. Bert closed the door and sat behind the desk. He gestured to a chair, but John remained standing with one hand on the door knob.

"I need this like I need another ex-wife," Bert said. "First we got the Tabernacle thing, then the whole Bolero High School thing, and now this. I'm spending more time with officials and investigators and lawyers than I am with contractors and suppliers."

"I need to get the status from Deputy Lovejoy ASAP, Bert."

"I can tell you the status. Tyler is standing outside the storeroom door with his pistol drawn. Every ninety seconds he yells, 'Come on out with your hands up,' like a cuckoo clock." Bert waved at the phone. "And Cook is climbing up my back, saying that when he watches the news tonight, he wants the lead story to be Pastor Luke being hauled off to jail in handcuffs."

"We don't know that Luke Jackson had anything to do with this."

"It was his people."

"We don't know that, either."

"He got here soon enough, and with a news crew, so he must have known something about it."

"I'll get to him when the cameras leave. Right now the priority is getting the people out of the storeroom and off your property." John pulled the door open.

"And Luther called. He wanted me to keep him informed of how you're handling the crisis."

John froze, then shut the door slowly, turned to Bert and stared at him. Like the county sheriff, the county judge was elected and accountable only to the people. Luther Gibson had no authority over John, other than overseeing the budget.

He thought about why Judge Gibson would be monitoring things through a back channel. He suspected this was about the upcoming election. But why did Bert mention it instead of keeping it to himself. Gibson wasn't the shy type. If he had wanted John to know he was checking up on him, he would have called him directly. Was Bert giving him a warning or making a threat?

John considered what little he knew about Bert. It wasn't like they were close. They saw each other around town, at the Lion's Club fish fry and football games and such things. He knew Bert made his own beer and spent weekends all over the state competing in chili cook-offs. That was about it.

John had a skill essential for a law enforcement officer, the ability to process things without talking them through. A wordless but focused stare could make a nervous suspect blurt out all kinds of things, usually incriminating.

He stared at Bert, but Bert wasn't nervous and he didn't blurt. He just stared back. The only sound was the loud shush of the air conditioner vent near John's head. Then the AC shut off and the silence was deafening.

John opened his mouth to respond but was stopped by a noise coming from the duct. It sounded like the buzzing of flies. He stepped to the duct and put his ear against it. The droning morphed into a raspy muttering voice. An occasional word or two surfaced.

"*zzzz . . . zzzz . . . fortuitous concourse . . . zzzz . . . zzzz . . .*"

Bert cleared his throat. "John, you okay?"

John held up his hand for quiet.

"*zzzz . . . than nothing . . . zzzz*"

Bert walked around his desk and stood facing John, his ear to the vent. Their faces were inches apart as they stood motionless, listening intently. From outside they probably looked like two lovers gazing into each other's eyes just before kissing. John glanced out the window. Nadine stared at them from the filing cabinet, her head cocked like a baffled basset hound. John felt the sweat on his torso congealing into a second skin.

"*zzzz . . . fresco*"

Then a faint shouting. "Come out with your hands up!"

Bert shook his head. He started to speak, but his phone rang. He rushed to the desk.

John walked to the door, but heard a muffled thumping and Lovejoy's voice, again. "Hey, what are you doing in there?" He stepped back to the vent.

Then he caught a whiff of something. "Call the fire department," he yelled to Bert, who looked up, puzzled.

John tore through the door and down the hall, past offices with estimators and draftsmen who stared as he ran past. The hall ended at a door as he remembered. He burst through into the heat of the warehouse, barely noticing it. Lovejoy banged on the storeroom door with his fist. Smoke seeped around the door jamb.

John pushed him aside, tried the knob, which was locked, and then leaned back and planted a solid flat-footed kick next to the handle. The top of the door gave, the jamb splintered, and the door budged slightly, letting out more smoke. John pushed again, but it was blocked.

He stepped back. Drawn by the noise, people from the office trickled into the warehouse. John waved them back.

"There's a fire. Go out the front entrance and wait in the parking lot." Some of them hesitated, not wanting to miss the action, but others turned as Bert burst out of the office. John pointed to him. "Get a fire extinguisher."

He turned to Lovejoy and motioned to the storeroom door. Finally offered a task that was suited to his skills, Lovejoy holstered his weapon, took a three-point stance, and slammed his full weight against the door with his shoulder. There was the sound of wood splintering and the doorknob hung loose. The next two hits didn't make much difference. The smoke thinned out and wafted to the rafters of the warehouse. The fourth hit produced a screeching sound of metal on metal and a loud crash. John was able to see into the room.

A metal shelf had been leaned against the door under the doorknob, wedged against shelves on the opposite wall. The battering had finally bent the legs on the shelf upright on the far wall, causing it to fall on top of the first shelf and scattering cleaning supplies across the room. The extra space at the foot of the shelves allowed the door to open wide enough for John to squeeze through.

The heat inside rivaled that of the parking lot, but of a different sort, like an oven versus a heat lamp. Fire ringed the room along the walls, concentrated in the back corner where several file cabinets had been vandalized. A large black trash bag hung from the ceiling, duct-taped to the sprinkler, which slowly created a giant water balloon. No humans were visible, but they might be behind the door.

The gap was too narrow to admit Lovejoy. John pulled out his weapon and nodded to Lovejoy, who did the same. John stepped to the opening and yelled hoarsely.

"This is the sheriff. Step to where I can see you with your hands up." He paused for three beats. Nothing. "I'm coming in. Stand away from the door."

John slipped through the gap as quickly as he could and took a stance next to the desk. He focused his attention and the gun in the back corner, behind the door. No one.

He stood in the middle of the ring of fire and swept the room with his gun. The room was about ten by twenty. The walls were lined with shelves, filing cabinets of various sizes, a supply cabinet, a table, and the desk. He began to sweat from the heat of the fire. There was no other door, but one supply cabinet was big enough to hold a person. He stepped to it and kicked the handle, the gun held out in front of him. The door swung open. No one.

He gave the room one last hard look, holstered his weapon and shouldered the shelves away from the door. Lovejoy rushed in, his weapon drawn, and cleared the room, following his gaze with his gun.

"Where are they?" Lovejoy yelled.

John didn't answer. A fire extinguisher hung on the wall by the door. He pulled the pin and emptied it on the epicenter in the back corner.

Bert rushed in with another extinguisher and worked on the fire along the front wall. Lovejoy checked under a desk.

Soon the fire was contained. The back corner was a smoking pile of paper and charred, melted plastic. Bert stepped back and looked around the room. "Where are they?" he asked John.

John shook his head.

Lovejoy walked back to the smoldering pile. "Looks like they just got an upgrade from breaking and entering to arson."

John noticed an air conditioning vent on the wall near Bert's head. Too small for a person to crawl into. He looked up at the drop-tile ceiling.

Billy walked in, carrying the axe handle in one hand and a pad of paper in the other. He stopped in front of the bloated trash bag. "Whoa. What's that?" He poked it with the axe handle and it burst open, soaking the pad of paper and his pants, flooding the room. The ashes hissed as the water reached the corner where the fire still smoldered.

Billy looked down at his pants. "Dang it!"

Lovejoy whirled around. "This is a crime scene. You just destroyed physical evidence."

Billy squished guiltily away from the bag, which hung limply from the sprinkler, channeling the water straight down to the floor like a particularly lame water feature.

"What evidence?" he said, defensively.

"Footprints, fingerprints, cigarette butts, hair samples, DNA," Lovejoy said.

"Yeah, right. Like you got a DNA lab down at county."

John took the axe handle from Billy and poked a few ceiling tiles.

Bert looked from Lovejoy to Billy and shook his head. "I'll go turn off the sprinklers."

John called over his shoulder. "Bring a ladder." He poked a few more ceiling tiles and then checked the room for flare ups. Why did they lock themselves in the storeroom? Why did they start a fire? If they were with the church, why didn't they make any demands?

Lovejoy joined him and looked at the smoking ruins. "Looks like payback to me. Fight fire with fire."

John didn't comment. It was probably payback, all right, but not how Lovejoy thought. "Go out front and see if Pastor Jackson is still here. I want to talk to him."

Lovejoy nodded and turned. Billy stood next to the desk, holding a muffin. It was halfway to his mouth. Lovejoy's shout nearly deafened John. "Stop!" He held up one hand like he was directing traffic.

At that moment, the sprinkler shut off with a thud.

Billy flinched and the muffin popped in the air. He fumbled for it and it bounced between his hands several times before he got a good hold on it. He looked at Lovejoy, irritated. "What?"

"Where did you get that muffin?" Lovejoy shouted.

Billy shrugged. "It was on the desk."

"Did you bring it?"

"No."

"Did anybody else from the office bring it?"

"I don't know. People bring stuff all the time."

Lovejoy strode across the room and held out his hand. "That could be evidence."

"This? It's a muffin."

Bert walked in with an eight-foot A-frame ladder.

Lovejoy turned to him. "Sir, do you recognize this muffin?"

Bert looked at him blankly.

Lovejoy pointed at the muffin in Billy's hand. "Is this a preexisting muffin?"

Bert looked at John for an explanation, and then back at Lovejoy. "What, do you think they disguised themselves as a muffin to escape capture?"

"The perps could have brought it here. It could have DNA on it." He snatched it from Billy's hand and held it up toward John. "I'll bag it for chain of custody."

John looked back as blankly as he could. "Pastor Jackson."

Lovejoy took the muffin with him as he walked out. "I'm on it."

John turned to Billy. "Why don't you go mind the gate?"

"They all left."

"Then go get some dry pants."

Billy grabbed his axe handle and sulked out the door.

From outside the room Lovejoy's voice boomed. "This is a crime scene. You must stay outside the perimeter."

John walked out into the warehouse. The KHIL news crew had evidently slipped through the fence and come in the warehouse door. The camera was live and a Latina reporter was talking excitedly into a microphone.

"Get them outside the fence," John said to Lovejoy.

Billy strode toward them. "This is private property," he yelled. He held the axe handle horizontally and used it like a cow catcher to railroad them out the door, which he closed with an echoing thud.

John went back into the storage room. Bert stood on the ladder, pulling the garbage bag off the sprinkler head. He handed it to John, who set it on the desk and motioned for Bert to come down.

John moved the ladder to the door. His pants clung to his legs, stretching as he climbed up. He felt his shirt slide across his torso, slick with sweat. He popped a ceiling tile and stuck his head up into the plenum. Guy wires led up to a framework that supported the ceiling, wiring, and plumbing. He climbed higher to see the top of the framework. It had an unbroken layer of dust half an inch thick.

Behind the opposite wall of the storage room, the side of the warehouse extended up twenty feet to the roof. There was a window halfway up for light and ventilation. It was open a few inches. He looked toward the offices. He could see all the way to the front wall of the warehouse. No signs that anything was disturbed. No picketers or ninjas or *Mission Impossible* spies hung spider-like from the rafters.

John climbed down and scanned the floor. All the water seeped out the door. None of it seeped down into some hidden escape tunnel in the concrete slab.

He looked at Bert. "So, where are they?" John nosed the air. "You smell that?"

Bert nodded. "Paint thinner."

John walked over to the smoldering lump of plastic and paper in the back corner. "What is this?"

Bert joined him. "It's the archives. The paperwork for all completed projects is transferred out here." He pointed to a set of legal-sized file cabinets toppled over, the contents now a pile of soggy ash. "Anything over five years old is scanned to microfiche." He pointed to a set of smaller file cabinets, the contents now a lump of smoking plastic slag.

"Why did they burn it?"

Bert shrugged and looked at the ring of charred wall around the room. "Looks like they were looking for fuel to keep the fire going."

"Do you have copies anywhere?"

"These are the copies."

"Is that a big loss, these files?"

Bert shrugged. "It's an inconvenience. The financial stuff would be in our accounting system on the computer. Permits and that type of thing are on record at the courthouse, so we could get a copy if we had to, but it would slow things down. Any correspondence is lost, unless the client kept a copy."

Lovejoy walked in with a paper evidence bag, red tape sealing the opening. "Pastor Luke is out front." He held the evidence bag out to John. "Bagged and tagged."

Bert watched. "What is that?"

"Evidence," Lovejoy said.

Bert looked at John. "What?"

John sighed. "Ask Billy." He took the bag which he assumed held the muffin. "Deputy Lovejoy, tape off this room and then take a statement from Billy."

Lovejoy walked out.

John turned to Bert. "It may be a week before you can get back in here."

Bert scanned the room. "Looks like we'll have to dump most of what's in here, anyway. I can't wait to tell Cook about the archives. And that nobody's been arrested."

John bristled. "You tell me how two men got out of your storage room while it was on fire without going through the door and I'll make an arrest."

"It seems pretty simple to me. This is retaliation. That preacher is behind this."

"So, you're saying he prayed them out of there? You want to sign a statement to that effect?"

"Ask the muffin. I don't know how they got out. I'm not a detective."

"That's right, you're not. So keep that in mind. And I'd tone down that talk about Pastor Jackson doing this if I were you. Cook Brothers isn't the only one who can file a defamation lawsuit."

Bert splashed out of the room. Lovejoy returned with the crime scene tape.

John walked up the hall to the reception area. Bert sat in his fishbowl, his head resting sideways in one hand while the other hand pressed the phone against his head. Probably getting a chewing out from Cook.

John nodded to Nadine, touched the brim of his hat. "Have a good day."

She sighed. "I wish."

He went out the front door. The heat enveloped him like a blanket. He thought the storeroom fire was hot, but it was no match for a Texas summer.

Luke Jackson stood by the flagpole watching the news crew pack up. He was dressed much like John, a black suit, white shirt, and black tie, but Jackson's suit cost four times as much. Maybe more.

John walked up to him. "Pastor, you have a minute?"

Jackson turned away from the news van. "How can I help you, Sheriff?"

"I need a list of the people who were here protesting today."

Jackson shook his head. "There is no list."

"I'll need a list of your members."

"That's not public information."

John sighed. His eyes felt gritty from the smoke. He noticed his shirt was streaked with ashes and flame retardants. "I can get a warrant."

Jackson looked over his shoulder at the departing news van and then back at John. He didn't seem to notice the heat at all. "The constitution has protections against religious persecution."

John nodded wearily. He didn't know which was more exhausting, the heat or Jackson. "But there is no constitutional protection against breaking and entering, destruction of private property, or arson."

"My people didn't do this."

"You've said some pretty strong things against Cook Brothers, enough to incur a defamation suit—"

"Entirely unwarranted."

"And somebody in your congregation might have decided to take things into their own hands. Do you know anybody who might have leanings in that direction? Somebody a little too zealous?"

"Too zealous?" Jackson's TV voice came out. "Zeal for thy house consumes me." He looked John in the eye. "You cannot be too zealous about the house of the Lord."

John felt his eyebrows rise. He brought his expression back into check, but didn't say anything. He didn't need to. Jackson would talk. The hard part would be to shut him up.

"But this act is not the work of my people." He turned the voice on again. "Dearly beloved, avenge not yourselves, but rather give place unto wrath: for it is written, Vengeance is mine; I will repay, saith the Lord."

"So you're saying God started the fire?"

"Cook Brothers started that fire when they raised their hand against the Lord. Be not deceived; God is not mocked: for whatsoever a man soweth, that shall he also reap. They that take up the sword shall perish by the sword."

John figured that if God wanted to burn down the warehouse, he wouldn't need paint thinner to get the job done. Talking with Jackson was always like this, like following the White Rabbit down a bottomless hole. That was why John avoided it. It left him feeling like he had taken drugs. He turned back toward the office.

"I'm going to need to see that membership list, Pastor."

"And I'm going to need to see a warrant, Sheriff."

John stepped inside the door of the office. Billy and Lovejoy sat in the orange plastic seats. Lovejoy wrote laboriously in his notepad while Billy waited.

Nadine looked up with a deep sigh. John nodded to her and then turned to Lovejoy. "You got that list of protestors?"

Lovejoy looked up and nodded his head toward Billy, who held up a soggy pad of paper. The names still appeared to be legible.

"Good. Maybe you can get Nadine to make a couple of copies." He heard the sigh, but didn't look over at Nadine. "Split the list with Sam and get statements from everyone for the incident report."

When he walked out the door, he realized he still had the evidence bag with the muffin in it.

22

The Bolero Volunteer Fire Department arrived as John walked to his truck. He walked over to the fire truck as the chief climbed down from the cab.

"I think it's contained, but your boys should check it out. Lovejoy's inside. He'll show you where it is."

"Got it." He motioned to the three men climbing out of the truck and turned to walk past John.

"Another thing," John said.

The chief stopped and turned back around.

"It looks pretty simple. Doused the place with paint thinner and lit a match. But let me know if you see anything unusual."

"Will do." He followed his crew into the building.

John walked to his truck. His shirt and his hat brim were soaked with sweat. His pants clung to his legs like a second skin, but not as pliant. He didn't hang around for the report. What could they tell him? That God had sent down fire from heaven?

He opened the door and felt the heat blast pour over him like lava. He reached in and started the ignition. As the compressor got up to speed, he hung his hat on the rack behind his seat, peeled off his jacket, hung it next to the hat, and climbed into the truck.

He tossed the evidence bag containing the muffin in the passenger seat and waited until the interior cooled into the nineties before he closed the door. The cab was filled with the aroma of ribs and onions. He tossed the newspaper in the back seat and looked at the bag. He could still have a hot lunch, in every sense of the phrase.

He pulled onto the highway and pointed his truck toward a picnic spot that overlooked the river where it was wide and shallow, good for wading and skipping rocks, but no good for swimming. In the middle of the week and the middle of a baking summer afternoon, it was deserted, as he expected. He left his jacket in the truck and found a table under a pin oak that offered refuge from the sun, but not from the heat.

Humidity wicked up heat like a worn blanket and spread it into every corner of creation, every crevasse you might crawl into, every hidey-hole you might hunker down in. A breeze could give momentary respite, but eventually all things succumbed to the pervasive warm moisture that invaded everything like the sand on Mustang Island.

John wiped the grime off his face with his sleeve, opened the sack, and spread his feast before him. First he tossed the coleslaw, which would be iffy by now, in a nearby trash barrel like a bouncer ejecting a party crasher. He opened the okra. It was mushy, but still tasty, like an old friend in reduced circumstances. Then he slowly opened the butcher paper to reveal the guest of honor—three hulking beef ribs looking like they had been plucked directly out of the TV from a Flintstones cartoon. They glistened in the sunlight, reddish at the bone but otherwise a rich brown, tinged with scorched patches at the extremities.

They called to him, sang to his unplumbed depths, urged him to the brink of the abyss. He munched on a soggy bit of okra, regarding the ribs with fear and lust. He snagged a red onion from the butcher paper and bit into it. He closed his eyes, his senses floating on the sharp twinge mixed with buttery grease.

Then he remembered the phone call. His father, such as he was, back in town and threatening to disrupt the space-time continuum. He opened his eyes. He couldn't enjoy this moment with unfinished business on his mind.

The ribs still taunted him, but now they looked less like rungs on the stairway to heaven and more like road kill. He balled them up in the butcher paper and crammed them back in the sack. He jammed his hat on his head and left the okra for any foraging animal with the strength to brave the heat.

He tossed the bag of ribs on the seat next to the evidence bag, cranked the engine, and left a cloud of dust hanging over the picnic tables.

He avoided the *Battles for Sheriff* sign by cutting across on a gravel road to the farm-to-market road that lead to his childhood home, but he couldn't avoid the thoughts, specifically Bert's comment that Gibson was checking up on him.

John had no proof, but he suspected Gibson had encouraged Battles to run against him. Gibson was evidently going to try to use any mismanagement of the Cook Brothers case as ammunition for Battles in the campaign. As he thought about the vanishing suspects, John took slow, deep breaths, a calming technique his mom advocated. On rare occasions, her advice was actually useful. But the exercise did nothing to dispel the dread as he realized how easily Battles could spin the incredible facts.

And he wouldn't need Gibson to spread the news. He pictured Lovejoy taking Billy's statement in the reception area, with Nadine noting every word. Between the three of them, it would span the county in a few hours.

As he turned off the gravel road onto asphalt, his thoughts turned to his errand and he felt his heart rate escalate. His radio buzzed.

"*zzzz . . . wise and black . . . zzzz*"

It wasn't Sam's voice, but it sounded familiar. He pulled the radio from his belt and keyed the mike.

"Sam, come again?" He waited and tried again. "Sam, 10-9. Repeat your last transmission."

After a moment, Sam responded. "Uh, go to Cook Brothers?"

"Are they back?"

"No, my last transmission was two hours ago, telling you to go to Cook Brothers."

"Okay. Must be interference on the radio."

He set the radio on the seat.

"*zzzz . . . argot ergo . . . zzzz*"

He picked it back up and held it to his ear. Nothing.

"*zzzz . . . Why now?*"

The sound had not come from the radio. He set it down and looked around the truck. There were not many places for a prankster to hide, but he wasn't the kind of man to take chances. He pulled off the highway into the grass shoulder, got out, his shirt sticking to his body, and searched the cab. Behind the seat, under the seat. He found nothing and nobody.

He climbed back into the cab, closed the door, and sat with his left hand on the wheel, his right on the key, but not turning it. He was sure he heard something, but there was no explanation for it. Like the storage room and the vanishing suspects. Sweat rolled down his forehead and dripped onto the inside of his sunglasses.

"*fortuitous concourse*"

This time he recognized the voice. It was the raspy voice he heard through the air duct in Bert's office, the voice he assumed belonged to one of the suspects. He looked at the evidence bag, a paper bag not too different from what a coffee shop would use if you bought a muffin for breakfast.

He picked it up. It didn't say anything. He broke the chain-of-evidence seal and looked inside. The muffin sat there quietly on its side.

He didn't want to touch it. Despite the absurdity of Lovejoy bagging it as evidence in the first place, it was remotely possible it had some kind of recoverable prints, fiber, or DNA. But if it was talking to him in the voice of a suspect, it might also contain some kind of wireless receiver. And a speaker.

John set the bag down on the seat. It sat askew against the bag from Stella's, giving him a view of the muffin inside. He looked at it with concern. This was too absurd, even for him, and, considering his parents, that was saying something.

"*Why now?*"

"Why not now?" he asked back, and immediately felt like an idiot.

Which was worse? Hearing a muffin talk to you or answering back?

Actually, the better question was, "Why *what* now?" but he couldn't bring himself to ask it out loud. He waited out the muffin like he would sweat out a suspect in an interrogation room. But the muffin wasn't susceptible to his interrogation techniques. It didn't blurt out a confession. Instead, it lay nestled in the confines of the evidence bag and kept its own counsel. In this regard, John thought, it displayed a higher level of intelligence and composure than most humans.

John turned the key. The engine and the AC roared to life, and he continued down the road to his mother's house.

On John's eighth birthday, he had a pirate party. A half-dozen kids came over. While Mom got out the cake and ice cream and punch, Dad made newspaper hats for all the kids. While they loaded up on sugar, Dad went in the front yard, pulled down half the rose trellis, hacked it into pieces, and tacked together little swords for everyone. They had a treasure hunt in the backyard, following a set of clues

Mom wrote the night before, and discovered a cardboard treasure chest full of chocolate gold doubloons hidden under a washtub in the middle of the yard. Fortunately his birthday was October 2, so the chocolate was still in solid form when they found it.

The big present was a motorcycle, a motocross bike. It was wildly overpowered for his spindly eight-year-old frame. In the driveway, Dad showed him how to start it, and how the clutch and throttle worked, and turned it over to John. The first thing he did was pop the clutch and lurch straight into the garage, knocking a huge dent in the door of the family car, and then crash into the workbench, releasing an avalanche of a dozen different half-finished projects that had been piled there for years.

Dad dug him out. They pried the fender away from the front tire and hammered it back into a semblance of its former shape. In the next three months, John spent more time on the ground than on the bike, and even more time straightening fenders and reattaching mirrors and tail lights and pegs.

Then the finance company came and got it.

When John pulled up to the house where he grew up, the first thing he saw was a sparkling Rangoon red Mustang next to his mother's gecko-green VW Beetle. The old man had nerve, but that wasn't news.

John parked in the driveway, got out, wrestled his jacket on over his soggy shirt, and walked around the Mustang. It looked identical, but John couldn't be sure. He'd only seen it for a few minutes over twenty years ago. Twenty-three years, ten months, and two weeks ago, to be exact. Not that John was counting. He checked the plates. Florida. Was that where he had been the whole time?

John walked up onto the porch and through the door without knocking. The living room was empty. A paperback copy of *Idylls of the King* lay spread-eagle on the coffee table in front of the armchair, as if it had just been set down and the reader would return at any moment. He hadn't seen an open novel in this house in years. Probably twenty-four years.

A sudden memory assailed him–John supine on the couch after dinner as Rusty read aloud from his armchair. Lewis Carroll or Ray Bradbury or Sir Walter Scott. He shook it off and looked around the room.

"Hello?" he called.

A rustling sound came from the hallway leading to the bedrooms. In a few moments, Mom came out wearing one of those gauzy robes she favored, over a loose, flowing silk blouse and trousers. "Honey, you finally made it." She hugged him. She smelled of cigarettes and Old Spice, neither of which she used. It was Rusty's smell.

John looked at the hallway. "Where is he?"

Rusty Lawson emerged from the hallway, buttoning up a Hawaiian shirt. His conspiratorial smile raised John's blood pressure several dozen millibars. Like John, he was tall and lean. Unlike John, he always seemed to be on the verge of being everybody's best friend, if they could be so lucky.

"Deborah and I counted you among the missing in action hours ago," Rusty said. "But there should be the vestige of a margarita in the blender. The old Lawson special." He winked.

John stared at him without expression, refusing to encourage him.

The old man's face relaxed, transforming from a pixie to a penitent. "Okay. Conscience compels me to confess that I stole the recipe from Jimmy Buffet." He stared at John, waiting.

"I'm on duty."

Mom spread her arms to embrace the whole glorious situation and the world. "I'll make tea. You two sit and catch up." She wisped into the kitchen, trailing gossamer robes of glory.

As she left, John felt the atmosphere in the room change. His father didn't look any different, but John sensed his presence expanding as hers diminished.

Despite Mom's suggestion, neither of them sat. They looked at each other. John assessed the old man like a suspect. He noted that Rusty's hair, while thinning on the crown, was still jet black, unlike his own, which had entered the salt-and-pepper stage. A puka shell necklace rested against his golden bronze tan. Both necklace and tan genuine. He wore a silk, flagrantly-understated-but-obviously-expensive Hawaiian shirt, raw hemp trousers, and leather sandals. The entire wardrobe was new, the mark of a player recently flush.

He thought about the car out front. A first generation 1964 1/2 Mustang in mint condition. Probably not the same one he drove out of town a quarter of a century ago. That also represented a significant investment. A recent investment, because men of Rusty's character couldn't maintain such a vehicle in such a condition for more than a few months.

Rusty Lawson was a dangerous man, but never more dangerous than when he had money. Or access to credit.

"You can't stay," John said quietly. He felt he might explode with all the unsaid things roiling under the surface.

"Did you see the car?"

"Yeah, I saw it. Just the kind of thing a manic would buy on impulse."

Rusty pulled a set of keys from his pocket and held them out. "It's yours. Paid for, unencumbered."

John stared at the hand and the keys, saying nothing.

"Son, I know it can't make up for the years we missed, but I'd like to think it's a start."

"The only start I'm interested in is you starting that car and leaving. Now." John glanced at the kitchen. "Before she gets her hopes up."

"Too late for that, I'm afraid." Despite the words, it was said without a hint of apology. More like a challenge. "I have returned."

"Why now?"

"Somebody told me it's never too late to do the right thing."

"She doesn't have any money."

"I'm not hurting for cash."

John stepped closer and lowered his voice further. "You can dye your hair and buy expensive clothes, but you can't change what you are. She'll see through it."

Rusty held his gaze without blinking. "Deborah never asked me to leave. Never."

"When was the last time you took your meds?"

Mom looked in from the kitchen. "The tea's ready and I have banana bread. Let's bring it in here, boys."

John held Rusty's eyes. "I can't stay. There's a situation I have to deal with."

She stepped into the room. "Oh, honey, can't it wait?"

"No. It's urgent."

"Then come to dinner. And bring Liz. She's never met Rusty."

John pulled his gaze from Rusty and mentally debated how to play it. Based on her response in the phone call, it was clear she intended to forgive and forget, to pretend nothing had happened. It had to be dealt with, but this was not the time to begin what could be hours of discussion.

"I don't know if I'll be done by then."

"Then call as soon as you're free." She hugged him. "And be careful, honey."

He shot a final look of warning at Rusty and walked out the door.

When John opened the door to the truck, the aroma of ribs and muffin wafted out on the hot air escaping the cab. His stomach reminded him that it was closer to dinner than lunch and he still hadn't eaten. He looked longingly at the ribs and then sternly at the muffin, daring it to make a noise.

On the drive home, he called the captain of the fire station and got a report. As he expected, the suspects had doused paint thinner around the perimeter of the storage room, focusing on the microfiche cabinet. There were a few Camel cigarette butts among the detritus, but no sign of how they escaped from the room without going through the one door.

John drove through the twists and turns, rises and falls of the Hill Country with the muffin and the ribs riding shotgun in their respective bags. The smell of the ribs now pervaded the cab, soaked into the upholstery. It would probably take days for it to fade. He would put the ribs in the fridge for later.

The muffin, well, it hadn't said anything recently. John began to wonder if it had said anything at all, or if . . . well, he didn't want to think about the *if*.

Over two hours of daylight remained before the lingering Hill Country twilight, the time of day when the sun disappeared behind a ridge leaving behind a blue sky until it dropped below the true horizon. Liz was bringing dinner, probably from Flo's, since she knew he was getting his test results today. He looked at the Stella's bag and considered eating one of the ribs, but decided against it.

Christopher would be home by the time John got there. Christopher got a full engineering scholarship at A&M, having aced the SAT, not to mention all his calculus classes and the valedictorian thing. When he came home at the end of his freshman year, he took a summer job on a Cook Brothers bridge crew. For him it was early to bed and early to rise to beat the heat.

When John pulled into the drive, he saw Christopher's 4x4 parked under the oak out front. Christopher bought it himself by working summers during his high school years at the Rio Frio Ranch taking tourists on trail rides and campouts, much as John had done.

John parked in front of the garage, which was too full of stuff to accommodate a car. He grabbed the two bags from the passenger seat. He'd have to find a way to hide the ribs in the fridge or they would disappear down the bottomless Christopher pit before sunset. He walked through the garage and shoved the Stella's bag into the deep freeze under a slab of venison from last season.

He set the evidence bag on the desk in the corner of the den where he sometimes worked after hours. He headed for the shower, but heard it running. He decided to take a quick shot at "Nobody's Dirty Business" instead.

He turned on the TV, muted it, picked up his guitar, and kicked back on the couch. As the network news broke to commercials, he ran through the progression.

John didn't look at himself in the mirror and think, "guitar player." He doubted anybody else did, either. But when disaster strikes, you survive by grasping for anything that keeps you from sinking, and for John it was the blues.

Christopher was seven when Jennifer took him and left for the house on the opposite ridge. It was the cusp of the new millennium, but despite the festivities in Times Square, John didn't party like it was 1999. He wandered through the little two-bedroom house feeling like a ghost in a Gothic novel.

One night the following January he realized he was sitting on Christopher's race-car bed, the kind with matching sheets and bedspread, staring at the carnage left behind. She'd left in a hurry, but that was probably his fault. He hadn't taken the announcement well, particularly because she left him for an older man, much older. And not particularly attractive, either.

In the ensuing histrionics, she tossed clothes into suitcases and fled like a southern belle who has just received the news that Sherman's army is over the next ridge. Later she returned for more clothes and toys, but didn't linger to tidy up. Christopher' room had looked like an explosion in a toy factory and John didn't touch it for years.

On that winter night he sat on the bed, half drunk, and looked at the toys littering the floor, the clothes Christopher had outgrown slung halfway off hangers in the open closet, the Transformers posters she hadn't bothered to take down. The things discarded in her flight, all evidently as unsuitable for her new life as he was.

Then his eyes fell on a three-quarter-sized guitar in the corner, a gift from one of Jennifer's brothers. He dragged his finger across the strings and it reminded him of the opening chord in "Hard Day's Night." He picked it up and tried to play "Mary Had a Little Lamb." It only took him ten minutes to figure it out.

A Mel Bay instruction book peeked from under outgrown pajamas. John opened it and tried out a C chord, using his right hand to guide the fingers on his left hand to the proper position. He strummed with his thumb. It sounded more like a pair of platform shoes falling down a staircase than a chord. He pushed down harder with his left hand, the thick steel stings cutting into his fingertips, and tried again. Better.

He moved on to a G chord, then to an F, gave that up and went back to the G. He flipped over a few pages, saw "Blowing in the Wind" and gave it a shot, stumbling when he had to play a D. At the end he realized that for the first time since she'd left, he'd gone an hour without thinking about Jennifer.

He spent the next few weeks drinking Shiner and learning chords. It took him a month to build up calluses sufficient to dull the pain from long sessions of playing. By that time he'd cut back on the drinking because it interfered with his dexterity.

For a while the guitar took over his waking life. He found himself thinking of chord patterns while driving, his left hand miming them in the air. He tried to guess the progressions of songs on the radio and then tried them out when he got home.

He'd never been much of a Dylan fan, so he looked for other material to play. He remembered an old album Rusty used to play, Lightnin' Hopkins. He stopped by Mom's place, dug through the box in the closet, and found it.

He started with "Hello Central" and graduated to "Short Haired Woman Blues" after a few months, playing everything with a pick. But he couldn't get that Lightnin' sound. On a trip to Nashville he went to the Gibson factory at Opry Mills and got a real guitar, a Gibson Hummingbird.

The guy at the factory also gave him the inside story on Lightnin's thunder thumb. Lightnin' used a thumb pick to play the rhythm while picking out the melody with his index finger. It took a few years to learn all the songs on the record the way Lightnin' played them. Or pretty close.

John's phone signaled a voice mail, even though he hadn't heard it ring. It was Mooney, the justice of the peace.

"John, you'll never guess what I'm looking at right now. A 1964 1/2 Rangoon red Mustang driving past the Lone Star. Is that your dad? It kinda looks like him. Wow. Call me and tell me what's going on."

John deleted the message, glanced up, and noticed that the local news was on. He grabbed the remote and turned on the sound.

The fire was the top story. There was footage of the protestors dragging their signs out to the bus and driving off. Of the charred walls visible through the yellow crime scene tape across the door to the storage room. Of Billy outside the fence, holding the axe handle, his pants wet from the ruptured garbage bag, relating his part in the events. Of Bert yelling, "No comment!" through the glass wall of his office.

And there was the interview with Pastor Jackson, which went much along the lines of what he had said to John. The hand of God, justice for the righteous. It was a lot of Bible verses and theatrics, but John noticed that he was careful not to say anything actionable.

Christopher walked in, his hair wet from the shower, and immediately stopped and raised his head like a hound scenting spoor.

"Stella's ribs? For dinner?" He smiled largely.

Liz came in the door with bags with the Flo's logo on the side.

"No. Boneless, skinless chicken breasts with a cracked-peppercorn herb rub and sautéed garlic brussels sprouts." She dropped a smaller bag on the counter. "And whole-grain bran muffins with local honey for dessert."

Christopher's face fell as he dropped into a chair. John turned off the TV, set the guitar against the couch, and walked to the table. Liz set their dinner on the counter and kissed John. Then she sniffed, stepped back, and looked at him.

"Barbecue? Were your test results that good?"

John reached into his pocket and pulled the stack of paper he had stuffed in there from Doc. He handed it to her. "I've been too busy to eat anything since breakfast. Even herb chicken with vegetable balls sounds good right about now." He looked at Christopher. "Get some plates." He began decanting their dinner from the containers.

Liz flipped through the papers, looking first at the results, then at the prescriptions. By the time she set them on the counter, dinner was on the table. The conversation centered on the first day of school. Liz's middle-school English class had to share a room with the history class to make space for high school students displaced by the collapse of the Bolero High gymnatorium the week before.

After she described the tag-team arrangement she and the history teacher worked out, Liz brought the conversation back to John's test results.

"Maybe you should drop out of the election and retire. High stress can affect your cholesterol levels."

It was the same conversation every four years. The reasons varied, stress, danger, work hours, pay, politics.

"Any law enforcement job is going to have stress."

"You can change careers."

"At forty?"

"You're not forty for another month." Liz smiled.

"Speaking of changing careers," Christopher said. "I'm taking off a year from A&M to dig water wells in Africa."

John waited for the punch line, but Christopher's mouth was already full of chicken. Liz didn't contribute anything beyond a pregnant glance at John. She had strong feelings about education, but from the day they met she let the relationship between John and Christopher alone.

"Don't classes start next week?"

"Yep."

"Is this Caitlyn's idea?" John attempted a disinterested tone, but was unsure how successful it was. After years of arguments with Jennifer and Christopher, it took Liz to enlighten him that his questions tended to sound more like an interrogation than a conversation. He'd been working on changing that.

"She doesn't know about it yet. I'm telling her tonight."

Christopher's girlfriend was typically the driving force of any do-gooder activities.

On his weekends home, Christopher went with her to church, a source of conflict with Jennifer, who viewed all church people with suspicion. So, when he came back to Bolero for the summer, Christopher moved back to the house he left when he was seven.

His old bedroom looked just the same as it had thirteen years earlier, and being men of action, not accessories, neither of them took steps to redecorate. He slept in the race-car single bed, put his clothes in the matching dresser, and left the Transformer posters up. It was nothing more than a place to sleep, anyway. He spent all his time working or hanging out with Caitlyn or his high school buddies.

John assumed that if Christopher was going off to Africa to dig wells and convert the savages, Caitlyn was behind it. If not Caitlyn, then who? "How does a fellow decide where in Africa to go dig a well?"

"A guy on the bridge crew just got back from three months over there with a group called Water Friends For."

"How much does it pay?"

Christopher snorted. John ignored it and the look from Liz.

"You have to pay your own way," Christopher said. "He's working this summer to save enough to go back for a year. I'm going with him."

John set his fork down and abandoned his attempt at detachment. "And you have a year's worth of money socked away somewhere you're going to use?"

"It costs almost nothing to live in Africa. The big cost is getting there and back. I'll sell my truck. It's almost paid off. With what I make on the bridge crew, I'll have more than enough."

"What about your degree? What happens to the scholarship?"

Christopher shrugged. "I'll have to check. Maybe they'll hold it for me."

"Maybe? Don't you think you should check on that before you start making plans?"

"If they don't, I'll figure things out when I get back."

"You can—" John took a deep breath. Christopher was the only one still eating. Liz watched from the sidelines. John changed tactics. "How long did it take you to pay off your truck?"

Christopher thought for a second. "About four years."

"And how much does one year at A&M cost compared to what you paid for your truck?"

"About twice as much."

John nodded. "So, to complete your degree, you're looking at six times as much as the cost of your truck. If you lose the scholarship, it would take twenty-four years to pay off the rest of your degree."

"I'll make ten times as much as an engineer. So it would only take me a few years to pay it off."

"Or you could finish the degree and then take your year in Africa if you still wanted to."

Christopher set his fork down. "And how many children die drinking contaminated water while I'm saving money?" He stood, took his glass to the refrigerator, filled it from the door dispenser, and took a long drink. "See that? In a few seconds I have a full glass of clean water. In Kenya, a woman has to walk for hours to find some puddle of dirty water with who knows what in it. I can take a few weeks to drill a shallow well and she'll have clean water five minutes from her home. Or I can make sure I don't lose any money getting my degree while her children die from dysentery."

John suddenly realized he didn't know his own son at all. He'd tried to be a good dad even after the divorce. He went to all of Christopher's games, took him fishing and hunting occasionally. This summer they hadn't talked much, just hung out, two bachelors sharing a house. They watched a little TV together, worked on a few home-maintenance projects.

"It's just not practical," he finally said.

"Practical? What's practical about children dying in the twenty-first century because they can't get clean water?" Christopher sat down at the table. "I'm not a kid anymore, Dad. I've thought about my career. You hire people. You tell me, which is easier to explain to a recruiter, a year gap between graduation and job interviews or a year gap between my freshman and sophomore years?"

John was impressed by both the passion and the logic, but it seemed crazy for Christopher to throw away a year of a sheriff's salary to dig wells for complete strangers on the other side of the world. He looked at Liz for assistance, but she just sat there, waiting to see what he would do. John fell back to an old, comfortable script.

"What did your mother say?"

"I haven't told anyone about it. Not until just now." Christopher took a muffin from the serving plate, poured local honey over it, and consumed it in three bites.

John searched for something of substance to respond with, but came up empty. He pulled rank instead. "You're not walking out on the scholarship. Africa will still be there after you graduate."

"It's my scholarship and my decision." Christopher pushed away from the table and walked toward the door.

John turned to follow him. "You come back here. This conversation is not over."

"I think it is," Christopher said, his words cut off as the door slammed behind him.

John stood and strode to the door. As he pulled it open the truck roared to life and down the ridge to the highway until it faded into silence.

Liz walked over, stood by his side and looked out into late afternoon sun. John closed the door against the heat.

"He's got a good head on his shoulders," Liz finally said. "He'll be okay no matter what he decides."

"He can decide whatever he wants, but he's not quitting school." He walked back to the table and began stacking plates.

Liz followed. "I'm not sure you can stop him."

John grunted and took the dishes to the sink. "There's just so many ways to screw up."

"And he's already avoided most of them," Liz answered. She took the dishes out of his hand, set them on the counter, and pulled him to her. "He's like his father."

John wrapped her in a hug, his chin against her ear. "That's what I'm afraid of."

Liz slapped him on the butt and pulled back, looking into his eyes. "I don't want to hear that kind of talk in here." She sounded like she was in front of her classroom, scolding a kid for bad language. She softened and ran her hands up his chest to his face. "You're a good man, John, and he's going to do you proud."

She kissed him lightly, then more aggressively. John felt her body melt against his. She was only a couple of inches shorter than him, but fortunately not as skinny.

She slid her lips off his, across his cheek to his ear, and whispered. "How long do you think he's going to be gone?"

Her blonde hair obscured his vision, sticking to his lips as he replied. "Based on that door slam, I'd say several hours."

"Mmm," she said.

After Liz left in a hazy afterglow of pheromones and Christopher returned and crashed in his improbably prepubescent bedroom, John took another shower, dressed in jeans and a black shirt and left for his Tuesday night game of Texas Hold 'Em. There were a dozen individuals in semi-regular rotation, with no more than half that showing up on any given night. It was a small-stakes informal affair played with chips, which kept it nominally legal. Players settled accounts off-site as they saw fit.

Instead of taking the truck, John drove the Crown Victoria he had picked up at the police auction in Uvalde a few years back. He crossed the county line and turned onto Horseshoe Road, stopping at the roadhouse called the Horseshoe Road Inn. It was a long, low frame building painted dark brown. He pulled past the dozen cars out front and parked on the side next to the quartz-halogen security light. As he got out he sampled the air and thought it was starting to cool down. It might even be dipping into the eighties.

He walked under the neon sign and into the building. Beer signs on the wall glowed in the general gloom of the large room. Islands of light spilled over the bar, the pool table, and the dart boards. On the jukebox, Hank Williams complained about being lonesome.

Eight regulars at the bar all looked up as he walked in, nodded, and turned back to their drinks, except for Billy Swallow, who smiled and waved at him.

John walked up to the bar. "Hey, Billy."

The TV above the bar showed Pastor Jackson in front of Cook Brothers making his case for religious persecution. The reporter nodded very seriously. John pulled his gaze from the TV and toward Buzz. He placed his order via a three-finger salute and walked past the empty bandstand to the back room. He was late and they had already started. It was a light night, only three other guys at the large round table.

A bourbon and branch sat at Matthew Lindsey's elbow. He was the oldest of the bunch, in his sixties, owner and editor of the *Bolero Bulletin*, the local weekly. He'd spent the first two decades of his career working his way up to city editor at the *Houston Chronicle* before escaping to the Hill Country twenty years ago.

On Lindsey's left, Paul Mooney, John's age, justice of the peace and owner of the Rio Frio Ranch. He was a fifth-generation Boleran, his ancestors having arrived during Reconstruction.

Mooney had already folded, which was no surprise. He refilled his glass from a bottle of Falls Creek Tempranillo. He'd never been much of a drinker, being raised Baptist, and he only drank wine because that's what they drank in the Bible. In the last few years he had become a Texas Hill Country wine snob, taking the tours and boring the poker group with talk of noses and body and legs until they forced him to shut up on pain of bodily harm. He had to bring his own selections to poker night since the Horseshoe only carried wine in a box. That wasn't strictly legit by the Texas Alcohol Beverage Commission rules, well, laws really, but they weren't around to complain.

On Lindsey's right, Roberto Guzman. He was in his thirties, a handyman turned independent contractor. A black and white dealer button sat next to his Bud Light.

John took his usual seat facing the door, opposite Lindsey.

Mooney set the wine bottle on the floor and took a sip. "Hey, did you get my message? Was that your dad?"

Buzz entered with a boilermaker consisting of a shot of Johnny Walker and a bottle of Lone Star. John didn't drink Lone Star by itself, but the selection was limited at the Horseshoe and it was good enough as a back for whiskey.

"Thanks, Buzz." John ignored Mooney's question.

Buzz nodded to John, tossed a dismissive glance at Mooney and his wine, and left. Buzz had recently confided to John that Mooney was gay, this impression based on Paul's preference for wine over beer. Buzz didn't know any guys who drank wine by choice, and his suspicions were confirmed when Mooney told him that the tempranillo was like a bowl full of cherries with the finishing grace and fragrance of roses and violets. John told Buzz that Mooney had memorized the description from the label on the bottle, but it did nothing to disabuse Buzz of his conclusion.

As Lindsey and Guzman played the hand through, John took a sip of the whiskey and chased it with the beer. The thought of his visit with Doc and the test results leapt unbidden to his mind. The beer and whiskey wouldn't affect his cholesterol numbers, but it could affect his glucose. He made a mental note to do some Internet research on the glycemic index of Johnny Walker.

"Red wine has a lower glycemic index than beer," Mooney said.

John stopped with the longneck halfway to his mouth. He set the bottle back on the table and squinted at Mooney. "How the—"

"I saw you coming out of Doc's. Your face kind of told the whole story."

John took a drink of the Lone Star. It was pretty rough. He decided to sip the Lone Star and use the scotch as a chaser.

Lindsey and Guzman tossed their cards on the table and Guzman dragged the chips in. Guzman passed the dealer button to Lindsey.

Lindsey picked up the cards and shuffled. "Good of you to make an appearance. We were in need of someone to share the burden." He nodded to the pile of chips in front of Guzman. He set the cards down for Guzman to cut and stacked $200 of chips in front of John, making a note on a pad.

"I'm proud to be of service," John said.

Lindsey picked up the cards. "Blinds, please."

Mooney put two red five dollar chips in front of his stack and John put four out.

Lindsey dealt a round of cards to the players, facedown, and then another. Everyone took a peek at their cards by lifting up the edge, except for Mooney, who picked up his hole cards and held them. John had a five of clubs and a three of hearts. A trash hand.

"Raise," Guzman said immediately, and slid forty dollars of chips forward. "Been busy down at Crook Brothers?" It was his pet term for Cook Brothers. He'd been trying to get in with them as an independent contractor for five years with no success. He said they only gave work to guys who gave kickbacks, but John had always figured that for sour grapes. It was more likely that he was too small and inexperienced to handle the volume. His stable of subcontractors was limited, consisting mainly of his high school buddies.

"A bit," John said.

"Fold," Lindsey said with undisguised disgust and sipped his bourbon.

"They've had a run of bad luck," Mooney said. "First the church, then the school, and now this."

"I'd say the chickens are coming home to roost," Guzman said.

"The story on the high school comes out tomorrow," Lindsey said.

"I hope you ripped them a new one."

"I don't have Woodward and Bernstein on staff," Lindsey said. "It's a local weekly."

"It's to you, Paul," Guzman said.

"Fold." Mooney dropped his cards on the table.

"*Caramba*, Paul, you didn't even give the hand a chance," Guzman said.

Mooney frowned at the cards. "That's not a hand, it's a foot."

It looked like it was catching. Everyone had been dealt a turkey, probably Guzman included, but you could never tell with Guzman.

"Fold," John said.

Guzman smiled and pulled the chips in, adding them to his already appreciable stash.

Lindsey shoved the dealer button to Mooney and turned to Guzman. "I wouldn't expect a common laborer like you to understand, but every paper has to find its market. A small-town weekly is about school lunch menus and honor roll lists and daily police reports and human interest stories. People around here care more about the new coach than the gym caving in. We don't do exposé pieces."

"Maybe you should start," Guzman said.

"The only thing to expose around here is who your wife is sleeping with," Lindsey said. "You want that in the paper?"

John almost smiled.

Guzman shrugged. "You want to print that I'm having sex with my wife, you go right ahead."

"Stop the presses!" Mooney barked from his corner.

Guzman had five kids under ten years old. John doubted his wife had the energy or privacy to carry on with somebody else, even if she had the interest.

Guzman scowled at Mooney. "And are you going to deal, or what?"

"Blinds," Mooney said, a bit snippy, and shuffled the cards.

John put out the small blind and Guzman the large blind. Mooney passed the cards to Lindsey to cut and then dealt the hole cards.

John looked at his cards. Hearts, a nine and a king. Things were looking up.

"Call." Lindsey shoved twenty dollars forward. "Did Jackson's people really start that fire, John?"

"Call." Mooney matched Lindsey's bet.

"I can't comment on an ongoing investigation," John said. He checked his hole cards again. It was a decent hand, not strong, but strong enough to stay in and see what happened next. "Call."

"Raise." Guzman set forty dollars down and looked at John. "I'd check for insurance fraud, I was you. Probably had a bunch of material they wanted to write off. They don't call them Cook the Books Brothers for nothing."

"Nobody calls them that but you, Guzman," Lindsey said. "Call."

Mooney hesitated, looking from his hand to the chips in front of the other players. He swapped his cards around, but they still told the same story.

"It's forty to you, Paul," Guzman said.

"Call."

John was surprised at Mooney's play, since he folded more often than a paper airplane. But there was no question of his own play. He called, placing his chips quietly.

Mooney dealt the flop, burning the top card and then laying three cards face up—seven of hearts, king of clubs, and jack of hearts.

John was now sitting with a pair of kings, hearts and clubs, or four hearts into a flush, depending on how he played it. His only concern was that Mooney was sitting on a pair of sevens or jacks and now had three of a kind. It was the only thing that would account for him staying in. But there was no sense in checking. Guzman would jump all over him.

"Raise." He pushed twenty dollars forward.

"Raise," Guzman said predictably. He put in forty.

"Fold." Lindsey consoled himself with his bourbon.

"Well shucks, Matt, it just ain't your night," Guzman said, smiling.

Lindsey offered a simple gesture to Guzman while sipping the bourbon.

Mooney looked at Lindsey, evidently confused. He looked back at his hole cards. "Call." He pushed forty dollars worth of chips forward gingerly like he was sliding a mousetrap into a corner.

Now John was really puzzled. Mooney must have three Jacks to be so bold, but why the hesitation? John was still sitting on a pair of kings, in no position to raise. "Call."

Mooney burned the top card and played the turn card, a nine of diamonds, and smiled.

The smile confused John. He'd misread Mooney's hand. He obviously wasn't sitting on three of anything. He checked the board. Seven, nine, jack, king. Surely Mooney wasn't holding out for a straight. John shook his head and looked at his own situation. He now had two pair, nines and kings, and four hearts. He decided to push Guzman's buttons.

"Raise." John slid forty dollars forward.

Guzman stared at John without blinking, then at Mooney, who broke the gaze to refill his wine glass. John leaned back in his chair, waiting.

"All in." Guzman shoved all his chips forward, a stack that dwarfed the others.

Mooney looked at the stack and back at his hole cards. He sighed, threw the cards face down on the table, and picked up his wine glass with an injured air.

John looked at his cards. The river card could give him a full house or a flush. Or it could leave him with two pair.

As John considered his future, Mooney spoke, oblivious to the tension. "You didn't answer my question. Was that your old man driving that Mustang?"

"That was your dad?" Guzman asked. "I thought it was a confused snow bird." Guzman was barely in elementary school when Rusty left, so it wasn't surprising he didn't remember the situation.

John didn't respond. Instead he called. He wouldn't give Guzman the satisfaction of bluffing him out of the game. He shoved all his chips forward.

Everyone looked to Mooney. He burned the top card and played the last card up, an eight of hearts. John's pulse bumped up. He had a flush. His excitement was checked by a smile from Guzman, but it was eclipsed by Mooney, who picked up his hole cards and checked them.

"Sunny beaches! I would've had a straight!" Mooney threw the cards down—an ace and a ten.

"Coulda, woulda, shoulda," Guzman said. He turned over his cards, two jacks. He had three of a kind.

John shook his head. He had pegged the wrong player for the jacks. He looked at Mooney's cards. Nobody in his right mind would have held out for an inside straight, anyway. Except for Guzman, who would have bid everyone else off the table before he even knew what he had.

All eyes were on John. He checked his hole cards one last time and then flipped them over.

Guzman snorted in disgust and shoved his cards to the middle.

"Way to stick it to him!" Mooney said. He slapped John on the shoulder and passed the dealer button to him.

John gathered the cards and shuffled while Guzman fumed. He took his time and then set the cards down between him and Mooney, but didn't take his hand off them. He looked at Guzman.

Guzman scowled back, then looked at Lindsey. "I'm buying back in."

Lindsey raised an eyebrow. He pulled $200 worth of chips from the box and set them in front of Guzman, making a note on his pad.

John took his hand from the cards and Mooney cut them.

John picked up the cards. "Blinds, gentlemen."

Guzman tossed ten dollars down. Lindsey set out twenty.

Mooney broke the silence. "What's he been doing? He been in Florida the whole time?"

John looked the question at him.

"Your dad."

John frowned.

"The plates. On the Mustang."

"No idea." John placed his thumb on the deck to deal the first card.

"At least he's back," Mooney said, and picked up the wine bottle. "After twenty years, I figured he was dead."

"He's not staying."

The table went silent and John realized he'd spoken with more force than he had intended. He looked up. Guzman looked away, then down at his chips. Mooney busied himself with refilling his wine glass. But Lindsey looked at him with a calculating stare that said he sensed a human-interest story. John tried to imagine the headline. Then tried to forget it.

Lindsey had arrived in Bolero about the time John graduated from the academy and started on at the sheriff's department as a deputy. As far as John knew, Lindsey knew nothing about Rusty. And he'd like to keep it that way. Just a few months remained until the election and John had no doubt Rusty could wreck it like he wrecked everything.

"At least, that's what he says," John commented in as nonchalant a manner as he could achieve.

He looked down at the deck in his hand, his thumb and forefinger holding the edge of the top card, ready to deal.

John had just turned eleven. Dad still had his job teaching English at Bolero High. He wouldn't get fired for another two or three years.

John and Paul Mooney went camping in late October, the first weekend after the rainstorm that usually ushered in the fall season in the Hill Country. A flash of green had returned to the valley and the Frio River ran full.

Mr. Mooney, Scoutmaster for the local den, suggested the camping trip. It would be just the two of them out alone for the first time, a celebration to mark earning the last Cub Scout rank, the Arrow of Light.

On Friday afternoon, John and Paul loaded their provisions into backpacks. Then John grabbed the handle of the stove, Paul shouldered the tent, and they made the half-mile hike through the back acres of the Rio Frio Ranch to a bend in the river that created a swimming hole. They set up the pup tent and John built a fire pit while Paul took the hatchet and gathered firewood. In the twilight, they heated up a can of beans and roasted wieners, washing it down with lukewarm root beer.

After the sun dropped behind the western ridge, the temperature dropped into the fifties. They pulled on their jackets and sat by the fire, retelling old ghost stories and making up new ones. When they ran out of wood and the fire burned down to embers, Paul pumped up the gas lantern like Mr. Mooney showed him, John got the deck of cards from his pack, and they played spades inside the tent, their shadows projected on the tent walls like a revelation of their inner monsters.

Even with four players, John thought spades was too predictable. Because there were only two of them, they each played two hands of thirteen cards and soon John found it painfully boring. As they argued whether to keep playing, find something else to do, or pack it in for the night, a noise struck them mute. The sound of something big moving around in the blackness outside the tent.

John stiffened and looked at Paul, who looked back, eyes large, darting to the tent flap. There weren't any big animals in the Hill Country, other than cows and deer. But there were mountain lions and bobcats. John repented of making up a story about a panther that attacked without warning and dragged small, screaming children into the woods. His breaths came quick and shallow, his pulse pounding in his ears. Then he heard the clattering of the cans they had left around the fire, and the sound of a man swearing softly.

As they sat frozen, staring at the tent flap, a hand reached in and pulled it aside. A face loomed into view, an unearthly face, illuminated from below by the glow of the lantern, casting weird shadows.

"Dad?" John said, relieved to hear that his voice held steady.

"How you boys doing?" Dad smiled and crawled into the tent with them, letting the flap fall back into place.

John and Paul made room and the three of them sat cross legged, knees touching.

Dad looked at their hands. "Cards? That's a capital idea. What's the buy in?"

John was embarrassed and annoyed. Mr. Mooney knew enough to let them navigate this rite of passage on their own. They weren't kids anymore. Paul was already twelve. They were Boy Scouts now, or soon would be. "What are you doing here?" he said.

"I heard you got the Light Foot Award, wanted to congratulate you."

"Arrow of Light," John said. He pointed to the patch on his shirt.

"Yes, that's what Deborah told me." He gestured to the cards. "What's the game? Five card draw? Mexican sweat?"

"Spades," John said.

Dad shook his head, sharply. "No, you don't want to play that. That's a kid's game. You're not kids anymore." He took the cards from their hands and gathered up the rest. "You boys know how to play poker?"

Dad wasn't checking on them in case they were scared. He was here to prepare them for their new role as Boy Scouts, where the older boys would already know poker. John smiled at Paul, who grinned back like Dad had suggested they put a frog in the pulpit on Sunday morning.

Mr. Mooney was not only the Scoutmaster, he was also a deacon at the Baptist church in downtown Bolero. He kept a short leash on Paul and his older brothers. John figured Mr. Mooney had probably never played poker in his life.

Dad explained the basics, talking about flushes and straights and full houses, spouting off odds and other confusing numbers. John and Paul watched in a trance as Dad dealt out one trial hand after another, faceup, showing the play each hand had, until the lamp dimmed down and Paul had to pump it up again.

"You ready?" Dad asked. "Got any change?"

Paul dug in his pocket and found two quarters, a dime, and two nickels. John held out three nickels and two pennies.

Dad shook his head. "All I got is twenties. How about matches?"

Paul opened the waterproof tube he'd brought and poured out a dozen matches.

Dad shook his head. "I guess we'll have to play strip poker."

John looked at Paul, who looked back nervously. Was this what the older guys did in Boy Scouts?

Dad dealt out the cards, five to each of them, facedown. "Five card draw, no betting. The losers have to remove an article of clothing."

John picked up his cards. Eight of hearts, nine of spades, ten of hearts, jack of clubs, jack of diamonds. He tried to remember what Dad said. He had a fuzzy idea about what hand beat what and no recollection about the odds of making any specific hand.

To his left, Paul held his cards up in two hands like a chipmunk eating a nut. He shuffled his cards around, frowning at them. Dad held his cards deep in one hand, only the top edges showing above his fingers. He looked up at John with a raised eyebrow.

John looked back at his hand. He had two jacks, but he also had four cards of a straight. He tried to do the math. He could throw away three cards and hope he got another jack. Or he could throw away a jack and hope he got a seven or a queen. If he went for the jacks, he'd get three chances at picking up one of the two jacks left, assuming nobody else had one or both of them. Or he could drop a jack and have one chance at the eight cards that could give him a straight. That sounded better to him. He put a jack face down and Dad dealt him a card. John picked it up. Seven of diamonds. His pulse quickened. He looked up at Dad. Dad looked back, his face blank but his eyes twinkling in the lamplight.

Paul put all his cards down.

Dad shook his head. "You have to keep at least one."

Paul picked one up without even looking at it.

"If you have an ace," Dad added. "Otherwise, you have to keep at least two."

Paul picked up another card.

Dad gave Paul three cards, set two of his own cards down, and dealt himself another two. Then he set them down, face up. "Three twos."

Paul put his cards down. "Two threes."

John put his hand down. "Straight."

"Outstanding," Dad said, smiling. "Inside or outside?"

John frowned.

Dad pointed to John's hand. "Which card did you draw?"

"The seven."

"Outside." Dad looked at Paul. "Good thing it's a cool night or this would be a short game." He leaned over on an elbow and pulled off a shoe, tossing it to the side.

Paul looked around uncertainly. He slowly shrugged off his jacket. Dad dealt another hand.

After an hour, Dad wore pants, a t-shirt, and one sock. John had on a t-shirt and underwear. Paul shivered in his tighty whiteys, arms crossed over his chest.

Dad laid down his hand. "Read them and weep, gentlemen." A full house.

John groaned and dropped his cards on the sleeping bag. He slowly pulled off the t-shirt. He and Dad both looked to Paul, who just shook his head.

Dad laughed. "I forgot to tell you. The winner throws the losers in the river."

Paul's eyes went wide. "No!" He shivered, rubbing his arms.

"It's not that cold. I'll lead the charge." Dad rolled to his hands and knees and crawled out the tent flap.

Inside the tent, Paul and John looked at each other.

"I'm not going in that water," Paul said.

John shrugged. "Let's see how bad it is."

Paul hesitated. With Dad gone, the life seemed to have been sucked out of the tent. It felt stuffy, the hissing of the gas lantern suddenly loud.

Then came a loud whoop and a splash. John scrambled over the cards scattered on the sleeping bag, past Dad's shoes and shirt, and out of the flap. Paul followed close behind.

A t-shirt, pants, and boxers lay in a pile in front of the tent. Ten yards away the water in the swimming hole frothed as Dad splashed around.

"Whoo hoo!" Dad's voice echoed off the limestone ridge across the river. "Come on in boys, the water's fine!"

He swam away from them, got his footing on the sand bar that jutted from the ridge, and stood. The water hit him at the base of the ribs, his pale, hairless body luminescent except for his left forearm and his forehead, a trucker's tan.

John looked up at the full moon. It must have cleared the ridge while they were playing poker.

"Come on. It'll put hair on your chest." Dad dove toward them, his white butt flashing momentarily above the water line.

John pulled off his t-shirt.

"You're not going in, are you?" Paul said, his teeth chattering, his hands shoved into his armpits.

"Why not? We're in the middle of nowhere. Who's going to care?" John stripped off his underwear.

"What about water moccasins?"

"Too cold. They're reptiles, remember? Cold blooded."

Dad splashed to the shore, climbed out, hollered, and did a cannonball off the bank. John took a last look at Paul, who shook his head, and ran to the river, leaping into the pool while screaming.

Dad had lied about the water. It was as cold as Satan's back forty. It knocked the breath out of him as he sank into the pool, trailing bubbles. He felt like a discarded boudin casing, the sides stuck together. Then his feet hit the bottom, he curled into a ball and shoved off the sand, rocketing to the surface.

He broke through to the air and tried to suck in a lungful, but he was too cold to take a deep breath. He gasped a few times, and then whooped. "Whoo! Oh man!" He thrashed around thinking it might warm him up. It didn't. He swam to the bank and treaded water.

"Come on in, Paul! It's great!"

He didn't get a response. John climbed up on the bank and the cold air buried him like an avalanche. Paul had disappeared. He saw Paul's monster silhouette on the tent wall as he pulled his pants on. John turned and jumped into the river to escape the cold air, yelling as he flew across the divide between land and water.

He and Dad floundered around, hollering to drive the cold from their bodies, jumping from either side of the river, diving down to grab a handful of sand as proof they hit the bottom, and generally doing their best to convince themselves they were having a good time.

After a while the sting of the cold dulled down and it really did become fun. Paul stood on the bank, his hands jammed into his jacket pockets, and watched them without comment.

They eventually exhausted the limited entertainment possibilities in the pool. John decided to get out. He swam to the bank and was about to climb out of the water when a thought hit him. He turned back to Dad, who stood on the sand bar across the pool, agitating the water like a washing machine.

"Towels."

Dad stopped and looked up. "What?"

"We don't have any towels."

John saw a light flash on the ridge behind Dad and come to a rest, throwing Paul's shadow against the limestone. He turned around.

Paul stood on the bank, lit up like a prison break in an old movie. He turned toward the light, shielding his eyes with a hand.

John heard an engine rumbling from beyond the height of the bank, race for a bit and then fall to an idle. Then the sound of car doors and two more silhouettes on the bank, two men, one with a cowboy hat.

"Paul, what's going on out here?" That was Mr. Mooney, the one without the hat.

"Nothing, pa." Paul shrugged toward the water. "They was just taking a swim."

"They?" Mr. Mooney stepped past Paul to the edge of the bank and looked down at John. Then he looked across the pool to where Dad stood waist deep in the black water, glistening in the moonlight. "Who's there?"

"Evening, Carlton." Dad waved.

"Rusty?"

"Just taking the boys for a midnight swim. No harm in that."

"Tell that to the Jeffcoats up on the ridge. You been keeping them up for the past hour. They called the sheriff here," he nodded back to the silhouette with the hat, "asking what the heck I got going on out on my ranch. Figured it was a bunch of kids drinking."

"Nobody drinking. Just swimming. Didn't mean any trouble."

"Well you got trouble, anyway. Come on out and take your boy home."

Paul turned to Mr. Mooney. "Dad, we're camping and every-thing."

"Not tonight you're not. Get in the truck."

John watched the outline of Paul's figure deflate like he'd just jumped in icy water. John started to climb out, but remembered he had no towel and his clothes were in the tent, thirty feet away. He looked back at Dad, who remained standing on the sand bar.

Sheriff Weiss spoke for the first time. "Come on out, Lawson, you and your boy. Where's your car?"

"I walked."

"I'll give you a ride home."

"Thanks for the offer, Sheriff, but my son and I will just finish our swim and take ourselves home."

"Mr. Mooney asked you to leave. You're trespassing."

"Last time I checked, the river is public land. It doesn't belong to Carlton or anyone else."

"You'll be trespassing when you get out."

"Perhaps we'll float down to the bridge and get out on public property. No trespassing involved."

Irritation crept into the sheriff's voice. "Don't make trouble, Lawson. I'm going to let the drunk and disorderly go if—"

"I haven't even been drinking."

"I'm going to let you off on disturbing the peace, but you got to leave now."

"Or?"

"Or, I'll take you and the boy in. Cost you a couple hundred each to bond out."

"No need to drag the boy into it, Weiss."

"Near as I can see, they boy's already in it over his head." He adjusted his belt. "Unless you're saying that's somebody else's boy I see treading water down there."

Dad swore and dove toward shore. He broke water next to John. "Come on, son, let's go home."

John was reluctant to climb out naked into the spotlight, but Dad paid it no mind. He climbed up the bank, strode over to his clothes, and used his t-shirt to dry off. Then he pulled on his pants, not bothering with the boxers. John followed suit, very conscious of Paul, Mr. Mooney, and Sheriff Weiss watching as he walked the thirty feet wet and naked, but he refused to give any indication that he cared. He grabbed his t-shirt and darted into the tent to get the rest of his clothes.

He stood on his knees in the pup tent and dried off with his t-shirt as best he could. His jeans refused to slide up his wet legs without a lot of coaxing. Dad poked his head into the tent to grab his shirt and shoes. He winked.

"They don't know what they're missing, do they?"

John grunted as he rolled around on the sleeping bag, pulling on his jeans. He finally got them snapped, put on his shirt, and crawled out of the tent with his shoes.

When he stood up, he saw Paul and Mr. Mooney in the cab of the truck. The sheriff stood by the spotlight. "You can jump in back until we get to the house and let the Mooneys out."

"No need, Sheriff. We'll walk."

"Mr. Mooney wants you off his land. Once we get to the road, you can do what you want."

John and Dad jumped in the bed of the truck for the half-mile ride to the ranch house. Mr. Mooney got out without saying a word. Paul glanced back toward John as he got out, and then followed his dad into the house.

"Come on in," Sheriff Weiss hollered from the cab.

Dad leaned around to talk in through the open passenger door. "Just stop on the road and we'll jump out." He grabbed the door and slammed it shut.

They rode in the bed the mile drive to the highway, John dreading the walk home. It was a good five miles. It would take three hours even if they walked fast.

When the truck pulled to a stop at the highway, Dad jumped out. John followed.

Sheriff Weiss rolled down his window. "You sure, Rusty? I'm going that way."

Dad walked away, waving his hand. "You take care of yourself, Sheriff. Give my regards to the little woman."

John looked at the truck wistfully for a second, then turned to follow Dad. He heard the truck pull onto the highway and then watched it drive past them and away, ten times as fast as they were walking. Maybe twenty times.

They walked in silence for a few hundred yards, on the highway facing oncoming traffic, although there wasn't any, since it was probably one a.m. The road went over a creek and then Dad crossed to the other side and walked down a two-rut track that lead back into some woods, probably to a fishing hole or an illegal dump.

John followed. A few yards in he caught the reflection of a taillight. Dad walked to the car and pulled the door open. The light came on. It was Dad's Pontiac.

They got in. Dad pulled the keys from the passenger side visor and started the car.

John leaned against the door and looked at Dad. "You told Sheriff Weiss that you walked."

"Exactly."

"Why?"

"No need to tell the sheriff my business if it's none of his." He put his arm across the seat and craned his neck as he backed the car out onto the highway.

"But what did it hurt for him to know you had a car?"

"It's not about hurting. It's about needing to know, and he didn't." He put the car in drive and returned his arm to the seat back. "There are many things the law has no need to know." He looked over at John and nodded to drive the point home. "Remember that."

Even though his head wasn't in the game, John finished the night way ahead. Guzman lost most of his second buy in. John had plenty of chips for power plays of the type that Guzman liked to make and the momentum stayed with him for the rest of the night.

Of course he'd never see the money. The game was more of a battle of egos than a financial transaction. Lindsey kept the books so that players could settle, if they wanted, on a per game basis, but it rarely happened. When it did, the guy who insisted on getting paid got the cold shoulder until he realized his faux pas or dropped out of the rotation.

But even if he were of the mind to settle up, he'd never ask Guzman for the money. He had five kids at home, after all.

DAY 2: WEDNESDAY

Wednesday morning, John went from sleep to consciousness in a moment, as he usually did. He had been dreaming about the muffin and it left him disoriented. It took him a second to establish his surroundings.

He heard Christopher in the bathroom and checked his alarm clock. 5:12 a.m. John waited until the sounds moved to the kitchen before he got up. By the time he was showered, dressed, and in the kitchen, Christopher was heading out the door. They exchanged a look, but neither spoke.

There was plenty of coffee left over. In deference to his test results he didn't make bacon and eggs. Instead, he poured some local honey on a saucer with a muffin from dinner, poured a mug of coffee, and went out on the deck to watch the sunrise. Almost seven and it was already in the eighties.

He looked first to the west. The sky there was still black. Above him the heavens were a rich blue black. He settled in a chair facing east and looked across the valley. At the horizon, just above the opposite ridge, the sky was bleached out to a grey white. He watched that spot and tried not to think about the muffin in the evidence bag. Or the dream. He thought about the first time he looked out over the town from this ridge, the day he realized he had the power to change the future.

When John proposed to Jennifer, he came back to this ridge west of town and bought it. It was accessible only by a graded road that washed out after a good rain. Most of the fifteen acres was on an incline. The one somewhat level area was barely wide enough for a trailer, which was why he could afford it. He installed the single-wide a month before the wedding.

But he had bigger plans for his ridge. First, he built a deck. With no other structure in the way, it had 360-degree views. To the east it overlooked Bolero. To the west a higher ridge blocked out half the sky. To the north his ridge rose to the backbone of the range in a steep grade of limestone outcroppings dotted with mesquite, cedar, agave, and stunted oaks. To the south the trailer sat on cinder blocks well away from the future building site.

On the few evenings when neither of them was working, they drank margaritas on the deck and watched the sun set behind the western ridge. Then they turned their chairs around and watched the shadow creep across the city of Bolero spread out like a small quilt a few miles away, across the ranches and farmland beyond, to the Frio and another limestone ridge, the highest in the county. It had views of and access to the river and its sunset vista encompassed the valley and John's ridge.

John would watch the town and wonder what mischief the teenagers were getting up to and if he would be called out to subdue a group of boys who had been in junior high when he left for the academy. Jennifer would watch the last rays of the sinking sun sparkle on the summit of the opposite ridge where a developer was clearing ground for a new gated community called Bella Vista Estates.

Over the months a house gradually emerged from the caliche of John's ridge, a multilevel, two-bedroom bungalow that climbed the ground between the trailer and the deck and hung over the eastern side of the ridge, supported by pilings driven into limestone.

On the opposite ridge, on the highest point with the best view west, a very different kind of house materialized, more levels, more rooms, spacious multilevel patio, hot tub, pool. The new home of Judge Gibson, the politically ambitious son of an oil family.

Since John did most of the work himself when he wasn't working double shifts, their bungalow took several years to build. By the time Christopher was in the middle of potty training, they were saved from insanity by moving from the trailer to the house.

That was almost twenty years ago. John sipped his coffee and watched the sun rise behind the house where Jennifer now lived, the one at the top of the opposite ridge.

Jennifer had always loved the sunset, but John preferred sunrises. The gaudy show of a sunset felt like an overly earnest assurance from someone moving on to the next party that he would stop back by later. A sunrise was like a promise kept, like the one guy who said he would help you move and then actually showed up at seven a.m. on moving day.

The light slowly crept across the deck to the eastern edge of his ridge. There were a few late flowers on the clumped barrels of the claret cup cactus that grew there. The dew on the petals caught the light, glistening like cut glass. It would be gone in an hour as the day heated up.

Some mornings he wondered if he and Jennifer were sharing the quiet affirmation of the sunrise from opposite sides of the valley, but he knew better. In retrospect, he realized that although they had been married seven years, they had shared very little. Proximity didn't guarantee affinity.

He finished the muffin and the coffee and went back inside. He decided to get to the office early to read the incident report and statements gathered from the day before. He grabbed the prescriptions and stuffed them into his shirt pocket. He holstered his gun and his radio, grabbed the evidence bag, and headed out.

It was a quiet drive into town, the muffin silent inside the bag on the passenger seat. John began to wonder if he had dreamed the voices, and the dream he was trying to forget replayed itself in his mind.

Like in reality, he broke in the door of the storeroom only to find it devoid of suspects. The table sat in the middle of the room, surrounded by smoke and fire. In the center of the table, the muffin glowed in the spotlight originating from the belly of the mother ship. He didn't see a mother ship; he just knew that was where the light, and maybe the muffin, came from. In that moment he was certain, as one is in a dream, that the suspects had not escaped, but rather had transformed themselves into this muffin. He took the muffin into custody, read the transformed suspects their rights, and locked them in the back of a cruiser for transport to the county lockup.

Despite his memory of the incident, how he put out the fire, how Billy burst the trash bag and flooded the room, how Lovejoy commandeered the muffin and bagged it, this was now how John saw that moment. A muffin bathed in an otherworldly glow. He glanced at the ordinary-looking evidence bag, its red tape violated. It said nothing.

He was early to the office.

Ted, the night dispatcher, scrambled to get his feet off the desk while tossing a magazine aside. "Hey, chief."

"Hey, Ted. Fresh coffee?"

Ted jumped up. "I'm on it."

John went into his office, set the evidence bag on the desk, and pulled the papers from his inbox. The first witness statement was relatively free of typos, which meant Sam had keyed it in. John sat down and began reading. It was Bert's statement and it contained no new information. Ted came in with a cup of coffee. John thanked him and moved on to the next statement. It was from an accountant who worked in the office. He skimmed it and moved on. They appeared to be arranged in pecking order. The last statement from the set was from Billy. John didn't have to check to see who had typed it. The number of typos indicated it was Lovejoy.

The reports were good background, but there was no new information for John in them. He set them aside and looked at the evidence bag. He opened it, dumped the muffin out, set it on a notepad and looked at it. It had been in the room when the suspects barricaded themselves in, when they set the fire, when they escaped. If it was going to talk, why not tell him something useful, like what happened?

He turned to the next pile, statements from the protestors. They were even less helpful than the first set. By the time he finished, Ted was gone and the day crew was in. He called out without getting up. "Lovejoy."

Lovejoy stepped into the room. "Yessir?"

John pointed to the chair in front of his desk and Lovejoy sat down.

"Any clues on how they escaped?"

Lovejoy shook his head. "One way in. One way out."

"But still they got out."

"Yeah." Lovejoy's gaze dropped from John's face to the muffin. "Did you find any fingerprints or anything?"

John shook his head. "I didn't try. No suitable surfaces."

"What do you think it means?"

"Means?"

"The muffin. You think they left it behind like a calling card? Like a serial killer?"

"We don't know who left it there. It could have been an employee, not the suspects."

Lovejoy shook his head. "Too fresh. And I asked around the office. Nobody knew anything about it."

"Forget the muffin. Let's talk about the arson. You think it was a true believer?"

"You mean Jackson? He couldn't find his butt with a flashlight and a GPS." He blushed. "I mean . . ."

"I know what you mean." In a small town like Bolero, it was hard to maintain objectivity when everyone you had to arrest or caution or ticket was someone you knew. One thing he tried to impress on all the deputies and jailers was the need to avoid getting too familiar or personal with the citizens when they were in uniform. Hence Lovejoy's embarrassment at his slipup. "What about one of his disciples?"

Lovejoy snorted.

"Yeah," John said. "I think this looks more like a disgruntled employee. Talk to Bert. I want a list of all employee write-ups for the past eighteen months. And a list of everyone they let go." He leaned forward. "And check at corporate. It could be someone from another location. Also, we need a list of what was in the files that burned. That would be all contracts over five years old. Maybe you should write this down." John tipped the notepad to slide the muffin off it and handed it to Lovejoy.

He started writing while talking under his breath. "Write-up. Eighteen months. Corporate." He looked up. "What was after that?"

"A list of the files in the archives, contracts over five years old."

"Right." Lovejoy scribbled it down and stood. "I'm on it, sir." He strode out.

John watched him go, and then looked at the muffin.

The rest of John's morning was filled with the minutia of administering the sheriff's department. Budgets and e-mails and commissioner's court agendas and complaints about green bologna at the county jail and employee reviews to read and sign. The next time he looked up it was after twelve and he realized he was hungry. Then Sam stuck her head in the door.

"Charles Cook on line two."

John looked up at Sam. Despite her thirty-two years, her two kids, and the shapeless brown sheriff's department uniform, she wasn't hard to look at. Many were mystified by why she was a dispatcher instead of modeling or acting. John knew it was the two kids. She hadn't always made good decisions, but when it came to the kids she was like a cornered mama bear. And her steady income was their ticket out.

"Did he say what he wanted?"

"Nope. Just left the number. But he sounded impatient."

Cook was always impatient. He probably considered it the secret to his success, the fact he moved while others waited. Most likely he wanted to complain about the lack of an arrest for the arson. John punched line two and put it on speaker.

"Sheriff Lawson," he said, as if he didn't know who was on the line.

"John, how's life treating you?"

"Can't complain, Charles."

"And your folks? How they doing? I hear your daddy's back in town."

"Just visiting."

"Oh?" Cook said, as if he had heard otherwise. "Well, we're both busy, so I'll get straight to the point. Have you thought about where you want to be five years from now?"

This was getting to the point? "Like you said, Charles, we're both busy. What do you need?"

"It's more what you need, John. Your talents are wasted in the public sector. I've been looking for a head of security and I think you're the man for the job."

Cook Brothers covered a fourth of Texas. The offer was a quantum leap beyond sheriff. John didn't say anything. He looked at the muffin, waiting for more.

Cook filled the silence as John knew he would. "It would involve a significant increase over your current salary. More than double." More silence. "Triple. Plus benefits."

"I already have a job, Charles. Right now it's finding out who torched your storeroom. Do you know of any employees or former employees who have a grudge against Cook Brothers?"

"Talk to Bert about those details. I'm calling about your future. Every four years you're at the mercy of the voters, who God knows *zzzz . . . zzzz . . . psycho fish . . . zzzz . . . zzzz* and don't pay well."

John looked at the phone, but said nothing.

Cook finally spoke. "What do you say, John?"

"What was that you said about fish?"

"Fish? Did you say fish?"

"Didn't you say fish?" John looked from the phone to the muffin.

"No, John, I didn't say anything about fish." Cook's voice sounded wary, as if he couldn't decide if John was mocking him or going crazy.

"Okay, Charles, thanks for the offer. I'll give it some thought. But right now, I have an arson to solve."

John hung up the call, leaned on his forearms on the desk, and studied the muffin. Evidently he hadn't dreamed the episode in the truck on the way to Mom's house. He rotated the muffin slowly, viewed it from all angles.

"*zzzz . . . zzzz . . . catch the psycho fish . . . zzzz . . . zzzz*"

He jumped like he'd been stuck with a bread knife. Then he called out. "Sam. Could you come in here for a second?"

Sam walked in the door. John kept his eyes on the muffin. She stopped halfway to his desk and turned as if to leave.

"You want some coffee to go with that muffin?"

"*check the microfiche*"

John glanced up and locked eyes with Sam. She stood there, balanced in a half turn, waiting. She didn't look at the muffin. She didn't look disturbed.

"Black, right?" she asked.

"Yeah, black," John said.

Sam started toward the door.

"Oh, Sam."

She looked over her shoulder, waiting. This was a ticklish moment. If she didn't hear the muffin, the last thing he wanted to do was mention he had heard it. Especially considering his family history. "Did you hear anything?"

"About what?"

"Microfiche."

She turned back around. "Micro fish?"

"I mean just now, when you came in, did you hear a noise?"

Sam looked around the room. "A fish noise?" She didn't even look at the muffin.

"Never mind." John leaned back in his chair and smiled. "Just the coffee. Thanks. And ask Lovejoy to come in."

He watched the muffin while he waited, but it remained mute.

He thought about the message. *Check the microfiche.* He couldn't do that. It had been destroyed.

Lovejoy walked in and stood in front of his desk. "You wanted me, chief?"

John waited a few seconds to see if the muffin would speak. He looked up at Lovejoy.

"Did you make those calls to Cook Brothers?"

"Yessir."

"Corporate?"

"Yessir."

"When?"

Lovejoy checked his watch. "About an hour ago."

They were on the right track. The inquiries had stirred up things. Something had happened with an employee that Charles didn't want to come out. Maybe sexual harassment or some EEOC issue and the victim couldn't get justice through normal channels. In that case, the person might still be working at Cook Brothers.

"Let's also check for complaints the other direction, from an employee toward the company or another employee. Like discrimination or harassment."

"Yes, sir."

Sam came in with the coffee and set it on the desk next to the muffin.

John smiled at her. "Thanks."

Sam looked at the muffin. "That's a pretty nice muffin. Where did you get it, Flo's?"

"That's evidence," Lovejoy said. "We bagged it at the scene."

Sam looked at John to see if Lovejoy was serious. John nodded slowly. Sam shook her head.

John drove south toward town, the muffin beside him in the evidence bag. The more he thought about it, the more he liked the vindictive employee take on the arson. Digging through the write-ups and firings from Cook Brothers would be mind numbing, but that's what deputies were for. He passed Mabel's Beauty Parlor and on impulse pulled into the parking lot next to a 1980s Impala idling in front of the door, a girl in her twenties in the driver's seat, texting.

Mom never changed the sign after she bought it. John thought it was a good decision. Even if she had changed it to Deborah's, or something regrettable like The Clip Joint, everyone would continue to call it Mabel's anyway. Small towns like Bolero were slow to change. He knew old-timers who still gave directions according to landmarks that had been gone for decades.

"Go down to the old Arco station and hang a left." No matter that for the last fifteen years the Arco station was a coffee shop run by a couple from Colorado. If you didn't know about the old Arco station, you deserved to get lost.

Mom kept the shop like a walk-in freezer and the sudden chill refreshed him. He said hi to Mabel, the former owner. After a few years of retirement she missed the excitement of downtown Bolero and came back as the morning receptionist. She was in her eighties and still sharp. The downside was that customers had to yell into the phone when making appointments. And Mabel sometimes took a mid-morning nap at the counter.

"What's up, Johnny?" Mabel was the only person who called him Johnny. He never understood why. "Come in to get your ears lowered?" She chuckled.

Mom saved him from answering by walking up to the counter with a customer, a friend of Mabel's, her wispy hair styled from the available material. She was a papery-dry corn husk of a woman hunched over from osteoporosis.

"Trim and a set," she said to Mabel, "with the senior discount." She set her hand on the woman's shoulder. "Enjoy yourself at the wedding. Maybe next year you'll have some great-great grandbabies."

The woman smiled, displaying pristine dentures slightly too large for her face. She looked up at John.

"Is this your boy, Deborah?" she asked in a raspy half shout.

"Yes, ma'am."

She looked at John through glasses like decorative glass bricks from the fifties. "You must be mighty proud of him."

"Oh, I am. Bring me back some pictures, honey."

The woman plopped her purse on the counter and excavated the contents in search of cash.

Mom turned to John. "John, how sweet of you to drop by. And so unexpected." The crinkle of a smile around her eyes seemed to say otherwise.

"Lunch?"

Mom turned to the receptionist counter. "Mabel, how's the afternoon look?"

Mabel slowly counted the bills and coins extracted from the purse one at a time. John looked around the shop. Three cutting chairs, two shampoo stations and one ancient hair dryer like a mind-meld machine from a fifties sci-fi film. All empty. Tiffany, one of the stylists, swept up microscopic hair remnants.

John noticed the new issue of the *Bolero Bulletin* on the coffee table in the waiting area. As Lindsey said the night before, the lead story was about the new football coach at Bolero High and the scandalous loss of the preseason game. He picked it up and flipped it over. The story on the high school dominated the page below the fold.

The Bolero ISD school board has selected a San Antonio firm to lead the investigation into the cause of the collapse of the Bolero High gymnatorium late last week.

The collapse caused the school board to condemn the remaining five buildings on the campus, including the classrooms, until the investigation verifies their structural integrity. Classes began on Tuesday as scheduled, some in trailers brought to the campus over the weekend and others in classrooms on middle and elementary school campuses across the district.

The six buildings of the high school campus were built by Cook Brothers from 1988 through 1993, with classes beginning in the fall of 1989. The investigation will focus on the foundation and environmental factors.

This is the second Cook Brothers building in Bolero County to make the news this year, the first being the Abundant Life Tabernacle fire in April. In that case, the investigation revealed that the music pastor disabled the fire detection and suppression system during rehearsals for the Easter pageant because they repeatedly set off the smoke detectors. However, he failed to enable the system after rehearsal.

During the televised Easter morning service, a Roman guard tripped on his cloak during the Gethsemane scene, inadvertently setting fire to the papier-mâché forest. Access to the control panel was blocked by the Golgotha set, preventing anyone from engaging the system once the fire started. Although there were few injuries and no deaths, the building was declared a total loss.

"Ready, hon?"

John folded the paper twice and slipped in into his back pocket. "Where to? Anywhere in Bolero County. My treat."

Mom looked at Mabel with a big smile and back to John. "Well, since you're being so generous, let's go to Flo's."

John held the door open and the heat poured in like a tide surge. Mom went out, followed by the old lady inching her way to the Impala. Her great granddaughter stopped texting long enough to help her into the car. John opened the passenger door of his truck, moved the evidence bag to the dash, and helped Mom up to the seat.

In a few minutes they pulled into the parking lot at Flo's, the most recent of the three main eateries in Bolero after Stella's Kitchen and the Lone Star Grill. Flo made comfort food, the unleaded version, and compensated with more flavor. The diehards could get a chicken-fried steak, lean ground chuck coated in pepper panko bat-

ter and fried in safflower oil, but her menu focused on the female cli-
entele and the occasional diet-conscious male, such as Mooney. The
plate lunch specials devoted half the acreage to green stuff, a quarter
to starches, and a quarter meat.

John followed Mom as she greeted everyone in the dining room
and eventually settled on a table near the front window. She ordered
for both of them, doing her part to counterbalance his more carnivo-
rous proclivities, and gave the menu to Ginger.

"So, how's Liz doing?"

"She's fine."

"Be sure you treat her right, honey. She's one of a kind."

"Yes, ma'am."

Mom fell in love with the girls John dated long before he did.
She had nagged him into pursuing Jennifer back in high school. Not
that Jennifer had played hard to get. When they got married, Jennifer
did nails and facials at Mabel's during the day and waited tables at
the Lone Star Grill at night. She always got big tips, especially from
the men. Mom said it was because she was friendly and attractive.
The other waitresses said it was because she was flirty and a tramp.
But that was just jealousy. At least that's what he told Jennifer. And
himself.

But John didn't bring Mom here to talk about Liz or Jennifer.
"Do you really think he's changed?"

Mom looked puzzled. "Rusty? Who said anything about that?"

"Don't you remember what it was like?"

"Of course, honey. I was there."

"And you want to go back to that?"

"Oh, I forgot." Mom dug into her handbag and pulled out a
folded paper. She smoothed it out on the table, scanned down the
page with her finger, and read aloud. "This is truly a day of new be-
ginnings. You can start a fresh cycle of emotions and understanding
that can help you develop the quality and depth of your relationships." She looked up at him and smiled.

Ginny set a basket of whole-grain bread slices on the table and
left.

"What was Rusty's horoscope? All the bridges you burned have
miraculously regenerated?"

Mom reached past the bread basket and touched the hand John had wrapped around his iced tea. "John, honey, we're long past that now. Whatever you think Rusty did a quarter century ago, it's time to let it go."

"What I think—" John stopped himself as the stares from the surrounding tables converged on their table.

"Honey, the past is an anchor. You have to let go of who you are to become who you will be. This is our chance to grow beyond that moment so long ago. Remember what the Buddha said. Holding onto anger is like grasping a hot coal to throw at someone. You are the one who gets burned."

"Do you really believe that?"

"Of course I do. Which has more power, the past or the future?"

John calmly took a sip of tea, looked out the window, and turned back to Mom.

"I can't pretend like that stuff never happened."

"Twenty years ago, John. This is your chance to have a deeper relationship with your father."

"Sure, right up until he disappears, again. Which will be today if I have anything to do with it."

Ginny arrived with their lunch, shrimp over baby spinach. The shrimp was sautéed in olive oil and crushed red pepper, the baby spinach garnished with toasted pine nuts, hard-boiled eggs, and roasted red bell peppers. All covered with warm honey-sweetened vinaigrette.

Mom grabbed John's hand and said a quick prayer, then let go. John began eating without comment.

"I heard about that business at Cook Brothers," Mom said.

John grunted. No telling what the grapevine had turned that disaster into.

Mom leaned forward and whispered loudly. "Did those boys really disappear?"

John thought about how to answer. He realized for the first time that he had never actually seen or heard the suspects. If you didn't count the voices coming through the air duct, a detail he'd not mentioned to anyone and didn't plan to. All he had was Billy's story and vague comments in some of the protester's statements. He'd have to ask Lovejoy if he'd heard anything from the storeroom after he got there.

"You know I can't talk about an ongoing investigation."

"You know what it was, don't you?"

John struggled to subdue the natural flinch that accompanied Mom's revelations.

"Astral projection. Soul travel."

"How does that work, Mom?" John asked, knowing it was useless.

"While your physical body stays where it is, your astral body travels through the astral plane on a journey of discovery."

"But their bodies didn't stay there. They disappeared."

"Their bodies were never at Cook Brothers. That was the astral projection everyone saw."

Despite previous experience, John responded with logic. "So what can your astral body discover by barricading a door with a shelf and setting the room on fire?"

"That could have been an accident. Neophytes can get clumsy, project too much energy."

"Especially when they bring in their own paint thinner."

"Don't attribute to malice what can be explained by inexperience."

John returned to munching spinach leaves. He couldn't believe his career had come to this, talking to Mom about accident-prone astral arsonists and eating a shrimp salad in public. He speared another shrimp and a pine nut.

Actually, the salad was pretty good. He wouldn't mind eating it again, but did he really want to be known as the SaladShooter Sheriff? Would that cost him votes against Battles, a meat-and-potatoes lawman? Just like John, up until yesterday.

As they finished lunch over lemon pound cake with tea (Mom) and coffee (John), Mom caught his eye and held it.

"Honey, you remember the story of the prodigal son? How his father waited for him to return and welcomed him home with a party?"

John grunted.

"Well, your prodigal father has returned. You have a choice. You can welcome him back with rejoicing, or you can grumble like the brother who stayed home. Can you give him another chance?"

John stared at her. He hadn't been completely surprised by her reaction to Rusty's return, but he couldn't believe she expected him to do the same.

"For me? Can you do it for me?"

John took a slow sip of coffee and set the cup down. "No, Mom, I don't think I can."

John dropped Mom off at the shop and returned to the office. Before he got settled in his chair, Lovejoy popped in and stood in front of his desk.

"I got something, sir."

John rolled his chair up to the desk and looked up at Lovejoy.

"About the disgruntled employee thing."

"They gave you a list already?"

"Nosir. Bert said he couldn't release confidential files without a warrant. But I talked to Nadine."

A conversation with Nadine was better than a warrant. Lovejoy sat down in the chair. He was as wriggly as a Labrador puppy.

"Cindy Ellis used to be the receptionist at the Cook Brothers yard in Uvalde." Lovejoy paused meaningfully.

The implications were not lost on John. Cindy was the wife of Dr. Ellis, the dentist present at the protest. And Lovejoy had spoken in the past tense. John gestured for him to continue.

"Last year she complained about the calendars in the office. Girls in bikinis on the hood of muscle cars. That kind of thing. They ignored her and she filed a harassment suit. They had to take the calendars down."

Lovejoy looked at John.

John waited, but nothing was forthcoming. "So she won. Why would she have a grudge?"

"So, the guys in the office complained about her religious stuff. Bible, footprints poster, that kind of thing."

John frowned. "Footprints poster?"

"Guy has a dream about walking with Jesus on the beach and sees scenes from his life and footprints in the sand, sometimes two sets, sometimes one. The spots where there is only one set of footprints were the tough times in his life. He complains to Jesus that he had to walk alone through those times. Jesus says those were the times that he carried the guy. They were Jesus's footprints, not the guy's."

John nodded.

"She claimed freedom of speech. One of the guys filed a harassment complaint, said it created a hostile workplace environment. The ruling was that she had to remove the religious artifacts. She refused. They fired her."

"When was this?"

"March."

Five months ago. And then The Tabernacle burned down in April. John leaned back in his chair and considered this information.

"But there's another thing. Cindy has two brothers, one older, one younger. And they match the description of the suspects in the arson."

"You get names and addresses?"

"Yessir. Frank Berger is the older one. Leonard is the baby of the family. They're down outside of Utopia."

"Work address?"

"Frank's a painter. Self-employed. Leonard is between jobs."

"Any record?"

"Frank's got half-a-dozen tickets, all paid. Leonard has a few D and Ds. None recent."

John checked his watch. Only one thirty. "Maybe we can catch him at home. I'll give Sheriff Fuentes a courtesy call to let him know we'll be in the area."

Ten minutes later John was headed south with Lovejoy in the passenger seat, the AC cranked. John had left the muffin behind in a desk drawer. He reached into the backseat, pulled out a Mapsco book, and dropped it on the seat next to Lovejoy.

"See if you can find the Berger's house on there."

"No need, sir." Lovejoy pulled out a phone, entered the address, and a map popped up. A red line indicated the best route to their destination. He held it up to John. "That circle is us, the arrow shows our direction. This will take us all the way there."

As far as John knew, his phone just made phone calls, serving mainly as a horoscope delivery device. "That's handy." John tossed the Mapsco into the backseat. "By the way, did you ever see the suspects?"

"Nosir. They were already locked up before I got there. I just took their descriptions from Billy."

"Did you hear them talking or moving around inside the storeroom? Did they ever answer you?"

"Nosir, not so you would notice. There may have been some bumping around, but no talking."

"And the witness statements were pretty vague."

"Yessir," Lovejoy said, cautiously. He paused to recollect. "Only two people noticed them. Short, dumpy guy in a trucker's cap, faded black t-shirt, and jeans, larger solid guy in a white cowboy hat, wife beater and jeans. They're not sure about the paint thinner. One says he may have seen one of them carrying a crowbar."

"And they didn't see the suspects actually go into the storeroom, only into the warehouse."

"Correct."

John thought about it for a while. Why didn't anybody else see the suspects? "Is Billy tight with the witnesses?"

Lovejoy shook his head slowly. "Nosir, I don't think he is. They're a few years younger and Billy don't take to the church crowd, so to speak." He looked over at John. "What are you thinking, sir?"

"All this time we've been wondering how two grown men got out of a locked room with either Billy, you, or me watching the only exit the entire time. Perhaps we should have been wondering if they ever were in there in the first place."

They rode in silence as the truck curved down to a stop sign and turned south.

John finally connected the dots for Lovejoy. "It's possible that all three of them made up the story."

"Why? And who set the fire?"

"Or the suspects really did break through the fence and run into the warehouse. They might have even doused the room with an accelerant and left before you got there."

"But the door was locked and a shelf was knocked over against it."

"It was just a lock on the knob. Whoever did this could have leaned the shelf against the door, locked it, then let the door close behind them. The lock clicked and the shelf slid down farther against the door."

"Then how did they start the fire?"

"A fuse or some kind of timer."

"The fire department didn't find anything but cigarette butts."

"They weren't looking for it. It could have been as simple as a cigarette. And it might have been something that burned up completely, leaving no trace. Or washed away when Billy flooded the room. That little stunt may have not been an accident."

Lovejoy looked stunned. "But why would Billy set Cook Brothers on fire?"

"Maybe he wouldn't. That's up to us to find out."

They passed Vanderpool. John looked at Lovejoy's phone. "Where's our turn?"

Lovejoy used his phone to guide them, a blacktop road to a gravel road to a dirt road to a small frame house ten years overdue for a paint job. The yard was mainly dirt, bisected by a concrete flagstone walkway that jutted up from the yard like a causeway, put in a long time ago when somebody cared. There was a vehicle to the right of the house, an old F-150, but the rotting tires and waist-high weeds indicated that its last trip had probably been to the hardware store to pick up the paint for the house.

John pulled up to the edge of the yard and killed the engine. He spoke without taking his eyes off the house.

"We're going to take this nice and easy. I'll ask the questions. You'll be the silent partner."

"Yessir."

"I don't think we'll have any trouble, but keep your eyes open."

"Yessir."

Despite the air conditioning in the truck, John had to peel himself from the seat as he got out. He pulled on his jacket and hat. They walked up on the porch, barely big enough for the two of them and two metal lawn chairs placed on either side of a window air conditioning unit.

John approached the door. Lovejoy stood to the side by the air conditioner, which sounded like a 1952 Studebaker with a blown head gasket. It spewed hot air at them, piling on in the humid afternoon like a late hit in a ball game. The plank below the unit was damp with mold from the condensation.

There was no screen door. John knocked. A click of toenails on wood and a piercing yap told them Leonard had a small dog. After thirty seconds of barking he knocked again, louder. After another ten seconds he banged on the door and yelled, "Mr. Berger, we need to ask you a few questions."

John heard the sound of something knocked over, of someone stumbling and cursing. The door opened a few inches and a face peered out, probably midthirties. The white-tinged snout of a brown short-haired dog wedged into the gap a foot above the floor and snarled.

"Leonard Berger?"

The face squinted into the searchlight of the afternoon sun and took in John's black suit and tie over a white shirt. The smell of cheap whiskey hung heavy in the stifling heat.

"My soul don't need saving."

His attempt to close the door was blocked by the snout of the dog. John pushed the toe of his boot into the gap as the dog yelped and jerked his nose away.

"We're with the sheriff's office. We have a few questions."

The squint intensified. "About what?"

The dog returned to the gap in the door, growling, but keeping clear of the frame.

"Can we come in, Mr. Berger? I don't want you to lose any air conditioning." John looked down at the snarling lips curled back from yellowed canines. "And you'll need to restrain your dog."

The face examined John, then Lovejoy, who stepped into view, and disappeared. The snout of the dog disappeared, although the growls intensified. Then the door opened wider.

John and Lovejoy stepped into the dark cave of the Berger house, only marginally cooler than the outside, despite the labors of the window unit. The place smelled of stale cigarette smoke, sour laundry, and dog. The man lumbered barefoot to a broken-down couch, his back to them, the growling Chihuahua in his arms, and dropped into a sprawl.

74

He looked as disheveled as the furniture, moving like a much older man. His stained wifebeater and cutoffs were rumpled, as if he had been sleeping in them. His head gleamed with sweat, slick and shiny on the top with a thin fringe of hair, long around the sides and back like a monk in need of a trim. His nose was narrow and pointed. Combined with the squint, he had the look of a disreputable rat.

Lovejoy closed the door and stood in front of it. John walked up to a much abused coffee table covered with the evidence of a binge. Beer cans, vodka bottles, fast food containers, an overflowing ashtray, a Peterbilt cap.

"Leonard Berger?" John asked again.

The man looked near him but never directly at him. "Yeah, I'm Leonard. What's this all about?"

"Is Frank here? We'd like to talk to you both."

The dog barked and squirmed in Leonard's grasp. "Stacy, settle down!" Leonard yelled. The struggles diminished marginally. He glanced near John's ear and then away. "He's out on a job."

"And you're not?"

Leonard almost made eye contact. "I'm between positions at the moment."

"Where is Frank's job?"

"I don't know. I don't keep his schedule."

"Does he have a cell phone?"

"Yeah." Leonard gave the number.

Lovejoy pulled out a notebook and wrote it down.

"Where were you yesterday at one thirty?" John asked.

Leonard reached for a pack of Camels on the table, knocked a cigarette from it, and fired it up. "Right here."

"Can anybody vouch for that?"

A slow, crooked smile formed around the cigarette in Leonard's lips. "Yeah, Stacy."

At the mention of her name, the dog, which was restrained with only one hand, wrestled free, shot past John, and attacked Lovejoy's ankle. He managed to shake the dog free from his leg, but it maintained a hold on his pants. A swift kicking motion sent Stacy flying across the room and rolling into the kitchen, where she came to rest against the stove with a crash. The kick plate clattered down on her and she ran skittering across the worn linoleum kitchen floor back to Leonard's arms.

"Hey!" Leonard yelled, almost moving from his sprawled position on the couch. "I told you I was here. You don't have to beat my dog."

John ignored his outburst. "Can anyone confirm that you were here yesterday at one thirty?"

Leonard cradled Stacy in his lap. "I should sue for police brutality."

"Or we could take Stacy in to be put down for distemper," Lovejoy retorted from the door. He fingered the ripped hem of his pants.

"There ain't nothing wrong with Stacy," Leonard yelled.

"Let's calm down," John said. "We just need to establish your whereabouts yesterday at one thirty and we'll be gone."

"Why?" Leonard said. He squinted at them and sat up suddenly on the couch, looking closer at the shoulder patch on Lovejoy's uniform. Stacy offered a tentative growl from within the shelter of Leonard's arms. "Bolero County? You got no jurisdiction here. I don't have to answer your questions."

"Or we could call Sheriff Fuentes. You know him, don't you? If he has to drive all the way up here from Uvalde to persuade you to cooperate, he'll be in a great mood when he walks in."

Leonard flopped back into the womb of the couch, squinting his left eye shut at the smoke curling up from the cigarette. "I'm cooperating. You just don't believe me."

"It's just a matter of confirmation."

"Nah, you don't believe me. Freaking cops, don't believe anybody."

"Maybe that's because—"

John threw up a hand to cut off Lovejoy's comment.

A light flickered on behind Leonard's eyes. He pulled the cigarette from his mouth with his free hand and opened both eyes. "Hey, you're here about that fire. At that construction company."

"What makes you say that, Mr. Berger?"

"I saw that on the news. Somebody set a fire and got clean away." Leonard leaned back on the couch, took in a long drag, and blew a column of smoke into the middle of the room. "Good for them. Too bad they didn't burn it to the ground."

"Why would you say that?"

"I have my reasons."

John saw that they would get nothing else of significance from Leonard and the evidence was too slim to take him in. He glanced back at Lovejoy. "Make a note that Mr. Berger has no alibi for the time in question."

"Hey, I got a alibi. I was right here. I done told you."

"No confirmed alibi," John said.

Lovejoy made a note and fixed his gaze on Leonard. John walked to the door, stopped, and turned back.

"Do you have a phone here?"

Leonard shook his head. "Cut off. Last month."

"We'll be in touch," John said.

"I can't wait," Leonard said, lighting another cigarette off the first one.

They left, saying nothing until they got to the truck. John pulled out onto the dirt road and headed back toward Bolero. Lovejoy pulled his foot up onto the seat, pushed his pants leg up and his sock down, and inspected his ankle.

"It was just a Chihuahua," John said.

"Broke the skin." Lovejoy showed the bite mark to John.

John had Lovejoy call Frank on his fancy phone as they drove back to the office. Frank had been on a job yesterday, but by himself. Another unconfirmed alibi.

"What do you think?" Lovejoy asked. "Are they good for it?"

John shook his head. "Something doesn't add up, here."

"The thing about Billy?"

"Yeah."

They rode in silence the rest of the way.

Back at the office, John caught up on his messages. By the time he was finished, it was after seven. John grabbed the muffin and headed out for the Lone Star Grill for a Shiner and a patty melt with fries. He got a three-top facing the door with the front window to his left. Most of the window tables were open because they were in the sun, which was about an hour above the horizon and dumping the last of its load before calling it a day. John could wait it out and he liked to see what was coming.

Ginger took his order. He wasn't surprised to see her. She supplemented her lunch shift at Flo's with a night shift at the Lone Star. Lots of folks in Bolero worked multiple jobs.

When his order arrived he remembered his test results, which made him think of the prescriptions in his pocket. It was too late to get them filled, now. He'd have to do it tomorrow. He looked at his plate. It was all carbs and cholesterol. The only green thing was the pickle spear.

His thoughts were interrupted by a large man walking in through the front door. He wore black slacks cinched up with a leather belt and large buckle half buried under a paunch obviously cultivated over decades in greasy spoons. A white shirt covered the expanse of his upper torso, a bolo tie at the collar. He held a white straw hat in one hand as he scanned the room, his eyes coming to rest on John. His eyes narrowed, then his face broke out in a smile and he walked over.

"Sheriff Lawson. How's the wife and kids?"

John nodded without setting down his patty melt. "Can't complain, Battles." One of the reasons John suspected Judge Gibson of putting Battles up to run against him was that Battles had adopted Gibson's greeting. They were the only two in Bolero who asked him that inappropriate question. "And you?"

"I've seen worse, Lawson. Much worse."

John didn't doubt it. Like most peace officers John knew, Battles was divorced. It was a profession notably tough on marriages, especially in big cities like Dallas. Only the most determined, or the most masochistic, kept a spouse for the long run in their business.

Uninvited, Battles pulled out the chair opposite and sat. It creaked under his weight. "Can't visit long. Meeting someone, but I'm a little early." He nodded to Ginger. She brought him a Bud Light, which made John smile.

How quickly Battles had ingrained himself into the social fabric of Bolero. Ginger already knew his drink. Battles held up the bottle. When John didn't respond, he clinked it against the Shiner sitting next to John's plate, took a drink, and set his bottle on the table.

"Nasty bit of work at Cook Brothers, Sheriff." Battles winked. "You let the media get out ahead of you. That's going to come back to bite you."

"I was elected to keep the law, not spin stories for a TV station in San Antonio."

"That's where you're wrong, Sheriff. Everybody in Bolero gets their news from KHIL-TV. You talk to a few people a day. KHIL talks to all of them every day. And when a story goes national, and I'll bet you a grand right now that this one will, based on Pastor Johnson's track record if nothing else, the takeaway for the locals is that their sheriff has just made them look like bumpkins to the whole country."

"You think the people of Bolero care what they're saying in New York City and D.C.?"

"You bet they do. And about what their family in Houston and Beaumont and Austin and Shreveport and Little Rock is saying. You think the people in Waco cared about what the country said about them?" Battles leaned forward. "Here's a little tip from the big leagues. You have deputies to man the oars. The sheriff's job is to set the course, not rig the sails."

John took a gulp of his Shiner. Battles evidently figured John was out of his depth with this case and the election, incapable of controlling the course of events.

He set his bottle down and kept his expression blank. "Mighty neighborly of you to help me out like this, Battles."

"My pleasure, Sheriff."

The front door opened and a third-generation rancher with influence across several counties walked in. Battles heard the bells on the door jingle and twisted in his seat. He nodded at the rancher and stood up. He held out his hand to John.

"Good chatting with you, Sheriff."

John nodded at him and took another bite, ignoring the hand. "The pleasure was all yours," he said around the patty melt.

John had thought he would be able to enjoy the guilty pleasure of his patty melt in peace, but he was mistaken.

As Battles walked away, Rusty stepped into the door, walked to his table, pulled back the chair Battles had just vacated, and sat down. He tossed a two finger salute at Ginger and then turned to John, smiling. "Saw your truck out front and thought we could catch up a bit."

John didn't respond. Ginger arrived with a Corona and left just as quickly. John shouldn't have been surprised, but the man had only been in town two days. It was unnerving and more than a little annoying.

Rusty took a long pull from the bottle, exhaled with satisfaction, and looked back at John. "Did you ever ask out that filly you were so taken with back in high school? What was her name?"

"Jennifer?" John blurted out before he could stop himself.

"Oh yes, I remember now. Val's daughter, if I recall. It was always a mystery to me how a misshapen lump of humanity such as Weiss could sire such a creature." He watched John expectantly.

"We divorced thirteen years ago."

"Oh. You married her, then. Any kids?"

"One. Christopher."

Rusty pondered on that while he took another drink of his beer. "So I'm a grandfather, then?" He pulled a pack of Camels from his shirt pocket, slipped a cigarette from the pack, and thumped the filter against the table. "Live with his mother?"

"You can't smoke in here."

Rusty looked around the room, surprised. "You don't say." He looked wistfully at the cigarette balanced between his thumb and forefinger. "Things have really changed around here."

"A lot of things can change in a quarter of a century."

Rusty shifted his gaze to John. "I suppose you're right." He slipped the cigarette back into the pack and dropped it into his pocket. He picked up his beer and leaned back in his chair. "See you got an election coming up in a month or so."

John shrugged.

"Who is this Battles character running against you?"

John glanced involuntarily at the table across the room where Battles was in deep conversation with the rancher. He turned back to his dinner and took a bite of the pickle, followed by a bite of patty melt.

Rusty followed his glance, watched for a few seconds, and turned back. "The guy just sitting here?"

John nodded, washing the bite down with beer.

"And I'm guessing this thing out at Cook's equipment yard isn't helping things any in that department."

John didn't respond. How could he know so much about current events and not even know he had a grandson?

"What do we know about Battles?"

"*We* don't know anything," John replied with a sudden passion. He'd tried to maintain an objective distance, but the situation overwhelmed his reserve. "Whatever part you might have had in this ended twenty-four years ago."

He stood, his chair scraping against the floor, intending to leave, but suddenly Liz was standing next to him. She kissed him on the cheek.

"I was going home from a PTA meeting and saw your truck out front."

Rusty stood, taking in Liz with one long glance. She turned to him. He smiled.

"Is this your father?" Liz asked without taking her eyes off Rusty. She held her hand out.

John watched the shrinking gap between her hand and Rusty's. He had a sudden urge to sweep Liz out of the Lone Star before their hands met, as if by preventing that touch he could keep his history safely in the past and out of their relationship. He placed his hand on her shoulder, but it was too late.

Rusty took her hand in both of his. "I have that honor. Rusty Lawson." He seemed to bow without actually moving.

"Elizabeth Huxley. I heard you were in town. But not from John."

She looked a mild reproof in his direction and reached for the chair between them. Rusty stepped forward, pulling it out for her. She flared her eyes at John. A raised eyebrow asked him why the Lawson chivalry hadn't passed down to him. As she sat, John looked over her head. Rusty smiled back. John tamped down his anger to a smoldering glare and dropped into his chair. Rusty sat and waved Ginger over.

"What is your pleasure, Elizabeth?"

"A cabernet."

Rusty nodded at Ginger and she disappeared.

Liz leaned forward on her elbows, her chin resting on her thumbs. She looked like a schoolgirl. John felt a pang of desire. And maybe a little jealousy.

"What brings you to Bolero, Mr. Lawson?"

"Rusty," he corrected.

"He's just visiting," John said.

Liz kept her gaze on Rusty. "From?"

"Florida," John said.

Liz and Rusty both looked at John like he was the one who had just crashed their dinner. He looked from Liz to Rusty and back, shrugged, and picked up the patty melt he had tossed down on the plate a few moments before. Liz frowned at the remains of the sandwich and turned back to Rusty.

"What is it you do in Florida? John's told me so little about you. Nothing, really."

John washed the sandwich down with the last of his Shiner and handed the bottle to Ginger as she delivered the cabernet, signaling for another. In the eight years that he had been seeing Liz, he had intentionally avoided conversations about his father. That plan was about to go up in smoke.

Rusty took a longer pull from the Corona, set it down, and leaned back dismissively. "I have a hand in on several ventures. A few well-placed gambles have paid off. I can't complain." He pushed the bottle aside and leaned forward to match Liz's posture. "Did you say you came from a PTA meeting? Do you represent the P or the T?"

"Oh, the T, definitely." Liz glanced at John before continuing. "I love teaching kids, but I can't imagine having to live with them. One must have a sanctuary, don't you think?"

"Perhaps you are right. I taught senior English for many years, and the bell at the end of the period was sometimes a blessing." Rusty sipped his beer, reflecting. "But perhaps it's like the difference between dating and marriage. Those who embrace life with complete abandon reap rewards that are denied to the cautious."

Rusty looked at Liz as he spoke, but that didn't fool John. Was that why he left, because he couldn't be encumbered by a cautious soul? Then why had he come back?

Liz nodded slowly, forehead furrowed in thought. She sipped her wine. "Tell me a story about John. What was he like when he was younger?"

John couldn't think of a worse idea, or of a way to derail this line of conversation without looking like more of a jerk than he did already. Ginger appeared with the Shiner. John accepted it gratefully and took a long drink.

Rusty looked at Liz like he was trying to figure out what she was made of. He glanced at John and turned back to Liz. "You know John's ex-wife? Jennifer?"

"It's a small town and she's a big presence."

Rusty nodded appreciatively. "Well said. Back when John was in high school, Jennifer was his best friend's girlfriend." He looked at John. "What was his name? Carlton Mooney's boy."

"Paul?" Liz asked. "Jennifer and Paul?" She turned to John. "You never told me that."

"It never came up."

"Thing was, John was smitten the first time he saw Jennifer. Way back in grade school. Never told a soul, but we knew, me and Deborah. And Jennifer. She knew."

"Okay, that was a nice story," John said. He placed a hand on Liz's forearm. "Ready to go?"

"That's just the setup," Rusty said.

Liz patted John's hand, but otherwise ignored him.

"She was a high-spirited colt and a frisky filly. Old Carlton practically spit nails when he heard she was dating Mooney. She wasn't old enough for my class, but I knew what she was. The Mooney boy was entirely out of her league. Not much to look at and the personality of a wounded duck. And him paired with a vixen with a natural talent for maximizing potential? But she took up with him. Probably to torment John with her constant proximity."

Liz gave John a pitying look and patted his hand again. He withdrew it, pushed his chair back, turned it at an angle, kicked his feet out past Liz's chair and crossed his boots. He drank his Shiner with his left elbow on the table, looking out across the room.

"But John uttered not a word of his feelings to anyone. He was Lancelot, sans betrayal. Or perhaps not." Rusty looked at him. "How did you come to marry her if she was with the Mooney boy?"

John didn't give the answer, that when Jennifer heard the rumors that he had run his own father out of town at the age of sixteen, she began to suspect there was much more to him than she had seen. She cut Paul loose, for which Paul seemed relieved, and took up with John.

He didn't realize at the time what a life-changing moment it was. Jennifer's dad took him under his wing, launched his career in law enforcement.

It was a silent coup. One day she was Paul's girl, the next she was John's, and they never spoke about it. Until after the divorce, when Paul thanked John for his sacrifice in saving him from marrying Jennifer.

John stood. "Okay, are we done, here?"

Liz smiled at him and turned to Rusty. "From what I've heard of Jennifer, I don't know that John had much say in the matter."

"True, she was an elemental force," Rusty said.

John sat back down and leaned across the table toward Rusty. "So, when are you headed back to Florida?"

"I thought I'd stay a while, catch up with old friends, meet my grandson. You know." He shrugged.

"No, I think it's better that you keep your visit short. Very short." Liz eyed John.

Rusty shook his head. "I don't want to disappoint Deborah. She's expecting me to be here a while."

"She'll get over it. She did fine the last time."

"John," Liz gasped.

John leaned back with an arm over the back of his chair and looked at Liz. "He's going to leave anyway. It's what he does. Better to do it now, before anyone gets their hopes up."

"You seem very sure of yourself," Rusty said, quietly.

"The fact that you're here right now proves it. You left someone or something back in Florida, didn't you? How many someones did you leave in the last twenty-four years?"

Liz grabbed his arm. "John! What are you doing?"

Rusty shook his head. "No, it's alright. He's upset. I left twenty-four years ago. I understand that."

John leaned forward again, and spoke in a forced whisper that took the varnish off the table. "You don't understand anything. I'm not upset because you left. I'm upset because you came back."

Liz pushed back from the table. "Perhaps I should leave."

John stood. "I'll walk you out."

Rusty signaled Ginger for another beer. John threw a twenty on the table and walked out with Liz. The sun had disappeared behind the western ridge and the security lights over the parking lot sputtered to life, but the heat persisted, more the glow of a gas oven turned off than the blast furnace of the day. It didn't even raise a sweat. Not yet.

Liz walked to her car and then turned on John. "How can you treat him like that? He's your father."

"Who abandoned his family twenty-four years ago."

"And who has come back to make amends."

"You don't know what—" John bit the word off and walked toward his truck, but turned back after a few steps. "He's a vampire, Liz. Yes, he's charming and witty and endearing, and he seduces you into believing in him, but in the end he just sucks the life out of you."

"Maybe he's changed. It's been twenty-four years after all."

"You have no idea how many times I've heard those words. He's changed. This time it will be different."

"No, I don't. Because you never talk about him."

"There was nothing to talk about. He was gone. And even if I do nothing, in a few days or weeks or months, he'll be gone again. So why doesn't he just leave now and save everyone the trouble?"

Liz closed the distance between them. John watched her come, unsure of her intention. She slipped her arms under his and around him and pulled him to her. He slowly released the tension in his body and put his arms around her. They hugged in silence for a few moments, then she pulled away.

"Why don't you come over for dinner tomorrow. Just you and me. Christopher can fend for himself."

"That seems to be his specialty," he said.

When John got home Christopher was already in bed. He went out in the garage, opened the freezer, and stood there looking at the ribs and the smoky air cascading down the front of the refrigerator. He closed the door without touching the ribs.

He dropped onto the couch and tortured the intro to "Nobody's Dirty Business" out of his guitar, having to stop several times.

After several years of playing the same songs, he'd gotten bored. Last year he quit playing, but he found himself walking around the house in the evening, restless and vaguely annoyed for no good reason.

Then he heard about Travis-style picking. John got a book from a music store in San Antonio. He had to unlearn just about everything he had figured out on his own, but it gave him a new reason to pick up his guitar and he stuck with it, practicing every day for an hour after he came home.

Next, he discovered Mississippi John Hurt and a whole nother corner of blues. He picked a song to learn and now, after three months of submitting himself to therapeutic abuse, he could almost play it. Almost. The trick of getting the thumb and fingers on his picking hand to work independently always defeated him. It was like trying to pat your head and rub your stomach.

He tried again, muttering the verse as he tried to keep his thumb and fingers from confusing each other. It came out in spurts. At the end of the first line he stopped, realigned his fingers, and continued.

It was always that spot in the first measure, beats three and four. It was unfair for John Hurt to put that lick right there at the front. He should have given people a running start at it.

After half an hour of getting no closer, he gave up. He leaned the guitar against the couch, grabbed a Shiner from the fridge and a cheap cigar from his humidor and went out on the deck.

It was an hour after sundown, a good time for deck sitting even if he couldn't see the view. The thick atmosphere grudgingly relinquished the last of the pent-up heat of the day and the female mosquitoes retired from their bloodlust to ponder their own short life spans.

There was the constant love of a good woman, a welcome if undeserved windfall after the passionate but mercurial Jennifer. There was Christopher's career-jeopardizing humanitarian scheme. There was Mom, and now Rusty, both seemingly incorrigible and somehow cosmically deserving of each other. There was the arson, puzzling and annoying.

His thoughts turned to the unexpected job offer from Cook. The money would come in handy. The tiny house was in need of serious renovations—a new roof, a decent paint job, bringing the bathrooms and kitchen into the twenty-first century. All left undone for the past two decades because of his income. Or lack thereof.

Why not take the job? Battles would probably win the election, anyway. And the hours couldn't be any worse than law enforcement. He could splurge a little on Liz. Maybe take her to Hawaii.

The prescriptions that were still in his pocket reminded him that he'd also live longer if he got out of law enforcement. A proper meal was the exception in his schedule. Most of the time he was grabbing high-carb, high-cholesterol fast food on the way to some incident, eating at odd hours, fasting and bingeing. A proper job with proper hours and proper pay would mean a proper diet. Or at least a better one. He couldn't see giving up Stella's ribs.

He ignored the siren call emanating from the freezer and considered the muffin. It sat beside him on the small X-frame folding table he kept on the deck for his ashtray. He took a long, slow drag from the cigar and exhaled, wreathing the muffin in smoke. He had probed its depths with a paper clip and discovered nothing that would explain its cryptic transmissions. But he remained strangely reluctant to tear it apart, dreading at some primal level the verification that it was nothing more than an ordinary bran muffin, just like the mute muffins Liz brought for dessert the night before.

The thought of the muffin speaking both intrigued and terrified him. Was it proof that the universe did indeed speak to those tuned to its mystical wavelength as Mom believed, or was it proof that he was his father's son?

Rusty was about the same age as John was now when he disappeared. He'd left his meds behind, the lithium that he was so reluctant to take when things seemed to be going okay. On and off through the years John had worried over the fact that manic depression was genetic. Or bipolar disorder, as they called it these days. But he'd never had cause to suspect the worst. Until now.

Because on Tuesday two religious extremists trapped in a bran muffin, or two malcontents, depending on your interpretation of the case, talked to him, asking cryptic questions and making random comments. If he had to hear voices from a muffin, he'd prefer one that supplied answers instead of creating more questions. He already had plenty of those.

He went to the fridge for another Shiner, came back with this week's copy of the *Bolero Bulletin*, and flipped through it under the yellow bug light, having already read the front page. It was filled with the usual info about local happenings. A lengthy letter to the editor devoid of paragraph breaks caught his eye.

The heading read *Bolero High School Collapse No Surprise*. John skipped down to the end, saw it was written by the local conspiracy theorist, and decided to read it anyway. He skimmed through quickly and then read it a second time, more slowly.

Dear Editor,
    It will come as no surprise to the few remaining readers of your yellow sheet that the trained monkeys you call reporters were themselves surprised when Bolero High School collapsed last week. In fact the only real surprise was that it took twenty years for it to cave in. Twenty-three years four months and eleven days ago the pinhead Commissioner's Court committed age discrimination upon my person by forcing me to retire. My last official act before I was unceremoniously escorted from my office with nothing but two cardboard boxes of plaques and commendations to show for the best forty-five years of my life that I gave Bolero County was to file the site report on the unsuitability of the proposed location for that very high school, or for any structure more substantial than a brick [outhouse]. Of course nobody was less surprised than I when construction began ten months later by the infamous Crook Brothers and no that isn't a typo. I meant to spell it that way because that's what they are. They got rid of the inconvenient facts the way they always have by burying them in bribes financed by the Rothschild syndicate. I don't know why I even bother to waste the typewriter ribbon on this letter since nobody will listen to me now any more than they did twenty years ago when I predicted this would happen. The only happy moment in this otherwise miserable fiasco is that the inevitable demise of the ill-conceived structure occurred three weeks after the spring term and beyond a janitor who sustained a broken arm while waxing the floor of the gymnatorium at the time of the catastrophe there were no casualties. The fact that your publication is little more than a mouthpiece for the New World Order and therefore will

never print this letter makes the writing of it that much more of a futility. My only consolation is that if nothing else this letter puts the forces of evil on notice that there is at least one good man remaining who will not stand by and do nothing. And this is no hollow threat. I can produce the evidence to give the lie to the baseless claims of plausible deniability by all malefactors concerned.

Edward Crookshank
    Bolero County Inspector, retired

John set the paper down, sipped his Shiner, and looked at the muffin. It declined comment for the record. John looked back at the paper. Maybe he would pay Crookshank a visit before he went in tomorrow. Old men were often up early, and Crookshank was closer to ninety than to eighty.

He called it a night and carried the muffin back inside.

DAY 3: THURSDAY

John poured the last of the coffee from the pot into a travel mug, shoved the prescriptions into his shirt pocket, and grabbed the evidence bag on his way out the door. The muffin was inside.

The drive to Crookshank's cabin took twenty minutes. He lived in a remote canyon, the only house for miles. John had been there once after reading a letter to the editor complaining about raves in the neighboring canyon. He took the highway to a blacktop road to a gravel road to the mouth of the canyon.

The driveway was a mile-long dry creek bed. It was not the place to visit in your Lexus, but Crookshank didn't get visitors. He was the last of his line, an old Scottish bachelor with no friends. He drove into town once a month, loaded his Jeep with supplies, and spoke only the words required to make his purchases.

John found the house up on a limestone shelf, high enough to avoid the flashfloods that hit these canyons in the rainy season. He pulled up next to Crookshank's Jeep, sounded his horn once to let the old man know he was there, and took his time getting out of the truck. The homestead was still in shadow. The canyon only got a few hours of sun a day.

He stood by the truck, sipping coffee from the travel mug, and waited for the old man to come out on the porch. John was certain he was up because he could see smoke rising from the chimney. Crookshank didn't have electricity, not willing to pay to bring it out this far. He grew up during the Depression and had been a doughboy in the second war. Privation was his middle name.

John decided the old man had finally gone deaf and walked up to the cabin. He knocked on the door and called out, but got no response. He tried the door. Unlocked. He pushed it open and looked inside.

One large area served as living room, kitchen, dining room, and office. Crookshank sat with his back to the door in the gloom at the kitchen table, his upper body collapsed on the table. An oil lamp sat next to him, but it was not lit.

John walked quickly to the table and looked down at the man. His head rested on an ancient typewriter, his arms trapped under his body, his hands clutched to his chest. The body was cold to the touch.

John knew his radio would not work in the canyon. He tried the cell phone, but it had no reception. And Crookshank didn't have a phone, of course. He would have to drive out to the highway to call it in. He returned to his truck, drove far enough to get a signal, and called Sam. He outlined what needed to happen and hung up. As he turned the truck around, his phone made the voice-mail noise. He checked it. It was Mom.

"Honey, call me as soon as you can. I have some important news."

He deleted the message and headed back to the cabin. The news was most likely some highly instructive bit in his horoscope designed to adjust his attitude regarding Rusty's return.

Back at the cabin, John parked his truck to the side so he wouldn't get blocked in by the deluge of officialdom on its way, and resumed his inspection of the scene.

He started with what Crookshank had been writing when he died. The paper in the typewriter began with a date, the words "To the editor" and a few sentences regarding public sanitation visible without moving the body. The date was two days ago. John left Crookshank's upper body as it was. He knelt down, grabbed a pants leg, and pulled it forward. The leg moved freely with only a little resistance. Rigor mortis had come and gone. He had been dead somewhere between twenty-four and forty-eight hours.

John checked the oil lamp. The reservoir was dry. He had sat down to type at night, possibly, although given the gloom of the canyon twenty-two hours of the day and the failing eyesight of an octogenarian, he might have burned the lamp during the day when writing. Then again, Crookshank was very frugal, so perhaps not.

Based on the rigor and the lamp, John guessed that Crookshank had died not last night, but the night before. He looked more closely at the body. There was nothing to indicate foul play, no blood or wounds or bruises or ligature marks around the neck. He looked around the room. Nothing looked out of order. Dishes in the sink, a clean skillet on the woodstove. Then he remembered the smoke.

He stepped to the stove. It was cool to the touch. He opened the grate. The ashes were cold. He walked out into the front yard and looked at the chimney. No smoke. He stepped back further and saw that smoke was rising from behind the house. His earlier impression of smoke coming from the chimney had been an illusion.

John walked around the cabin. In the back yard, smoke rose from a fifty-five gallon drum. John scanned the area, but saw no one. He looked in the barrel. Inside, a pile of smoldering ashes mixed with a few scraps of unburned paper. John snatched up a fragment and inspected it. It was the top left corner of a legal document containing a filing date, June 10, 1977, and part of a document number.

John looked at the barrel again. Ashes filled the bottom half. He touched the side. Warm. Crookshank had been dead for at least thirty-six hours. If he had started the fire, it would be cool to the touch by now. Not to mention the fact that Crookshank would have never burned the files he had taken such trouble to duplicate and store.

John went out front and inspected the area where the vehicles were parked. It was mainly gravel. He took a look at his own tires and the Jeep's tires, got his camera out of the truck, and walked back up the creek bed. A hundred yards later he found a patch of sand in a bend. Because the sun wouldn't shine down here until the afternoon, the sand was still damp from the morning dew. His incoming tracks showed very plainly. He looked closer and saw that his tracks overlapped other tracks that didn't match the Jeep. The man who never got visitors had suddenly become popular.

John took several pictures and went back to the cabin. In the central room, he noticed doorways on either side. The one on the left led to a bedroom so neat it looked like Crookshank was preparing for a showing. He walked across the central room to the other doorway.

Inside, cardboard bank boxes lined the walls from floor to ceiling. They were labeled by year, starting with 1945. He surveyed the collection. It stopped at 1975. Thirty years. In the letter to the editor Crookshank had said he worked for forty-five years. And he said he had the site inspection report he had filed for the construction of Bolero High School, which happened in 1990. So where were the last fifteen years of documents?

He looked out the window to the smoking trash barrel. Cook Brothers archives destroyed in a fire. Crookshank's archives destroyed in a fire. Within twenty-four hours of each other. And Crookshank was dead. In the letter, Crookshank implied that the original report filed with the county had been destroyed as well. He would verify that.

Bert Masters had assumed the warehouse arsonists were connected with the Tabernacle. John had suspected they were ex-employees with a grudge. But he now realized they both might be wrong. It was beginning to look less like revenge and more like a cover-up.

John went back to the kitchen table and looked at the body again. He didn't want to move anything until the team was there. The death certainly looked like natural causes, but given the circumstances he was no longer sure.

As justice of the peace, Mooney was responsible for declaring the cause of death, but he was mainly a rancher and knew nothing of medical forensics. In most cases it didn't matter. When people died in Bolero, the cause was usually quite obvious. Mooney had called Doc in a few times when things got beyond him, but even Doc would be out of his depth on this one. John might be able to get assistance from the Bexar county medical examiner, but that would cost a few thousand dollars that wasn't in the budget.

The sound of a siren drew him onto the front porch. Not surprisingly, Lovejoy was the first to arrive, enveloped in his trademark cloud of dust. He'd evidently driven the whole way, including a mile down a dry creek bed in a canyon in the middle of nowhere, with lights flashing and siren blaring.

John waited for him on the porch. Lovejoy skidded up next to the Jeep and shut down the carnival on his roof. The dust cloud drifted across the limestone ridge to the porch. John just held his breath instead of waving it away from his face, blinking to keep his eyes clear of dust.

Lovejoy followed the cloud to the porch and John walked him through the scene, explaining the details and their implications. He left Lovejoy behind to photograph everything and see if he could pick up latent prints that didn't belong to Crookshank. More help was on the way in the form of other deputies, Mooney, and an EMS truck to transport the body. John wanted to get to the county clerk's office before they got busy.

At the turn from the gravel road to the blacktop, he passed the EMS truck headed in. He gave them a three-finger salute and pulled onto the blacktop.

Once he was on the road, he pulled out his phone and called Mooney, who answered immediately.

"I'm on my way out the door, John."

"Good. No hurry. Crookshank's not going anywhere. But I want you to take a close look at this one. Somebody was there after he died, destroying files. It's possible the old man had some help into the next life. I'm thinking we send him to the ME in San Antonio just to make sure."

"An autopsy? Are you sure? He was almost ninety."

"I just have a feeling about this one. You take a look, see what Lovejoy has to say about the scene, and let me know what you think."

"Aren't you there?"

"I have to check out something."

"I'll check it out and let you know."

"Thanks." John disconnected and set the phone on the ledge on the dash in front of the speedometer.

A few miles later, he heard it as he turned off the blacktop onto the highway.

"*zzzz . . . swallow the honey . . . zzzz*"

He looked at the evidence bag. The muffin had been silent all morning, through breakfast, through the drive to the cabin, and on the drive out of the canyon.

He thought about the muffins Liz had brought for dinner on Tuesday. "Local honey?"

He knew that the suspects weren't really trapped in the muffin. But he also knew muffins didn't really talk, even while this particular muffin interrupted his thoughts.

"*zzzz . . . follow the money . . . zzzz*"

He'd avoided thinking about the talking muffin precisely because he knew it couldn't talk, and the thought of what might really be happening scared him.

"Which is it? The honey or the money?" He pulled the muffin from the evidence bag and set it on the ledge next to the phone.

"*follow the money*"

The phone rang. He checked the caller ID and shook his head with a sudden and overwhelming sense of weariness. He put the phone on speaker and set it back on the dash next to the muffin.

"Hey, Mom."

"Honey, did you get my message?"

"I've been up in the canyons where there's no signal. What's the news?"

"You won't believe what I saw on the way to the shop this morning. No, she's not in the book, but she called last night and I told her we could work her in first thing. Highlights and a set. Get Tiffany to do it."

"What?"

"Not you, honey, I was talking to Mabel."

"What did you see this morning?"

"You know the bridge over the Frio just past the Y?"

"Yeah."

"There was a sign that said 'watch for ice on bridge.'"

John waited.

Getting no response, she continued. "Don't you think that's strange? It's already 97 and it's only ten o'clock."

"I'll have Elmer take care of it."

"No, honey, that's not why I called. It's a sign."

"Of course it's a sign. For when there's ice on the bridge."

"No, not that kind of sign. It's a sign from God."

John sighed, figuring the road noise would cover it. "How is this a sign from God, Mom?"

"Don't you see? Rusty has come back and you've been very cold."

The Crookshank thing had pushed Rusty out of his thoughts for a few blessed hours, but now he was back. John felt his heart rate rise, just like yesterday. "What's this got to do with the sign?"

"He's trying to build a bridge, but you're putting ice on the bridge. God's telling you to watch out. To not be so cold."

John knew better, but he never could let these things go unchallenged. "If God wanted to tell me, why didn't I see the sign?"

"He knows I talk to you. And there aren't any bridges between your house and your office."

John opened his mouth to speak, but then saw a yellow diamond on a pole where there should have been a yellow triangle, just before Tenderfoot Creek. He stared at it as he drove by.

Watch for ice on bridge.

He didn't mention it. "Mom, do you not remember what it was like?"

"John, you don't understand Rusty at all. He always wanted the best for you."

"The best for me? How is spending all the grocery money on a dirt bike the best? If he wanted the best for me, why didn't he just hold down a job, pay the bills, make sure we had electricity and water and dinner?"

"Of course he's impractical. He's a Gemini. That's why he needs a Virgo to balance him out."

"Mom, you should kick him out, right now. But whatever you do, don't let him near the bank account."

"Watch for ice on bridge, John. That's your sign from God. Watch for ice on bridge. The Buddha says 'Those who are free of resentful thoughts surely find peace.' Oops, my ten o'clock is here. I have to go."

She hung up. He dropped the phone in his shirt pocket and felt it crumple the prescription forms he'd put there this morning. It reminded him of the ribs hidden in the freezer. If he had eaten them for dinner last night he wouldn't have run into Battles. He should have pulled them out before he left the house this morning. They would have thawed by lunch. Too late now.

In town he turned off the city square and parked behind the courthouse.

John leaned on the counter in the county clerk's office while Yvonne used her terminal to search through the document management system.

Yvonne shook her head. "I'm not getting anything. What year would this be?"

"Either 1989 or 1990. It was just before he retired."

She frowned at the computer. "That's what I searched for. Let me try something else."

"You're doing a great job, Yvonne. You should get a raise."

"Tell that to Linda," she responded.

"I heard that," Linda said without looking up from her work. She was the office manager and had the large desk in the corner by the windows.

John was confident Yvonne would find the document. Even though she was only a few years out of the Southwest School of Business in Uvalde, she was the sharpest of the three-woman team. In ten years she would probably be sitting in the corner desk. If she stuck around that long.

"That's strange," Yvonne said.

"What?"

"It shows up in the document index. But when I search on the document number, it's not there." She turned her screen so John could see.

He leaned over the counter. A box in the middle of the screen said "Document Not Found" followed by a document number. Yvonne clicked the OK button and used the mouse to highlight a line in the ledger. It showed the document number, the date, the title of the document, and the name of the person who filed the document, Edward Crookshank. John pulled out his notebook and wrote down the information. Before he was done, Linda stood next to Yvonne, looking at the screen.

"That's not supposed to happen," Linda said.

John knew how she felt. That phrase summed up the last forty-eight hours. "These electronic copies were scanned from the originals, right?"

Linda nodded without looking from the screen.

"When was that done?"

Linda finally looked at him. "The end of 1998, beginning of 1999. There were hundreds of thousands of documents to scan, back to 1883. It took almost a year."

"And where are the originals?"

"In a climate-controlled warehouse in San Antonio. The RFP required the company with the winning bid to store the originals."

"Can we get a copy of the original from them?"

"Yes, if it exists." Linda cut off his next question. "If it exists, it should be in the system. I guess it's possible it got skipped somehow, but it's never happened before."

"Could you request a copy for me?"

"Sure. Yvonne." She returned to her desk and resumed her work. "And be sure to charge it to the sheriff's office," she added without looking up.

One more thing not in the budget. Might as well go for broke. "Also, can you print off everything in the records related to Bolero High School and send it over to my office?"

Yvonne nodded.

"Thanks."

"You see what I have to work with," she answered in a loud whisper.

"I heard that," Linda said without looking up.

John turned to go, but a thought made him turn back. "Who else would get a copy of the inspection?"

Yvonne looked back at Linda, who actually looked up from her work. "The contractor, the architect . . ." She thought for a second. ". . . any law firm associated with either of them."

"Who was the architect?"

Linda looked at Yvonne. Yvonne's fingers danced on the keyboard. "Wainwright." More typing. "In Uvalde." She turned around to the printer which was already spitting out a page. She handed it to John.

"Thanks." He looked at Linda. "She really is good, you know."

"That's why I hired her," Linda said.

Yvonne smiled. John left.

98

He was halfway down the curved stairway to the lobby when he heard his name called from above. He looked up. Luther Gibson, county judge and current husband to John's ex-wife, stood at the balcony railing. Smiling.

John sent a deputy on courthouse errands and this was the main reason. He could usually avoid Gibson because the sheriff's department was no longer in the courthouse. It was a few miles north of town. The old county jail, three cells and an office in a little limestone building on one corner of the square, now housed the historical society. The modern jail, if you could call it that, was across the street from the sheriff's department. John turned slowly and walked back up the stairs.

In the last thirteen years, John had come to terms with the fact that Jennifer had wanted more than he was able or prepared to give her. At first he had taken it personally, but he eventually concluded that his main failing was financial.

When John started dating Jennifer, her dad, the sheriff, took him on as a project, talked him into getting a jailer's certificate right out of high school. John worked nights at the three-cell Bolero county jail until he was old enough to go to the academy. He got the certificate and got on as a deputy. Sheriff Weiss had pretty much made John what he was.

They got married not long after he made deputy. Romance and hormones had been enough at first. But sometime during the seven years in a tiny two-bedroom house on an isolated ridge, it had ceased to satisfy. He remembered her sitting on the deck and watching the last rays of the sun reflect off the disappearing-edge pool of the mansion on the opposite ridge. The budget of a sheriff's deputy was too limiting for the scope of her vision.

John could understand that, even while it destroyed him.

But what he could not accept was the county judge seducing his wife while John worked double shifts as a deputy to pay for the house that was already too small, the county judge smiling at him when he came to testify in court, the county judge buying his lunch in the day and banging his wife at night.

The day Jennifer left for the mansion on the higher ridge, taking Christopher with her, was the day John filed to run for the office of county sheriff. He knew it was too little too late. Not even a sheriff's salary would satisfy her ambition, but he had to do it, if for no other reason than to prove to himself that there was more to him than her limited vision could see.

After the divorce Jennifer's family sided with her, so some might have seen to run for sheriff as a grudge match. Weiss had no intention of retiring and he had lots of friends, including Luther Gibson, who by that time had been the county judge for almost twenty years. But public sentiment favored the betrayed husband over the father of the unrepentant tramp and he won by a large margin.

John never got another invitation to Thanksgiving at the Weiss house, which was a shame because he was partial to deep-fried turkey, the old sheriff's specialty.

John reached the top of the stairs. Gibson held out his hand.

"Sheriff, how's the wife and kids?"

John ignored the hand. It was a thirteen-year-old ritual that Gibson never seemed to tire of. Gibson was large, both tall and broad, with the swagger of a man who sees no need to prove that he can lick anyone in the room. He lowered his hand to the balcony railing.

"Did I hear right? You want to ship Crookshank to the Bexar County ME for a full autopsy?" He said it like it was a joke he'd just heard.

John wasn't surprised, even though it was barely an hour since he had left the scene. Gibson had informers all over the county and beyond. John trusted his staff, but there were others at the scene who would have heard of the plan from Lovejoy. "There's reason to believe that he may not have died of natural causes."

"The man was older than Methuselah's goat, Lawson. Old people die."

"And some of them have a little help."

"There's no room in the budget for an autopsy."

As if John's life wasn't complicated enough, the county judge controlled the budget, a point of control that Gibson exercised at every opportunity.

"We'll have to make room."

"No, we won't."

John caught Gibson's eye and held it. "You have no authority over this investigation."

"I do have authority over the budget," Gibson said in a tone that said he was amazed he had to explain something so simple to the sheriff. "This is a waste of taxpayer money."

"I know that you already know that the last fifteen years of Crookshank's files have been burned by somebody. After Crookshank died. And after Crookshank publicly threatened to produce information implicating a local contractor in the collapse of the school. That's enough reason to order an autopsy and I mean to do it."

"The man was a crackpot. He invented the aluminum foil hat. You can't take that threat seriously."

"Somebody did."

Gibson regarded him for a second, and then spoke quietly. "You're not thinking of going up against Cook."

"I'm following the evidence wherever it leads."

"As a friend, I counsel you to reconsider. This can't end well for you."

John snorted and started to walk away. He stopped and turned back. "Are you recommending I back off a legitimate suspect?"

Gibson shook his head as if saddened by what he heard. "Don't be absurd, Lawson. If you want to hang yourself, I can't stop you. But I won't authorize additional taxpayer funds to help you do it."

John walked down the stairs without responding. He'd find the money somewhere.

Back in his truck, John checked his watch. Almost eleven. He decided to drive down to Uvalde, get lunch, and then pay a visit to Wainwright and Associates. He looked at the muffin on the dash, daring it to speak, and drove around the city square, turning south on the highway.

He checked in with Sam, who had a few nonurgent messages. He left a message on Lovejoy's voice mail to give him an update. He passed a "Watch for ice on bridge" sign and called Elmer to take care of it. But that reminded him of Rusty. He thought about turning around, but decided against it and continued south.

The whole Rusty thing bothered him. Why return now after twenty-four years?

When John was growing up, every few years or so Rusty would disappear, usually for a few days, sometimes a week, once two weeks. But he always came back. When John got old enough to notice, he asked Mom where he was. She said he was just blowing off steam, that a man needed a little space every once in a while.

The last time Rusty left, John was sixteen. After two weeks, Mom started to get anxious. She didn't say anything, but John noticed her looking out the kitchen window while supper burned on the stove, or with her hands submerged in cold dishwater, the head of bubbles reduced to soap scum. She'd lose her concentration in the middle of a conversation, often in midsentence.

Three weeks in, they sat at breakfast in their usual morning routine. First, she read his horoscope. "Good friends are faithful companions. Look for romance in your own backyard." She looked up. "Did you ask Jennifer to the homecoming dance, yet?"

John didn't answer. He hated personal questions, especially from his mother. She returned to the paper and her own horoscope.

"Advanced preparation makes for smooth sailing. Keep a weather eye for opportunity."

She continued reading silently and John knew she was reading Rusty's horoscope, like she did every day. Then she set the paper aside and sat thoughtfully, sipping her herbal tea. After a few minutes she pushed back from the table and took her dishes to the sink.

"I think I'll see if Mabel needs any help." By the end of the day she had a job at the beauty shop.

John talked Mr. Mooney into giving him odd jobs around the ranch after school and on weekends. He was surprised at how quickly he got used to a full pantry and refrigerator, to regular meals, even if he did have to cook most of them himself because Mom was at the shop, to how easily he slipped into the assumption that turning the faucet would always result in a stream of water, that he could go to bed at night without wondering if he would awaken late to the sight of a darkened clock-radio display.

By the time John graduated high school, Mom was the main beautician, and by the time Christopher was born, she had taken a second mortgage to buy the business when Mabel retired. Her customers got more than a perm or highlights, they got a life coach for no extra charge with advice tailored to their birth sign.

Although she seemed to move on, Rusty's clothes still hung in the closet untouched, with the evident assumption that his return was imminent. It was a tactile illustration of the difference between mother and son.

Mom believed in things. She believed that people meant well, that things would work out, that it was all for the best, that the universe was run by one or more benevolent forces, that every cloud really did have a silver lining. She always clapped for Tinkerbell, even after John was grown, and always said with Dorothy that there was no place like home. And she believed it. She seemed capable of believing practically anything effortlessly at a moment's notice.

John found belief difficult. He questioned good fortune. He was skeptical of coincidence, suspicious of unwarranted favors, and was certain that a good thing would not last and that people rarely got what they really deserved, reward or punishment. He doubted that there was some force up there watching out for him or sending him messages. And he never clapped for Tinkerbell, not even as a kid.

Although at first he had expected Rusty to return, just like all the other times, within a few weeks he suspected it was different this time. After a few months John concluded Rusty was gone for good. He worked through various theories as the mood took him. Hit by a train, murdered by hoboes, seduced by a Latin temptress. That he had planned to return but was struck with amnesia and didn't know where home was anymore. That he had a second family all along that he finally decided he liked better.

As he grew older and thought more about Rusty from the perspective of an adult rather than a kid, he came to the conclusion that Rusty had stayed away to punish him and was waiting for John to beg him to return, this despite the fact that they had no idea where he had gone or how to contact him.

By the time John was in his thirties and had lived over half his life without Rusty, he had stopped thinking about him altogether. Life went on, life intruded, life intervened, and Rusty became irrelevant. But now Rusty was painfully relevant, fresh in from Florida. That was a bad combination with no silver lining, despite Mom's predilection to the contrary.

The cell phone interrupted John's musings. It was Lovejoy. The EMTs had taken the body to the mortuary in Uvalde. Mooney was drawing up the papers to send the body to San Antonio. The only prints in the house belonged to Crookshank. The rocky soil of the canyon was not conducive to footprints, but he had found a few by the trash barrel one set of which was probably John's, that didn't match any shoes in the closet. John complimented Lovejoy on the work. The boy might be overeager, but that could have advantages.

The Uvalde city-limit sign raised a more pleasant topic, where to eat. John turned left at the Grand Opera House, drove past the court-house and the county lockup, taking the neighborhood streets east. Uvalde offered the usual range of cuisine—burgers, barbecue, pizza, home-style, and the usual smattering of chains. He turned south to-ward Main Street and was surprised to see that The Fez was open. He hadn't expected a Moroccan restaurant to survive in Uvalde, but somehow they had weathered the economy.

John never would have set foot in the place had it not been for Jennifer. The owners had bought an abandoned Howard Johnson restaurant, boarded up the windows and painted faux mosaic figures, domes and crenellated arches on the exterior in vibrant Mediterra-nean colors. Topped with the trademark HoJo orange tile roof, the effect failed to instill confidence in the typical South Texas epicurean.

At first glance, John immediately got the impression that The Fez was the sort of establishment that did most of its business late at night in back rooms on a cash-only basis. But as soon as Jennifer saw it she had to try it, and John discovered to his surprise that he was a big fan of Middle Eastern food. Right up to the divorce they dined there at least once a month. He hadn't been back since.

There were only a few cars out front. John parked his pickup at the far corner of the building, left the muffin in the car, and walked in out of the heat. John hadn't checked the temperature, but he was pretty sure they had hit three digits already. He stopped just inside the door and waited for his eyes to adjust to the dark. Even though it was half past noon, the room was as dark as a romantic dinner place.

Or a dive bar. At least it made him feel cooler. There were a dozen or so tables scattered around the room and a handful of three-paneled folding wooden screens to give the illusion of privacy. Three of the tables were occupied.

The owner greeted John, remembering him even though it had been over a decade since he'd been inside. He went through the buffet, took a table in a corner facing the door, and scanned the room again.

At a table against the opposite wall he saw Jennifer's unmistakable profile. She was dressed sedately, for Jennifer, in a tight fuchsia skirt and matching cropped jacket and a white blouse, the first button of which was halfway between her neck and her navel. Her lunch date was a younger guy in a pricey suit, obviously not from Bolero or Uvalde. They were engaged in conversation, oblivious to the world.

He remembered Gibson's smug face at the courthouse and wondered if he knew about the guy in the suit. Was this guy her first dalliance since trading up to the county judge? John doubted it. She'd been married to Gibson twice as long as she'd been married to John. Who knew how many notches she had on her belt, now?

It was an unkind thought and it made him feel a little mean. He looked away and considered leaving before she saw him. He regarded his plate filled with food—chickpea and lentil soup, baba ganoush, tabbouleh, and half a pita. It looked healthy to him. He was behaving, if you didn't count the lamb kabob concealed under the pita. He considered taking his lunch to the counter and asking the owner to pack it up to go, but it was hot outside and it was an awkward meal to eat in the truck.

He moved around the table to a chair that let him see the door without facing Jennifer. Based on the experience with the ribs, he chose to attack the kabob first and save the soup for last. Between bites of lamb he tore off a piece of pita, dipped it in the paste-like baba ganoush, and then dabbed up a clump of tabbouleh with it. He was probably violating half-a-dozen rules of Middle Eastern etiquette with this procedure, but he liked it and there were no Middle Easterners at the table to be offended or correct him.

It reminded him of the time Jennifer had dragged him to Hawaii. The first night they were bussed to a luau. He hadn't known what to do with the little plastic cup of white goo that came with the meal, so he used it as a dip for the kalua pig, which was evidently the Polynesian version of pulled pork. He was enjoying the combination when a passing busboy stopped in front of him and said the white stuff was haupia, a coconut-based dessert. By then most if it was gone, so he just shrugged and continued on. The memory made him smile and he recalled how Jennifer looked in the sarong they bought in Hale'iwa. If ever a woman had the body to do justice to a sarong, it was Jennifer.

He chanced a glance at her table and caught her looking at him. He looked away, but it was too late. She crossed the room, sat down opposite him, and smiled.

"Well look at you, Mr. Shish Ka Bobby. Is lamb on your diet?"

He studied her face, but didn't answer. How did she know about his test results?

She looked him over. "Have you lost weight?"

"No." Actually, he had gained weight, which meant she thought of him as fatter than he was. The idea annoyed him.

"I guess I always remember you as bigger than life."

Her drawl made her words sound like honey. She had an aura, the power to make you forget what had been and instead dream of what could be. But all he had to do was think about the deck, about watching the sun rise over the Tuscan villa, and the spell was shattered. He knew that her finesse was affectation, not affection.

John looked at the suit across the room. The guy looked back as if John were his natural enemy.

"Who is he?"

"A nobody. A defense lawyer."

John had assumed that the stare was a territorial glare aimed at a competitor. But it could be the natural animosity of a defense lawyer toward a cop. "San Antonio?"

"Houston."

John nodded. Gibson was the top of the food chain in the Bolero County legal and social ecosystem. The suit, if he was any good, could make five or ten times the salary of a county judge. And despite the disdain with which Texans outside of Houston view the city, it did have its version of high society, which was more than could be said for Bolero.

"Does Gibson know he's just the next stepping stone?"

Jennifer's eyes flared and she flushed. John decided it was anger. He doubted anything could make her blush. The reaction passed quickly and she looked at the suit for a moment before answering.

"Luther only knows what he wants to know." She turned back to John. "I hear your daddy is back in town."

By now everybody knew. They would have known as soon as he drove through the square in the Mustang. "Not for long. If I have any say."

"I always thought he was a sweet man."

"You didn't live with him."

"Your mama didn't kick him out. And Bolero could use a little excitement."

John didn't say anything and Jennifer's demeanor changed. It was a subtle thing, but John had learned to see past the cleavage and the makeup, to sense the subterranean shifts communicated with the slightest of clues. It was something about her eyes and the set of her shoulders. He realized he had leaned forward slightly. He picked up the cup of soup, set it in front of him, and began to eat.

At last she spoke. "Can you talk to Christopher?"

He watched her, waiting for the rest, but she had stopped. "About?"

"I was hoping he would move back in for the summer, but . . ." She looked away at nothing in particular, away from John, away from the suit. "It's okay if he . . . I can understand if he wants to stay with you now that he's grown. And he's never been fond of Luther, but . . ."

She looked at John and for a second he felt sorry for her despite himself. He suspected she didn't realize how naked she was at that moment. Or maybe she did.

"But he hasn't even come by once."

John knew why, but he couldn't say it. Regardless of what she had done to him, it would be too cruel. He had watched the gradual change in Christopher as he passed through adolescence and became aware of how different his mother was from the other mothers in Bolero. It wasn't easy overhearing the whispered comments in study hall, the lecherous laughs in the locker room, to realize that your mother was the subject of your friends' fantasies.

Other mothers were suitably asexual, dumpy and domesticated. But Christopher's mother was Dorianna Gray as seductress, all the more desirable to his classmates for being unattainable.

"He's working long hours on the bridge crew," John said, hoping the excuse would placate her. "And he's talking about dropping out for a year to dig water wells in Africa."

"What?" She recovered enough to be confused. "Africa." She said the word like it was the name of an ugly girl Christopher had asked to the prom.

"He's selling his truck to pay for the trip. He told me last night."

"But what about the scholarship?"

"That's what I said."

Her eyes narrowed. "It's that girl. Caitlyn. Isn't it?"

"He said she doesn't know about it. He's been talking to some guy on the crew who just came back from there."

"He can't do this." Jennifer grabbed his hand, the one holding the soup spoon. "You have to stop him. He listens to you."

John shook his head. "Not anymore."

Twenty years ago when John realized he was going to be a father, he was terrified. He certainly had no role model to follow in that regard. He'd bluffed his way through, praying that Christopher wouldn't discover that John had no real power, only words and spankings and the granting and withholding of favors. He dreaded the day that Christopher discovered that he had the power to defy the rules and choose his own path. But now that day had come. He supposed he was lucky it had taken this long.

Jennifer looked him in the eye, still clutching his hand. "You can do it. Your words matter. More than you know."

John looked back at her, wondering if she was still talking about Christopher. A loud throat-clearing broke the spell. Jennifer glanced irritably at the suit and released John's hand. John nodded toward the suit.

"I think Houston has a problem."

"You don't know the half of it." She stood, but didn't leave immediately. "Will you talk to him? About coming to see me?"

"I'll do what I can."

She leaned across the table, her hands planted on either side of his plate, her cleavage blocking everything else in his view, and kissed him on the forehead. Her scent enveloped him, musky with a hint of sandalwood. It was almost masculine, but made her seem twice as alluring, as if she had the power to turn everything to her own ends.

"Thank you, John," she whispered, and then returned to the suit.

John took a moment to shake off the assault to his senses and psyche and right his world. Then he finished his soup, paid his bill, and left without looking back.

John found Wainwright and Associates a mile from the town square in a two-story limestone and redwood building. He parked between two Uvalde PD cruisers and walked through the entrance arch into a courtyard shaded with semitropical plants. The heat of the day had kicked in, but between buildings and vehicles he'd spent very little time in it. That was the way to deal with a Texas August—minimize your minutes outdoors.

The temperature drop of ten degrees in the shaded courtyard was offset by a humidity gain of twenty percent. A rock fountain fed into a stream. A curving pebble walkway hugged the stream, swinging out to the building at the various office entrances.

He found the architect's office, pulled open the glass door, and stepped inside. A guy in a forest green polo shirt sat at the front desk. Half a burrito lay on the desk in the foil-lined paper it was delivered in. He ignored it, flipping through a printout and copying numbers from the printout onto a form. John noticed the Uvalde Police Department logo at the top of the form. He leaned closer and saw it was a supplemental page to an incident report.

"I'm here to see Larry Wainwright. Is he in?"

The man looked up with a confused expression, his pen hand hovering above the page. Midfifties was John's guess. He didn't look the type to be manning the front desk.

"Larry?"

"Yes." John scanned the room. Desks, filing cabinets, a conference room with a glass wall on the left, where a police officer sat at a table with a woman in her twenties. An office with glass walls on the right where another officer sat with a man in his thirties.

"What do you need?"

"I need to talk to Mr. Wainwright about a project in Bolero County that he worked on." John showed his badge.

The man looked at it and then up at John. "He's dead."

"What?" John looked around the room again. The officers were obviously taking statements from witnesses, but there were no signs of anything else amiss. Other than this overaged receptionist.

"He was my father. He died eight years ago. I'm Rod Wainwright. I run the firm now."

John indicated the room with a nod of his head. "What's going on?"

Rod set his pen down and rubbed his eyes. "We had a break-in last night."

John scanned the room again. Nothing seemed amiss. Then he noticed the empty area on all the desks where computers had probably been the day before. "What's missing?"

"Just the electronics. They knew what they were doing. They got all the computers, monitors, printers, servers, tape backup system, battery backup system, cables. The works. It's like they were going to set up their own office network." He gestured around the room. "They disabled the alarm and left no traces as far as the police can tell. Their evidence technician couldn't find a thing."

"Sorry to hear it." It would be easy to turn the equipment in San Antonio for a quick buck. "I won't take much of your time. I'm looking for an inspection report from a job in 1989."

Rod shook his head. "It's gone."

John pointed to the filing cabinets. "They took the files, too?"

"Ten years ago we digitized all the old records and recycled the paper. We used the saved space to build the conference room." He pointed to the room where the officer and the woman sat at a long table. "But they took all the tapes from the archives, too."

"They took the backup tapes? What for?" The data would be useless to the thieves or the buyers.

Rod shrugged. "Maybe to record over. 'Here, buy this tape drive and we'll throw in all these blank tapes for free.' Who knows?" He noticed the burrito and took a bite, washing it down with a soda.

John remembered what Linda had said about how the county had off-site storage. "Any off-site backups?"

"Nope. Not for anything older than ten years. We can get back our current projects, thank God. We'll be back in business as soon as we get new hardware. But the archives are gone."

John resisted the urge to ask to look around. It was pointless, but he wanted to do something, to dig around and find the report, even though it had been shredded a decade ago. Instead, he held out his hand. "Thanks."

Rod shook his hand. "For what?"

John smiled. "For not much, I guess." He pulled out a card, borrowed Rod's pen, and wrote "Bolero High School 1989" on the back. "If the backup tapes are recovered, give me a call."

"Sure," Rod said, but the single word communicated the futility of the gesture.

"Good luck," John said, and walked through the humid jungle in the courtyard to his truck.

On the drive back to Bolero, John pondered on the situation. Tuesday the Cook Brother's archives are destroyed. Thursday morning he discovers that Crookshank's personal archives have been destroyed. Thursday afternoon he discovers that the Wainwright archives are missing. What did these three things have in common? Bolero High School. Crookshank's report, which was also missing from the county clerk's records.

The Wainwright burglary was a cover to throw the scent off the inspection report, the same as the Cook Brothers arson was staged to make it look like a Tabernacle vendetta.

This brought him back to the call from Charles Cook. At the time, John had interpreted it as an attempt to distract him from a personnel issue. But that was before he had these two additional data points. He recalled Mr. Pickard, his tenth-grade geometry teacher, who used to drone on at the front of the class as everyone struggled with the assignment. "Two points make a line. Three points prove a line." It looked like he had a line, now.

He looked at the evidence bag in the passenger seat. The fold at the top wasn't as crisp as it was two days ago and the tape no longer held it closed. He set the muffin on the dash and stared at it.

"Now what?"

The muffin didn't answer. John tried to recall the first words he heard it speak. Two big words, something about an airport. And a painting. No, a kind of painting.

Fresco. That was it. And the other words, course something. Of course . . . recourse . . . discourse.

John hit the steering wheel in frustration. Then he wondered why it mattered. It was just nonsense. The muffin didn't know anything; it didn't even talk. The words were nothing more than the random noise in his own head. They held no more meaning than the words of his mother's horoscopes, just a delusion that things happen for a reason, that something out there is trying to tell you something.

"*zzzz . . . fortuitous concourse . . . zzzz*"

That was it! Fortuitous concourse!

His foot lifted off the gas as he realized that he didn't know if he had remembered it or if the muffin had said it. The AC was on MAX, as usual in August in Texas, but the chill he felt had nothing to do with the air conditioner. It had to do with another summer night. A long time ago.

It was August. John woke up sweating and suddenly sleepless. The light of a full moon poured into the bedroom in aluminum sheets, perverting the colors of his bedspread into an otherworldly palette.

The old house had an attic fan, a gigantic contraption five feet across that pulled air in through the windows and pushed it into the attic, where it leaked out through the vents in the eaves. The fan roared in the hallway, providing a nice sleep-inducing drone, but John figured the air it pulled in was at least ninety degrees.

He turned onto his back and tried to relax, willing himself to fall asleep. He didn't want to wake up tired on his first day of junior high.

It was useless. He got up and padded into the kitchen in his pajama bottoms, opened the freezer door on the top of the fridge, and rested his head on the sill, letting the cold air cascade over his shoulders and down his back like a waterfall. He waited until he was chilled to the point of shivering before he closed the freezer and turned to go back to bed. But in the three a.m. stillness he heard a low noise, a murmuring sucked into the kitchen window by the fan.

John peered out. He slipped to the back door, which was ajar, and out onto the screened in porch. On the wicker daybed, his mother slept in a thin nightgown, her blonde hair silvered in the moonlight. She often slept on the screened-in porch on hot nights.

But the noise came from beyond the screens. John saw the silver-limned silhouette of his father looking down into the birdbath, his hands held out as if he were on the verge of capturing a butterfly in his cupped palms.

John stepped out the screen door into the backyard. The creak of the springs made no impression on Dad. John moved slowly into the backyard, keeping to the shadows of a large crepe myrtle, its pink flowers painted yellow in the weird light. In the summer, the neglected waters of the birdbath became a mosquito farm when it wasn't dried up altogether. But on this night John could see the blazing orb of the full moon painted on its surface, the reflection unwavering in the thick air.

As he crept forward, he picked up whispered phrases.

". . . muskadine, turpentine, dandelion wine . . ."

The voice trailed off. John inched closer.

". . . sin abasement, window casement, in the basement, when the lace rent . . ."

John shivered in the ninety degree night. Dad raised his head and his arms and addressed the goddess of the night.

"Yes, yes, yes . . . for the two of us of course, forty-two from the true source, fortuitous concourse . . ."

John shuddered, shocked back into the present by the last phrase. He realized that the white stripe of the highway was crawling past. He got back up to the speed limit.

Was the phrase something he remembered from that night long ago? Or something he remembered from the afternoon two days ago? Or something else entirely?

Fortuitous concourse. Who had spoken those words? His father? The muffin? His own fractured mind?

He jerked the muffin off the dash, shoved it savagely into the evidence bag and threw it across the cab against the passenger door.

This was nonsense. He was not his father and the muffin was not an oracle.

He slowed to turn the truck around and drive out to Charles Cook's three-hundred acre ranch. He would confront the old man in his office. He swung to the shoulder, checked his mirror and pulled the wheel to the left. But before he gunned the engine, he realized he had nothing more than speculation. He stepped on the brake, dropped his arm across the steering wheel, and thought about what to do next.

Evidence. He would check with Lovejoy and find out what the team had learned from Crookshank's cabin.

But first he would check out the source like he should have done on Tuesday.

John pulled into the Cook Brother's parking lot and got out into the blazing heat. He scanned the equipment yard through the chain-link fence, but saw no signs of Billy. He walked past the flagpole and into the overly refrigerated office. Nadine looked up, startled at his abrupt entrance.

"Sheriff?"

"Where can I find Billy?"

"Somewhere else. He usually works nights. Bert called him in for some overtime when the church folks showed up with signs."

John glanced at Bert's window. Bert was inside, on the phone as usual. He held up a finger, but John had no desire to get stuck in a conversation with him.

"I'm going to take a look around."

He walked past Nadine, waving at Bert, and pushed through the door out into the warehouse. It was hot, but a different kind of hot. Softer, more like a blanket or an oven full of chocolate chip cookies than the fist-in-your-face, steel-melting blast furnace of the parking lot.

The crime-scene tape was gone and the furniture that could be salvaged was out in the warehouse. Inside the storeroom, a guy was pulling down the scorched, soggy drywall. John stood in the doorway and looked at the metal wall behind the studs for signs of an opening or some other way the suspects could have escaped, but saw nothing. He nodded to the worker and walked out the warehouse door into the lot.

He looked to the gate, still catawampus from the break-in, held in place by the chain. He looked down at the ground. Hard-packed, sun-baked, tough as cement. Most of the yard was gravel or dirt, but on the edges, prairie grass and weeds made inroads.

John walked to where the fence met the front corner of the office and skirted the inside perimeter, a hundred yards per side at least. It was a hot walk with only his hat between him and the afternoon sun. The grass was calf high and thirsty. It rustled like old newspapers against his pants leg as he pushed through with his boots. But the weeds were doing just fine, which was the way of it. The good guys had to push uphill both ways just to stay even.

The cicada buzz enveloped him. It was the sound of heat, the rays of the sun made audible, resonating in his brain like the hum of a cosmic generator. It was the buzzing in the air conditioning duct and the static from the muffin and the hoarse whispered words of his father. Fortuitous concourse. He pushed the thought aside and kept walking.

He walked all four sides of the yard, coming to a stop where the fence hit the back corner of the warehouse, without seeing any indication that the suspects had scaled the fence to escape. There was one section of the perimeter he had not explored, the outside wall of the warehouse. He entered the warehouse through a set of double doors on the back side, through the office without a word to anyone, out the front door, and turned left.

He turned the corner and walked down the side of the building. The ground sloped away from the warehouse slab and there was a slight wash where the runoff from the roof flowed toward the parking lot. In a spot near where the fence met the back of the warehouse, the gravel was disturbed, as if someone, or maybe two someones, had recently passed through it.

He turned around and looked at the woods bordering the lot. A few yards in, he found traces of their escape. Vines pulled aside, broken branches, scuffed-up ground cover. After a quarter mile, he found a utility road, two ruts with the grass bent where a vehicle had parked.

Maybe they did walk through walls, but after that, they drove away like regular folks.

It was only four o'clock. John reviewed the case as he drove back to the office. It all came back to the missing report. Something about Bolero High School that Cook thought had been papered over.

The report on file at the courthouse had disappeared over a decade ago. Then the foundation failed, Crookshank's letter was published, and Charles Cook realized it could hang him out to dry. So he sent someone out to the canyon to make it disappear. And to silence Crookshank.

John thought about Crookshank. There was nothing about the body to suggest foul play. Either Cook's boys were far more sophisticated than one would expect, or they had just lucked out. The ME in San Antonio would answer that question.

But what about the copies at the Cook Brother's warehouse and Wainwright's office? Why didn't he destroy them years ago, the same time he got rid of the courthouse copy? John looked to the muffin bag for an answer, but it wasn't on the seat.

He lifted his foot off the gas and scanned the cab, glanced into the back seat. It was gone. Somebody had been in his truck.

John stomped on the brakes, and then belatedly looked in his rearview. Fortunately nobody was behind him. He jerked the truck to the side of the road and rifled through the papers in the passenger seat. He twisted around and looked into the back seat. No muffin bag.

He left the motor running, got out into the heat, and flipped the seat forward for a thorough search of the back. Nothing. He went around to the passenger side. The ground fell away sharply into a ditch. The door handle was at shoulder level. He jerked it open. The evidence bag tumbled out, dropped at his feet, and rolled halfway down the incline.

John felt relieved and embarrassed. He'd thrown the bag against the passenger door just a few hours before. Paranoia couldn't be a good sign. He retrieved the bag, verified that the muffin was still inside, and put it in the glove box.

Back at the department, he nodded at Sam and walked to his office. A pile of reports sat on the middle of his desk. He flipped through them. Lovejoy had already given him the highlights and the reports added nothing of importance. He logged into e-mail, but Sam walked in with a pile of message slips in her hand before he had a chance to knock down the count in his inbox.

"Anything urgent?"

"Not really." Sam set them on his desk.

John picked them up and flipped through them. Nothing that couldn't wait. He set them back down and turned to his computer, but realized Sam was still there, standing in front of his desk. He looked up at her.

She looked away.

"Is there something else?"

Sam looked back at him. "Tyler says the man in the Mustang is your daddy."

John nodded.

"I always thought he was . . . dead."

John didn't have a response. He waited, watching her.

She searched his face. "Are you happy he's back?"

John tried to keep his expression blank, but it was an effort. Of course he wasn't happy, but how would Sam know one way or the other? She was in elementary school when Rusty left.

"Sam, what's going on?"

Her face flitted through a range of emotions so quickly John couldn't follow them. She sat down and pulled the chair up to the desk.

"Did you miss him? Did you wish he had been around? Do you regret not having a dad around?"

John was overwhelmed by the questions and her intensity.

"I mean, you turned out okay. It didn't hurt you none, him being gone."

The light came on. She wasn't asking about him. She was thinking of her kids.

"There are worse things than not having a father around."

She watched him without responding, waiting for more. Lovejoy walked in, but stopped abruptly when he saw the look John gave him. John nodded at the door. Lovejoy closed it on his way out. Sometimes the boy surprised him.

John looked back at Sam. "Like having the wrong kind of father around."

"Really?" She leaned forward. "Is that really worse?"

John nodded. He remembered the night she had called him six years ago, well after midnight. He arrived at her two-bedroom frame house just off the Bandera highway within minutes. Jason was out front, drunk, hammering on the door and yelling.

He was far enough gone that John's badge meant nothing to him. He turned all his rage on this new target. He had thirty pounds on John, but John had the advantage of height. And the fact that he wasn't drunk. In a few minutes Jason was on the ground with a bloodied nose and an eye that would be swollen shut by morning, handcuffed, and screaming obscenities into the dirt.

Jason spent a few weeks in jail. He got out early under the condition he make himself scarce. The last John heard, Jason was down in Vidor, working an offshore oil rig, and sending back occasional child support payments. Just enough to keep the heat off.

John leaned back in his chair. "Do they ask about him?"

Sam shook her head. "They did for a few months, but not no more."

"Sam, don't you worry about it. They'll do fine," he said with more conviction than he felt.

There had been two or three losers since Jason, none quite to his level, but bad enough. Sam needed to improve her selection process or swear off men completely. But this wasn't the time for that talk. In fact, John couldn't think of a time when he would be willing to have that talk. Some things just couldn't be fixed with talking.

John opened a desk drawer and pulled out a tissue. Sam took it, dabbed her eyes and blew her nose. It wasn't a ladylike noise, more like a wounded goose. John smiled and she blushed. Beauty had a way of making awkward things cute. A honking nose on a homely girl would have just been annoying.

Sam pushed the tissue into a pocket. "Why did he come back?" She noticed John's confusion. "Your daddy. I don't remember him at all. He must have been gone since forever. Why did he come back?"

"I don't know."

Sam stood and smoothed out her uniform. "Maybe he missed you."

"I don't think that was it."

Sam opened the door. She stopped with her hand on the knob and turned back. "Thanks, boss."

John waved her off. "Sure."

She smiled at him and walked out, leaving the door open. Lovejoy appeared immediately and walked up to John's desk.

"Your daddy's here."

John stood, knocking his chair back from the desk. It bounced off the wall behind him. "What?"

"I mean, there's a Rusty Lawson here to see you."

John looked at the door and then back at Lovejoy.

"He's out in reception, sir." There was a hint of apology in his voice.

John retrieved his chair and sat down. "Well, send him in."

As Lovejoy reached the door, John shot up again. "No, wait. I'll go out there."

Lovejoy turned around, looking curiously at John.

John didn't want to encourage Rusty to hang around in the office. Or Bolero. Or Texas. He walked past Lovejoy, grabbed his hat from the hook by the door, and strode past Sam and through the bullpen without acknowledging anyone, although he could feel their eyes following him.

He went out the security door. Rusty sat reading a paperback. He was dressed much the same as on Tuesday—Hawaiian shirt, white linen slacks, boat shoes. A white Panama hat sat on the chair beside him.

When the springs pulled the heavy door shut with a thunk, Rusty looked over, saw him, and smiled. John didn't smile back. He walked across the room.

Rusty closed the book, stood, and held out his hand. "Hey, son—"

John ignored the hand and leaned in close, speaking in a forced whisper. "What are you doing here?"

Rusty looked confused. He didn't lower his voice to match John's tone. "Wanted to see my son in his natural habitat. Establishing justice. Insuring domestic tranquility. Thwarting evildoers." He smiled again, but with less conviction.

"There's nothing to see. Paperwork, phone calls."

"Well, in that case, let me buy you a drink." Rusty nodded to the clock above the receptionist's window. "It's almost five." He took in John's expression and frowned. "You're not one of those bosses are you? A clock-watcher?"

John glanced at the receptionist, who watched through the reinforced glass of the window. She looked down at the paperwork she was processing. John turned back to Rusty.

"Come on." He shoved the front door open, walked out into the blast furnace of the Bolero afternoon, and waited. The red Mustang sat in the handicapped spot.

Rusty emerged, adjusting the hat on his head. "How about the Horseshoe?"

John turned back to Rusty, their toes almost touching. He was a good head taller. His shadow fell across Rusty's upturned face. "How about I give you a full tank and a thousand dollars and you go back to where you came from?"

Rusty returned his gaze without expression. "I don't think so."

"Ten thousand," John said, without pause or thought.

Rusty smiled slightly. "Son, before you start bargaining, you have to know what the other guy wants."

"Okay. What's it going to take to send you back to Florida?"

Rusty shook his head and walked to the Mustang. "It's too hot to stand out here and listen to nonsense. Let's take a ride, at least."

John wiped away the sweat that was already forming on his face with his sleeve. Rusty stood by the Mustang, the door open, his hand on the window.

"We'll take my truck."

Rusty nodded and slammed the door. John walked around the corner to his reserved spot by a side door. He climbed in and cleared off the passenger seat.

Rusty climbed in the passenger door and looked around. "Nice." He set the paperback on the seat between them. *Idylls of the King.* John remembered back to junior high and Rusty quoting Tennyson over dinner. Back when he still found romance in the old man's erratic ways.

John cranked the engine and the AC without a word and pulled onto the highway headed north.

Rusty twisted around and looked behind them. "Horseshoe Road is the other way."

John would have paid three prices for a decent whiskey, but he didn't want the camaraderie that Rusty would infer from the gesture. "I'm on duty."

Rusty regarded him. "Didn't stop Weiss back in the day."

"I'm not Weiss."

"There's a mercy. When did that wolf of woman born retire?"

John drove for a bit. "He didn't exactly retire," he finally said.

"You ran against him?"

John replied with a slight nod.

"And beat him?"

John almost smiled. Rusty looked out the passenger window and chuckled.

He took the road east toward Bandera. Things were getting too chummy. John realigned his expression, focused a thousand yards ahead at the ridge, and drove. He thought about the fact that Rusty was right here, sitting a few feet away, after twenty-four years. About what Mom had said about letting go.

It was easy for her, for some reason John never could understand. She could dismiss an offense with no more effort than the wave of a hand, even though a repeat performance was a near certainty. But John was more of the fool-me-once-shame-on-you school. He didn't allow for the possibility of a repeat offense.

Rusty's voice startled John from his thoughts.

"There's not a day has gone by that I haven't thought of you and Deborah."

Here it comes, John thought. The manipulation. He had no patience for it. "Thoughts. You can imagine how helpful that was to us as we tried to keep the bank from foreclosing."

Rusty nodded. "Too little, too late. I understand that."

John clenched his teeth and felt his jaw muscles bulge. It was like conversational judo. He threw a punch, Rusty accelerated the follow-through and pulled him off balance. The only way to win was not to play. John didn't respond.

"Son, if I could turn back the clock, I'd do a lot of things differently, but all we have is now, and the next day, and the next. I spent a lot of years avoiding this day, thinking there's no way to undo what's been done." He pulled a fresh pack of Camels from his shirt pocket and slapped the top against his palm. "Maybe that's so." He pulled the tab, spiraling the cellophane off the top, and crumpled it, tossing it onto the floorboard. "Or maybe we don't have to. Maybe we just leave that alone and move forward." He peeled the foil off one corner of the pack and dropped it on the floorboard, too.

John looked at the trash Rusty had just thrown on the floor. What if he did stay? How long would it be before he once again had little incidents, things that needed smoothing over? Incidents he would come to his son, the sheriff, to do the smoothing.

Rusty knocked a cigarette from the pack and broke the silence. "If we're not going for a drink, then where exactly are we going?"

John breathed in deeply through his nose, exhaled noisily, and pulled his gaze from the road. He caught Rusty's eye and held it. "We're taking the long way back to the sheriff's office. Then you're getting into that car and going away. Go find yourself, do whatever it is you've been doing for the last twenty-four years, and leave us alone."

They were out of the hills now, down in the valley halfway to Bandera. John turned south toward Hondo. Rusty thumped the butt of the cigarette against the dash a few times.

"You can't smoke in this truck."

Rusty looked from the cigarette to John, back to the cigarette, and slipped it behind his ear. He put the pack into his shirt pocket.

"I'm back, son. You're going to have to wrap your brain around that idea. The sooner you do, the easier it will be for everyone."

Up to now the conversation had been conducted in calm and measured tones, but John became instantaneously and inexplicably angry. He felt his heart rate increase, his breathing become shallow.

He recognized it as an influx of adrenaline, like when a routine traffic stop suddenly escalated into a knife fight or shots fired. His mind turned down a narrow lane bounded by rock walls, fixated on a single thought. *The old man must go.*

The old man was talking, saying something about how it was never too late and how he had come to see things differently, but it might as well been Swahili. John heard the words, but not the sense of it. It was all overlaid by static, like the crackle of the radio as Sam keyed in to update him with a breaking development.

"*zzzz . . . swallow the honey . . . zzzz*"

John jerked his head, looking at Rusty. He was talking to the windshield, maybe baring his soul, but John didn't hear it.

"*swallow the honey*"

His eyes drifted to the glove box. Was the muffin telling him to accept the bogus story Rusty was spinning about some belated experience of enlightenment and repentance?

Then he remembered the last message from the muffin. "Swallow the honey" was code for "follow the money." Rusty was after money. But he had just turned down ten thousand dollars. And a full tank of gas. That didn't make sense. Then he realized he was arguing with a muffin.

John smiled grimly to himself and his encroaching lunacy and took the cutoff back to Bolero.

Back at the sheriff's office John waited while Rusty got in the Mustang and left. He thought about heading back to Cook Brothers to see if Billy was guarding the fort, but instead he went inside to his office and brought up the website the county used for background checks. He tried every permutation of Rusty's name possible and limited the search to Florida. He spent a frustrating twenty minutes digging through the dozens of Rusty Lawsons who were twenty-three or ninety-three or African American.

He expanded the search to nationwide, but got thousands of hits. It would take days to go through them. He limited the search to Alabama, Georgia, and South Carolina and began to scroll through the hundreds of results when his cell phone rang.

He checked the caller ID. Liz. Dinner! At her place! He checked his watch. It was almost seven. He turned off the monitor and walked to the door as he took the call.

"Hey, honey, I got tied up at the office, but I'm on my way right now."

"I don't hear any road noise."

"I'm walking out the door."

"Then pick up some brussels sprouts and balsamic vinegar at Toolie's."

"Is this my punishment for being late?"

"Apple walnut cranberry vinaigrette salad, baked salmon, and garlic brussels sprouts."

"Sounds . . . wonderful." He got in his truck.

"And frozen yoghurt with raspberries for dessert. Did you get your prescriptions filled?"

He patted his front pocket. The prescriptions crinkled softly.

"Could we make it grilled salmon?"

"No charcoal."

He cranked the engine. "See you in a few." He hung up, put the truck in gear, and backed out onto the highway.

He set the bag on the counter. Liz gave him a kiss and a glass of white wine. She pulled out the balsamic and opened the jar.

"Rinse the sprouts, peel the outer leaves, and cut them in quarters."

She measured out some vinegar, poured it into a blender with some other stuff, and hit the button. John dumped the sprouts into a colander and ran water over them.

"Been working late on the arson?" Liz yelled over the blender.

John grunted a response. It was too small a town for secrets, but he felt the confidentiality of the confessional extended to his work. People did things they weren't proud of, but nobody should be defined by their moments of desperation. And he had no intention of mentioning the background search or the conversation in the truck.

Liz talked about her day and school. John responded in all the right places as he plucked and sliced the sprouts and she prepared the salad. Then she sautéed the sprouts in butter and garlic, before handing the job over to him so she could pull the salmon out of the oven.

A few minutes later they were at the table. The salad was pretty good, but John felt it would betray his manhood to admit it. The conversation died out and they ate until Liz broke the silence.

"You were a little hard on your dad last night."

John took another bite of the salmon. It would have been better grilled, but it wasn't half bad. Not Stella's ribs, but pretty good. "He's earned it," he finally said.

"I know he hasn't been the best dad—"

John grunted at her understatement.

"But he's family. You don't give up on family."

"You're talking to the wrong Lawson. He's the one who gave up on us."

"He came back, John. Okay, he did the wrong thing. Sure, he took too long to come around. But he's back. You owe it to yourself, to your mom if for no other reason, to try to make it work."

"He didn't come back to us. He ran away from something."

"What, exactly?"

"I'm working on that."

Liz was quiet for a few minutes. "What he said about you and Jennifer. Was that true?"

John chewed on his answer for a long time. "Which part?"

"Any of it."

John took that as a good sign. At least she was asking the right questions.

"Close enough."

"It doesn't sound like you."

"Which part?"

"Standing on the sidelines. Letting someone else call the shots."

"I was young."

By now their plates were empty. They both had an early morning tomorrow. Liz should be clearing the table, preparing dessert, but instead she poured the last of the wine into her glass, swirled it, and took a long sip.

"What if Jennifer tossed Gibson aside like she did Paul and came back to you?"

"You have to ask?"

"After last night I realized I don't really know you. I know what's happened since I moved to Bolero. But you're like an iceberg. The rest is submerged. What else are you hiding below the surface?"

"I'm not hiding anything."

"You never told me about your dad."

"It never mattered. He was gone."

"It matters, John. Everything matters."

John stacked the plates and took them to the kitchen. Liz followed. He rinsed them and put them in the washer. She watched. He closed the washer and turned to her.

"Dessert?"

"I heard about how Jennifer treated you, how she left. Not from you, of course, but I heard. But it's not about her, is it? It's about him. I saw that last—"

"I don't—"

Liz crossed her arms, wrapping herself. "Why did he leave? I did the math. You were sixteen. What happened?"

John was as lost as a West Texas hick in Times Square on Saturday night. "What?"

"Was it something to do with Jennifer?"

"Jennifer? What does he have to do with her?"

"You tell me. That's about the time you started dating her, right?"

"Why would you even ask?"

"Because I know nothing about four-fifths your life."

"You know all that matters."

"I don't know anything."

In the silence that followed, Liz seemed to shrink in on herself. John stood by the dishwasher and she leaned against the island, hugging her arms around her body and shaking. She began to cry.

John stepped toward her, tentatively. He felt he should do something, but he feared that whatever he did would be wrong. He reached toward her. She didn't respond. He stepped closer, brushed away the hair that had fallen into her face. His fingers followed the line of her jaw to her neck, down to her shoulders and around her. He held her to himself with both arms, trapping in the arms she had wrapped around herself.

Liz buried her face into his chest and talked into his shirt.

"Whatever is going on with you and him, it's going to spill over into you and me. If you don't stop it."

John held her, wondering what she meant.

John pointed his truck in the general direction of his godforsaken ridge and gave it rein. It knew its way home. He tried to wrap his mind around the evening, but it wouldn't bend that far. Was it just a mood that would pass? His only previous experience with women was with Jennifer, but she was the action that provoked the opposite reaction. She didn't talk about it first.

He reached across the cab and popped open the glove box, trusting the truck to keep to the road, and dug around in the darkness until his fingers recognized the evidence bag. He tossed it on the passenger seat, rooted it open, slammed the muffin on the dash, and glared at it.

"What's going on?"

The muffin sat on the dash, smugly mute.

"What does she want? What do I do now?"

The muffin remained as silent as an unanswered prayer.

It was all Rusty's fault. He came back when he had no right to, no reason to. No rhyme or reason, no time or season, no crime or treason.

John shook his head, took the wheel with both hands, cleared his thoughts, and focused on the road. He was splitting the white line. He jerked the truck back into the right lane and wondered. Had he thought that or heard it? Was he finally losing it?

"the name of the game is the dame is the same"

He tore his eyes from the road to the muffin.

"No more riddles."

"the name is not the same"

"What name? The same as what?"

The muffin was not forthcoming.

The name. The name. It was telling him something. The name of what? Why was it not the same?

He thought back through the day. Crookshank's place. The courthouse. Luther Gibson. Lunch and Jennifer. Wainwright. The

Cook Brothers yard. Sam and her ex. The drive with Rusty. The failed background check. Dinner with Liz.

The chirp of a siren startled him. A searchlight flashed into the cab from behind. He checked the rearview and saw the gumball lights of a cop car. He realized his foot was off the gas and he was idling down the highway at five miles per hour. He parked on the shoulder, got out of the truck, and squinted into the headlights behind him.

A dark shape emerged from the car and walked to him, silhouetted in the headlights. He shaded his eyes from the lights and recognized Lovejoy.

"Boss, you okay?"

"Yeah. I dropped my phone. Was trying to find it."

"For half a mile?"

"It fell under the seat. I think."

Lovejoy inspected him. John suddenly felt transparent under his piercing gaze. He hadn't been on this side of a traffic stop for two decades. He thought back to dinner. Liz emptied the Gewurztraminer, but how many glasses did he have?

"You want me to follow you home?"

John shook off the sudden sense of vulnerability. He was the sheriff and this was his deputy. There was no need for paranoia. "No, I'm fine." He started to climb back into his truck but stopped and turned back around. "Lovejoy."

"Yessir?"

"I'd like to bring Billy in tomorrow for a little talk. He works nights, so he should be at home tomorrow. Let's get him around ten, when he's still groggy."

Lovejoy looked him over again, but John could see his thoughts shifting from John's behavior to the case. He nodded slowly, as if impressed by the strategy. "Yessir."

John nodded back and climbed into the truck. He pulled away, careful to keep a normal speed. He watched the rearview until Lovejoy turned around and his taillights disappeared around a curve. Then he took a cutoff and headed out to his mother's house, the house of his childhood.

He knew what the muffin meant. The name was not the same.

Halfway down the block John turned off his headlights and killed the engine. He coasted to the curb across from his mother's house and put the truck in park. The Mustang sat next to her Beetle, just as he expected.

He grabbed his flashlight, a notepad, and a pen. He flipped the switch to kill the dome light and opened the door.

Next to the driver door of the Mustang, he focused the beam of the flashlight on the windshield and copied the seventeen-digit vehicle identification number onto the pad. He slipped the pad and pen into his shirt pocket and tried the door. Unlocked.

He opened the door and the light came on. He closed the door, walked to the passenger side, dropped into the seat, found the switch to kill the dome light, and opened the glove box. A quick search with his flashlight turned up the registration information.

He focused the light on the card. Reggie Loftin. The muffin was right. The name was not the same. He wrote down the name and the Fort Lauderdale address. Tomorrow he would find out what Rusty had been up to in Florida, and maybe even where the money came from.

He returned the registration card to the glove box, returned the dome light switch to its original position, got out of the car, and eased the door closed. Before he turned to go, he gave the house a final inspection. He realized a glow limned the east corner. He checked his watch. Almost midnight. He pocketed the flashlight and walked cautiously around the house.

As he passed the master bedroom he heard the sound of the shower. He continued forward slowly.

The light came from the screened porch. He knew from experience that at night he could see in, but from inside, anything beyond the overspill of the porch light was invisible. He stepped around the corner.

Inside, his mother reclined facing him on a profusion of pillows on the wicker daybed she favored on summer nights. Several books lay open on the bed around her. Her attention was focused on a multipage chart unfolded on a lap desk. She made a notation on the chart. He could hear the scratch of the fountain pen over the insects singing around him. She set the pen down and consulted one of the books.

He stood just outside the reach of the light and watched her. She turned the pages, found the passage she was seeking, read for a moment, and then smiled. She set the book aside and made another notation on the chart, pausing to assess her progress.

Something seemed different. He studied her face, looking for a clue. He leaned closer and felt the porch light wash across his face. He pulled back into the shadow and then it hit him.

It was the face from old photos on the mantle. Old snapshots, some in black and white, others in the yellow-hued tones of cheap 110 cameras from the seventies. Photos of her and Rusty around the time they got married, around the time he was born.

The screened-in porch was a time machine flashing a glimpse of his mother four decades ago. He suddenly felt twelve years old. He shook it off.

John walked around the porch to the door and scratched on the screen, careful not to startle her. She looked up.

He waved. "Hey."

"John?" She set the lap desk aside, shuffled on a set of slippers, and flipped back the latch on the screen door.

He stepped in. "I was passing by and saw the porch light."

He could see that she saw through that lie immediately, but gave it no space in her mind. She cleared a stack of astrology books off a wicker chair and motioned him to it. She returned to the daybed and considered him with a benevolent gaze. "How is Liz?"

John flinched inwardly, but was careful to keep it from his face. He had no illusion that Mom was fooled. Tonight she seemed to him to be an oracle, the Earth Mother, connected by unseen strands to everything and everyone. He wondered why he'd never seen it before. Then he realized it was probably the wine.

"She's fine," he said, and the second lie burned on his lips.

"You do right by her, John. She's a keeper."

"Yes, ma'am. She is."

The silence of the night enveloped them with its symphony of sounds. The crickets. The cicadas. A lone coyote. She waited. He

called the number for Brian Rogers and got a voice mail
g. He left his number and a message saying he would like to
fishing trip, hung up, and leaned back in his chair.

ow did Rusty get the money to buy a boat? He assumed Rogers
pilot, because Rusty knew nothing about boats. Or maybe
. A lot of things can change in a quarter of a century. Or so he
ard.

didn't know what he thought he'd find in this fishing expedi-
f Rusty had a fishing business in Florida, perhaps he really was
iting, despite his protestation to the contrary.

afternoon John had a budget meeting in town at the tax as-
office. John did his usual sparring with Gibson. The autopsy
up and John shuffled some funds from the fleet budget. When
eeting adjourned, John tried to slip out, but Gibson caught
the lobby.

ibson offered his hand. John ignored it. Gibson chuckled.

ny developments on the arson?"

Nothing solid."

ny idea how they got past Deputy Lovejoy?"

There's no evidence that anyone was actually in the storage room
Lovejoy arrived."

omebody set the fire."

hn nodded without comment.

re we sure Lovejoy's coverage of the room was uninterrupted?"

hn held Gibson's eyes for a long moment before responding.
t is it, Gibson? Not enough excitement in the judge racket?
ps you'd like a supervisor position in the department. I can have
end you an application."

ibson's chuckle rippled up through his barrel body. "We can't
is thing get out of hand. Especially this close to an election. It
reflect poorly on us all."

Your concern is touching, but there is no we, Judge. It's my
em and the fallout ends with me."

By the way, I hear your father is back in town. Give him my
ds. I always felt he was an underappreciated asset in Bolero. This
an always use a visionary. Fresh ideas keep us from stagnating."

fidgeted in the wicker chair. This was no good. He should have gone
directly home.

"What has he been doing the last twenty-four years?" he blurted
out, regretting it immediately.

She looked back, unperturbed. "Does it matter?"

That rattled him from the trance that had enthralled him since
he turned the corner in the dark. "If it doesn't matter, then what I do
doesn't matter."

"John," she said in a mixture of love and pity that he found unen-
durable. "Do you know what Jesus said to Peter when he asked about
another disciple?"

John shook his head.

"He said, 'What is it to you? As for you, follow me.' What someone else does matters not at all. But what I do matters more than
anything."

John refused to be drawn into her web. "He's just back for another round. Whatever he was doing in Florida didn't pan out. You
know what he is."

He saw a transformation in her that made him wonder if he had
ever known her at all. Her spine stiffened and she spoke with a stern-
ness he had not heard in his forty years.

"I've known him longer than you've been alive. If anyone in this
room can claim to know what he is, it's me."

"Then what is he?" John asked, quietly.

"He is the same as you. Human. Nothing more. And nothing
less."

She retrieved the lap desk and the chart. John felt that he had
just been dismissed. He stood, leaned over to kiss the cheek she pre-
sented, and said goodnight.

He thought about going in to do the search on Reggie Loftin,
but it would keep until tomorrow. Plus, he needed to be fresh for
Billy's interrogation. He smiled. The boy wouldn't know which way
to turn. He would crack open like a three-egg omelet.

DAY 4: FRIDAY

During the interrogation, Billy was clearly confused when John leaned on him, pressing him for physical descriptions of the arsonists. His responses ran along the lines of medium height, medium build, medium hair. Whatever specifics he did give didn't match the statements from the witnesses, but he stuck with his story and the lack of physical evidence eventually forced John to cut him loose.

He asked Lovejoy to keep an eye on him in case he took a drive south. It would have been nice to put a wire on his phone to see if they had made him nervous enough to call someone, but this wasn't CSI and his budget was already stretched with the Crookshank autopsy.

They were essentially at a dead end. No extant copy of the mysterious inspection report. No actionable evidence from the crime scene. Nothing of use from the witnesses. In an act of desperation, John called Matthew Lindsay at the *Bolero Bulletin*, which was basically an office rigged up in the second level of Lindsay's barn. It looked out over the bull pen. A real pen with a bull in it.

"Sheriff, what do you know good?" Lindsay growled over the line.

"Very little. What can you tell me about Crookshank's letter in the last issue?"

"It's like every Crookshank letter. One gigantic paragraph in serious need of editing for grammar, punctuation, style, length, and libel."

"Did you see the document he mentioned?"

"It was a letter to the editor, not a news article. it and demand sources."

"No need to get a burr under your saddle."

"Speaking of Crookshank, what can you give tion out at his cabin?"

"What situation? He's dead."

"Is it true you're ordering an autopsy?"

"We're pursuing several lines of inquiry at this

"Is this your new media face? You're starting tles."

"See you Tuesday."

"Thanks for the warning, Sheriff."

John spent the next few hours reading ove School documents Yvonne had sent over, gettin players in the project. Nothing stood out. He skim and then stared at the wall for a few minutes, loo There were none. He'd have to wait for the result until a break opened a new direction.

He pulled out his notebook and ran a searcl the Mustang. The owner came back as Reggie Lof the card in the car. The sale was registered two wee out the former owner, a collector in St. Petersbu name and address and continued his search.

A few vagrancy charges surfaced in Miami fr so evidently he'd lost the Mustang within a few ye streets for a while. There were a few arrests for c from the nineties, which was not surprising. T those in Bolero from the seventies and eighties. tickets, that was it.

He found a disjointed chain of apartment years ago. But the biggest reveal was a 2007 DBA Lauderdale for Captain Reggie's Sport Fishing, a dently owned along with a Brian Rogers. They address. Another search revealed it to be the R But it was not the address on Rusty's vehicle reg search on that and got nothing.

"Right."

John walked out into the heat, a welcome change from the company of Judge Gibson.

Back at the office, John went through his messages. Routine stuff and a call from Charles Cook. John tossed it into the trash. He already had a job.

The rest of the day was uneventful. The rift with Liz kept surfacing in his mind as he revised budget numbers and answered e-mails. He called her after school got out and suggested they spend Saturday at Medina Lake, camp the night and come back Sunday afternoon. She had a school thing. The conversation was short, with long silences. John gave up and hung up.

Mom called with his horoscope and an invitation to dinner for him and Liz. John said he was taking Christopher camping before he went back to school. Mom thought it was a great idea and said they could have dinner next week. John gave a noncommittal grunt.

At five he headed home. Christopher's truck was already there. He walked in to the aroma of barbecue and set the evidence bag on the kitchen table.

Christopher sat on the couch, watching *Duck Soup* and eating beef ribs. Three of them. A crumpled ball of foil lay next to the microwave.

John glanced back in the direction of the deep freeze out in the garage and turned back to Christopher. "You're home early."

Christopher wiped his hands on his jeans and muted the TV. "Last day. They let me off early. With pay."

John's eyes never left the ribs. "Must be nice."

Christopher nodded. "And guess what? The guys took up a collection for me for the Africa trip. Three hundred dollars."

"So you're still thinking about taking a year off from A&M?"

"No."

John looked up from the ribs.

"I'm not thinking about it. I'm doing it." Christopher snagged the last bit of meat from the bone and set the plate on the coffee table.

John opened his mouth for a Hail Mary attempt to stop the boy from ruining his career, but he could think of nothing he hadn't already said. Christopher unmuted the TV and leaned back on the couch to watch *Duck Soup*.

John stood by the table, watching Christopher watch TV. He grabbed his guitar, sat on the edge of his recliner, leaned forward and played a few scales while watching Groucho and Harpo do the mirror scene. He fumbled through "Nobody's Dirty Business" in fits and starts while watching the movie. He chuckled when Groucho spun around and Chico just stood there and matched his flourish afterward, but he kept playing. When Chico miraculously whipped a white straw hat onto his head after having carried out a top hat, John laughed out loud.

As the scene played out with Groucho picking up the hat Chico had dropped and handing it back to him, John realized he was playing the song without any fumbling pauses. With a quiet rush of adrenaline he played it through several times.

He stopped, kicked back in the recliner and let the guitar rest on his stomach. The sense of accomplishment was exhilarating. He had the sudden and unprecedented impulse to jump up and whoop, but instead he tried the verse again, thinking it was probably a fluke. It came out just as flawlessly as before. He played the whole song, muttering the words under the soundtrack of the movie.

A commercial break came on and Christopher muted the TV again. He got up, dumped the bones in the trash, and set the plate in the sink. Then he came back slowly, sat on the couch, and watched John, who sang a little louder until he finished the song. John looked up.

"Wow," Christopher said. "That was pretty good. When did you learn to do that?"

"Just now."

"You just sat down and played it?"

"Yep."

Christopher shook his head. "Man."

John let a soft smile break across his face. It had been years since Christopher had been impressed with anything he had done. He almost told him he'd been working on it every night for three months. Almost.

He looked at his son, now a man, making his own reckless, irresponsible decisions and sticking to them. Liz was right about that, at least. He was a good kid. And any day now he would disappear into Africa, the Dark Continent where tribal war and religious war and revolutions and AIDS and other devastating diseases wiped out millions at a toss without even trying. He would go there in the blithe immortality of youth, believing in the invincibility that was his American birthright until some random plague or act of violence snuffed him out with no more regard than the windshield has for the bug. Then he remembered what he had told Mom.

"Hey, what say we head out to Medina Lake, get a camping spot for the weekend?" John was surprised to hear himself say it, but not as surprised as Christopher.

"What about Liz?"

John's brain caught up. The summer break was coming to an end. "You have plans?"

Christopher shook his head. "Caitlyn is at Disneyworld with her family. You?"

"Wide open."

John sat in silence for a few seconds, waiting for reality to kill the moment. But before it could intrude, Christopher jumped up.

"Let's do it!"

John put his Gibson in the case and snapped it shut. A hurried consultation began as they rushed around the house, packing clothes, emptying the ice maker into a cooler and throwing food from the fridge into it, tossing clothes into duffle bags, digging out the musty sleeping bags, the tent that exuded a slight aroma of mildew.

Within an hour they were in Christopher's truck headed north to the Bandera cutoff. They had the tent set up by sundown, caught a few fish in the twilight, and cooked them in a skillet over a wood fire by the light of a gas lantern. After dinner they stretched out on the grass along the shore, watching the Milky Way turn in the sky like the dial of a cosmic egg timer. The orange yolk of a quarter moon boiled over the tree line across the lake.

After a half-hour of silence, Christopher spoke. "What was your dad like when you were a kid?"

"My dad?"

"I saw him at Toolie's."

John pulled himself up onto an elbow and squinted at Christopher in the dark. He should have said something when the old man first got into town. "Did he talk to you?"

"He doesn't even know I exist."

John didn't correct him. "How did you know it was him?"

"Mooney told me."

It was more accusation than information. Of course Paul told his son, who told Christopher. A school friend tells you the stranger at the cash register is your grandfather. What is that like?

John walked to the cooler and pulled out a Dr Pepper for Christopher and Shiner for himself. He fired up a cigar, took a few drinks, and spoke into the darkness without looking at Christopher.

"It was great when I was a kid. Elementary school. Even junior high. Some of it."

"But not in high school?"

John shook his head.

"What happened?"

John looked out across the lake at the lights on the other shore. "I grew up. He never did."

John felt Christopher look at his silhouette in the darkness. He could almost hear him frowning. He turned and looked at the dark spot that was his son.

"You're more responsible than he is." He looked away, out across the lake. "Or maybe not. I mean, you are the one throwing away a scholarship to dig holes on the other side of the world."

Christopher ignored the jab. "What was so bad about him? He seemed nice enough at Toolie's."

"He was always nice, right up until he left. He would be the nicest person to ever wreck your life. You were better off with him gone."

"But what did he do that was so bad? Besides leave?"

John stared into the night sky. Smoke from the cook fire intermingled with cigar smoke and the aroma of dead fish wafting up from the shoreline. Frogs and insects competed for airtime against the backdrop of a powerboat throttling down as it approached the boat ramp, nothing more than a noise and a few running lights gliding through the dark.

What did he do? He did a lot of things, but it was more who he was than what he did, the hand of chaos scattering fragments of your carefully arranged life. He was at his worst when he meant well, when with the best of intentions he scuttled your ship that had just come in.

"He's bipolar," John said.

"What's that mean?"

"It means as long as he's on his medication, he's normal, or what counts for normal with him. But he doesn't like to take the medication."

"Then what happens?"

"Oh, I don't know. Any number of things. Like leave his English class a week before finals, spend everything in the bank account for a down payment on a brand new Harley, and drive straight through to Tahoe."

"Did he do that?"

John nodded.

"Why Tahoe?"

"A college friend was playing Hamlet at the Shakespeare festival. He thought he could swing a part. Guildenstern, if nothing else."

"Did he?"

"Polonius got food poisoning, so he got the part. Stayed for the whole summer season."

"Sounds like it worked out."

"It worked out fine for him. He supported himself by playing poker in the casinos. We were back at home with the bank account cleaned out and not much to worry about, either. Just little things like the mortgage, electricity, food."

"How old were you?"

"Thirteen. I worked with Mooney on the ranch during the summers for spending money. That summer I didn't see a dime of it. It all went to keeping the lights on. Mom worked at Mabel's. We got by."

"He came back that time, right?"

"He always came back, eventually. But the school wasn't happy about being left high and dry the week of finals. They didn't renew his contract. That was the end of his teaching career. At least in Bolero."

Neither of them spoke for several minutes. John got his guitar from the truck and tried "Nobody's Dirty Business" again. The melody seemed to roll off his fingertips, as if the song had been trapped inside him and something in the guitar was pulling it out. He smiled in the darkness.

Ragged strips of clouds eased in soundlessly from behind him like a tattered flag in search of stars. Soon the Milky Way disappeared behind the unornamented banner. The cook fire was down to dull red embers in a bed of dark ash. The anonymity of the night emboldened John. He sang through the chorus softly in a rough, almost tuneless style, more talking than singing. He knew it sounded bad, but he didn't care.

He played it through a few more times and stopped, letting the notes die out slowly on the strings.

Christopher broke the silence. "You think I'm like him? Running off, being irresponsible?"

"I think you're wasting a once-in-a-lifetime chance. If I could stop you, I would."

"But you can't."

"Evidently not."

The silence that was the soundtrack of night animals returned. Back in junior high when John's summer job was turned into rent money, he came to the conclusion that his father, while seemingly the nicest person in the room, was actually the most selfish person he knew. It was also how he saw Christopher's decision. It seemed big-hearted and well intentioned, but it would cripple his career and place a burden on his family to cover the next three years of college.

"What he's got, is it genetic?"

"Who?"

"Your dad. The thing he takes medicine for. Can it be passed down?"

"No." The differences between John and Rusty were so great that it had never occurred to him that he might be at risk. Not until this week. Now he wasn't so sure.

"Does he still need the medicine?"

"There is no cure, only treatment. He'll always need the medicine."

"Is he taking it?"

That was the million-dollar question. Had he returned because he was finally stable? Or had he returned in the throes of a manic episode?

"I guess we'll find out."

They didn't talk much after that, just sat and watched the clouds swallow the stars. John's fortieth birthday was only a few weeks away, but his thoughts were on a birthday twenty-four years earlier, the last time he saw Rusty.

For a while after Rusty left, John struggled with guilt for the part he played in the whole sorry affair. A few weeks later, when he walked into the kitchen and saw Mom standing at the sink, staring out the window, holding a cup that dripped suds into cold dishwater, there was the guilt for how it affected her. He even carried guilt for the sense of relief he felt when he finally realized Rusty wasn't coming back, even though he knew they were better off, that the town was better off.

With Rusty gone, Christmas was a small affair. Their checks went to keeping the lights on and the mortgage paid. As always, Mom made the best of it, refusing to allow her Christmas cheer to be diminished the slightest by circumstances. They made hot cocoa from scratch, strung popcorn garlands for the tree, crafted ornaments from old Christmas cards she had stockpiled in the attic.

Knowing she would find some way of buying a present with money they didn't have, John insisted that all he wanted for Christmas was a week in the hills and canyons west of town, camping, hiking, quail hunting.

He and Mooney set up camp in the ridges west of Bolero the night after Christmas. It had been a mild winter, but halfway through the week a cold snap hit. A quick trip back to town in Paul's truck provided the wardrobe and supplies they needed to survive the last few days.

An hour or two after midnight they sat bundled in old horse blankets around a small, hot fire of pine and mesquite. In a silence that lasted for hours they watched a Cheshire moon climb above the eastern ridge and smile over Bolero, painting the rooflines of houses and the steeples of churches in a pale, glittering outline of frost. It looked like a Christmas card. A phrase from a Christmas program came to his mind.

"*For this reason I have come into the world.*"

Suddenly, in that moment, everything felt more real, more right, more purposeful than he had ever suspected possible. Life wasn't something that happened to you; it was something that happened in you, through you. He began to see what Mom had always said, that things happen for a reason. They happen because someone makes them happen. And he had made this moment happen the day he ran Rusty out of Bolero, which was the way he saw it now.

He looked over the town, his town, and felt a sense of peace and kinship. He looked at the fire, the one he and Paul had built, purposefully selecting wood that would burn hot, and felt a warmth that reached deeper than the flames. He looked at Mooney, his best friend, and saw in him the brother he never had.

Paul had felt his gaze, had turned to look back, and had eventually said, "What?"

But John had no words. He just smiled and looked back over the town. Things were going to be different, because he would make them different.

Four years later, he bought the ridge he and Paul had camped on that Christmas with money saved from double shifts and moonlighting and built a house on it with his own hands. Built his own future.

And now, twenty-four years after that Christmas, he was camping with his son, searching for glimpses of the waxing moon when the clouds thinned.

By the time John's birthday rolled around Christopher would be in Africa and who knew when he would return? Who knew if he would return at all, whether he would stay there by choice or be felled there by fate, by some random act of human or cosmic violence? Suddenly his sense of control seemed stunted, the foolish dream of a teenager drunk on his first false sense of power.

The campsite was dark now. He could barely make out Christopher's shape in the light of the dying embers. John grunted to his feet, put his guitar away, cleared up the remains of supper, and retreated to the tent.

John spent the weekend watching the sands of life plummet to the bottom of the hourglass with nothing much to show beyond fishing, eating, sleeping, playing guitar, playing poker. As they navigated the lethargic agenda of camp life, John surreptitiously studied his son, memorizing his face, his shape, his manner, looking for antecedents. Was he his mother's boy or his father's son, or some uneasy or fortuitous mixture of the two? Or had he skipped a generation, melding the numerous strands of his ancestors into something John could not apprehend?

Sunday evening arrived without John achieving enlightenment. They broke camp, loaded the truck, and returned to civilization with John no wiser.

DAY 7: MONDAY

Halfway through Monday morning John debated whether to call Liz, show up at the school during her lunch break, or wait it out. Sam patched through a call from Rod Wainwright in Uvalde.

"You asked me to let you know if we recovered the stolen computers."

"Where did you find them?" He hadn't expected anything to come from leaving his card with Wainwright, but two decades of law enforcement had taught him that a case could break from the most unexpected source. Cards were cheap and he scattered them like seeds during an investigation, never knowing which ones would sprout.

"We got a hit on the serial numbers from a pawn shop in San Antonio. Sheriff Fuentes got a copy of the security video and he seems to know the guy. He's gone to pick him up."

"Did you get the tape from 1989?"

"We're still digging through the boxes trying to sort everything out."

In five minutes John was driving to Uvalde. The tattered evidence bag sat on the seat beside him, now a regular fixture in his truck, the muffin safely inside and keeping its own counsel for the moment.

The phone rang. He checked the caller ID. Mom. Always available to provide guidance when muffins failed. He put it on speaker.

"Morning, Mom."

"Are you going somewhere? Sounds like you're in the truck."

"Uvalde."

"Then I'm not interrupting anything. And you'll want to hear this." After a short interlude of rattling paper, her voice returned. "'Your ability to work miracles is waxing, so make the most of it.' That might come in handy in Uvalde. What are you doing there?"

"Recovering stolen property. Might be a break in the arson."

"See? It's already working."

John thanked her in the manner of one with a long history of enduring unsolicited encouragement. The phone fell silent for a few moments. John crested the last rise where the terrain fell away from Hill Country to the southern plains. It was his favorite point on the drive. He could see halfway to Mexico.

"John," Mom finally said. "When did you see your father last?"

"Last week. Thursday, I think it was." She didn't respond. "Why?"

"Don't jump to any conclusions, but I haven't seen him since Thursday night."

"He's gone? Already?"

"Now, John . . ."

"I knew he wouldn't stay, but I thought he'd hang around at least until he got in some kind of trouble."

"John! Shame on you."

John thought back to the last thing he said to Rusty. *Go do whatever it is you've been doing for the last twenty-four years and leave us alone.* That was Thursday evening. It couldn't be that simple. There must be some other reason he left. Maybe he really had gotten into trouble, God knew what kind.

John felt a sudden and sickening premonition of what kind.

"Mom, tell me you didn't give him access to the bank account."

She laughed. "Oh, honey, he doesn't need money. He's got a suitcase full of money."

"What?"

She lowered her voice. John had to pick up the phone and hold it to his ear.

"When he unloaded the car, I unpacked for him while he was in the shower. The top half of the second suitcase had clothes in it, but the bottom half was full of bundles of one hundred dollar bills. Thousands of them."

"Where did he get it?"

"The point is that he didn't come back because he needs money."

John glanced at the muffin, knowing what it was going to say before it even said it.

"*swallow the honey*"

John nodded at it and smiled. He turned back to the phone. "What about the suitcase now?"

"His clothes are still in the closet."

He'd expected that. Just like last time. "The other suitcase."

"Oh." There was another pause, a longer one. When she came back to the phone, her voice was softer. "It's gone."

John could picture her sinking down to the couch slowly, the phone to her ear. This wasn't the same as before. It was a new thing and it wasn't good.

"Mom, the first thing you have to remember is that he's a grown man, making his own decisions. Nobody else is responsible for what he's done, least of all you." It was true, although John would like to claim responsibility for Rusty leaving town.

"But what does it mean?" Mom asked. "The money."

"I don't think we need to know. It's probably better if we don't. "

"You know what the Buddha said. Three things cannot be long hidden: the sun, the moon, and the truth."

"A million dollars in a suitcase is never good news."

"Do you think he stole it?" Mom whispered.

"Has he told you anything of what he's been doing for the past twenty years?"

There was silence, long enough that it was clear she was having a hard time thinking of anything specific.

"He talked about sunsets on the beach. About sailing and sunrise on the ocean with no land in sight. He told me about some of the people he'd met. A retired organ grinder who still had his monkey. A Norwegian shipbuilder who sailed the world on an authentic Viking ship he built himself. A worm grunter. But I doubt any of them had a million dollars to steal."

"A worm what?"

"You pound a stick into the ground and run a big file across the top and catch the worms that come up. He put his kids through college by grunting."

"Did he mention any names? Any locations?"

"I don't recall. The stories were so fascinating, I didn't listen for those kinds of details. Although I think the worm grunter was named Marvin."

"Did he say anything about a charter fishing boat captain named Brian Rogers?"

"No."

There was nothing to go on. He made a mental note to call Rogers again as soon as he got the Wainwright thing squared away.

"Mom, I think you have to assume he's gone for good."

"Why would he leave his clothes?"

"You can buy a lot of clothes with a million dollars."

John sat in Sheriff Fuentes's office nursing a cup of coffee strong enough to launch a campaign for governor. Fuentes had a coffee cup and a spit cup on the desk.

He was almost as wide as he was tall, with a belt buckle like a dinner plate. John wondered how the wintergreen of the snuff paired with the coffee. And he wondered if he ever sipped from the wrong cup.

"We recovered most of the hardware and some of the tapes. Don't know where the rest went. He says he found it in a dumpster."

"Let's see the jacket."

Fuentes pushed a slim file across the desk. John skimmed over it. Minor stuff. Mostly D and D.

"You sure he's the guy?"

"Got him on video. He was selling the stuff while the city was taking statements at Wainwright's office. The judge arraigned him this morning."

John looked at the top of the file for the name. Leonard Berger. He looked up at Fuentes.

"You got him here?"

Fuentes nodded. "I think the boys are about done with him."

"You mind if I ask him a few questions?"

Fuentes studied him. "About that Cook Brothers thing? How does he figure into that?"

"I'm not sure he does. That's what I want to ask him."

Fuentes took a sip of coffee, then spit into the other cup. "Don't see why not. Jimmy!"

A deputy poked his head in the door. "Yes, sir?"

"Y'all done with the Berger boy? Sheriff Lawson here wants to pick his brain."

"I'll check, sir."

Jimmy disappeared. Fuentes studied John again. "Bad timing, this Cook business, a month before the election. Two guys disappear from a locked room with your deputy guarding the only door. Have you figured out how they did it?"

"That's what I hope Mr. Berger can tell me."

Fuentes snorted, pulled a neatly folded hanky from his back pocket, opened it up, and wiped his mouth. "Leonard?" He carefully folded the hanky and replaced it in his pocket. "He couldn't find his way out of an igloo with a flamethrower."

"What do you know about his brother?"

"Frank? He's the smart one of the pair, but that's like saying Moe was the smartest of the Stooges. But you can see for yourself if you hang around. He'll be here soon as he finds a bondsman that takes personal checks."

Jimmy poked his head into the room. "He's all yours, Sheriff Lawson."

Leonard looked down at the handcuffs trapping him at a metal table that was bolted to the floor. Like before, his head was shiny with sweat. This time his wifebeater was supplemented by an equally stained short-sleeved plaid shirt. His hair had been trimmed, making him look more like a pasty version of the monster in *Young Franken-stein* and less like Fagin in *Oliver Twist*. He squinted at John when he walked in, scowled, and looked away. There were dark circles under his eyes.

John sat in the chair across the table. Leonard waited. John didn't talk. Leonard looked up, waited, and looked away again. He shook his head. He glanced at John, and then looked in the direction of the door before speaking.

"What do you want?" he finally asked.

"You did the Cook Brothers job and the Wainwright job."

"I told you I don't have a job."

"Did they tell you why?"

Leonard's gaze gravitated somewhere in the same zip code as John's face. "I don't know what you're talking about, man."

"Billy Swallow knows what I'm talking about."

Despite his best efforts, Leonard's eyes met John's for a second before skittering to the far corner of the room.

"Billy had a lot to say about you and Frank."

Leonard grunted.

"He's ready to make a deal with the DA. He gives us you and Frank for the arson, he walks."

"That Boy Scout? He knows better."

John waited. Nothing. "Knows better?"

"That's all I'm saying." Leonard looked away pointedly. He tried to cross his arms but the gesture was jerked back like a junkyard dog on a short chain. He glared at the handcuffs, slammed his hands down on the table, and jerked his head to the side, looking at the door.

"You might want to check on that, Mr. Berger. He's looking at two to twenty in state prison right now and he's feeling pretty chatty. I don't think your welfare figures very high on his radar."

"It's his own welfare he should be worried about."

The door opened. Jimmy stuck in his head. "His brother's here to bond him out."

Leonard leaned back in the metal chair. John stood, looked at Leonard's smile, and walked out. He stopped at the door and turned back.

"Use your time on the outside wisely, Mr. Berger. It's likely to be short."

Fuentes stopped him on his way out. "Did you get what you needed?"

"Enough to work with."

As he walked past the front desk he saw two men, one in a fresh pearl-button western shirt and new blue jeans, obviously the bondsman, the other in stained and worn painter's whites with a pack of cigarettes rolled up in the left sleeve of his t-shirt. Frank Berger. He studied the man. He looked nothing like his brother. Where Leonard was soft and slumpy, Frank was hardened muscle. His strong features, like a leading man in an action movie, were in stark contrast to Leonard's weasel face.

The only similarity was in the eyes, which viewed the world through narrowed slits. He looked up from the paperwork at John, assessing his appearance as if to figure out John's culpability in this inconvenience to his workday.

John noted that he matched the description of the taller suspect and responded with a distant nod that took in Frank, the bondsman, and the deputy at the front desk. He stepped out the door and checked the time. A little after one. He called Lovejoy.

"Let's get Billy in. I'll be back around four. I'd rather not wait until tomorrow." He hung up, got in his truck, drove to the Wainwright office and found a parking place along the back of the lot.

Inside the tropical courtyard the humidity offset the shade like the week before. He was sweating by the time he stepped into the overly conditioned air of the office. A girl in her early twenties sat at the front desk, the one who was giving her statement in a conference room the last time he was here.

"Is Rod Wainwright in?" he said before she even looked up from her computer screen.

She reached for the phone. "Can I say who is calling?"

"Sheriff Lawson."

John stepped to the side and looked around the office. It appeared things were nearly back to business. A kid in a plaid shirt and skinny jeans pushed a cart next to a desk and unloaded the computer onto it. Several of the desks had people working at computers, others lacked computers, but everyone seemed busy.

Through the glass of the office on the right he saw Rod Wainwright hang up the phone and wave him in. John thanked the girl and met Rod at the door of his office. They shook hands. Rod motioned him to a chair and took his place behind the desk. He was in a much better mood than the last time they talked.

"You certainly work fast, Sheriff."

"Working a case is like working concrete. You have a small window to get it all done."

"Then I have bad news. We didn't recover everything from the pawn shop. A computer is missing and some other stuff, including half the backup tapes."

"Nineteen eighty nine?"

"Afraid so."

John thanked Rod and left him sitting at his desk. He nodded to the girl on the way out, returned to his truck, and drove to The Fez. It was just going on two o'clock. There might still be something on the buffet. If not, he could order from the menu.

The owner greeted him at the door as always. The buffet was closed, but he insisted on giving John all he could eat of anything on the menu at the buffet price. John couldn't talk him out of it, so he took a seat facing the door and pondered yet another dead end.

Cook was certainly making up for his lapse in judgment twenty years ago with a scorched earth policy this time around. But nobody launches a campaign of that magnitude without making some kind of mistake. All John had to do was find one loose thread and keep pulling it until the thing unraveled.

Perhaps he could match the tire tracks from Crookshank's cabin to a vehicle owned by Frank or Leonard Berger, placing them at the scene. It would be a start, but he needed something stronger. His best bet was to follow the connection from Billy through the Bergers to Cook himself. A solid confession beat circumstantial physical evidence all the way to Albuquerque and halfway back.

His mind wandered to Liz. He thought about calling her, but the owner arrived with his lunch. He ate, thinking of his conversation with Jennifer the last time he was here. He pulled out his phone and called Christopher.

Christopher answered. "Hey."

"Have you been to see your mother at all this summer?" The silence was all the answer he needed. "You're about to leave the country for who knows how long and probably get yourself killed. Go see her. No matter what you think about her. Go see her. In person."

Another silence, and then, "Okay."

"Today."

"Okay." A little exasperation this time.

"If I find out you haven't visited her, in person, I will burn your passport and your birth certificate. That should set you back a few months."

"Okay, Dad. I said I'd do it."

"See that you do."

John hung up and continued his lunch. Christopher would do it. He was too much of a Good Samaritan not to. And maybe Jennifer would say something that would get through his iron skull and change his mind. Or not.

When John got back at four, Lovejoy had Billy stashed in the interview room. Lovejoy stood in front of John's desk as he flipped through messages.

"I figured that would rattle him a bit, being in that room instead of your office like last time."

"Did you Mirandize him?"

"Yessir. Told him it was just routine. He didn't ask for a lawyer."

"Good work." John looked up from the messages. "Get some prints of the tire tracks from Crookshank's cabin. They might match Frank Berger's truck."

Lovejoy raised an eyebrow and nodded once. John picked up the Bolero High School file, followed Lovejoy out the door and turned down the hall to the interview room. He looked in the tall, thin window with chicken wire embedded between the two planes of tempered glass. Billy sat in a chair in his Cook Brother's security guard uniform, his fingers drumming nervously on the table top. Three walls of the room were blank. The fourth had a built-in tinted window. There was nothing behind the window but wall. But Billy didn't know that.

John opened the door. Billy flinched and then grinned weakly.

"Hey, Sheriff." He stood and held out his hand.

"Have a seat." John ignored his hand and took the seat opposite. He pulled a digital recorder from his pocket, pushed the record button, stated the date, his name and Billy's name, and set it on the table. Billy stared at it like it was a cottonmouth coiled between them.

John started out easy, but distant. He thanked Billy for coming down to help them out, verified that he'd been read his rights and that he didn't want a lawyer, all while paging slowly through the report in front of him, which had nothing to do with Billy.

Not that Billy knew that. His gaze moved slowly from the recorder to the two-inch file. John glanced up and saw Billy squinting, trying to read the page upside down. John turned the pages a little faster, and Billy's head followed them like a dog watching bites of steak disappear into a man's mouth.

John continued to turn pages, keeping his eyes on the paper. "Last Thursday we found the body of Edward Crookshank in his cabin." John looked up. "What can you tell me about that?"

Billy's confusion was plainly written on his face. "What? I don't know nothing about a body."

"The medical examiner in San Antonio is determining the cause of death and looking for evidence on the body. We'll know something soon. Do you have a truck, Billy?"

"Uh, yeah." Billy frowned at John. "But I didn't kill any old man."

"Did you know Mr. Crookshank?"

"No!"

"Then how did you know he was an old man?"

"Well, I heard people talking about it this weekend."

John looked at him for a long moment, then resumed turning the pages. "Is your truck out front?"

"Yessir."

John stepped to the phone on the wall by the door and dialed two digits. "You have those prints of the tire tracks from Crookshank's place? Good. Do a comparison with Billy's truck. Thanks."

He hung up the phone and returned to the table.

Billy leaned forward on both arms, looking earnestly into John's eyes. "I didn't kill anyone. I never been there. Don't even know where he lived."

John nodded once. "Good. Then you have nothing to worry about, do you?"

Billy nodded absently, but he didn't appear to stop worrying. He frowned and leaned back into his chair. John flipped through a few more pages quickly, stopped on a page, and looked up at Billy.

"I've been talking to some friends of yours. Frank and Leonard Berger."

Billy's eyes flared, but he said nothing.

"Let me tell you how this works, Billy. Frank and Leonard are old hands at the game, so they have an advantage on you. They know the first one to squeal gets the deal, and they've already fingered you as the lead man on the arson at the warehouse."

Billy shot up out of his chair. "That's a lie."

"Sit down, Billy."

Billy stood facing John, taking quick, shallow breaths. He sat down slowly.

"Here's the thing," John said. "I know that the arson and Crookshank's death are related. For arson, you're looking at a state jail felony. That's two years in prison and a $10,000 fine." John glanced down at the paper and back up at Billy. "As for the murder, that's a whole different story."

"But I didn't kill anyone," Billy said in a voice halfway between whining and crying. He looked around wildly and focused on the door. "I gotta get out of here."

Billy rushed toward the door. John didn't move from his chair. Billy grabbed the handle and looked back at John.

"Billy, if you get a lawyer, you don't get the deal."

"What deal?"

"That's what I'm trying to tell you. Sit down and listen."

Billy looked out the tiny window, slowly released the door knob, and returned to the chair. John waited until he was settled before he spoke.

"The thing is, I don't believe Frank and Leonard. I think Frank planned the warehouse break-in and the little incident with Crookshank, and a few other things. And if you help us out, we can make sure that Frank is the one who pays, not you."

"I don't know anything about that guy. And I didn't plan anything."

"Of course not. So why don't you tell me what happened, in your own words, and we'll get it all sorted out."

"And I don't go to prison?"

"I don't think so."

Billy took a few breaths and spilled his guts like a disgraced samurai with a sharp sword. John glanced at the recorder to make sure the red light was on, and listened.

Billy liked to stop by the Horseshoe Road Inn on the way home from the warehouse. Last week Frank showed up and they got to talking at the bar. They bought each other a few drinks and soon they were at a back booth by the bathrooms, far from prying ears, where Frank laid a proposition before him. Five hundred dollars for two minutes of work.

Frank would take advantage of the presence of the church protesters to break through the gate and lock himself in the storage room. Billy would follow him in, stand at the door, and demand he come out.

"Why?" Billy asked him.

Frank scanned the room slowly. "There's something in there I want. It's a small thing, not worth much to anybody but me."

"How is locking yourself in the room going to do any good?"

"That's the point, right? You'll be outside the door. And once the coast is clear, you'll give me the signal and I'll come out and leave by the back fence, but you'll keep standing there, yelling for me to come out."

"But you won't be in there."

"Right. Exactly."

Billy sat in silence for a moment and then began to smile. "They won't chase you, because they'll think you're still inside."

"Right. Not much to do for five hundred dollars, is it?"

And Billy had agreed. It would be the easiest half-grand he had made in his life. He was thinking differently now. He looked at John with desperation.

"But I didn't know they was going to be two of them, and he didn't say nothing about starting any fires."

"What was the signal?" John watched Billy's eyes for a tell.

Billy answered immediately without looking away. "I'm calling the cops."

"So, when you hollered 'I'm calling the cops' instead of 'Come out with your hands up' he would know the coast was clear."

Billy nodded.

"How did he start the fire if he wasn't there?"

Billy shook his head. "I been trying to figure that out. Remote control?"

John pulled a legal pad from the folder, set it in front of Billy, and set a pen on top of it. "Write that down and sign it and we're good." John stood.

Billy grabbed the pen like it was a life preserver. He looked up at John. "And I don't go to prison, right?"

"I don't see you going to prison, Billy." He picked up the recorder and the file and walked out. No prison for Billy. A little county jail time, maybe, but no prison. John would fix it with the DA.

John walked through the bull pen. He stopped in front of Lovejoy's desk. "Once Billy is through with his statement, book him for accessory to arson, and process him." He turned to Sam, had a second thought and turned back to Lovejoy. "He might be a little surprised, so be on your guard."

"You got a confession?"

John nodded, turned to Sam, and set the digital recorder on her desk. "Let's get that transcribed ASAP and fax it to Sheriff Fuentes."

"If you're in a hurry," Lovejoy said, "I can e-mail him the MP3 file right away and get him the transcript later when it's done."

John picked up the recorder and turned to Lovejoy. "You think Fuentes will know what to do with it?"

"Jimmy does. I'll call him so he knows it's coming."

"Good. I'd like both the Berger boys in jail before sunset. Let him know we'll pay for the room and we'll provide transport if we need it." John turned to Sam. "But I still want the transcript."

At his desk, John called Fuentes to give him a heads up on what was coming and requesting they pick up the Berger brothers ASAP. He hung up, checked the time, and called Ernst Boyd, the Bolero district attorney. As he expected, the deal with Billy would not be a problem, but the Berger brothers deal could be ticklish. John gave him the full background and they discussed details. That settled, he skimmed through his e-mails. Nothing that couldn't keep.

His phone rang. He picked it up. "Sheriff Lawson."

"Thank you, John."

"Jennifer?"

"Christopher came by this afternoon. He just left."

"Really? I never got around to telling him."

"Of course not."

"Did you talk him out of going to Africa?"

"I just wanted you to know I appreciate it."

She hung up. John looked at the phone, smiled, and set it down. He thought about Liz and looked at the phone. It had been four days. He reached for the phone, but Sam walked in with the transcript of Billy's interview.

"Here it is." She handed it to him.

John skimmed through the pages and handed them back to her. "Thanks. Did you fax it to Fuentes?"

"Yes, sir," she said, but she didn't leave. "What you said last week, I appreciate it. I took the kids to Schlitterbahn yesterday. There was a boy screaming at his girlfriend and Claire said, 'She ought not to put up with that loser.' And I realized I must of done something right."

"How old is Claire?"

"Eight."

"Let's hope she still thinks that in ten years."

Sam smiled. "I'll make sure of it. Anyway, I just wanted to thank you again. Like you said, we're better off without him."

John nodded. Sam left with the transcript. John looked at the phone again. Maybe he did know how to talk to a woman after all. At least Jennifer and Sam seemed to think so. He picked up the phone and dialed Liz. She answered on the fourth ring.

"Hey, John."

"How about dinner tonight? I'm buying."

There was a long silence. "John, I don't think . . . I don't know if we should."

"I could grill some steaks on the deck instead."

"John, I love you and I want us to be together, but this thing with your dad . . . it's a big thing, even if you don't see it. Especially if you don't see it."

"Then you'll be happy to know that it's all worked out. Problem solved."

"What do you mean?"

"He left town Thursday. Like I said, it was just a matter of time."

Liz processed this and finally responded. "John, that doesn't change anything. It doesn't matter if he's here or gone. It's not about him. It's about you. About you dealing with whatever happened twenty-something years ago."

"There's nothing to deal with. He left. We did fine without him, even better, in fact. He came back for a few days and then disappeared, just like I knew he would. He's gone. It's over. End of story."

"That's the problem. You think the solution is to run him off instead of dealing with why he left the first time and what that did to you."

"Liz, he's gone. He was never here when he was here. You're making something out of nothing." He realized he was on the verge of yelling. He glanced at the door to his office and talked softly. "Look, let's have dinner and we can talk about it then."

"What happened last week, that night in the grill, it was like you were a different person."

"He has that effect on people."

"No, he doesn't John. Everyone I've talked to thought he was charming. Even your mom—"

"Mom is . . . you know Mom. She would find something good to say about an axe murderer."

"The point is that whoever that person is, the one that came out at the grill last week, that's some part of you. And that's not good for you. Or for us."

"It was only because of him and he's gone."

"He's just the catalyst, not the problem. And what if he comes back? Or what if something else sets it off?"

"Or what if it doesn't? We can't live by what-ifs."

"But we can face reality. Or at least I can. John, I love you, but until you face this—"

"What does that mean? What is it you want me to do?"

"Talk with someone about it. A professional."

"You want me to go to a shrink?"

"Get counseling."

John didn't respond because he couldn't. He didn't know where to start. The idea was obviously absurd, but it was just as obvious that he couldn't say that.

"For us." There was a long pause and what might have been a sniffle. "For me? Would you do it for me? If I'm wrong, it should be a short session."

John thought about the election. If it came out that he was seeing a shrink of some kind, well, he didn't want to think about that. He was unsure how to handle it.

"Liz," he said, softly. "I'm not sure . . . Can we give it a little time, first?"

"Okay."

From her voice, John was pretty sure she was crying. He got a sinking feeling.

"But I need some time, too, John."

"For what?"

"To figure out what I think about this. About you. About us."

"What?"

"Goodbye, John. I love you."

The background noise on the connection abruptly ended. John stared at the phone, then set it down. He wasn't sure what Liz meant, needing time to figure it out. Was he supposed to avoid her? Was she making the relationship conditional on him getting counseling?

John checked the clock. It was closer to six than five. He grabbed his jacket, walked out to his truck, and headed home. He glanced at the evidence bag. The muffin hadn't said anything new since Rusty left. He pondered the connection, but didn't come up with anything. Did that mean he was really sane after all? Or that Rusty drove him crazy? Literally?

He decided it didn't matter. Rusty was gone. The muffin was silent. It was a good thing. He had a break on the arson case, the kind he could ride all the way to a conviction. Things could get back to normal.

As he pulled up to the house, something Billy had said hit him. Frank and Leonard were gone before John arrived. Even before Lovejoy arrived. So what was it he had heard in the AC vent in Bert's office? Up to now he had been operating on the assumption that the voice of the muffin was just his mind recycling the real voices he had heard through the ductwork. But there were no real voices.

He thought back to that moment in Bert's office. Had Bert said anything that indicated he heard the voices from the vent? He thought so, but couldn't remember.

He put the truck in park, turned off the key, and opened the evidence bag. He peered into the shadows, saw the muffin resting in a corner. Maybe the muffin had nothing to do with it. He set it back down in the passenger seat and went inside.

The fridge contained nothing of interest and Stella's ribs were no longer available, although he could always get more. As he closed the fridge, he saw the crumpled prescriptions on the counter. He should get them filled.

With any luck, Fuentes would have the Berger boys in lockup in a few hours. A reason to drive to Uvalde, a chance to fill the prescriptions. He picked them up and tried to read Doc's writing. He gave up and decided to put them in the truck so he wouldn't forget them.

He climbed in the driver's side and leaned over to stuff the prescriptions in the glove box, then decided as long as he was in the truck, he might as well get some dinner. He went over his options as he drove into town. He toyed with the idea of Stella's, but the weight of the prescriptions won. He ended up at Flo's.

He looked over the two or three options he would normally order, the burger, the patty melt, the chicken-fried steak with mashed potatoes and gravy, and began seeing them in terms of carbs and cholesterol. The pleasure he used to feel when looking through the menu drained away. What had Doc said? Divide the plate in half. One half green vegetables. The other half split evenly between protein and starch. And while you're at it, split your heart in two and beat yourself in the head with a sledgehammer.

Defeated, he ordered the shrimp salad and iced tea, changing it at the last minute to unsweet. He heard himself thinking that the salad wasn't half bad and wondered how it had come to this. How could he be as thin as a rail fence and twice as good looking, and be forced to eat from the old lady's side of the menu? To forever consider the good side of the menu the forbidden fruit? That was for other people, overweight, out of shape, undisciplined people.

Well, now he was one of them and he had to get used to it. Or did he? What was the point of living longer just so you could eat salad? He felt like a dissident in the Lubyanka, being resuscitated and kept alive so he could endure more torture.

He looked across the room and saw Battles digging into a monstrous steak drowned in butter next to a baked potato the size of Enchanted Rock with a snowcap of sour cream on it. The strings of his bolo tie rested atop a bulging gut that strained the buttons on his white shirt.

Here was a man so intent on drowning himself in lard that he went beyond the menu to guarantee it. His cholesterol must be off the charts. Perhaps he would have a heart attack before the election.

John smiled at the thought and then noticed that Gibson was also at the table, his plate loaded with lean pork chops and couscous, the special for the evening. They were so intent on conversation that they evidently hadn't seen him come in. Probably planning some scheme for exploiting the fiasco of the disappearing arsonists. He smiled again. They were in for a surprise.

His salad arrived. He took a bite. It was better than he remembered.

The sun was setting when he left Flo's, the heat dropping into the nineties. On the drive home he got the call from Fuentes. The Berger brothers were sharing a suite courtesy of the county, with the complimentary continental breakfast.

"You sending someone down for them tonight?"

"They can keep for seventy-two hours before we have to let them go. Let them stew until morning. Should be ripe about ten a.m."

"It's your nickel."

The phone rang before he had disconnected from Fuentes's call. Lindsey.

"Hey, Sheriff, what do you know good?"

"Not much, Lindsey."

"I'm writing up the arson story for Wednesday's paper. Got anything for me?"

John considered how to play it. Surely Cook already knew about Billy. He might even know about the Bergers. He thought about what Battles had said about the media. "You can say we have a person of interest in custody."

"Would that be Billy Swallow?"

John didn't answer. They'd just booked him a few hours ago.

"The daily strength report is public information, Sheriff."

"Yes, sir, it is. But I can't comment on Billy or anyone else." At least the Bergers wouldn't be in the story, since Lindsey didn't know to check Uvalde.

"You think he set the fire himself?"

"I can't comment on speculation."

"Off the record."

"There is no such thing as off the record. We have a person of interest in custody. That's all I can tell you."

"Got you. Later."

John pulled up to the house. Christopher's 4x4 had a For Sale sign in the back window. Inside, he found Christopher lounging in his recliner with a laptop, flipping through the REI website.

"You guys going to be roughing it? I figured you'd be staying in a compound of some kind."

Christopher craned his head around. "Hey." He climbed out of the recliner and moved to the couch. "They have a home base, but you have to go out to remote villages to dig the wells."

John grabbed a Shiner and dropped into the newly-vacated recliner. "No Motel 6 out there, huh?"

"No electricity," Christopher said without looking up.

"They going to pump it by hand?"

"Solar power. With a manual pump backup system."

John nodded. Not their first rodeo, evidently. He checked the clock. Barely eight. "You're home early."

"Had dinner with Meemaw. She likes early."

"What is this, old home week? First your mother, now Meemaw? Who's next?"

Christopher looked up. "Actually, I wanted to talk to your dad, but he wasn't there."

They looked at each other without speaking for a good minute or more. John spoke first.

"I knew he wouldn't last long. Thought he'd last longer than three days, though."

Christopher bristled. "So you knew? This weekend, you knew he was already gone."

"She told me this morning. What did she say about it?"

"She told me stories about him. He sounds okay to me."

"Yeah, sure. And he's gone. Don't forget that part."

"Too bad I didn't get to know him when I was a kid."

"And whose fault is that?" John finished off the Shiner, kicked the footrest down on the recliner, and leaned forward. "Look, you have to realize he's . . . he's like the Easter bunny or the tooth fairy. You might get something nice occasionally, but he's not going to be there for you when you need him."

Christopher snapped his laptop shut and stood. "Right. Got it." He disappeared into his bedroom.

John watched him go, figuring it was somehow his fault, but not sure how. Here the boy was with a place to stay, rent free, and meals when he wanted them, all summer long. Would he get that from his Granddad? No, he would not. Did he ever get one blessed thing from his Granddad his whole life? No, he did not. But here he was, romanticizing this idea of the nice-guy Granddad that he'd somehow been cheated out of, when the only reason he'd missed out was because that very same nice-guy had abandoned his family long before Christopher was even born. How was that John's fault?

John got another beer and a cigar and went out on the deck. The lights of Bolero twinkled below. The lights of the faux Tuscan villa on the opposite ridge gave off a soft glow in the humid air like a glamour photo, tinted aquamarine from the lights in the vanishing-edge pool.

Was Jennifer in the pool, taking the edge off the heat, or out somewhere with her Houston gigolo? Was Gibson back, cloistered in his home office scheming plots to rid himself of this meddlesome sheriff? And what was Liz doing?

He remembered her words, that she had cut him some slack because of Jennifer, which had galled him. He didn't need her pity. And what was so wrong with him that she suddenly couldn't stand to be with him? He'd treated her right, gave her space, respected her career, been there for her. She acted like he was some kind of abuser. He didn't deserve that and he knew it. And she used to know it.

Until she met Rusty. That was the moment everything changed. Like Christopher, she was seduced by the masquerade. Christopher had been seduced without even meeting the man, seduced by proxy through Mom's rosy-tinted stories, her photogenic memory that made everything look better than it actually was.

And worse yet, the man had abandoned them again, and for some reason everyone thought John was the one with the problem. It was absurd. He slammed the Shiner down on the table, slapped his cigar into the ashtray, and stalked into the house. From a back shelf in his bedroom closet he retrieved a bottle of Longmorn 16. He grabbed a glass on the way out to the deck, dropped into the deck chair, poured a generous splash, and held it up to his nose, breathing in the spirits. He took a sip, allowed it to roll across his tongue, and swallowed, feeling the warmth spread through his viscera, down his limbs, and out the extremities.

He took another sip and resumed the cigar. He'd expected more of Christopher, but he was young and passionate. But he was abandoning a scholarship to go to Africa, so perhaps logic wasn't the right tactic for him.

He reached for the scotch, but his hand froze as a whispered voice tickled his spine.

"*zzz . . . hollow the dart . . . zzz*"

It was quiet, barely perceptible, but unmistakable. The muffin.

John jumped to his feet and stared into the dark toward the truck invisible in the driveway.

"What?" he shouted in its general direction. He stalked off the western edge of the deck, around the corner of the house to the truck, and ripped the door open. He jerked the evidence bag from the passenger seat, dumped the muffin into his hand, and held it up.

"You have something to say to me, you say it to my face."

"*zzz . . . hollow the dart . . . zzz*"

It was louder this time.

"Hollow the dart? What the hell is that supposed to mean? Why don't you just say what you mean? Own up to it like a man."

"*zzz . . . hollow the dart . . . zzz*"

"I'll hollow your dart."

John shoved the muffin back into the evidence bag, wadded it up, and with a mighty swing of his arm threw it over the house. He slammed the door of the truck, strode back to the deck, finished off the scotch in the glass, dropped into his chair, and picked up his cigar. He took a deep breath, then a long draw from the cigar. As he blew out the smoke, the back door opened. Christopher stuck out his head.

"What's going on out here?"

"What?"

"I heard some yelling."

"Just chasing a raccoon off the trash can."

Christopher looked around, then back at John. "Uh. Okay." He popped back inside and closed the door softly.

John poured more scotch, sipped it, and smoked the cigar. After his heart rate returned to something resembling normal, he thought about what had just happened. The muffin had talked to him, despite being shut up in the truck twenty yards away. He leaned forward, peering over the edge of the ridge into the dark where the muffin now doubtlessly rested fifty or a hundred yards below. Would he still hear it, even after throwing it over the ridge?

He waited. Nothing came wafting up from the depths to haunt him. He resumed the scotch and cigar and tried to pick up where he had left off, but he found he couldn't concentrate, or even remember what it was he had been thinking about.

He turned his mind to the case. He expected his interview with the Bergers to lead him back to Cook, who wanted evidence of the original report to disappear permanently. He had somehow engineered its disappearance from the county clerk's files long ago. Then Crookshank's letter to the editor made him realize that other archival copies of the report could still exist. Hence the arson in the warehouse, the destruction of Crookshank's files, the burglary at Wainwright's office, the job offer designed to pull John off the case.

John smiled. Tomorrow he would pull the thread that would unravel Charles Cook's world and render impotent the schemes of Gibson and Battles to exploit the fiasco at the warehouse for their campaign.

He raised his glass to the scintillating aquamarine reflections off the western façade of the faux Tuscan villa on the opposite ridge, downed the last of the scotch, and went to bed.

John wakes in a sweat in a dark room. The voice of the muffin plays *"hollow the dart"* on a loop in his head. He checks the clock radio. Three a.m. He kicks the sheets aside and sprawls, trying to get back to sleep, but the three words won't permit it.

Wearing only his boxers, he moves stealthily through the dark rooms to the back door and out onto the deck, where the phrase crescendos, echoing in his skull.

Hollow the dart. Hollow the dart. Hollow the dart. Hollow the dart. Hollow the dart.

He walks to the edge of the deck, laps the toes of his right foot over the edge, and squints down into the tangle of grass, agave, cactus, and mesquite outlined in the silver of the gibbous moon. The muffin is down there somewhere.

As he stares, he slowly becomes aware that he is talking, saying words.

"Hollow the dart. Swallow the tart."

He clamps his mouth shut, refusing to echo the syllables, but the words continue in his mind. "Wallow in art. Follow the cart."

He knows that it won't stop until he returns the muffin to the truck. He steps off the deck, his left leg dropping three feet until it hits the caliche of the ridge, which crumbles under his bare foot. His right foot slips over the edge of the weathered boards of the deck, gathering splinters from his ankle to his knee as he skis awkwardly down the incline of the ridge, coming to a bone-jarring, bruise-inducing stop against a limestone spur.

Hollow the dart. Hollow the dart. Hollow the dart. Hollow the dart.

He rubs his shins viscously until the sting recedes, wiping the blood on his boxers, and then strikes out to the right, descending incrementally via the Braille method. The elements of the slope—dirt, rock, live plant, dead brush—speak to him as he handles them, guiding him with psychic GPS.

Hollow the dart. Hollow the dart. Hollow the dart.

"Follow the cart," he mutters as he stumbles down the slope in a controlled fall.

He clutches at a cactus, the spines piercing his hands, embraces a stunted mesquite that directs him farther to the right, lunges across a limestone ledge, steps off its edge, and tumbles like a gymnast until he comes to rest against the succulent spines at the base of an agave.

Hollow the dart. Hollow the dart.

"Swallow the tart," he rasps between ragged breaths. "Hallowed in art."

He slowly unfolds himself, hand-over-hand up the stalk of the agave like a drunk up a lamppost, and stands erect.

Hollow the dart.

A dark spot, little more than a blur against the moon-caressed caliche, teases the periphery of his vision. He inches toward it without looking directly at it, sliding his feet along the incline to dig a foothold.

"Hollow the dart."

He bends down and claws at the bag with his left hand, clutching it like a running back saving a fumble. With his right hand he begins the ascent, guided by the waxing moon as it races to the western ridge.

The muffin no longer speaks to him. In the void left by its silence he hears only the pounding of pulse in his veins, the scouring of breath through teeth, the scraping of feet against scree, the creaking of branches seized for support, the skitter of rubble loosed down the ridge.

He emerges to the south of the house, on the opposite side from the deck. He staggers to the truck and inters the bag in the glove box.

Day 8: Tuesday

John walked into Fuentes's office. "Is he ready?"

Fuentes looked up, then took a second look. "You wrestle a chupacabra?"

John shook his head. "Mesquite. Clearing land."

Fuentes nodded doubtfully. "Yeah, he's in there. Need some company?"

"Thanks, I got it."

He walked down the hall, favoring his left leg, the greatest of the mysterious injuries he sustained during the night. The rest were mainly cuts and abrasions. A soak in the tub and some judicious first aid addressed most of the injuries, but he couldn't hide them all under his suit.

He stopped at the interview room and looked through the chicken-wire glass. Leonard was in there, handcuffed to the table, looking like he'd spent his few hours on the outside hiding under a rock in a damp cave. He still had on the same clothes. John figured it was an even call on whether to throw them in the washer or the dumpster.

He opened the door and stepped in, greeting Leonard's frown with a quiet smile. The frown deepened into a scowl and Leonard looked at the other corner of the room, his eyes bouncing back to John and away for a millisecond every so often.

Before he left the house, John had called and requested that Leonard be put in the room as soon as possible. Anticipation and uncertainty would play in John's favor. He had selected Leonard as the more malleable of the pair. John had been on a fishing expedition the first time around, but now he had the backing of the DA and charges of arson and possibly murder.

John held the smile, dropped the file on the table, and sat down. He waited. Eventually Leonard's attention skittered close to his vicinity like a nervous mosquito.

"Welcome back, Mr. Berger. I hope you found Stacy a good home. It may be a few years before you see her again."

A frisson of fear rippled through Leonard's body. He looked at John directly, if only for a second. "You got diddly on me."

John started the recorder, leaned back in his chair, and flipped the file folder open. "Well, that's where you're wrong. I've got charges from the DA. We'll transport you up to Bolero tonight. Doubtful you'll make bail. Should come to trial in three or four months. If you're a good boy, the judge might count that as time served toward your prison sentence." He flipped a page and pretended to read it. "Two to twenty. I'd figure toward the twenty end if I were you."

Leonard looked at the stack of paper. "You got no evidence."

John sat up and flipped through the pages. "Here we go. I have eyewitness descriptions to match you and Frank. From good, upstanding churchgoing citizens who will look good on the stand." He turned a few more pages. "I have physical evidence in the storage room and along the escape route, right to where you parked the truck."

He turned more pages, picked up a page and looked at Leonard. Leonard looked at the page, then at John.

"And I have testimony that describes how Frank recruited Billy Swallow and how you pulled off the disappearing act. All of which matches the physical evidence."

John set the paper down and closed the file. "The DA feels good about this one. He's going for the maximum penalty. With time off for good behavior, you might get out in twelve or fifteen."

In the stillness of the room, John could hear Leonard's rapid, shallow breaths, furred with a smoker's rasp. Leonard's eyes darted around frantically, examining every corner. Then he leaned forward on his elbows with his hands on either side of his face, his fingers sliding along the dull shine of his head. A low groan slipped out.

John gave him a few more seconds.

"However . . ." He let the word die out and waited.

It seemed to break like a wave on Leonard's gleaming skull and wash over him. His head came up slowly and he looked into John's eyes, frightened and hopeful.

"What?"

"There's just one thing. We don't think you torched that warehouse for fun. Somebody hired you to do it and he's the guy we want."

"Yeah, that's right. It wasn't our idea. Me and Frank, we would never do anything like that out of meanness."

"Whose idea was it?"

"I don't know. Some guy called Frank couple weeks ago. That's the guy you want. We were just following orders."

"You don't know the name? Not even a first name?"

Leonard shook his head. "Frank never said."

John had expected that. He knew he would have to use Leonard's confession in his next interview, the one with Frank, where he would get the ticket to the next level, Charles Cook.

He mined Leonard for the details of the arson starting from when they got the materials and drove up to Bolero to when they climbed over the fence and hoofed it back to the truck. Then he removed the handcuffs, left Leonard writing out his statement in his childish scrawl and stopped by Fuentes's office.

"I'm headed to lunch. When Leonard gets done writing, let's swap out the brothers, but don't let them talk to each other."

Fuentes took in the scratches on John's face and the bruise on his left cheekbone. "It went okay, then?"

"Fine as frog hair. But Frank's holding the face cards. He needs to spend an hour in speculation. I don't need him talking to Leonard and working out a plan."

Fuentes nodded. "Where you going for lunch?"

"Gonna grab some drive-thru and see if I can catch Wainwright in his office."

He walked out to his truck and headed to The Fez. He felt bad about the misdirection, but he didn't need company. He had too much on his mind.

He had a shadowy recollection of a dream, of clawing through an alien landscape after an elusive muffin that taunted him with riddles as it receded into the swirling center of a black-and-white Hitchcockian spiral. He had a clearer memory of awaking next to his bed, his body a mass of aches and scratches, blood smeared in finger-sized streaks across his boxers.

At The Fez he cruised the parking lot, checking for Jennifer's Infinity before going in. He had no idea how often she hooked up with Houston. Inside he scanned the room, satisfied himself that he was surrounded by strangers, and took a table in a corner with a view of the door.

With his plate filled from the buffet, he settled down to lunch and rumination. His last clear memory was throwing the muffin over the house, out into the eastern abyss beyond the ridge. And before that, sitting on the deck, hearing the voice of a muffin that wasn't there.

He didn't know what it meant, but he was sure it wasn't good. And then waking up in that condition. Something had happened. He didn't know what it was, but he was sure that wasn't good, either.

Rusty was gone. He no longer mattered. But this felt too much like Rusty for comfort. Childhood scenes flipped through his mind like a multimedia show.

Rusty diving naked into the Frio River, splashing in the frigid moonlight. John remembered the short-lived thrill of the evening, the total abandon of an eight-year-old cutting loose. But what kind of adult does that?

Rusty looming over the basin of the birdbath, staring into the watery reflection of a full moon, chanting nonsense. Even as a twelve-year-old John had wondered what Rusty felt in the moment. Serenity? Compulsion? Confusion?

The next spring, when John was in seventh grade, voices woke him. Moonlight streamed through the window, lighting up his bedroom like a night scene on a community theater set. He looked at his alarm clock. Two a.m. He walked squinting down the hall, following the noise to the kitchen. Rusty limped around the room, facing appliances in a stance like he was prepared to tackle them and wrestle them to the ground. Mom followed, pleading with him to sit down so she could tend to him. When Rusty turned, John saw the torn shirt, the cuts on his arms, the black eye, the blood trickling from his nose. He walked stiffly, protecting a broken rib, it turned out.

The next day, John learned from Mooney that sometime around midnight Rusty had lured a bull from its pen into a pasture and squared off against it. The bull successfully defended its honor and turf, but Rusty had acquitted himself well, considering the bull outweighed him by two thousand pounds. John endured some taunting from the eighth graders. By the end of the day he had a shiner to match Rusty's. When the last bell rang, he walked to the high school and waited for Rusty, like always. Rusty walked slowly out of the door and down the steps, smiling at a passing group of students and yelling something back to a girl standing just inside.

John tried to match the image before him, the favorite teacher in his natural habitat, to the scenario he had built in his mind throughout the day. A fit man in his late thirties crouching like a linebacker. A ton of annoyed beef snorting and pawing the pasture. Moonlight rendering the scene in gray tones. That much he could picture, but never what came next. Did they clash like knights jousting? Did Rusty prance and taunt the bull like a matador? Did he charge first, grabbing the horns and flipping over the bull's back like the bull dancers of Crete?

Most of all, he tried to imagine what Rusty had felt, what would lead him to provoke certain injury, possible death. What was that state of nonthought coupled with deadly action? How could one become so divorced from his rational self while still apparently acting from volition?

And had he done something similar last night?

The last image that played in John's mind was from the following summer—Rusty returning from three weeks in the state hospital in Big Spring, head shaved and eyes vacant, his personality scooped out with pharmaceuticals. Twenty days earlier he'd taken the car and started driving out I-10 to El Paso, where he evidently got turned around after dinner at a truck stop and headed back east, taking I-20 at the split.

Doing ninety or more, around Midland he came upon a state trooper driving east and taunted him—tailgating, flashing his brights, pulling alongside and making faces. It had taken three cop cars to pull him over. He didn't fight them when they pulled him out of the car. Instead, he wriggled like an eel, flopped like a fish, and chanted doggerel. When they finally got him cuffed, the trooper drove past the jail, directly to the state hospital in Big Spring.

Mom learned all this from the doctor, plus that Rusty spent the first day in confinement talking to a tumbleweed outside his window like Moses arguing with the burning bush. Was this the next step for John, to move from talking muffins to talking plants?

For the first time John thought that maybe Liz was right, that he should talk to someone, but he rejected the idea immediately. For starters, who could he talk to? Mom? Who knew what inanity she would prescribe? Not Liz, who would only use this episode as a confirmation of her diagnosis that he see a professional. And going to a psychiatrist was out of the question. No sense in solving the mystery of the vanishing protesters only to hand Battles and Gibson victory on a stick.

John finished his kabob and thought about the prescriptions. He reached for his pocket, knowing that they were most likely on the floor of his bedroom along with the bloody boxers. He shrugged and drove back to the Uvalde Sheriff's office where Frank was waiting to be flipped.

Frank didn't say a word. He sat with his hands cuffed to the table and studied John from across the table. John did the same, appraising the bronzed, muscular arms splotched with baby blue paint, the solid, bristled jaw, the close-cut hair, the startling grey eyes sheltered under a ridge of brows like a pair of rat snakes on a shelf halfway up a cliff. He wouldn't look out of place on the cover of a bodice-ripper romance novel. How could he be related to Leonard?

John knew this wouldn't be the cakewalk he'd had with Leonard, but he had confidence in the evidence and the signed statements from Billy and Leonard. Frank might be tough, but the fact that he had relied on the material at hand instead of finding more competent accomplices indicated that he wasn't as smart as he thought he was.

John worked through the preliminaries–starting the recorder, waving the right to an attorney, the "where were you on the night of" type questions, all of which Frank answered dismissively. Then he began laying out the bricks with which he would build the prison around Frank. The witness descriptions at the warehouse, the paint thinner used as an accelerant, the tire tracks at Crookshank's cabin that matched Frank's work truck, the chips of plastic in the truck bed that matched the damage to the equipment stolen from Wainwright, the video of Leonard fencing the gear.

Frank had little to say as John piled up the raw material. He alternated between boredom and irritation. But when John laid on the mortar of the testimony from Billy, Frank's demeanor changed. He didn't speak, but his breathing became audible and the snakes in his eyes writhed. John thought that if Frank bonded out, they might have to take Billy into protective custody.

But it was Leonard's testimony that broke him. It was rich with detail, right down to the time-delay fuse Frank built out of a chain of Camels, the brand they both smoked, using straightened paper-clips to keep them in place and ending in a book of matches nestled in thinner-soaked paper towels. The fury on Frank's face melted to something like resigned sadness, the look of a father when his son leads him with growing excitement to the den to present the chaotic mural he's just painted with permanent marker on the new white leather couch, confident of the effusive praise to follow.

"Maybe I should talk to a lawyer."

"You can do that," John said, "but a lawyer can't undo a confession. I conducted the interviews myself. They're solid, no procedural gaps to get you off on a technicality. You're going down on this one."

John let this soak in, watching Frank do the math in his head.

"Unless," he added.

Frank's thousand-yard stare focused back on John. "Unless what?"

John flipped through the pages of the file. "Taken all together, this will add up to quite a few years of hard time." He closed the file and leaned forward. "But I'm more interested in the guy who hired you." He watched Frank process this, saw the glimmer of hope in his eyes. "I already talked to the DA. He's willing to talk if you are."

"What about Leonard?"

After seeing the look on Frank's face when he heard Leonard's statement, John wasn't as surprised at the question as he might have been.

"He'll get the same deal you get, maybe better." The deal covered only the crimes committed in Bolero County, not the Wainwright burglary, but John saw no reason to mention that.

Frank thought for a long moment. "I want it in writing."

John nodded. "We can do that."

Frank thought some more. "I'm thinking I should get a lawyer to look over the deal, make sure it's legit."

John shook his head. "You get a lawyer, there is no deal for him to look at. You have to take your chances with the evidence. I hope you know a good one."

John leaned back, waiting. He watched Frank wrestle with the decision. After a full minute he swiped the file folder off the table, dropped it in his briefcase, and snapped it shut.

Frank looked up. "Okay."

John stood. "I'll get him on the phone and we'll work it out right now." He nodded at the cuffs. "I'll get somebody in here to take those things off. You want some coffee or something?"

Frank breathed out heavily with the air of a man committing himself to a direction he hopes is the right one. "Right. Coffee's good."

It took an hour to raise the DA. Jimmy set up an extension on the interview room table and John dialed Boyd's number. After twenty minutes they had a deal. Boyd faxed it in. Frank signed it. Then they got down to it.

John leaned forward, forearms on the table. "Who contacted you about the Cook Brothers job?"

"Lonnie Bates."

John was stunned. He pushed in toward Frank. "Bates?"

Frank nodded. "Right. Lonnie Bates."

John's mind raced, waiting for something to connect. It didn't. He suddenly felt tired. He leaned on an elbow, raised a hand, and massaged his temples with thumb and forefinger. He'd been primed for one answer—Charles Cook. Who was Lonnie Bates? An alias Cook used for his dirty work?

Boyd's voice came over the phone. "The septic contractor?"

"Right," Frank said.

That connected. John pulled the file from his briefcase and shuffled through the papers, coming up with something from the Bolero High School project. "Bates Excavations?"

"Right. That's the one."

"When did he contact you?"

"Sunday, right after the school fell in."

"Why did he want the files destroyed?"

"You know, I forgot to ask him that," Frank replied.

The rest of the interview supplied additional details. Bates had ordered the destruction of all the files, Cook Brothers, Crookshank, and Wainwright, but left it up to Frank on how to accomplish it.

John was curious about Bates placing such a high degree of trust in Frank. "Why did he go to you for this job?"

Frank waited a few moments before he answered. "I don't think that's part of the deal."

John let it go. No need to stall this investigation to uncover more evidence to burn Frank. He was already in the pocket. But despite repeated questions from John and Boyd, nothing led back to Cook. John could hear Boyd's dissatisfaction over the phone. He'd given away too much in exchange for a measly septic contractor.

They didn't get much further. John asked about Crookshank. Frank said he found the old man dead at his typewriter, like he had been writing his way to the gates of hell, and steered clear of him.

John sent Frank back to his cell. The deal only let the Bergers out once they had the next suspect in custody, a detail that prevented Frank from warning whoever it was.

On the drive back to Bolero, John and Boyd hashed out the next steps. John had no doubt that Cook was pulling the strings through Bates, but they had no evidence to support that theory. Only a direct link between Frank and Cook would work. All they had was the fact that Frank had fingered Bates, and that Cook often used Bates on jobs. Suggestive, but hardly compelling. Certainly nothing that would hold up in court and Bates would realize that immediately. With no physical evidence to tie him to any of the scenes, he wouldn't roll over and finger Cook.

John didn't want to bring Bates in until he was sure they could keep him. He cast about for some leverage. "If he's managing the dirty work for Cook, he's probably good for a lot of shady stuff we could pull him in for. We just need somebody to dig it up."

"My office doesn't have the funds to dig that deep, and you're scrambling just to pay for an autopsy."

"Thanks for reminding me."

"You'd do the same for me, I'm sure."

They finally settled on a game plan. John would have an informal talk with Bates, shake him up a little, and see if he got nervous enough to run to Cook.

John got back to Bolero after seven. He swung by the house, which was deserted, grabbed a sandwich, and played a little guitar to keep in shape. Then he changed to jeans and a black shirt and headed out in his Crown Vic to the Tuesday night poker game.

It was a light night at the Horseshoe Road Inn, only seven vehicles in the parking lot. John parked in his usual spot under the security light and walked in. Buzz caught his eye as he came in and immediately reached for the Johnny Walker. John nodded and walked to the back room.

Lindsey, Mooney and Guzman sat in their usual spots in the middle of a hand, but John hardly saw them because of the man seated in his spot, the chair facing the door.

Rusty.

John stumbled to a stop just inside the doorway, his involuntary reaction much like a week earlier, adrenaline and dread. Tunnel vision. Shallow, rapid breathing. Racing heart. Churning stomach.

Rusty looked up and smiled. That infuriating smile of genuine pleasure, no hint of an agenda. "Hey, son."

Mooney looked up at John, glanced back at Rusty, and then took a large gulp of wine and studied his cards. Guzman watched John with a hint of amusement. Lindsey craned around in his chair, saw John motionless in the door, and raised an eyebrow. He turned back to his cards and spoke without looking up.

"Come on in, Sheriff. You're blocking traffic."

A noise from the doorway caused John to step aside. Buzz entered, a Lone Star in one hand, scotch in the other. He looked at John, confused. Taking slow, deep breaths, John nodded toward the table. Rusty reached to the back wall and pulled up a chair between him and Mooney. Buzz set the boilermaker in front of the vacant chair and left.

Through the fading haze of his adrenaline rush, John noted that Rusty had placed the chair to keep the power position after John. He walked to the table, moved the drinks to the other side, dragged up a different chair, and pushed it between Lindsey and Guzman. They made room, grumbling.

"You're early," Lindsey said.

John drank the shot in one gulp and followed it with a third of the beer. "Set me up for the next hand." He stood, picked up the shot glass, and walked out.

At the bar, John caught Buzz's eye, slapped the empty shot glass down, and walked outside. He skirted the front of the building in the opposite direction from his Crown Vic to the dark side of the Inn. He rounded the corner and saw a familiar shape, ghostly in the moonlight.

Rusty had hidden his car, knowing John would come eventually. Despite the seemingly genuine smile, this was an ambush.

John spun around and retraced his steps to the bar, counting days. The Mustang was in the driveway late Thursday night when he got the VIN and talked to Mom. He must have been inside packing at the time. It was now Tuesday night. Five days. Where did he go and what did he do?

He thought of the charter business. Fort Lauderdale was about fifteen hundred miles, give or take. Doable in two days each way if you pushed it. But if he went back, why did he return? Was it about the money? Did he still have it?

He almost got the Slim Jim to take a look inside the car, but decided against it. He walked inside, grabbed the filled shot glass from the bar, and returned to the back room.

The hand was done. As he set the shot glass down next to his chips and took his chair, John scanned the table. Mooney was already down a third of the two hundred buy-in, as expected. Lindsey was up. Guzman was up more. Rusty was down to half. Not expected. John studied Rusty, knowing he would learn nothing.

The dealer button was in front of Rusty. He shuffled one last time and set the deck in front of Mooney, who cut them. John watched Rusty's hands.

Guzman set a white chip in the middle of the table. John slid two next to it, never taking his eyes off the deck.

"What say we make things more interesting?" Rusty said. "Two and four?"

"Raise the blinds?" Mooney asked, never one to welcome change.

John felt for two more chips and set them atop his first two. Guzman looked from John to Rusty, then added another chip to his.

As Rusty dealt them each two cards, Guzman broke the silence. "Okay, I'll bite. What's up with the face?"

Everyone looked at John, evidently wondering the same thing but too polite to ask.

John kept his eyes on the deal. "I don't complain about your face."

"Mine doesn't have scratches and bruises all over it."

"I can fix that for you."

Guzman shrugged. "Hey, it's your face. Wear it like that if you like."

Rusty set the deck down. Everyone checked his cards, Mooney holding his like always, like a squirrel with a pecan. Rusty held his with his fingers covering all but the top edges.

John bent back the edges of his cards enough to see them, and then let them fall back to the table. Two clubs, the jack and the ten.

Everybody called, adding their four chips, and Rusty dealt the flop—ace of clubs, king of clubs, jack of diamonds. John was one card away from a flush, perhaps a straight. Too good. Too easy. He looked at Rusty.

"How's the arson coming?" Rusty said.

John looked around the table. Mooney was the only other person in the room who had played against Rusty before. Just one game almost thirty years ago, but not one he would ever forget. Lindsey and Guzman knew nothing about Rusty except that they were winning and Rusty was losing. Just what Rusty wanted.

John caught Mooney's eye, glanced at the chips around the table, and back to Mooney. Mooney's face gave away nothing, but his eyes answered. It was every man for himself and the devil take the hindmost. And Mooney obviously had no illusions as to where to find the devil.

"I didn't come here to talk shop," John answered.

"No," Guzman said. "You came to get your butt kicked. Raise." Four chips.

"Less talk, more poker," Lindsey said. He took a sip of his bourbon and branch.

John called, as did Lindsey.

It was to Mooney. He pulled a bottle from the floor next to his chair and refreshed his glass. He noticed John watching him. He held up the glass. "Light and approachable with a wonderful, floral-driven nose," he said, much like a tour guide. He took a small sip, rolled it on his tongue, and swallowed. "Rich in cherry and plum on the palate with underlying notes of tobacco and cedar."

Guzman stood, reached across the table, and grabbed the bottle from Mooney's hand. He read the back label. "McPherson Cellars has executed a beautiful interpretation of sangiovese."

Mooney snatched at the bottle, but Guzman held it out of his reach. "Light and approachable with a wonderful, floral-driven nose, Stellare is rich in cherry and plum on the palate with underlying notes of tobacco and cedar."

He held out the bottle. Mooney jerked it from his hand, replaced the cork, and set it back on the floor. "Call," he said defiantly.

"Raise," Rusty said, pushing four chips to the pot. "Paul was always clever, even as a boy," Rusty said. "Made the Light Foot rank when he was only eleven. Not much for night swimming, though."

"Arrow of Light," Mooney said. "And I was twelve."

Guzman and John both called.

"Call," Lindsey said. "So, Mr. Lawson, what is it you do?"

"As little as possible."

"I heard that," Guzman said.

Mooney called. John inspected him. Could he be holding out for a straight?

Rusty played the turn card—the two of diamonds. John double-checked his hole cards. They were still clubs.

"Raise," Guzman said immediately and put eight chips in the pot.

John looked at him. Maybe he had the straight. Or not. Guzman would raise with a pair if he thought he could bluff you out of the hand.

John called and Lindsey folded.

"Here on vacation?" Lindsey asked.

Mooney also called. Whatever he had, it had to be solid. He was typically more timid about matching raises.

Rusty called. "I'm something of a speculator." Rusty added his chips to the pot. "I have a few lines of inquiry that look promising."

"You have a demolition company? Because somebody is going to have to haul away a high school." Guzman said.

"I'm more interested in bringing long-term jobs to Bolero. Help boost the local economy."

John wondered what that scheme might be, but before he could ask, Rusty played the river card. The two of clubs. John had made his flush. It didn't matter who had the straight, he was set.

"Such as?" Lindsey asked, no longer interested in the hand now that he had folded.

"My research indicates a severe shortage of correctional facilities in Texas."

John forgot himself and stared at Rusty.

"You want to build a prison in Bolero?" Mooney asked.

"A five-hundred bed, fifty-acre facility could provide full-time employment for over one hundred people."

"What do you know about building and running a prison?" John asked.

"It's not what you know, it's who you know."

"Check," Guzman said, evidently more interested in the game than the prison.

John turned his look of amazement from Rusty to Guzman. He'd never heard him check before. He must not have that straight after all. Or maybe he did and didn't see any reason in running everyone else out of the game.

"Raise," John said. He pushed ten chips forward.

"You can't bluff me out this time," Mooney said. "Call." He shoved almost half of his chips forward.

"You have investors lined up?" Lindsey asked.

"We are in negotiations with several interested parties."

"We?" John asked.

"My business partners and I."

"You mean Brian Rogers the fishing-boat captain?"

John didn't know how to interpret the expression on Rusty's face as they locked eyes. He had to be surprised that John knew about Rogers, but if so, he didn't let it show.

"Yes, he is a member of the syndicate in question. One of several."

"How about Reggie Loftin? Is he an investor?"

A longer pause. A slight narrowing of the eyes. "He's more of a silent partner." Rusty set his hands on his chips and slid the entire stack into the pot. "All in." He looked at John.

The whole table turned to John, even though it was Guzman's bid. John ignored them.

The whole discussion was absurd. Rusty might have most of a million dollars in his trunk, but he was not a business man. He was an English major who somehow stumbled into a charter fishing business, and John was guessing that Rogers took care of anything business related. Rusty probably sweet-talked prospects and kept them supplied with beer once they got under way.

And one million dollars wasn't even table stakes for a project of this magnitude. He was talking a minimum of fifty million just to build it and operational costs of over five million a year. On the other hand, a million dollars might be enough to grease the right palms to get the measure passed.

As he thought of this angle, it began to explain a lot. He might not be the guy to negotiate the details, but Rusty was definitely your man if you wanted someone to sniff out the suckers and see who could be bought. The million dollars in the suitcase was starting to make sense. Bad sense.

Guzman finally spoke up. "I think I'll back out of the line of fire." He pushed his cards away.

John held Rusty's eye. "What's it going to cost me this time?"

Rusty arranged the chips. "One twenty-four."

John set one hundred twenty-four dollars of chips in the pot.

"All in," Mooney shouted. He shoved two small stacks forward. "Sixteen."

Guzman snorted. Lindsey smiled. Rusty split the pot to account for the different call amounts and looked at John.

John smiled and turned over his cards. It would beat Mooney's straight and whatever Rusty had.

Rusty nodded. "Flush, ace high. How about you, Mr. Mooney?"

Mooney threw his hole cards down in disgust. A queen of clubs and a ten of hearts. "I flopped that straight. That should count for something."

Guzman pulled a chip from his pile and held it across the table. "Here you go, Mooney. I'm all out of gold stars"

Mooney batted his hand aside, sending the chip rolling across the floor.

John watched as Rusty set his hole cards down on the table—the two of hearts and the two of spades. He set them next to the two of diamonds and the two of clubs dealt at the turn and the river.

Guzman whistled. "Four twos."

"A fortuitous concourse of events," Rusty said. He smiled at John.

John held his gaze for a long beat, then looked slowly to Mooney. A barely perceptible nod passed between them. They both knew Rusty could make a pair dance the tango and elope to Niagara Falls if he wanted to. Setting up himself with four of a kind and then seeding everyone else at the table just enough to make them bet big was probably how he won the fishing boat.

John grabbed his hat and walked out the door. The old man had tipped his hand and John was going all in.

John used the Slim Jim to open the Mustang. The clutter in the backseat spoke of a road trip—fast-food containers, disposable coffee cups, crushed Camel packages—but no suitcase. He had no doubt it was in the trunk, but the car was forty-five years old. He couldn't open the trunk without a key unless he picked the lock or pulled out the back seats.

He flicked the dome light off, crawled into the passenger side, and closed the door. The car was low slung, but had plenty of legroom. He did the math. This car was twenty-four years old twenty-four years ago when he almost got it as a birthday present. Or one like it. He didn't have any experience with classic cars. It felt unexpectedly sleek and solid.

The upholstery was in perfect shape, probably recently installed. He settled into the seat and analyzed the prison project from multiple angles to find some interpretation that could be legitimate and they all led to the same bad place. Any outfit that used Rusty Lawson as their scout was either crooked or stupid.

The car was getting stuffy. He considered rolling down a window, but that would tip Rusty to his presence, so he just lived with it.

His thoughts turned to Liz. She hadn't answered her phone or returned his calls. He still wasn't sure of where they stood.

He pulled out his phone to try her again when Rusty came around the corner, pulling a cigarette from a pack. John shoved his phone back in his pocket, back on target. Rusty opened the door, but the dome light didn't come on, so he didn't see John. He sat behind the wheel, picked up a Zippo from the dash, and flicked it to life.

"What's the cash for?" John asked.

Rusty lost the lighter in the spasm. It fell onto his lap, still burning. He slapped at it, knocking it to the floorboard, and kicked it around. He finally rolled out of the door to his knees, snatched up the lighter, and snapped it shut. The smell of singed carpet filled the car.

John rolled down his window. Rusty searched around the ground until he found the cigarette, fired it up, and got back into the car.

"You startled me, son."

"You didn't come back for your family, did you? It was for this prison scheme."

Rusty blew a cloud of smoke out the open door. "It's not an either/or world."

"Are there really any investors? Or did you just make all that stuff up in there?"

"I've already identified a possible site."

"Where?"

"I'll show you." Rusty pulled his door closed, started the car, and put it in reverse. He stopped at the edge of the highway. "It's too rough for the pony. Let's get your truck."

That suited John. He'd rather be the one driving.

Rusty drove to the house without having to ask for direction. He pulled up to the left of the truck in the spot where the Crown Vic would be if they hadn't left it back at the Inn. John got out, walked around the truck, and opened the driver's door. As Rusty got out of the Mustang, Christopher pulled up in his 4x4. He stopped halfway in, his lights picking out the two of them like convicts in a prison break.

John climbed into the truck. "Let's go."

Rusty stood between the cars, shading his eyes with the hand that held the cigarette and squinting. Christopher got out of the car, the motor still running, and approached. John got out and walked back to where Rusty held out his hand.

"You must be Christopher." He took Christopher's hand.

"Yes, sir."

"I can see a bit of your mother in you."

Christopher flinched and withdrew his hand. John smiled. Strike one.

Rusty picked up on it immediately. "But anyone can see you're a Lawson. Lean. Mean. Independent." He took a drag off the cigarette and flicked the ash onto the driveway.

Christopher looked from Rusty to John. "What's going on?" He looked closer at John. "Whoa! What happened?"

"Nothing—" John began, but Rusty cut him off.

"We're headed out to look at a potential construction site for my next project." He looked past Christopher. "Is that a four-wheel drive?"

"Yes, sir."

"And a spotlight?"

"Yes, sir."

"Perfect. Want to drive?"

Christopher looked at John and shrugged. "Sure, I guess so."

Rusty claimed shotgun, leaving John to push aside the flotsam in the back to find a place to sit.

Christopher drove back down the ridge. He stopped at the highway. "Where to?"

"North out past the airport."

Rusty turned toward Christopher. "I hear you're headed to—"

John talked over him. This conversation was going to be about Rusty, not Christopher. He figured Rusty was less likely to stonewall him with Christopher in the car.

"So, how's the fishing charter business?"

"I can't complain."

"You have a charter fishing boat?" Christopher asked.

"Three."

"In Port Aransas?"

"Fort Lauderdale."

"Cool."

"What does a good charter boat cost these days?" John asked. "Quarter of a million? Half?"

"In that general neighborhood."

"Tell me then, how does a fired English teacher turned vagrant come up with a million dollars to buy three boats?"

Christopher looked at Rusty and then back to the road. He didn't say anything.

"It's not how much you have, but what you do with it."

"Would you like to translate that into plain English for the benefit of those of us who haven't mastered the skill?"

Rusty looked out the window. They drove through downtown Bolero. It was buttoned up for the night, parking lots empty, buildings dark, except for an occasional light in the back.

"I won the first one in a card game."

"Really?" Christopher asked.

"Absolutely," Rusty answered.

Christopher's enthusiasm annoyed John, but it was useful if it got Rusty to talk. "Did you win Brian Rogers in a card game, too?"

"I needed a captain, so I made him a partner."

"And the other boats?"

"We expanded. Brian's good with the business side of things. He got private financing."

"Private financing. Does that mean a private bank? Or guys who deliver cash in a suitcase and break your legs if you're late on a payment?"

They passed the sign for the airport. "Now what?" Christopher asked.

"I'm thinking of selling off my part of the business and retiring."

"No, I mean where do I go from here?" Christopher nodded toward the cutoff to the airport.

"It's another ten miles. I'll show you where to turn."

"These private financing guys, are they the same ones who want to build this five-hundred bed prison?" He could see Rusty joining the scheme just for the irony of the mob building a prison.

Christopher stared at Rusty. "A what?"

"Brian's handling that side of it. I'm the rainmaker."

"Like with the boat," John said.

"Why are you building a prison?" Christopher asked.

"A Lawson keeps his eyes open. Opens the door while opportunity is still wiping its feet on the doormat. There are more criminal bodies than beds these days. Especially in Texas."

The more Rusty talked, the less John believed. There were no investors, no plan to build a prison. Rusty was playing an angle. Why did he want everyone to think he was bringing a prison to Bolero County? To save face after having left in disgrace? But things would be even worse when the deal fell through. There must be some other plan.

And how did it fit in with the suitcase full of cash? Or were they two separate things? Maybe Rusty made up the whole thing after he got here. Or after he got back from wherever he went over the weekend.

"So, if I go out to Fort Lauderdale, will you take me out on a fishing charter?" Christopher asked.

"Absolutely," Rusty said. "In fact, if you want a job, you got one."

"Too late," John said. "He's headed to Africa."

"Hey, it's on the way," Christopher said.

John didn't know which would be worse, the dangers of Africa or the dangers of falling in with Rusty. He leaned toward Africa as the safer bet.

"Turn here." Rusty pointed at an unmarked gravel road angling off to the left.

It was little more than two ruts. Twenty yards in it climbed up the ridge at a severe grade. No place for a Mustang. John wouldn't even want to take his truck up there. At least not in the dark. He wondered how Rusty knew about the place.

The 4x4 scrambled up through several switchbacks, the view in the headlights alternating between limestone and scrubby vegetation. In no time at all they were at least a thousand feet up.

"You want to build a prison up here?" Christopher asked.

"Wait for it," Rusty said.

Then the headlights shone out into empty space. They crested the ridge.

"This is it. Pull forward to that wide spot over there and light it up."

They got out. Christopher killed the headlights, grabbed the spotlight from its base and shone it out into the void. The hill fell away sharply below them, and then undulated in rocky terraces to a dry creek bed. A quarter mile away it rose to another ridge on the opposite side.

Christopher swung the light back and forth. "Is this going to be some kind of Island of Dr. Moreau thing?"

"The fact that it is remote is what makes it attractive. No homeowners to complain. Think of it as an inverted Alcatraz."

"What are you going to do," John said. "Helicopter them in?"

"It opens up to the north. It's just a matter of building a road."

"And bringing in water and electricity," John said.

"No step for a stepper." Rusty swung out his arm, taking in the expanse of the unseen valley spreading out below them in the dark. "Imagine five hundred souls being rehabilitated in this primitive setting blissfully free of the corrupting influence of modern society, refreshing their spirits in the stark beauty of the Hill Country. This place will change lives."

John doubted himself for a moment. Rusty's face was partially illuminated in the backwash of the spotlight, glowing with passion and conviction. He spoke as if it were a real thing, as if it were his own vision, his lifelong dream to bring this gift to the downtrodden masses, those who had fallen victim to an oppressive system through no fault of their own. Then John remembered who he was dealing with.

He stepped closer to Rusty and lowered his voice. "Whatever it is you're doing, I can't cover for you. If you screw over Bolero like you did Mom and me, you're going down and I'll be the one to slap the cuffs on you."

He had not spoken softly enough. Christopher swung the light around, washing it over the two of them before he lowered his arm, bathing the limestone ledge beneath their feet in a blinding white, illuminating their faces with the reflection from below, the shadows exaggerating their expressions.

Christopher frowned at him with features that were a combination of Mom, Jennifer, and his own—an expression that was disappointed, reactionary, and censorious. John looked to Rusty. There was no mixture of emotions here. He was stricken, Shakespeare's Caesar, mortally wounded by betrayal.

John knew instinctively that his son's reaction was genuine. John felt remorse tempered with the knowledge that Christopher had no history, no experience to urge him to caution when dealing with Rusty. In time he would understand. It might take years, but John was willing to be misunderstood for a season.

But Rusty's natural ability to manipulate had been supplemented by years of training as an actor. His response seemed real enough, but so did his performances on the stage. And even if his distress were genuine, his perspective could change in a matter of minutes or hours as he rode the waves of his disorder. John had learned through bitter experience the dangers of staking anything on Rusty's reaction at any given time. It was as reliable as Texas weather.

It was time for plain speaking. No more whispering.

"Are you on your meds?"

"Dad!" Christopher flipped the light up into John's face, blinding him.

John closed his eyes and swung his arm to push the spotlight away. He connected much sooner than he anticipated, knocking it from Christopher's hand. It fell to the rock and the bulb shattered, plunging them into darkness.

Rusty's voice came out of the dark. "God be with you. Fare you well. This business is well ended."

"It's a legitimate question," John shouted. "It makes a difference." He inched toward the car until he felt the bumper. "It makes all the difference."

He felt his way to the driver's side and flipped on the headlights. Christopher stood in the glare of the beams, turning away, shading his eyes. John looked to the right.

Rusty was gone.

John ran to the edge. He could barely make out Rusty's form a few yards away, climbing down the ridge into the prison valley, no moonlight to guide his descent. He yelled down into the abyss.

"Is this what a Lawson does? Run away from the hard questions? This is the opportunity you were talking about. Come back up and face it. It's never too late to do the right thing. Isn't that what you said?"

The faint ghost of a man twenty feet below stopped. A pale oval appeared, the only hint of a face looking up.

"Dad!" Christopher stepped next to John and looked down.

John didn't take his eyes off the oval. He doubted Christopher could see it, doubted his eyes had recovered from the flash of the headlights.

Christopher reached for John, tried to pull him back from the edge. "What are you doing?" His voice was desperate, uncomprehending.

John pushed him away, back toward the car and the light. He continued to shout into the darkness.

"Why did you come back?"

He got down on his knees, grabbed the edge of the limestone, and leaned out into the empty air.

"This is your chance. I'm right here. Isn't this why you came back? To do the right thing? Tell me. Is this real? Are you taking your meds?"

John closed his eyes, took a deep breath, and leaned out further.

"Why did you come back?" he screamed into the night, his voice ragged and raw.

He waited. There was no answer. He opened his eyes. The faint oval was gone.

John pulled back from the edge, rolled to the side and leaned against a rock, breathing heavily. Christopher came over from the car and knelt beside him.

"What's going on, Dad?" His voice was shaky. He collapsed onto the ground next to John, pulled his knees up under his chin, and wrapped his arms around his legs.

John closed his eyes and felt the rush of adrenaline subside. He coasted it down to a more manageable heart rate. The fog in his head cleared. He looked around. Rusty was gone. His son sat next to him, his face buried in his knees.

Without thinking, John reached out. He wrapped an arm around the shoulders of his boy who was now a man but still his boy. He opened his mouth to answer, but there were no words. Instead, he just pulled Christopher closer to him and waited.

Sometime later, John had no idea how long, things seemed better. He gave Christopher's shoulder a final squeeze and stood. Christopher looked up. John held out his hand. Christopher took it and pulled himself up. John dusted off his pants and stepped to the edge, looking down. There was no sign of Rusty.

Christopher joined him. "Where is he?"

"Down there, somewhere. He could be down in that creek bed walking north, or ten feet away, hiding behind that rock or that mesquite over there." John was betting on the former.

"Why?"

John shook his head. "It's what he does. It's what he is without the meds."

Christopher looked aimlessly out into the darkness of the valley. "What do we do now?"

John turned away from the ledge. "We go home. We go on."

"But—"

"There is no but," John said, harshly, then thought better of it. He looked Christopher in the face. "Listen to me. He is what he is. He does what he does. We can't change that, no matter what we do."

He turned, walked back to the car, and opened the passenger door. "We go on. We live our lives. Maybe he comes back. Maybe he doesn't."

Christopher refused to step away from the ledge. "But . . . but he's out there. By himself."

John closed the car door and walked back to Christopher. "Listen to me, son. If you want to survive in the proximity of Rusty Lawson, you have to learn to think, not feel. He's out there because he chose to run away from his own flesh and blood. Nobody forced him over that ledge."

He waved his arms in the warm, humid night. "It's not going to get below eighty tonight. He won't freeze. He's only a few miles from the highway. He can walk back, or he might get lucky and catch a lift. Either way, he'll survive. He'll take care of himself. It's what he does best."

John reached out to Christopher and laid his hand on his shoulder. "But we go home. We can kill ourselves climbing around in the dark trying to save him from himself, or we can go home and live our lives and build something for him to come back to. If that's what he decides to do. He could disappear for another twenty-four years."

Christopher looked at John, his face stark in the glare of the headlights. "So, did you guys have a fight?"

John frowned at him.

"The bruises."

"No. I slipped off the edge of the deck last night."

Christopher weighed the answer, seemed to accept it, and walked to the car, veering to the passenger side. John took the wheel. They went home.

John drove the 4x4 south to the county line to his Crown Vic at the Horseshoe Road Inn. He got out and watched Christopher drive away. The parking lot was almost full, despite the fact that it was almost midnight on Tuesday. He glanced at his car and then veered to the door of the bar.

Buzz tossed a quizzical look in John's direction before turning away to take an order. The jukebox blared some modern country song he didn't recognize. It sounded more like rock than country. John glanced at the door of the back room. It stood open, the inside dark. He took an open stool at the bar and gave Buzz the nod. A minute later a boilermaker sat in front of him.

John sipped the whiskey, ignoring the Lone Star. He swung around on the stool and leaned against the bar, taking in the crowd. They were mostly young, in their twenties, contemporaries of Billy and Lovejoy. A crowd surrounded the pool table, drinking, shouting, laughing, occasionally putting cue to ball. All three dart boards were busy.

It was a typical Texas roadhouse. Plenty of cheap beer, loud music, and raucous celebration. Most of these kids would drag their sorry butts to a job they hated the next day, nursing a hangover, the voice of Johnny Paycheck echoing in their psyche.

It was exactly the kind of place that Rusty would own from the moment he walked into the door. Girls young enough to be his granddaughters would fall in love with him. Their boyfriends would go home talking about how great a guy he was.

But when those same kids looked John's direction, they made him in an instant, despite the jeans and black shirt. He was the law. They toned it down and watched their step.

John turned back to the bar. He'd rather be with Liz at her place. Maybe he'd give it a try. He checked the time. Way too late for that.

Buzz wandered in his direction, his eyes assessing John's face.

"Suspect get out of hand?"

John didn't answer, just stared back. Buzz looked away, glanced down the bar at the drink levels, and turned back to John.

"Was that really your daddy in here for the game?"

John nodded and winced down a swallow of the Lone Star. "I have a request," he said. "What say you stock a six-pack of Shiner under the counter on Tuesday nights?"

Buzz pursed his lips and nodded. "It could happen."

John raised the Lone Star in a toast, thought better of it, set it down, and picked up the scotch instead. "Have one on me, Buzz."

Buzz nodded and poured himself a Jack. They toasted and drank. Buzz leaned on the bar, wiping it with a limp towel.

"I hear your daddy is lining up investors to build a prison up north."

"I'd take that with a block of salt if I were you."

"No?" Buzz asked with arched eyebrows.

"No," John replied. "His bark greatly exceeds his bite."

Buzz considered this. "But he's a helluva guy."

"That he is." John finished off his scotch and pushed the shot glass toward Buzz. "That's one thing everyone agrees on."

"And a good tipper." Buzz replenished the glass.

With a million dollars in a suitcase, who wouldn't be? John drank the scotch, put a twenty on the bar, and left.

John drove north back into Bolero County, past his ridge, keeping an eye out for Rusty. He drove through town, past the airport and past the gravel road to the prison ridge. He kept on driving until the land flattened out up to the Bandera cutoff, past the point where Rusty would have walked out of the valley, turned around and headed home.

The Mustang was still in the driveway. John checked on Christopher. He was sprawled across his racecar bed. John put on latex crime scene gloves, went out to the driveway and began removing the back seat from the Mustang. As he suspected, the suitcase was in the trunk, a typical carry-on bag. He dragged it out, set it on the hood of the car, and opened it.

Hawaiian shirts. He pulled them out and set them aside. He did the same with the hemp slacks and the silk floral boxers.

Underneath was a layer of cash—Franklins. Those came from the bank in bundles of a hundred, ten thousand dollars to a bundle. He counted seven bundles across and two back. One hundred forty thousand dollars per layer. He dug to the bottom. Seven layers, nine hundred eighty thousand dollars. John figured the odd twenty grand for expenses—a new wardrobe, a vintage 1964 1/2 Mustang, gas, food, walking around money.

Mom was right. Rusty was driving around with a million dollars in a suitcase and some nameless scheme in his heart.

John carried it inside, pulled out twenty bundles, photographed the serial numbers of the top bills, and put them back. He repacked the suitcase, put it back in the trunk, and replaced the seats. Then he pulled out his notebook, wrote down the mileage on the odometer and from the title, and went inside to do some math.

The difference was almost five thousand miles. He checked Google maps. St. Petersburg, where he had bought the car, was only thirteen hundred miles. Somewhere around three thousand miles unaccounted for.

That gave him something to think about while he was falling asleep.

DAY 9: WEDNESDAY

When John looked out the door the next morning, the Mustang was gone. Christopher's 4x4 was also gone. He took a shower and studied his face in the mirror. The bruises were already fading to green, the scabs on the scratches starting to flake

Rather than go into the office and have to dodge more questions, he called Sam and told her he'd be available via cell and radio. He also read off the list of serial numbers from the hundred-dollar bills and asked her to get Lovejoy to check them out to see if they were related to a robbery or law-enforcement case. He wasn't hopeful, but it was worth a shot.

He headed east into Bandera County. He dialed Mom's number and put it on speaker.

"John, you're calling early."

"Have you seen him? Did he come back?"

"What, honey?"

"Rusty. Is he there?"

"No, he didn't come back."

John let that marinate for a few seconds. What was the old man up to?

"Did he tell you why he came back to Texas?"

"He didn't have to. It was time. You saw the horoscope."

"Mom, I need you to do something for me."

"What?"

"I need you to set aside the horoscope, the optimism, the always giving everyone the benefit of the doubt, and just think about this situation without any of that for a minute. Can you do that?"

There was a long silence. "Why would you ask me to do that?"

"Because I need to know something only you can tell me. But it's not going to work if you contaminate the information with your spin on it." He shook his head and held his hand out toward the phone. "Sorry, Mom, that came out wrong. I just need to know what really happened. Can you tell me that?"

A shorter silence. "Yes."

"He's been gone for twenty-four years, then suddenly he comes back. Something had to have happened, some catalytic event that made him do it right now. Not last month, not last year, not next year. Do you see that?"

"Yes," she said tentatively, as if expecting a trap.

"Did he say what that was? What caused him to come back?"

A very long silence. So long John checked the cell phone to verify the call was still active.

"No, he didn't say. And I didn't ask."

"Alright. I just needed to know. If you hear from him, can you let me know right away?"

"Of course I will."

"Thanks, Mom." He picked up the phone to disconnect, and then stopped. "Mom, you still there?"

"Yes."

"What's my horoscope say?"

He heard the crinkle of a newspaper.

"You might feel a bit pensive as your mind is flooded with several thoughts. Controlling your thoughts becomes a little difficult today."

"Thanks."

Halfway to Bandera he saw a large sign for Bates Excavations. Next to it was a ten-foot wooden ladder, its rails twisted into twin spirals. At the top several rungs split in the middle and the rails curved away from each other. The bottom was a tree stump.

John stopped in the driveway and took a closer look. The ladder was not a ladder. It was a sculpture carved from a tree, two feet of raw wood serving as the base. Then he noticed the sign on the fence—

Cedar Sculptures. John nodded. It was the best use for a cedar tree he could think of. He had a few on his ridge he'd like to donate to the cause.

The monstrosity wasn't something he'd put in his front yard, but whoever did it obviously had talent. He'd seen chainsaw sculptures before at Wimberley Market Days and like places. They tended to be rough-hewn depictions of various animals. Bears seemed to be popular. And eagles. But this was precision-crafted, finished, smooth, and delicate.

He eased past the sculpture, over the cattle guard, and through the open gate. The drive ran through the middle of a field. Every dozen yards or so a strange cedar sculpture stood sentry—a lean knight in armor in a spare art-deco style, a slender weeping willow, a geyser, a narrow replica of the Spindletop gusher, a spray of fireworks, a tornado, a fawn on its back legs stretching to nibble a leaf, and something that looked uncomfortably like some aboriginal phallic totem. All done in long, smooth, sweeping lines and intricate detail work. He was surprised they were left exposed to the elements, but they seemed to be bearing up.

In the east field at the far fence line, in the shade of trees crowded along a creek bed, a dozen cows lounged, their vacant faces turning to follow his progress like sunflowers seeking light.

Fifty yards ahead, set back on the right of the driveway, a large frame house nestled under the canopy of four massive oaks. Opposite the house, a metal warehouse squatted to the left of the drive. Two backhoes, one on a trailer, sat out front. Half-a-dozen septic tanks lined the far side of the building like doodlebugs of the gods.

John pulled up next to the large warehouse door, which was open, and got out of the truck. The sound of a chainsaw drifted from across the driveway. John squinted toward the house, but didn't see anyone. He stepped onto the concrete floor of the warehouse. He looked to his right. The space was cluttered with crates and tools and shelves. To the left, at a desk pushed up against the front wall a man sat, wrestling with paperwork.

John walked to the desk. The man looked to be five or ten years younger than John. His dark blue uniform had the name "Lonnie" stitched above the pocket. "Lonnie Bates?" he asked, doubtfully.

The man set down the pen like he wished he'd never picked it up and hoped he would never have to again. "You looking for a septic system or a cedar sculpture?"

"Neither. I'm looking for Lonnie Bates."

"Junior or senior?"

It wasn't a question John had thought to ask Frank. The man was obviously Lonnie Bates the septic contractor, but he was probably in Bandera junior high when Bolero High was under construction. Not a good candidate for a cover-up from two decades back.

"Senior."

Lonnie Jr. picked the pen back up and pointed it out the door toward the sound of the chainsaw. "Out back of the house." He tore off a strip of numbers from an ancient calculator and looked down at the half-filled form on the desk.

John followed his ears to the chainsaw. When he rounded the corner of the house, the noise doubled. A thick man in faded blue overalls and a black felt beret lumbered around what was left of ten feet of a tree trunk, wielding an odd-looking chainsaw. The blade was shorter than the motor. He revved the throttle in short bursts, lashing out with precise rapier thrusts to gouge shallow, narrow slashes in the wood.

The sculpture resembled a giant dried ocotillo cactus branch, riddled with diamond-shaped windows into the hollow interior. John couldn't imagine how the core had come to be hollowed out with a chainsaw. Perhaps Lonnie Sr. allowed himself a wider range of tools for his art.

John watched for a minute, then approached slowly. Lonnie eventually noticed him. He killed the motor and removed the goggles and noise-cancelling headphones. He smiled at John. Although Bates the son appeared to be younger than John, Bates the father appeared to be older than Rusty. Close to seventy. Perhaps older. But as solid as an oak.

"What can I do you for?"

John studied the sculpture. "Can you do a bear?"

"I got the number of a dozen fellers who can."

John didn't take his eyes off what Lonnie had done with the tree. "Impressive. What is it?"

"I call it Extruded Wood Number Nine."

"What happened to numbers one through eight?"

"This is the first one."

John pulled his gaze away from the sculpture. Lonnie Bates the septic contractor was not what John had expected. He appraised Bates carefully in the morning light.

"I'm working my way down," Bates said.

Without preamble, John flashed his badge. "Were you the septic contractor on the Bolero High School project twenty years ago?"

In an instant, Bates assumed the demeanor of a particularly dumbfounded deer caught in a set of quartz-halogen headlights. The chainsaw slipped from his fingers, nailed his right foot, and fell with a soft thump into the woodchips surrounding the sculpture. He bent to pick it up, glanced at John, then away, his eyes roving the area. He stepped to a workbench constructed of two sawhorses and a sheet of coarse plywood and set the saw there along two others with progressively larger blades.

John followed all this without moving. "Mr. Bates?"

"What?"

"When did you retire and pass the business on to your son?"

"What year is it?" Bates removed his beret to reveal a gleaming head, then resettled the cap. "I guess it was on about ten years ago. About the time Bush invaded Afghanistan."

"Did you notice any irregularities on the Bolero High School project?"

"That was a long time ago. I cut a lot of wood since then."

"Should I ask your son?"

Bates came out of his trance. "Lonnie Jr.? He wouldn't know nothing about it. Was playing junior varsity when I worked that job."

Now he had the man's attention. "Bolero High School collapsed two weeks ago."

"I heard."

"Did you expect it to happen?"

Bates frowned. "What is this about?"

"Did you have any reason to believe the structure was unsound? Anything you may have noticed?"

"No!" Bates backed up and hit the workbench, knocking the plywood and everything that was on it to the ground. He surveyed the mess and turned back to John. "I was just septic. I came in after the foundation was poured, put my tanks in, filled in the hole, left the fittings for the plumbers to tie into, and left."

Bates leaned down, grabbed the plywood and put it back on the sawhorses. He knelt down to pick up the chainsaws and other tools. "You're talking to the wrong guy. It's a foundation problem."

"What kind of foundation problem? How do you know that?"

Bates slammed the small chainsaw down on the plywood. "It collapsed, didn't it? What else could it be? Al Qaeda?"

John studied Bates and then his latest work. Intricate and impersonal. Clean lines. Pure design. No emotion. He suddenly recognized the sculpture at the gate. The double helix of DNA, the blueprint of life. A decade ago the man retreated into a private world of order and symmetry.

But if Frank Berger was telling the truth, Bates Sr. had emerged from his self-imposed exile from reality to orchestrate the systematic eradication of evidence related to the collapse of a high school.

"Do you know Frank Berger?"

Bates stared at John, his eyes clouded over with sheer panic. He shuddered and turned away, picking up the last chainsaw, the one with a large blade. "Frank who?"

"Berger. He's a paint contractor. But you knew that, didn't you? You worked on projects with him back before you retired." John was guessing, but he didn't see a downside to being wrong. Bates was on the defensive and any denial, even a valid one, would sound false, even to Bates.

Bates pulled at the starter on the chainsaw. It sputtered. "I got to get back to work." He pulled the rope again and the chainsaw roared to life. He stepped toward the sculpture.

"Mr. Bates," John yelled over the roar of the chainsaw.

Bates stumbled toward the sculpture, waving the growling blade, and hacked at the precision lines, leaving a gaping gash across three branches of the matrix of diagonals that provided structure.

"Bates!" John yelled again, louder. He wanted to grab his shoulder, pull the man away from his own handiwork, but it was madness to approach a crazed man with a chainsaw.

Bates swung the chainsaw one-handed, knocking out random chunks, leaving raw scars across the intricate detail of the surface. He hit the wood with such force that the whole thing began to totter under his blows.

John stood by, helpless to intervene. His peripheral vision caught a motion and Lonnie Jr. sprinted past John and grabbed his father from behind by the shoulders, yelling. The old man shook him loose, pushed him to the ground, and took a double-handed swing at the tower, the saw at full throttle. It cut through half of the sculpture at waist height and the superstructure canted in John's direction. John leapt aside as it crashed down.

The hornet-nest growl dropped away to the bubbly, full-throated chuckle of a chainsaw at idle, swinging unheeded at the side of Bates Sr. The saw slipped from his fingers and died in the dirt. Bates Sr. slumped down beside it, staring at the ragged stump, all that was left of *Extruded Wood Number Nine*.

In the silence that followed, John heard the heavy breathing of Bates Sr., the scrambling of Bates Jr. as he struggled to his feet, and the tattoo of his own heart marking the milliseconds until sanity returned.

"What is this?" Bates Jr. yelled, turning from his father to John. "What did you do?"

John flashed his badge. "I have a few more questions."

"I don't think so." Bates Jr. knelt down beside his father and helped him to his feet. "Come on, Pops. Let's get a little something to even things out."

"What do you know about the Bolero High School project?" John asked.

"What are you talking about?"

"Bolero High School collapsed two weeks ago. Your father worked on that project."

"Are you crazy? He was a septic contractor."

"I think he saw something, knows something about it. I need to find out what it was."

"You're out of your jurisdiction."

"I can get a warrant."

"Then do it. Until then, get off our land."

John watched the son help his father to the house. He took one last shot.

"Do you know Frank Berger?"

Bates Jr. stopped and looked squarely at John. "What's this about?"

"Destroying evidence, burglary, arson."

Bates Jr. stared at John a long moment before answering. "The Bergers are white trash and we got nothing to do with them. Nothing. Never. Now show me a warrant or get out." He ushered his father into the house.

John watched them disappear, heard the door slam behind them, followed by the snip of a deadbolt. He returned to his truck. He was on the right track. He'd obviously hit a nerve with Bates Sr., who would require delicate handling. The son could prove to be a problem. He'd have to get that warrant. A call to Mooney would take care of that. And a chat with the Bandera sheriff would be a good idea. John called them both on his way back to Bolero.

John nodded to the receptionist on the way in before he remembered he wasn't going into the office and why. He gathered looks along his path like a kid snagging candy on Halloween, but nobody said anything other than, "Morning, chief."

He sat down to check his e-mail and messages and noticed an envelope on his desk from the Bexar County Medical Examiner. He opened it and scanned. There was a lot of technical language, but the gist of it was that Edward Crookshank died of natural causes long before Frank showed up to burn his records. It took some pressure off his suspects, from Billy all the way up to Cook. But John felt relief that nobody had been murdered on his watch.

John called Boyd about Bates, got caught up on his e-mail, and had a quick status meeting with Lovejoy to bring him current.

"Pull together an arrest warrant for Bates."

"Junior or senior?"

"Senior. No, let's do one for each. Frank didn't specify which Bates, so it could be either one."

Lovejoy made a note and then reported on the currency serial numbers from the suitcase. No hits, as John suspected. Lovejoy didn't ask questions about the bills. He also didn't ask about the bruises and scratches, although it was clear he was dying to find out about both.

By then it was lunchtime. John took a break. In the bathroom he caught sight of the fading bruises on his face. He had a flashback of Rusty's pale face retreating down the ridge in the glow from Christopher's headlights.

He sensed a connection between the bruises and Rusty's retreat, but couldn't wrap his brain around why. He still had no clue as to how he had come by the cuts and bruises to his body on Monday night. He had a vague recollection of a nightmare, of a pit of vipers, of clawing his way up a cliff rife with cactus, only to be attacked by knife-wielding assassins at the summit.

He was not Rusty. He was not running away. But something happened Monday night. His body bore the proof of it. And his mind insisted on connecting it to Tuesday night on the prison ridge.

That made him think of Liz, of her insistence of unfinished business with Rusty. Of his conviction that Rusty was irrelevant, gone again, this time for good. It was now clear that John had no idea what Rusty would do next, if he would ever truly be gone. There might be something to what Liz had said.

He returned to his office, grabbed his hat, and directed his truck to the middle school. The parking lot was packed, double parked, as the facility tried to absorb as much as it could of the displaced high schoolers. He parked a block away and walked.

Inside, he nodded to the teacher on duty in the foyer during lunch and walked directly to the teacher's lounge. It consisted of three rooms, one with couches, chairs, coffee table, and snacks, another with tables and chairs for meetings or lunch, and a third a workroom with supplies, copier, and other tools of the trade.

John walked to the middle room and stopped inside the door. Liz sat at a table with her back to the door, eating a tuna sandwich. The other teachers looked up and fell silent. Liz turned around, half a sandwich in her hand.

"I told you he wouldn't stay."

"John? What are you doing here?"

"He came back. Then he left."

She didn't ask who. She just looked at him, and him at her. Then she set down her sandwich, got up, and walked past him, through the lounge and out the door. He followed.

She didn't stop until she was in the parking lot. The day had warmed up into triple digits again. The blacktop was like a sauna. Out next to the cars she turned on him.

"You can't just come in here like you own the place."

John looked around. "I pay taxes. I do own the place."

"We can't talk about this now."

"You don't return my calls. How else can I get you to talk to me?" He stepped toward her. "Look. The thing is, you don't get it. You don't know what he does. Last night he—"

"No, you don't get it. It doesn't matter what he does. It only matters what you do."

"I'm the sane one here, but I get all the heat and he gets off no matter how crazy he acts."

"He doesn't matter. I'm not dating him. "

"That's what I've been saying." John realized he was shouting. He stepped away, took a deep breath, walked in a small circle and stopped in front of Liz. "He doesn't matter. He's gone. We go back to how it was."

"Back to—" She took a close look at him. "What happened to your face?"

"Cleared the north end of the property last weekend. Chainsaw got hung in a mesquite."

"It doesn't have something to do with whatever you did last night?"

John waved her question aside. "Can you at least tell me why you're avoiding me?"

"I told you. You're just not listening."

John took a deep breath. Sweat trickled down his face, tickled his back. "Okay. I'm listening now. Tell me again."

Her silent gaze expressed her doubt, but she finally responded. "You've got something you need to work out with your dad—"

"There you go with the dad thing again. You just said he doesn't matter and now . . ." The glare from Liz would stun a goat at fifty yards, the look of a middle school teacher who kept her classes in line.

"Is this you listening?"

"Okay. I'm shutting up. Go ahead."

She waited a bit before continuing. "I don't know what things were like when Jennifer left—"

"Jennifer?" John stopped himself, held up his hands and gestured for her to continue.

"That night at the Lone Star Grill with your dad. I realized I had it wrong."

John bit back the question he wanted to blurt out. First Rusty, then Jennifer, then Rusty again. He wasn't following any of it. But he waited.

"The way she left you, first the affair, then clearing out and taking Christopher without even trying to work things out, well that would make anybody more cautious the next time around, so I understood why you might be a little distant, hold back, try to control things, fix anything you thought was broken. I just figured it was a reaction to what she did to you. I thought that as things went on and you learned to trust me then that stuff would slowly go away."

Her eyes glistened from rising tears. She blinked them back.

"But it didn't. And then in the Lone Star I realized why. You have probably been doing this ever since he left, and you'll keep on doing it until you deal with it. And I can't stay without some kind of hope that you'll let me all the way in."

John felt his jaw muscles bulging. He tried to relax his mouth while keeping it shut. His mind raced, trying to assimilate every-thing, and the heat didn't make it any easier to concentrate. He thought things were fine, but now it sounded like she'd been miser-able for years and never said anything.

"You couldn't make Jennifer want the same things you did, to be satisfied with life the way you thought it should be. Now you want to control Christopher, make him give up this Africa thing and go back to school. And you're trying to run your dad out of town like this is Dodge City and he's a horse rustler." Liz looked away. "And you're not willing to even consider that it's not everyone else, that maybe it's you."

John's jaw ached from clenching. This was all twisted around, like she refused to see what was really going on. But he kept his mouth shut.

Liz stopped. Maybe she had run out of steam. John waited, not sure if she was done. She stood, looking at him like she was trying to measure something. Maybe to see if he was really listening, or if he was getting mad, or . . . she opened her mouth, but then closed it again. He started to respond, but she blurted out one more thing before he could speak.

"Maybe Jennifer didn't leave you. Maybe you drove her away."

Her voice broke on the last word and she swept a single errant tear away from her cheek with the heel of her hand, but she didn't back down.

John's mouth hung open, the retort unspoken. He drove Jennifer away? Ridiculous. Jennifer did what she wanted, got what she wanted, damn the torpedoes and watch your back. She didn't need anyone to drive her to it.

But that single tear froze his answer in his throat. She said Jennifer, but she meant herself.

His pulse thundered, adrenaline swirling in his brain like a fog. To hear her tell it, he was responsible for half of everything that was wrong in Bolero County, and was suspect for the other half. Like if only he would get a clue, quit being a jerk, life would become some kind of Disneyland utopia, that Bolero would become the new happiest place on earth. He couldn't let this revisionist account of things go unchallenged.

But the tear struck him mute. If he had lost her, had driven her away, could he change that by arguing with her? By telling her how wrong she was, how absurd her account of things was?

In this silence, the school bell rang. Lunch was over.

Liz gave him a last look, waiting for his response, but everything she said made it impossible for him to respond.

She turned and walked back to the school and the rest of her tuna sandwich. He watched her go.

John drove back to the office in a haze, his mind struggling to gather all the threads and weave some kind of coherent narrative with a set of action items he could attack and resolve. They had a good thing. He just had to find a way to make her realize it.

He stopped by the Lone Star Grill for a sandwich to go and picked up a paper. The story on the arson stuck to the few known facts, but was unable to gloss over the fact that two captive suspects had vaporized. It did have the official "person of interest in custody" statement, with an observation that the only recent incarcerations were Billy Swallow and a DWI.

He skimmed over the rest of the paper. The "Bolero Busybody" column brought his skimming to a full stop.

> Has anyone else seen that sporty red Mustang about town and the dashing gentleman behind the wheel? Could it be that Rusty Lawson is really back after a quarter of a century?
>
> How many of us are left who can remember Mr. Lawson's English class? Here's looking forward to more juicy stories now that he has returned.

The Bolero Busybody, an apt name for the town gossip who got an early start in junior high, passing notes in class, planted in the center of a gaggle of girls at lunch, buzzing like a hive of hornets.

He walked through the building, distractedly acknowledging the greetings as he passed through, and checked his messages. Wainwright had called. A search of the Berger house turned up a computer they had kept for their own use and a shoebox with the missing backup tapes, including 1989.

John was out the door almost before he had hung up the phone. Lovejoy stopped him on his way out.

"I got the warrant for Bates. Jr. and Sr."

John looked over the paperwork. "Okay. Give the sheriff a call to let him know you're coming and then pick them up. " He handed the paperwork back. "I'll be back from Uvalde in a couple of hours." He continued out, but stopped halfway to the door. "And Mirandize them. If they do say something, we need to be able to use it."

He was halfway to Uvalde before he remembered the prescriptions. He didn't even think about turning around. He'd gone this long without the medications. A few more days wouldn't kill him.

In Uvalde he walked through the office courtyard jungle and nodded at the receptionist on his way to Wainwright's glass-enclosed office. Rod stood and waved him in. They shook hands and sat down. John skipped the pleasantries.

"You have something for me?"

Rod pushed a thick file folder across the desk to John. "A copy of everything on the Bolero High School project."

John opened the file and flipped through the pages, past materials estimates and invoices and scaled-down blueprints, looking for something signed by Crookshank.

"Is there something in particular you're looking for?"

John continued to turn pages. "A report from the county inspector."

"Allow me." Rod took the file back and fanned through the pages like someone looking for a dollar bill stuck in the middle. He stopped, set the bottom part down, flipped back a few pages, and set down the other half. He held a page with a Bolero County letterhead on it in his left hand as he gathered additional pages, then tapped them against the desk into a neat pile and handed it to John.

John flipped to the last page and saw Crookshank's signature. He turned to the front and began skimming for whatever the old man had ranted about in the letter to the editor. Three pages in, he found it. He read it over and then handed it to Rod.

"Can you interpret this for me?"

Rod skimmed through it. "The soil analysis revealed the presence of a mixture of soil types that would result in differential settlement." He looked up.

John looked back, waiting.

"That means special measures would be required to avoid some parts of the building settling more than others."

"What would that cost?"

Rod looked through the plans. "On a project of this size, it could be seventy, a hundred thousand. Give or take."

"And what if they didn't take the extra measures?"

"But they would."

"But if they didn't?"

Rod frowned and flipped through the pages in the folder. "I vaguely remember this project. It was one of the first ones we did after I moved back. Ah, here we go."

He pulled out another report with a similar letterhead and skimmed through it before handing it to John. "Yes, I remember now. Cook Brothers agreed to do the extra work and the inspector filed an amended report."

John checked the signature. Louis Hebert. "It's a different inspector."

"Right. The first inspector retired not long after filing that report."

John looked through the report. "This isn't an amended report. It doesn't even mention the foundation issues or the first report."

Rod took the report and skimmed it again. "That's strange. It should mention the problem and detail the steps taken to address it."

"So, based on Hebert's report, Cook Brothers could have completed the project without fixing any of the problems."

"They wouldn't do that." He looked up at John, his expression slowly changing.

John knew what he was thinking. If Cook Brothers had made the required changes, the school wouldn't have collapsed two weeks ago. He was holding the smoking gun.

John pulled the report from Rod's limp fingers, put everything back in the folder, and stood, the file in his left hand, his right hand extended. He shook Rod's hand.

"Thank you for your help, Mr. Wainwright. This report is significant to several investigations. That includes the school collapse, the Cook Brothers arson, and the burglary here. You should not mention it to anyone until they are all concluded."

"Of course."

"No one. That includes your wife. No one."

Rod nodded. "Yes, sir."

John left.

The two contradicting reports were the link between the events of the past seven days and Charles Cook himself. John doubted that something of this level could go on without Cook's direct knowledge. The inspection team from San Antonio could use it, but it was not a solid link to the arson, the burglary, the missing report at the court-house, or Crookshank's burned files.

Bates Sr. was the missing link. By now he was probably sitting in a cell in the Bolero County jail and John finally had the leverage to open him up like a Christmas present. He called Lovejoy and had him move the old man to the interview room and get him something to drink. He wanted him comfortable.

John started the recorder, stated the date, time, and people present, and then immediately asked Lonnie Bates Sr. about chainsaw sculpture. The old man was obviously surprised and confused. He pulled his black beret from his broad head, rubbed his hand across the gleaming scalp, and replaced the hat, but he answered the questions, becoming less guarded and more enthusiastic the longer they talked. John asked lots of questions and learned more than he ever wanted to know about the topic long before he felt that Lonnie was ready.

John changed the pace by leaning forward and lowering his voice to a confidential tone. "Mr. Bates, I think you've kept something from your son, something you're not proud of, something that might upset him."

Lonnie sat, suddenly silent, looking at the long, thin chicken-wire glass in the door.

"But I understand that. There are some things I haven't told my son. Things I hope he never hears about, from me or anyone else."

Lonnie looked at John, held his gaze as if testing the veracity of the statement. He shifted in his chair and looked back to the door.

"But we're going to have to talk about it, Mr. Bates. I'll try to keep it as private as possible, but it's a conversation we're going to have. Today."

Lonnie didn't volunteer anything.

John leaned back in his chair. "Now, let me tell you what I think. I think someone took advantage of your loyalty to your son, put you in a position with no way out but to do the thing he asked, even though you didn't like it. Even though it was illegal."

Lonnie stiffened, but didn't look away from the window.

"Is that right, Mr. Bates?" No answer. "Now I'm going to tell you what I know, so you can see where that puts you, which is right in the middle of things. But before I do, you need to know I see you as a victim of an unscrupulous man who has abused your love for your son."

John sensed more than saw the quickening of breath, the slight sheen of moisture in Lonnie's eyes.

"And it's that man I want to pay for this. If you can help me tie him to the arson at Cook's warehouse, to the burglary at Wainwright's office, I'll do everything I can for you."

John paused to let Lonnie talk, but he said nothing.

"Are we on the same page, Mr. Bates?"

Lonnie tore his gaze from the window. He looked at John. "I'm listening."

John set Crookshank's inspection report on the table. The one that Cook had gone to such lengths to destroy, using Lonnie and Leonard and Frank and Billy to make sure it was never seen by the inspection team or anyone else. He pushed it toward Lonnie.

Lonnie picked it up and flipped through it, frowning. He set it down and looked at John.

"What is that?"

John was thrown off balance. Why would Lonnie decide to bluff now? John had all the cards. "This is the report you paid Frank Berger to destroy."

Lonnie looked at it with more interest. "How'd you get it?"

"Why did you pick Frank for the job?" Frank the screwup, hired by Lonnie the screwup. John wondered that Cook would entrust the job to such rank amateurs, but he supposed options for that kind of work were limited in Bolero County. Actually, he'd gone outside of Bolero to recruit Lonnie.

Lonnie picked up the report and looked at it more carefully, turning the pages slowly. He stopped on page three and read for a full minute.

"That snake," he muttered. He shook his head and put the report on the table. "That slimy, lying snake." He looked up, fire in his eyes. John saw the spine of a much younger man shine through.

"He told me that the initial inspection showed that the septic installation had been botched and caused a leak that leeched away the soil around the footings over time." He looked at the window and did the hand-over-the-bald-head thing again. "That weasel." He turned back to John. "He said if I made the files disappear at the warehouse and the architect's office, he could make sure the evidence didn't point to Bates Excavations. Lonnie Jr. would be ruint. Flat ruint, and then what would they do, Bonnie and little Three?"

"Three?"

"Lonnie the Third. But this thing," he slapped his fist on the report. "This thing says it's Cook Brothers. They papered this over somehow and were too arrogant to bother to cover their tracks."

"What about the files at Crookshank's place?"

"A last-minute thing. He called after the paper came out Wednesday morning."

"Let's go back to the school collapse. How soon after the collapse did Cook contact you?" John figured it must have been the next day. The gymnatorium collapsed on a Friday and the arson happened four days later. Working backward, Frank talked to Billy on Monday. Lonnie talked to Frank on Sunday. So Cook must have talked to Lonnie on Saturday.

The confusion on Lonnie's face stopped John cold.

"Cook?"

"Charles Cook."

"He ain't never called me."

John looked from Lonnie to the report and back. "Charles Cook didn't hire you to destroy this report?"

Lonnie shook his head.

"Then who did?"

"Judge Gibson."

John stuck with the interview, hiding the shock. They went over it multiple times, digging into details that would either break Lonnie's story or provide more ammunition for John. Lonnie's story stood up under scrutiny. Luther Gibson called Lonnie Bates Sr. on Friday night around midnight. Lonnie lived alone since his wife died ten years ago. Gibson went out to Lonnie's house around one a.m. and they worked it out at the kitchen table over a bottle of vodka.

Lonnie spent the next day figuring the logistics, visited Frank at his place south of Vanderpool on Sunday, and worked out the plan of using the Tabernacle picket line as cover. Further questioning revealed this idea belonged to Gibson, as John figured. Lonnie wasn't stupid, but neither was he devious. The burglary was straightforward, especially with some information from Gibson about how to deal with the security system at Wainwright. Evidently the judge was adept at more things than politics and wife stealing.

They scheduled the arson for Tuesday morning, not only getting rid of the report but also leaving John with a career-damaging enigma, and the burglary for Wednesday night. Then Gibson called on Wednesday afternoon. They tacked the Crookshank job on the tail end of the Wainwright burglary, leaving the cabin a scant hour before John arrived Thursday morning.

There was little to connect Gibson to the scheme, but John held out hope for one thing, the midnight phone call. And who else had Gibson called? He would subpoena the phone company records. They might lead to Cook.

He took a break, had dinner brought in for both Lonnies, and called Boyd. It was after six and the DA was on his way home. John convinced him to turn around with a cryptic comment about a situation that could make or break both their careers.

Rather than have the conversation in the office, John met Boyd at the door. They took John's truck and drove on a long loop up north past the airport and the prison ridge, east toward Kerrville and back through Medina. It was a two hour drive. It took that long to convince Boyd of the evidence, absorb the implications, and plan a strategy.

It came down to evidence. There were enough holes in the case for the Spanish Armada to float through. They needed a recording of Gibson with unambiguous references to his involvement, and the key was the report. At this point only four people knew it had survived: John, Boyd, Lonnie Sr., and Wainwright. John thought it was containable.

Tapping Gibson's phone required a signature from the district judge in Uvalde backed up by enough paperwork to wrap all the Christmas presents in Texas. Fortunately, he needed the consent of only one party to record a phone conversation. Based on the interview, John thought Lonnie could pull it off as long as he kept his family in mind. John called Twink, a techie geek named for his fondness for the indestructible snacks, who ran sound at UtopiaFest and had a fascination with surveillance equipment.

Close to nine p.m., John dropped Boyd off to fill in the paperwork gaps and spent the next hour with Lonnie Sr., laying out a game plan. Lonnie latched onto the plan like a half-drowned possum on a trash-can lid in a flash flood.

John got home close to midnight.

DAY 10: THURSDAY

John was awakened by his cell phone from a sleep that would more accurately be described as a minor coma. He clawed his way to consciousness and groped for the phone. It was Lindsey.

"Put the coffee on. I'm coming by with a special edition of the *Bulletin* you need to see before anyone else."

Lindsey hung up without waiting for comment. John checked the clock. Four a.m. He rolled out of bed, dragged shirt and pants across his frame, and zombie-walked to the kitchen, flipping on lights. Normally Christopher would be up, preparing for his day on the construction crew, but he was off the job and in full Africa preparation mode, which allowed for a more humane schedule.

However, John took no pains to mute his actions. He flipped on the outside light, clattered in the kitchen to get coffee going, and then started preparations for an omelet, still in a minor-league trance.

Two eggs whisked with fresh ground pepper, a packet of parmesan, and a packet of crushed red pepper from Bolero Pizza. He swirled them into the pan and sprinkled shredded pepper jack across the surface, along with some crumbled bacon. After one minute, he broke the edges free with a fork, slid the thing around in the pan to keep it from scorching, and added chopped tomato and green onions. After a few more minutes he folded it over and slid it onto a plate.

He thought about this special edition. The weekly *Bulletin* had just come out yesterday. Seemed like Lindsey would have included whatever this was in that edition. He couldn't imagine what it was. No way he got wind of the Bates-Gibson connection. Surely not.

Christopher stumbled into the room in boxers, rubbing his hair and scratching in a general sort of way. John shoved the plate in his direction and started on another omelet. Christopher grunted, poured himself a cup of coffee and consumed the omelet with habanera sauce but without a word.

John finished a second omelet and was working on the third when Lindsey knocked at the door. Christopher let him in, directed him to the coffee, and disappeared into his bedroom.

Lindsey looked like he hadn't slept in a week and a half. He was an old guy and didn't carry it well. In fact, he looked like death on a popsicle stick. He dropped a paper on the table, got some coffee, and sat down. John set the fresh omelet in front of him, took the other for himself, and sat down across the table from Lindsey. He picked up the *Bolero Bulletin*, a one-sheet, four-page special edition.

The front page showed a surprised Battles holding three bundles of Franklins, ten thousand dollars per bundle, the photo surrounded by copy. John flipped to the inside. Half of it was photos of Battles. Eating dinner in a restaurant with some guy John didn't know. The two in conversation. The two passing a large envelope. Battles walking out with the envelope. Battles accosted outside. Battles opening the envelope. Battles with an expression of consternation and horror.

John started to read the story, which was quite long, but he didn't have the energy. He dropped the paper on the table and started on his omelet. "Give me the highlights."

"I got an anonymous call last night around six asking for the editor of the *Bulletin*. He told me if I wanted a scoop to go to the Turf and Surf in Uvalde and to bring my camera and recorder. I trusted the voice, so I did as instructed. I figured if nothing else, I'd have a nice tenderloin filet with grilled shrimp."

Lindsey shrugged. John nodded and reached for the habanera sauce.

"When I came in, I scanned the room for the voice, but saw Battles and knew this was the story. I got a table nearby, behind Battles, and snapped a few shots surreptitiously. I wasn't close enough to follow the conversation, but I did catch a few words here and there. Such as 'prison' and 'contract.'"

His expression was not lost on John, who felt the omelet turn to ashes in his mouth. He set his fork down.

"When the envelope changed hands, I knew I had been right to trust the voice. The other man excused himself to visit the bathroom and never returned. After twenty minutes Battles paid the bill and left. I followed him out and asked him what was in the envelope."

John knew what was in the envelope from the photos, but he was curious as to the answer Battles gave and why the master of the media so willingly dumped the contents out on camera.

"He said it was a proposal for a prison facility north of Bolero, a five-hundred bed, fifty-acre, high-tech, low-security facility that would provide full-time employment for over one hundred people. A proposal that he would unveil as part of his plan for his first term as sheriff, if elected."

Lindsey paused. John began to suspect the identity of the voice on the phone.

"I asked to see the proposal. He gladly opened the envelope and showed me." Lindsey gestured to the photo of Battles with the cash and took the last bite of omelet, washing it down with coffee before getting up for a refill. Lindsey sat back down. "He's not so glad, now."

John picked up the paper and skimmed through it. It said essentially the same thing, plus background on Battles's career and the coverage of the first contested sheriff's race in Bolero for over a decade. He looked the question at Lindsey.

"Your father's name will come up, obviously. He wasn't present at the meet, but we know of at least four people he told about the prison project. By now everyone in Bolero knows about it. When this hits the stands today, everyone will connect him with this bribe."

"You trusted the voice because . . ."

Lindsey nodded.

"Did Battles mention him?"

"Oddly, no. Hasn't talked to him, evidently. This character," he pointed to the photo, "Alonzo McKenzie, according to Battles, contacted him out of the blue, laid out his plan on the phone, and asked for a dinner meeting. Battles seemed to think it would seal the deal for the election."

John looked over the photo spread. "I'd have to agree."

He smiled at Lindsey, who let a small smile slip out.

"So, who gets this one, you or Fuentes?"

John thought on it for a second. "There's no evidence of a crime, really. Right now he's a private citizen and it's not illegal to hire him as a lobbyist or consultant to help them with the locals."

"There's still the matter of your father's part in this."

John looked at Lindsey for a moment, took a sip of coffee, and stood to clear away the plates.

"Let's talk about that." He walked to the sink and ran water on the dishes. "First, I assume as a respectable journalist, you don't reveal your sources."

Lindsey didn't bother to respond.

"So the tip will not become a matter of public record. Then we have the poker game. All hearsay. Somebody could try to look into it, but who exactly would that be and where would they look?"

"Gibson, perhaps?"

John shook his head, slowly. "I think Gibson has plenty on his plate right now. He'll cut Battles out like a malignant tumor." He refilled his coffee and sat down. "Plus there's the fact that nobody knows where Rusty is. He surfaced for the poker game and then disappeared."

Lindsey considered this information, killed his coffee, and stood. "Well, that's your lookout. I've got a paper to get out." He nodded to John and left.

All John could do was hope that Rusty stayed gone.

John pulled Lovejoy in on the operation. Around noon they drove out toward Bandera with Boyd and Twink and parked behind the Bates Excavations warehouse. They set up a command post in a spare bedroom.

Lonnie made the phone call at three p.m. He sat at a writing desk with a pen and a piece of paper with the major points. Everyone listened in on headphones.

    Gibson: Judge Gibson.
    Bates: Judge, you got a problem.
    Gibson: Bates? Why are you calling this number?
    Bates: Like I said, you got a problem.

Bates checked off the first item on the list.

Gibson: Where are you calling from?

Bates: Home.

Gibson: I'll call you back.

The line went dead. A minute passed, then five, then ten. Nobody talked. Lonnie slammed the pen down, got up and walked around the room, pulling off his beret, sliding his hand across his head, and pulling it back on. He walked out of the room. John wondered if they had spooked Gibson.

Lonnie walked back in with a bottle of vodka. John intercepted him and confiscated the bottle after a short struggle. Then the phone rang. Lonnie jumped back to the desk.

There was road noise on the line. Gibson was in his car, away from any ears in the courthouse.

Bates: Is that you, Judge?

Gibson: I thought you were in custody.

Bates: They let me out. Frank told them he was hired by Bates Excavations and they got Lonnie Jr. 'cause he's running the shop and they
didn't know no better. They asked me some questions but I played
dumb and they let me go.

Bates picked up the pen and checked another item.

Gibson: Frank? Who's Frank?

Bates: He did the work. You didn't think I did it myself, did you? A
seventy-seven-year-old man sneaking around like one of them ninjas?

Gibson: How much did you tell him?

Bates: Nothing. As much as he needed to know. What to do, when, and
where. No names.

Gibson: So what's the problem? Lonnie knows even less than this Frank
character.

Bates: They got a copy of the report.

Another check mark.

Gibson: Are you sure?

Bates: I saw it. And you lied. It was a known foundation issue that Cook
papered over somehow. It had nothing to do with me.

John looked at Lonnie, then over to Boyd. That wasn't on the list. There was a short silence. John could hear the gears in Gibson's Machiavellian brain locking in on a solution.

Gibson: That was not my understanding. I'm as surprised to hear that as
you are.

Bates: It don't matter what your understanding is. They got the report
and it points straight to Cook. So I'm out of it. I was just warning you.

Gibson: Warning me? My name's not on the report.
Bates: You set this whole thing up.
Gibson: And the only people who know that are on this phone call. You
 keep your mouth shut and you got nothing to worry about.
Bates: I don't take kindly to threats, Gibson.

John watched Lonnie closely. He was off the script, but there was
more passion in his voice. He decided it was a good thing as long as
he didn't get carried away.

Gibson: It's not a threat; it's just the reality of the situation. They'll pur-
 sue Lonnie, they'll run out of steam because he doesn't know anything, and it will go away.
Bates: They got that report. It ain't going away by itself and they ain't
 going to let it go. After a while they may figure they got the wrong
 Bates.
Gibson: That's simple enough. You take care of that copy like you did
 the others.
Bates: That ain't simple, Judge, and you know it. And in case you ain't
 heard, they got Berger locked up down in Uvalde. That's how they got
 the connection to Bates Evacuations.
Gibson: Berger?
Bates: Frank Berger. So what are you going to do about this report?
Gibson: That's my concern.

Boyd elbowed John and rubbed his thumb against his fingers.
John grabbed his notebook and pen from his pocket and scribbled
on it.

Bates: It's mine, too. They ain't going to leave me alone until they connect the dots.

John held the notebook up to Bates. It said, "$$ court costs."
Bates nodded.

Bates: And I'm needing some more cash to get Lonnie out. And a lawyer.

There was a silence and a sigh. John wrote on the pad and held
it up. $20,000.

Gibson: You don't take to threats, and I don't take to blackmail.
Bates: Ain't no blackmail. It's expenses. We're both better off if Lonnie
 gets out of there quick. I figure it will take twenty grand. Not much for
 a big time judge. Not like for a contractor with short margins."

There was another silence, longer than the others.

Gibson: Okay. You stay at home and don't talk to anyone.
Bates: I ain't in the mood for talking. Just want my boy back and forget
 about all this.
Gibson: Not a problem. I'll come by around midnight.

The line went dead. Lonnie hung up the phone and slumped against his chair, exhausted. They all looked at each other. Lonnie was the first to speak.

"Is this going to work? You going to let my boy out?"

John nodded. "As soon as we have Gibson. Your boy's safe. He's got nothing to do with it."

John and Boyd went back to town. They left Twink behind to wire up the kitchen where Bates and Gibson would meet. Lovejoy stayed to monitor the situation. When they left, Lonnie was out back with a chainsaw, cutting into a fresh piece of cedar.

Around nine p.m. John's nerves got the better of him. He decided on a quick boilermaker at the Horseshoe. He nodded to Ted, the night dispatcher, on the way out.

He found Rusty parked out front of the Sheriff's office, sitting on the hood of the Mustang. Despite the heat, he wore black slacks, a black shirt, and a black jacket.

"How about that drink? I'm buying." Rusty asked.

"I'm driving."

John walked to his truck. Rusty followed. They headed south to the county line. John didn't trust himself to talk, and Rusty didn't say anything. He pulled out a Camel and thumped it on the dash. John opened his mouth, but before he could speak, Rusty slipped it behind his ear.

Rusty appeared to be restless. He looked around the cab, glanced into the back, punched the button on the glove box. "You keep a gun in here?" He pulled out a crumpled evidence bag.

John regarded it with suspicion. He didn't remember putting it in there. In fact, he didn't remember anything connected with the muffin for a long time. He tried to think back.

Rusty pulled the muffin from the bag. "Is this your stash? Hiding some carbs from the little lady?"

John didn't answer. When was the last time the muffin talked? It was the last time Rusty was in the car, wasn't it? When it told him to follow the money? No, it was after, on the drive back from the catastrophic dinner with Liz, when it told him the name was not the same, the clue that led him to Rusty's alternate identity.

He looked at the muffin in Rusty's hand. Would it speak again now that Rusty was back? He remembered his theory, that Rusty made him crazy, made him hear muffins. He waited, but nothing came.

Then he remembered. Back on . . . Monday night it was, he threw the muffin off the ridge. The night of the . . . whatever. How did it get back in the truck? He didn't want to think about it.

Rusty put the muffin back in the bag and set it on the seat.

John didn't bother to stop by the house and switch to the Crown Vic. He just parked on the dark side of the Inn. It didn't make a lot of difference with the moon one day from full.

They took seats at the far end of the bar, away from the regulars. John nodded to Buzz and gestured to the two of them. On the TV above the bar, Pastor Jackson's face appeared in a box on the right of the screen, some Fox News Network show host in the box on the left. Buzz set a Johnny Walker and a Lone Star in front of each of them.

"Didn't know you was coming," Buzz said. "Won't have the Shiner until Tuesday."

John gave him a dismissive wave and he retreated back to the regulars.

Rusty picked up the scotch and held it toward John. John hesitated, then picked up his shot glass and clinked it against Rusty's.

"May you be in heaven a half hour before the Devil knows you're dead," Rusty said, and killed the shot.

John sipped, as usual, then changed his mind and killed his as well. They both took a pull from the beers. John winced and set it down.

"Did you see the papers?" Rusty asked.

John nodded, watching Rusty in the mirror behind the bar.

"I don't think you need to worry about Battles anymore."

John turned toward Rusty. "No. Instead I need to worry about an investigation leading back to my father."

Rusty shook his head. "I never said word one to Battles about anything, period. There's no connection."

"No connection? You talked up this prison idea two days ago right here in this bar. Everybody in Bolero knows about it by now, and knows it was your idea."

Rusty shrugged. "It's called salting the mine."

"What about the money?"

Rusty looked at him curiously. "What money?"

John leaned close and whispered fiercely. "The money in the envelope. The money in the suitcase."

Rusty raised an eyebrow.

"That's right, I know about the suitcase."

"Yes, and you also know it can't be traced, don't you?"

John nailed him with a frown and then picked up his shot glass and waved it toward Buzz. He was there in an instant. He refilled both glasses, left the bottle, and returned to his station. John nodded. Good man, Buzz.

Rusty slammed his shot. John sipped his and stared into the mirror. John broke the silence.

"You coming back, it's not going to work."

"Seems like it's working fine to me."

"Oh yeah, it was working fine Tuesday night when you climbed down into a canyon ten miles from town and walked back."

"I'm not afraid of a little walking, but as it turned out I didn't have to walk very far."

"And what was it that scared you over that ridge? One simple question you couldn't answer. And that's why it's not going to work. You won't take your meds, you'll cross the line, if you haven't already with that stunt with Battles." John turned to Rusty. "Do the decent thing. Leave before you take me and Mom down with you."

Rusty held his gaze. "I don't see it working out that way."

"Dammit," John yelled. "Why can't you just go? Why can't you—"

He choked off the sentence and looked down the bar into the faces of the regulars. He stared them down until they turned away, back to their conversation. He turned back to Rusty.

"What have you been doing for the past twenty-four years?"

"A lot of thinking."

"We were doing fine without you. Why come back now?"

"To make things right."

"It's too late for that."

John finished his shot and poured himself another. Rusty poured himself one. They both emptied the glasses.

"I tell you what," Rusty said. "Let's settle this like gentlemen." He pulled a deck of cards from his jacket. "We'll cut the deck for it." He pulled the cards from the box and shuffled them.

"Not on your life."

Rusty nodded his head once, his chin to the side. "It is my life we're talking about. And yours." He set the cards down and swiveled in his stool to face John. "Listen to me, son. We can't keep replaying this conversation every time we meet. I'm set on staying. You're set on me going. We both have our points. If you have a better way of settling the issue, I'm ready to hear it."

John stared at him. He thought about Liz, about their last conversation in the parking lot. He could go on, pushing this point until something broke, confident he would have the last word. But he would have to do it without Liz. He would have to choose between keeping her and getting rid of Rusty.

"Okay, but not with your cards." John signaled to Buzz. "You got a deck of cards back there?"

Buzz reached under the bar and produced a deck. John shuffled them five times, cut them half a dozen times, and set them on the bar. Rusty took the top card and held it up. A three. He looked at it without expression and set it on the bar.

John smiled, grabbed the top half of the deck, and held it up. He drew a two.

At eleven, John picked up Boyd and they drove back out to the Bates place. On his way, his cell rang. He checked the caller ID. Mom.

"Hey."

"John, you asked me to let you know when Rusty came back. He's here."

"Thanks. I'll talk to you tomorrow."

"You're welcome, honey. Oh, and I have your horoscope. Sorry it's late."

John waited through the rustling paper.

"Your artistic flow may be blocked by your fears of being judged or rejected by others. Learning to accept yourself exactly as you are can make a real difference in your ability to express yourself."

"Got it. Thanks."

"You take care, honey, and get some sleep."

"Will do. Bye."

They parked behind the warehouse and walked in the light of the moon to the back door where Lovejoy let them in.

The house was set up with a big central room with a vaulted ceiling, a half wall separating it from the kitchen. The master suite was off to one side, three bedrooms to the other. Twink had wired the central room with a few cameras, one taking in the large living area, the other focused on the kitchen table. It was also wired for sound, which eliminated the need to wire Lonnie with a mike.

Twink set up in the spare bedroom. The rest of them waited in the main room, watching the drive for headlights. John went over the plan with Lonnie a final time.

"He has to actually give you the money and you need to get him to say at some point what it is for—to pay you off for destroying evidence."

Lonnie nodded. John could see he was nervous. This was a different proposition than talking to Gibson over the phone. The man's physical presence was intimidating, apart from his personality and position. Together, they were a formidable combination. But they didn't have a lot of options.

A few minutes after midnight a set of headlights flashed across the double-helix sculpture and down the drive. Lovejoy and Twink retreated to the spare bedroom, John and Boyd to the master suite with wireless headphones and a black-and-white monitor. Lonnie remained alone at his kitchen table with a bottle of vodka and a pack of cigarettes.

Lonnie answered the door. Gibson stepped inside. Lonnie gestured to the table where a glass waited for Gibson.

"How about a drink?"

Gibson's voice boomed through the house, no need for headphones. "Lonnie, I've never seen your operation. Let's take a walk over to the barn." He gestured vaguely toward the warehouse.

John could see Lonnie blinking in the monitor. "The barn?"

"You have lights out there, don't you?"

"Sure, but . . ." Lonnie looked around the room, confused.

"Then let's take a look at it."

Lonnie's gaze settled on the bottle on the table. "Let me get the vodka."

John pulled off his headphones, opened a back window in the bedroom, and kicked out the screen. He ran to the back corner of the house and peered around. The moon was almost full, bathing the Bates acreage in a soft, otherworldly light. Fortunately the house was on the west side of the property, the warehouse on the east, so this side of the house was in shadow.

John buttoned up his coat to hide his white shirt, and stepped around the corner. A hand fell on his shoulder and he whirled around, reaching for his shoulder holster.

"It's me," Lovejoy whispered. "What do we do?"

John took a moment and a breath to calm his heartbeat and looked across the moon-drenched fifty yards of bare ground to the warehouse. The only cover was an oak ten yards from the house. He looked at Lovejoy, almost invisible in his brown uniform.

"We wait until they get past the tree, stay in the shadows, and follow as far as the trunk."

Lovejoy nodded. In a few seconds the sound of Gibson's voice preceded him like an advance guard as he and Lonnie approached the corner of the house. John crouched behind the shrubbery. Lovejoy joined him.

"What's he up to?" Lovejoy asked. "What was wrong with doing the deal in the house?"

"I don't know, but it doesn't look good. And Lonnie doesn't have a wire."

They watched the pair recede in the moonlight, Lonnie thick and stumbling, the bottle glinting in his hand, Gibson tall and wide and confident, leading the way. They crept to the trunk of the oak, first Lovejoy, then John.

Gibson and Lonnie crossed the driveway, walked past the back-hoes, and up to the door of the warehouse. Lonnie flipped a latch and pulled back on the door. It squeaked but didn't budge. Gibson reached past him and pushed the door aside with no apparent effort. They walked inside.

John pointed toward the near corner of the warehouse and Lovejoy sprinted in a crouch toward it. When he was set, John followed. He was halfway across the gap when the lights inside the warehouse flashed on, a large parallelogram of yellow splashing out onto the ground outside the doors. He froze for a few seconds, but no one appeared at the door. He sprinted the rest of the way.

He stopped next to Lovejoy. "You go around the back and take a position on the other side of the door. I'll take this side."

Lovejoy nodded and disappeared around the corner. John crept up to the edge of the light spilling out of the door and listened. Lonnie's voice had a high, strained quality.

"What do you mean the money isn't necessary? It durn sure is necessary after all you asked me to do."

"They have nothing on him and he knows nothing. If your boy just sits tight for a few days, they'll have to let him go and the case will peter out. While they're distracted with him, I can make sure the document disappears and the problem goes away."

"No, no, no. That don't work, don't you see?"

Lonnie was losing it, but they didn't have enough to make it stick, yet. John saw a motion in the darkness beyond the door and Lovejoy edged up to the opposite side, his back to the wall, his gun held vertical in both hands, like in the movies.

"Let's just go back to the house and sit down and talk it out."

"I don't think so."

"What?"

The upward rise of Lonnie's voice went beyond anything John thought his barrel chest could achieve. Something had happened.

Gibson cut off the wail. "Why don't you sit down at the desk and we'll talk this out."

"What are you doing?"

"Trying to get you to see sense."

John heard a noise behind him. He spun around, his weapon ready. It was Twink with a directional mike and a camera. John nodded and the tech crouched beside him, pointing the mike toward the open warehouse door.

"How is that going to make me see sense? That don't make no sense."

"If you'll sit at the desk and calm down, I'll put it away and we can talk. If you can make a case for bailing Lonnie out instead of using him as a distraction, I'll give you the money. But first you have to consider one question. How are you going to explain to Sheriff Lawson where you came up with twenty grand on a day's notice? You don't think that will create even more suspicion about your son?"

"I . . . I can't think out here. Why can't we go back to the house?"

"Sit in the chair, Bates."

John had heard enough. He looked around the corner. Lonnie stood next to the desk where John had found Lonnie Jr. laboring over order forms. Gibson faced Lonnie, his back to the door.

John yelled into the warehouse. "Gibson, this is John Lawson. Step away from Bates with your hands up. Slowly."

Lonnie glanced wildly at the door, then back at Gibson. Gibson's back stiffened. There was a motion with his arms and he turned slowly, pulling his hands away from his body. They were empty.

"Sheriff. What an unexpected pleasure. How's the wife and kids?" He walked toward John.

"Stop right there."

"Gun!" Lonnie screeched, pointing at Gibson. "He's got a gun."

Gibson frowned. "I'm afraid Mr. Bates has become—"

"Shut up, Gibson." John stepped into the warehouse, his gun pointed at Gibson's massive chest. "Lovejoy, come on in."

Lovejoy whipped around the door in a crouch, his gun following his line of sight, and zeroed in on Gibson. Bates scurried around Gibson and out the door.

Gibson shook his head, his right arm still extended for a handshake. "John, this is a bad idea."

John kept his gun on Gibson. "Here's what's going to happen, Gibson. You're going to lean against that wall and assume the position. Then I'm going to take the gun and cuff you and then you're going to explain why you're here."

"I think not."

"You're mistaken." John holstered his weapon and stepped forward. "Lovejoy, if he tries anything, shoot him."

Gibson took one step back. "This is about Jennifer, isn't it? You can't let go."

"Think whatever you want, Gibson, just get up against that wall."

"Lawson, I expect a certain level of deference for my position if nothing else."

"And I expect you to submit to the law. Spread them."

"Lawson—"

"Are you getting all this, Twink?"

Twink stepped into the warehouse, the shotgun mike pointed at Gibson. "Yes, sir."

Boyd stepped into the warehouse behind him. "You might want to do what he says, Judge. If he's in the wrong, it's all on the record to back you up."

Gibson looked at the great host of witnesses assembled before him, shook his head, and assumed the position. John stepped up, kicked his feet further apart, pulled back his coat and removed a Glock from a shoulder holster. He handed it to Boyd. "Anything sharp in your pockets I should know about? A needle, maybe?"

Gibson didn't answer. John grabbed his right hand and pulled it down, cuffing it. He pulled the left hand down and cuffed it.

"For the record, Luther, you can have Jennifer. You deserve each other. You got that, Twink?"

"Got it."

"Okay, Judge. Let's go to the kitchen and have a little talk. Love-joy, do the honors."

Lovejoy grabbed Gibson by the arm and escorted him out of the barn. Twink followed, camera rolling.

"You are under arrest for conspiracy to commit arson. You have the right to remain silent. Anything you say or do can and will be used against you in a court of law."

Gibson jerked his arm from Lovejoy's grasp. "I know my rights."

"You have the right to speak to an attorney. If you cannot afford an attorney, one will be appointed for you. Do you understand these rights?"

Gibson stumbled in the dark and fell. Lovejoy helped him to his feet.

"I need a verbal response for the record, Judge."

"I understand my rights," Gibson growled.

John, Boyd, Lovejoy, Twink, and Gibson walked the rest of the way to the house in silence. Inside, Lonnie Sr. sat in an overstuffed armchair drinking vodka from a tumbler, his hand shaking.

John nodded at Lonnie and guided Gibson to the kitchen table. Twink disappeared into the bedroom. Gibson stood next to the chair and glared at John. He had dirt on his forehead and cheek from the fall.

"I can't sit with my hands cuffed behind my back."

John looked back calmly. "Regulations say a prisoner under arrest must remain cuffed until he's in booking."

Gibson didn't sit. His eyes never left John. It was clear he was attempting a poker face, but a range of emotions bled through the mask—rage, fear, embarrassment. Behind it all, a desperate intelligence making calculations at high speed. He glanced at the camera and back at John.

"I can give you Cook."

John exchanged a raised eyebrow with Boyd, who nodded. John stepped around Gibson and removed the cuffs. Gibson rubbed his wrists, wiped the dirt from his face and clothes, and sat at the table. With a look from John, Lovejoy stood to the side, his hand resting on his sidearm. Twink emerged with a tripod, set up the camera, focused it on Gibson, and gave John a thumbs-up.

John and Boyd sat across from Gibson.

"Talk," John said. "Boyd will decide if it's worth anything."

Gibson licked his lips and cracked open like a stucco house in an earthquake.

Back at the Bolero County jail, Ted escorted Lonnie Jr. out of his cell and Judge Luther Gibson in. John found it strangely satisfying to see Gibson in an orange jumpsuit several inches too short in all directions, his forearms sticking out, his ankles bare, his barrel chest stressing the zipper to its limits.

While Lonnie Sr. waited for his son to get his personal items from the booking desk, John asked Ted to put on a fresh pot of coffee, gestured Boyd into his office, and closed the door. He sat down behind his desk, leaned back in his chair, and checked the clock. Almost four a.m.

"What are you thinking for Bates Sr.?" John asked.

Boyd nodded slowly. "I'm thinking he's a guy that got caught in the machine and made some wrong choices. But he's not a danger to the community. Quite the opposite."

"I'm thinking a suspended sentence and probation is the way to go."

Boyd kept nodding. "I can recommend it to the court. Bates could go back to his sculpting and vodka with a few stories for his grandchildren."

John leaned forward with his elbows on the desk. "About Cook—"

"Corruption of a public official is federal jurisdiction. When we call them in on Gibson tomorrow—" Boyd turned and looked at the clock. "—later today, they'll follow up on Cook."

"I'm going after Cook tonight. Before we call the Feds."

Boyd frowned. "You think that's wise?"

"Charles Cook is a private citizen, not a public official. He's in my jurisdiction."

"He's a private citizen who bribed a public official to destroy evidence, public documents."

John shrugged. "I'll save the Feds the trouble of rounding him up. Plus, there's always the danger he hears we have Gibson and destroys evidence. We can't be having that."

Boyd smiled. "No, I suppose we can't."

The eastern sky greyed into dawn as John turned his truck off the farm-to-market road onto Cook's driveway. Lovejoy followed in his cruiser. Over two miles later they arrived at the house, a rambling ranch-style mansion that served as Charles Cook's primary residence and headquarters for a working horse ranch. The stables, corral, and other outbuildings stretched out behind.

John hadn't called ahead. He figured Cook for an early riser, but he didn't care either way. He left Lovejoy leaning against the fender of his cruiser with a mug of coffee and a set of earbuds, watching the sunrise.

Cook answered the door just as John reached to ring a second time. He wore a puzzled expression and brown cotton pajamas covered with a midnight-blue silk robe. His steel-grey hair was disheveled. Perhaps not an early riser after all.

"John?" He looked over John's shoulder to Lovejoy and back to John. "What's the problem?"

"I wanted to talk to you about that security chief job."

Cook took another look at Lovejoy and studied John's face. "Let's do that in the office later today. I'll have Melba set something up and call you."

"Can't wait. Turns out you have a security problem right now."

"What?" Cook's doubtful expression tended toward a scowl.

"Time critical. Within a few hours, the FBI may be notified. We need to talk before that happens."

John could see the thoughts spinning feverishly behind Cook's eyes.

"Okay. Come on in."

Cook turned away and walked down the hall, leaving John to close the door. John followed him down a terra cotta tile hallway to a monstrous study with at least three separate sitting areas. Cook gestured to a leather chair and stepped to an alcove where he dropped a little pod into a coffee machine and punched a button.

"Coffee?"

"No, thanks."

They waited while the machine gurgled and spit a stream of coffee into a cup. Cook grabbed the cup and dropped into the chair behind his desk. He settled his elbows on the armrests, the fingers on his right hand gripping the handle of the cup, the fingers of his left holding the other side of the cup steady.

"Now what's this about?"

John studied the man behind the desk. At least twenty years older than John, but seemed younger. He'd built an empire from nothing, insulated and secure in his castle, annoyed at what was likely nothing more than an inconvenience that could have been handled without dragging him out of bed.

"You overplayed your hand. You shouldn't have offered me the job."

Cook waited.

"It made me curious. I found a loose thread and I followed it all the way back to you."

The dawn sound of birds filtered through the windows. Cook didn't respond. He just sipped his coffee. John settled back in the chair.

"You've been playing with a stacked deck, Mr. Cook. And you weren't the only one to get rich from it. I watched Gibson's little mansion go up from my trailer house on the other side of the valley. And what do you cover, maybe half the counties in Texas? I have a feeling I could follow this thread a long way, find a lot more mansions on ridges you've subsidized."

"You'd be out of your jurisdiction." Cook took another sip, seemingly unconcerned.

"That's where the Feds come in."

Cook set the coffee down and leaned forward. It was a simple movement, but it felt like a threat.

"But you didn't go to them. You came to me."

John nodded slowly.

"But you don't want the job."

John shook his head.

"Other arrangements are possible. And I suppose we should do something for your man out there."

"How generous are you prepared to be, Mr. Cook?"

"The real question is how discrete you can be. The job would account for a sudden jump in income. Other arrangements require a greater level of self-control to avoid unwanted attention."

John cleared his throat. "I think we have what we need." He stood.

Cook studied him, attempting to interpret his response. "Can you vouch for your deputy?"

"I think I can, but we'll let him speak for himself."

John stepped to the door, opened it, and looked down the hall. He stood aside and Lovejoy walked in. John gestured to Cook, who rose slowly from his chair, his hands planted on the desk.

Lovejoy crossed the room in three strides, reaching for his handcuffs.

"Charles Cook, you are under arrest for corruption of a public official. You have the right to remain silent—"

"What is this?"

"It's an arrest, Mr. Cook."

"Anything you say or do can and will be used against you in a court of law."

"But, you—"

Lovejoy walked around the desk. "You have the right to speak to an attorney. If you cannot afford an attorney—"

Cook backed away from the desk, away from Lovejoy. "You can't do this."

"One will be appointed for you. Do you understand these rights?"

Lovejoy reached for Cook's arm. Cook jerked away.

"I want an attorney. Right now."

Lovejoy slapped a cuff on Cook's left wrist. "You'll get a chance to call one after you're booked in."

Cook pushed Lovejoy away.

John crossed the room. "Charles, you can't stop this."

Cook backed away until he was against the windows that looked out onto the corral, backlit by the sun topping the barn.

A voice from the door arrested them all.

"Charles, what's going on?"

Melba Cook stood in the doorway in a kimono.

John looked to Lovejoy and tilted his head toward Cook. Lovejoy nodded. John crossed the room to Cook's wife.

"Melba, we have to take Charles down to the station."

She looked from John to Charles and back. "Whatever for?"

"Bribery of a public official."

Melba pushed past John. "Charles, is this true?"

John turned around. Lovejoy had the second cuff on Cook.

"Melba, call Henry and tell him to meet me at the county jail."

"But is it true, Charles?" Melba turned around and sought out John. "Can't he at least get dressed?"

John had hoped to avoid this scene. For the sake of preserving evidence, he couldn't let Cook go back to his room unaccompanied. "No, ma'am, I'm afraid we need to leave immediately."

Lovejoy led Cook out of the room and out of the house. Cook yelled over his shoulder.

"Call Henry, Melba. Call Henry."

Muffin Man

John watched as Lovejoy secured Cook in the back of his cruiser and left. Then he nodded an apology to Melba and got in his truck.

He had closed the loop, tracked the crime back to the source. Somehow, it didn't feel as good as he had expected it to. He pulled out his cell phone and called the FBI office in San Antonio.

DAY 11: FRIDAY

The Feds invited John along to search Gibson's house at nine a.m. The place was empty. Gibson was still in jail and Jennifer wasn't home.

It was the first time John had been in the house he had spent the last twenty years regarding from the opposite ridge, seven with Jennifer and thirteen without. It was a sprawling mansion, at least ten thousand square feet, six bedrooms, each with its own bath, a wine cellar stocked with at least a thousand bottles, and a tower guest suite.

John had no idea Gibson was living so large, and he wondered if anyone else knew. He walked out to the pool. It really was an endless pool, a disappearing edge that seemed to drop off into forever over the ridge.

He settled into a deck chair, pulled a Cohiba Churchill from his jacket, and fired it up. He wanted to find Gibson's liquor cabinet. There was probably a remarkable selection of twenty-five-year-old scotch in there. But he was on duty.

Instead he looked across the valley to his own ridge and the puny two-bedroom frame house he had built with his own hands while pulling double shifts as a deputy. The morning sun was at his back and it was barely in the midnineties, not enough to make him take off his jacket, yet.

He thumped his ash into the pool. Couldn't be too careful as dry as things were. He thought of Bates's sculptures. They would look good out here by the pool. Perhaps he'd mention it to Gibson the next time he saw him.

He wondered how often Jennifer sat out here at sunset, looking back the other direction. Probably never. She'd moved on months before she'd moved out.

He stood and walked along the edge of the pool and back toward the house. Gibson's office had a wall of windows facing the pool. Inside, the systematic dismantling and sifting of Gibson's files proceeded. An item in the corner window caught his eye.

He walked up to the window, then tapped on the sliding glass door to the office and put his hands in his pockets. A Feeb unlocked it and let him in. He walked to the telescope he'd seen through the window, bent over, and looked through the eyepiece. It gave him a splendid view of his own deck.

John straightened up and smiled. He kept the old man worried after all. Good. He should have worried more.

John got back to his office around three and caught up on his messages, spent some time on the budget figures, and shut down his computer around six. He stood, grabbed his hat from the peg behind his desk, turned around, and stopped.

Jennifer stood in the door of his office in three-inch black heels. She wore a silk leopard print blouse, the kind with most of the fabric in the collar, which hung down in folds. She had spray-on jeans, probably a notorious designer brand, but John had no eye for or knowledge of such things.

She walked in without a word and sat in the chair in front of his desk. He put his hat back on the rack and sat down. She looked at his face and he remembered the fading bruises, the hairline scratches.

"You should see the other guy," he said.

She looked around the room. "The last time I was in here, this was Daddy's office."

John followed her gaze. The walls were mostly bare, the nails that held all the photos of Weiss with celebrities still protruding from the sheetrock. John wasn't one for putting his stamp on a room.

Jennifer turned her attention back to John. "You arrested my husband."

"He had it coming."

She studied him for a moment. "Should I be worried?"

John looked back in silence for longer. "It might be too late to cash out. If the Feds establish a history of bribes, the court could seize his assets." He shrugged. "You could try."

"I meant about him."

They looked at each other for even longer. The scent of sandalwood drifted across the desk and teased his memory. Sitting on the deck with margaritas, back when there was no house, only a trailer and a deck, watching the sunset like a scene from *Raising Arizona*. Back when Christopher was barely a vague thought in the back of his mind, less substantial than a rumor. Back before he knew Gibson had a lens focused on him.

Back when John thought his high-school sweetheart was admiring the shadow as it crept across the valley to gradually engulf the town in darkness, not setting her sights on the villa on the opposite ridge.

"I underestimated you," Jennifer said.

"A lot of that going around."

"When I left, I mean. You had more potential than I realized."

John shook his head. "Maybe not. Still living in the same two-bedroom shack."

"I miss that shack, sunsets on the deck. I miss you. Liz is a lucky woman."

John didn't think she'd been drinking, at least not enough for him to smell it. "Somebody should tell her."

Jennifer stood and looked at him for a long time before speaking. "I should leave before I make a bigger fool of myself." She walked to the door and stopped. "You take care of yourself, John Lawson."

"Yes, ma'am." He stood and reached for his hat.

She turned to leave, then turned back. "And tell your daddy hi for me."

"Tell him yourself."

John went home to an empty house. Christopher was out with Caitlyn and he didn't have the energy to brace Liz in her den. He set the steaks he picked up at Toolie's on the counter, got a Shiner from the fridge, took a long swig, and went out on the deck to fire up the grill.

He turned to look across the ridge. Gibson would be back home by now, out on bail. He waved, held up the Shiner in a toast, and took another long swig. He imagined he heard cursing and the smashing of glass from across the chasm, but it was only wishful thinking.

He went back inside, coated the steaks with a hickory rub, seared both sides, then turned down the grill and closed the lid. Then he went to the closet, got the Longmorn 16, returned to the kitchen, and sautéed asparagus.

Back on the deck, he pulled one steak off early while it was still rare. That one would go in the fridge for Christopher, left rare so he could nuke it without overcooking it. He let the other get to one twenty and pulled it off. By then it was sunset.

He decided to eat on the deck, even though it was still in the nineties. It would cool down to the high eighties quickly enough. As he finished his dinner, a full moon crawled above Gibson's villa like a bulging orange tumor. It would be a bright night.

He refilled his scotch, went inside, and came back out with a cigar and a guitar. It had been almost a week since he had played and he was frustrated at how quickly he had become rusty. But after a few scales and Lightnin' Hopkins songs he was ready to tackle Mississippi John Hurt.

It flowed from his fingers and the words flowed from his mouth.

He was alone and he sang it loud. It felt good. He took a generous drink of the scotch and played it again.

He thought of Jennifer. Was she back across the valley on the other ridge, working out an exit strategy with Gibson? Or was she on her way to Houston, cutting her losses? Despite himself he wished her well. Yes, she had screwed him over, destroyed his life for several years, but in the end, like a cornered animal, she was only doing what she knew. It was all anybody could do, really.

He played the song again and thought about Liz. She brought her own baggage to the game, just like he did. Maybe he should quit taking it personally and try to understand why she felt the way she did.

For some odd reason, his thoughts turned to Mom and Rusty. No way could he live with Rusty, but it wasn't his place to make that decision for Mom.

He sat out on the deck, playing and smoking and drinking until well after midnight. He finished off the bottle of Longmorn. He shook his head. It would cost him a hundred dollars to replace it.

The cell phone woke up John at two a.m. It was Fuentes.

"Lawson, you need to come down here."

"Something up with the Bergers?"

"It's your dad. We got him in the jail."

"On what charge?"

"I'll show you."

"You'll show me?"

"Just get down here."

Somebody must have connected the dots between Rusty and the prison sting. John made the drive in twenty minutes. He walked past the duty officer without comment and went straight to Fuentes's office.

"Take a look at this." Fuentes hit play on a VCR. The monitor came up in split-screen view, showing twelve security cameras.

"Where is this?" John asked.

"Walmart. Here in town." He pointed to a pane.

Rusty walked down an aisle in men's clothes. He grabbed a package of white briefs, held the package up to the camera, then tore it open and pulled a pair on over his pants. He tossed the rest of the briefs on the floor and walked out of the shot. That answered the question about him taking his meds.

Fuentes pointed to another panel. Rusty appeared, still wearing the briefs, plus a Spiderman t-shirt over a Hawaiian shirt. He flipped through the CDs, selected a couple, showed them to the security camera, and then stuffed them into his pants in the clear view of the camera.

In another panel it was a bag of Nutter Butters in his shirt, and later a bottle of Drano. By now, an employee was following at a distance. Rusty appeared in another panel, grabbed an electric guitar, turned on the amp, turned the volume knob as far as it would go, and started playing. John didn't realize he could play guitar. From his left hand it appeared he was playing *Smoke on the Water*.

At last someone intervened. An older employee, probably the manager, appeared on screen, talking and gesturing. He unplugged the amp from the wall and held out his hand for the guitar. Rusty gave it to him. The manager set it down and escorted Rusty out of the frame.

An outside view showed a Uvalde PD officer waiting as Rusty removed various items from their secret locations. Then he cuffed Rusty and put him in the patrol car. Fuentes stopped the tape.

"What's the charge?"

"Shoplifting."

"How can that stand? The only reason he took anything out of the store is because they escorted him out without confiscating the merchandise first."

"Before you decide to spring him, take a look at this." Fuentes brought up a video surveillance feed on his computer, ran it back for a bit and hit play. Rusty was dressed in an orange jump suit. A deputy escorted him down a row of cells. He pointed to an open cell. Rusty grabbed the door and jumped on the cross bar at the bottom, riding the door as it slammed shut.

Fuentes let it run. "He said 'wheee.'"

"He said what?" John watched Rusty as he walked backward in a circle in the middle of the cell, talking.

"Wheee. When he was on the door. Like on a ride."

John turned away from the monitor. "Do you have his personal effects?"

"They were processed."

"Any medication, pills?"

Fuentes shook his head. "Matches. Camels. Keys. Cash. Lots of it." He looked at John. "And a driver's license under the name Reggie Loftin."

John dropped into a chair. "He needs lithium. Needs to be transferred to the mental health center." He rubbed his eyes. This was the exact thing he was trying to avoid. Cleaning up Rusty's messes. "I'd like to talk to him."

"If he's awake."

"He'll be awake."

"What about the ID? The name?"

"Evidently an alias he took when he left twenty years ago."

Fuentes turned back to the computer, clicked a few buttons, and the feed from the cell block came up. Rusty walked across the cell and touched the vertical bar in the corner, moving his finger slowly, then pulling it back quickly as it made contact. He turned deliberately and walked to the opposite end where he touched the matching bar in the same manner. Then he retraced his step, touching the second bar on the opposite end.

Fuentes swiveled around to John. "They'll buzz you back."

John stood. "Thanks, Ray."

The guard buzzed John through the mantrap and directed him to the right cell block. There were four cells, the other three silent except for snores and heavy breathing. In the fourth, Rusty continued processing the bars, now five from the corner and muttering slowly under his breath, one phrase per touch.

"Fell into a sadness, then into a fast, thence to a watch, thence into a weakness, thence to a lightness, and, by this declension, into the madness wherein now he raves, and all we mourn for."

With the last phrase he touched the center bar and looked up. His gaze fell on John and he smiled.

"Yet here, Laertes! Aboard, aboard, for shame! The wind sits in the shoulder of your sail, and you are stayed for." His words sped up as he spoke. By the last phrase, they tumbled over each other.

He snapped the fingers of both hands and danced a single step. "Come, and trip it as ye go, on the light fantastic toe." He tossed his head back into a pose, then looked back at John. "Five hundred beds, John, five hundred beds for five hundred souls. Into the valley of beds rode the five hundred!" He glanced over his shoulder. "Such as this."

He took two steps back and launched himself onto the bed, landing on his side, his elbow on the pillow and his head in his hand. "I'll call upon you ere you go to bed, and tell you what I know."

He sat up. "But we know what they know." He held up a finger. "And we know what they think they know they know, and what they don't know, and more importantly what they don't know they don't know, because we know it, not they."

He walked to the bars, and looked dead into John's eyes, and spoke in a high, lilting, nasal voice. "If you think we're wax-works you ought to pay, you know. Wax-works weren't made to be looked at for nothing, nohow! Contrariwise, if you think we're alive, you ought to speak."

John let the words die out into silence and then dug deep. After a moment he replied softly. "To thine own self be true, and it must follow, as the night the day, thou canst not then be false to any man."

Rusty eyed him with suspicion and replied in the same nasal voice. "I know what you're thinking about, but it isn't so, nohow. Contrariwise, if it was so, it might be; and if it were so, it would be; but as it isn't, it ain't. That's logic."

John ignored this and spoke softly again. "If you're going to stay in Bolero, you have to stay on your meds."

"Meds, schmeds, trundle beds. I've got the medicine in me head. You call it a zee, I call it a zed. Let's call the whole thing off." He blinked. "Fred," he added.

"You can do this to yourself if you want, but you can't do it to Mom. Not again. Not this time."

In a more erudite voice. "And now remains that we find out the cause of this effect, or rather say, the cause of this defect, for this effect defective comes by cause: Thus it remains, and the remainder thus." He bowed. "Perpend."

John shook his head and walked away.

Back in Fuentes's office he got the wheels set in motion to transfer Rusty to the local mental health center, talked Fuentes out of the keys to the Mustang, and walked out to his truck.

Cirrocumulus clouds covered the sky like a layer of cottage cheese. Across the highway to the west the full moon hung behind the clouds a few degrees above the horizon, bloated and yellow as a week-old bruise.

He got in the truck and drove north. The muffin lay beside him on the seat, encased in the crumpled bag where Rusty left it the day before. It had been silent for four days, at least. What was the first thing it said to him, almost two weeks ago? Fortuitous concourse? What did that mean, anyway?

He realized he had forgotten to ask Frank about the muffin. Did the Bergers really bring a muffin to an arson? If not, where had it come from?

"swallow the honey"

John didn't know if the muffin said or if he thought it. The money was probably still in the trunk of Rusty's car, a million dollars in cash, minus expenses and a bribe or two, abandoned in the Walmart parking lot. He'd take care of it later.

It bugged him that he still didn't know where the money came from. It would be a day or two before Rusty was lucid enough to even understand the question, but even then he probably wouldn't answer. It was like the muffin, of unknown origin and dubious provenance.

DAY 12: SATURDAY

It was close to five a.m. when John got back to the house. He tossed the muffin bag on the kitchen counter and took a shower. Then he dressed in jeans and a black shirt, drove to the old Arco station, bought coffee and a dozen assorted kolaches from the couple from Colorado, and drove to Mom's house. She would be up despite the fact that the shop didn't open until ten. She wouldn't eat the kolaches and he shouldn't eat them, but at this point he didn't care. Running on an hour of sleep, he needed the sugar.

He repented of his thoughts of the night before. Mom could make her own decisions about a lot of things, everything really, except Rusty. With Rusty, she had a blind spot the size of Hurricane Katrina.

She let him in with a hug and a question, but he didn't talk until they were in the kitchen. He dropped the box in the middle of the table, sat down, opened it up, and grabbed a sausage kolache for starters. He took a bite and washed it down with coffee while she watched him over her cup of herbal tea.

"Rusty's in jail."

"John," Mom said, spilling tea onto the table. "What have you done?"

"Uvalde County jail. Fuentes called me."

Mom wiped up the spill with a napkin and sipped her tea cautiously. "What did he do?"

"When did you see him last?"

"He left yesterday after lunch to run some errands."

"What was he like?"

"He was fine."

"You know what I mean. Was he manic?"

"He was full of energy."

John set his coffee cup down with a thud. "Mom, you're not doing him any favors by pretending." He leaned forward and lowered his tone. "He's in jail for shoplifting." He described the security footage.

Mom wilted, suddenly seeming weary. She grabbed a strawberry kolache from the box and took a large bite. "Did you talk to him?"

"It was all nonsense. Shakespeare, Carroll, Tennyson, some stuff I didn't recognize."

"The Tempest?"

"Hamlet."

She nodded. John selected a blackberry kolache and they ate processed flour and refined sugar for a while. Then John pushed back his chair and stood up. He looked at Mom, then sat back down.

"Don't you think it's time to cut him loose?"

The fire returned to Mom's eyes. "Now is when he needs us the most."

"What he needs is a reality check. If he doesn't get back on his meds and stay on them, next time it could be a lot worse."

"The Dali Lama said, 'Our prime purpose in this life is to help others. And if you can't help them, at least don't hurt them.' We just need to give him enough space to be himself."

"More like enough rope to hang himself." John stood. "You think the Walmart manager should have given him more space to be himself?" He picked up his coffee. "Take the kolaches to the shop for the girls."

He took a sausage kolache for the road and walked out. He stopped at the door to the kitchen.

"I know you want to think the best of everyone. I might even admit that it's a good thing and I should do more of it. But this is not one of those times. If you really want him to stay, and it looks like I can't do anything to stop it, you have to help him. And this is not helping."

She didn't look up. He left.

John went home, took another shower, drank a beer, and went to bed. He woke up around noon, feeling slightly more human than a yeti. He cooked a three-egg omelet, called Christopher and told him to come to the house.

John was out of the door before Christopher was out of his truck. John waved him back into the driver's seat.

"I need you to take me to Uvalde. I have to pick up a car."

Christopher froze. "You got a new car?"

"I'll explain on the way." John grabbed his jacket from his truck and climbed into the 4x4.

Christopher assaulted John with questions on the drive down. He had scoured the net for data on manic depression—the causes, symptoms, treatment, prognosis. John had few answers. Christopher wanted to see Rusty. John made a few calls and they ended up at the mental health center.

John pulled on the jacket on the way in. It would make him look more official, despite the jeans and black shirt. At the front desk he asked to see Reggie Loftin. His badge got them fast-tracked to the director. They sat in his office. The director pulled his chair up to his desk and flipped through the file.

"We got him stabilized with olanzapine but we'll be backing that off gradually over the next twenty-four hours."

"Can we talk to him?" Christopher asked.

The director looked over his reading glasses. "You can try. He's in the activity room."

The activity room was a large rectangular room with indoor-outdoor carpet, acoustic ceiling tile, and fabric-covered walls. The furnishings were a hodgepodge of couches, upholstered chairs, card tables with plastic folding chairs, Ping-Pong table, foosball table, televisions, and an upright piano in a corner.

Nobody looked up when they walked in. Most of the inmates watched television, or at least looked in its general direction. A girl with thin, stringy, mouse-brown hair to her shoulders sat at the piano picking out a Radiohead song.

John sighted Rusty on a couch, his elbow resting on the arm, his chin resting on his hand, looking out the tinted windows at an oak in a field of scorched grass in the hundred and three degree afternoon. He gestured to Christopher and they sat in the chairs across the coffee table from Rusty. He didn't avert his gaze from the window.

"Give every man thy ear, but few thy voice," John said. It was from *Hamlet*, the speech Polonius gave to his son Laertes as he boarded the ship to France. The role Rusty had abandoned his family for a summer to play. Rusty knew every inch of the part, every word, every syllable. John knew the major speeches.

But Rusty paid him no mind. He gazed out the window as if the hope of the second coming would reveal itself, as if at any second the trumpet would sound and the heavens would split open and he would be translated into paradise.

"What's going on?" Christopher whispered.

John talked without taking his eyes off Rusty. "He was manic. It takes serious meds to knock him out of orbit and back to earth."

"So he'll recover?"

John looked at Christopher. "From this trance? Sure. As soon as they back off on the meds. From his condition? There is no recovery. Only treatment." He looked back at Rusty. "And the reason he's in here now, drugged out like this, is because he refused to submit to the treatment."

Rusty's voice sounded out, though his eyes never strayed from the window. "Take each man's censure, but reserve thy judgment."

It was the next line from the speech of Polonius. John didn't know the line that followed, so he skipped to the end of the passage. "This above all: to thine own self be true."

"And it must follow, as the night the day, thou canst not then be false to any man."

John turned to Christopher, for it was his own son who finished the line, not Rusty.

"Farewell: my blessing season this in thee!" Rusty said, speaking much slower than the night before. He turned and looked at Christopher. "Africa awaits thee. Where the cannibals that each other eat, the Anthropophagi and men whose heads do grow beneath their shoulders."

249

Christopher looked at John.

"*Othello*," John whispered to him.

Christopher nodded, frowned in thought, and said, "How did you come to be here?"

Rusty nodded as if Christopher had uttered a profound truth, and then returned to his vigil, staring out the window.

After several minutes and as many failed attempts to engage him again, they left. John drove to the sheriff's office and asked Jimmy if he could set up the security footage from Walmart in the interview room.

"Less than twenty-four hours ago," John said, and hit play.

He pointed out the timestamp and the panels of interest as Christopher watched Rusty catapult through the store, his madness gaining momentum with each frame. They watched in silence.

"What was happening in his head during all that?" Christopher asked.

John shook his head.

"Have you ever . . ."

John shook his head again, but with less conviction. He had a faint recollection of scrambling headlong down a cliff in the moonlight, directed to a destination by a ghostly voice that spoke in italics.

"It's genetic, you know," Christopher said. "At the lake, you said it isn't, but it is."

John looked at him. "Have you ever . . . heard voices or anything?"

"No."

John nodded. "You'll be okay."

John had Christopher drop him off at the Walmart parking lot. Christopher wanted to drive the Mustang, but John pulled rank. He opened the doors to let the heat dissipate. Christopher jumped behind the wheel and checked it out. On the passenger side, John pushed the seat forward, gathered a double handful of trash, and walked it to the dumpster. After three trips he ran Christopher out of the car.

Once Christopher was out of sight, John opened the trunk. You could hide several bodies in a trunk this size, but all it contained was the legendary suitcase. He opened it. The money was still there, short a few bundles. He buttoned it all up, went to the driver's door, and looked inside.

The red interior looked new, but had a dusting of ash and a few cigarette burns. There was the burn from the lighter on the carpet by the clutch pedal. The ashtray was pulled open and held a grey powdery pyramid, the windshield greasy from thousands of miles of cigarette smoke.

He slid behind the wheel and pulled the door closed. A small avalanche of ash flowed into four streams at the corners of the ashtray, drifting down like sand in an hourglass, adding to four smaller pyramids on the console in front of the gearshift.

He put his hands on the wheel. It was skinny, maybe an inch around, and hard. It could crack a skull in a heartbeat.

He slid in the key, pushed in the clutch, and cranked the engine. It whined for a second and then roared to life. He felt the vibration in the steering wheel, a strangely comforting connection with the straight six under the hood.

An after-market AC hung below the red metal dash, four circular vents all pointed toward the driver. He turned it off and rolled down the window, leaned across and rolled down the passenger window as well. It was probably getting down to one hundred outside. Tolerable once he got moving.

He got back out and took off his coat, which was when he noticed the prescriptions in the pocket. He was in Uvalde and it was Saturday afternoon. Bound to be a pharmacy open. He found one, dropped off the prescriptions, got the car detailed, picked up his pills, and pointed the little pony on the grill toward Bolero.

Out on the highway it hugged the road like a cat. On the long flat stretches he punched it up to seventy, eighty, ninety. The large white numbers on the speedometer ran across the instrument panel in a straight line all the way up to one twenty.

He hadn't checked the tires, but expected they were in as good condition as the rest of the car, and pushed it to the floor. He pushed the needle until it pegged the right side, and then eased it back down.

Then he was climbing through curves as he continued north into the Hill Country. He thought about the day a car like this was almost his, or rather actually was his for a few minutes.

On John's sixteenth birthday he was late to school. He'd been taking showers in the field house at school because the water had been cut off the week before. When the sun shining on his face woke him up, he looked at his clock radio and realized the electricity had been cut off during the night.

He got up in a panic, threw on some clothes, grabbed his books, and set out on the three-mile walk to the high school. The old high school, because the school board was still in talks about building a new one. He got there in the middle of second period and muddled through the day, annoyed.

When the bus pulled up to his house to let him off, Mooney elbowed him and pointed out the window. A red Mustang sat in the driveway next to the family Chrysler. Mom and Dad sat on the porch swing waiting for the bus.

Mooney didn't take his eyes off the car. "Dude, is that yours?"

John sat in the seat, staring out the window until the driver yelled. "You getting off, son?"

John grabbed his books, rushed down the aisle, and off the bus. The door squeaked shut behind him and the bus rattled away. John stood in the driveway, emotion rising. Mom and Dad walked down the steps into the yard, smiling. John walked up to the side of the Mustang, bent down, and looked inside. Restored. Pristine.

Dad smiled and held out a set of keys, one for the ignition, one for the trunk. "Happy birthday, son. You deserve it."

John straightened up, turned around, and looked at the hand holding out the keys, at Dad's smiling face.

"I deserve it? You think I deserve it?"

Mom stepped up next to Dad. "Of course you do, honey. Straight A's. Beta Club. Debate team."

John ignored her. He didn't take his eyes off Dad. "What about being able to take a shower in my own house? Do I deserve that? How about my alarm clock working in the morning so I can ride the bus instead of walking three miles to school? Do I deserve that? Do I deserve some breakfast, maybe?"

Dad stood there, his arm outstretched, the smile frozen, uncomprehending.

John threw his books on the ground. "Why is it always something we don't need? What if one day you went crazy and instead of buying a bass boat or a motorcycle or a champion bull or a—" he jerked the keys from Dad's hands and waved them toward the car, "—a fully restored classic car that cost who knows how much, what if you bought us a year's worth of electricity or a freezer full of groceries?"

Mom stepped forward. "John—"

He cut her off. "No. This has gone far enough. The food is spoiling in the refrigerator, but hey, I have a sweet ride. I should be grateful, right?" He made a grandiose gesture. "There are starving kids in China who would kill for a car like this."

He turned on Mom. "And you. You just encourage him. You just act like everything is okay, no matter what he does, no matter what he puts us through, no matter that he refuses to take his meds unless somebody in a white coat locks him in a padded room."

He ran out of words and stood there, panting. A silence descended on the front yard as they looked at each other.

Dad was the first to recover. He held out his hand. John slammed the keys into it. Dad walked to the car, opened the door, slammed it shut, cranked the engine into a roar, and blasted out of the driveway, pelting them with gravel.

That was the last time either of them saw Rusty for twenty-four years.

John had assumed that Rusty had gone to return the car, to bring back the cash, or more likely the down payment. He was wrong about that. But he was right about everything else.

He thought about what would have happened if he had just let it go, had pushed down his outrage and had taken the car. What would his last three years of high school have been like? Taking Jennifer to the drive-in or out to Medina Lake or down to Galveston in a fully restored classic, hanging out on the main drag after football games, taking long drives alone through the Hill Country.

Of course, Rusty would never make a payment or would stop after a few months and the finance company would repossess it. Or John could have taken an after-school job and made the payments himself. As it was, when Rusty didn't come back he'd been forced to take the job anyway, just to help pay the bills, but without having the car.

If he'd kept his mouth shut, he would have had the car, but he would also have had Rusty. If he had known how Rusty would react, would he have kept his mouth shut? John shook his head. If he could have run Rusty off two years earlier, he would have done it.

Normal without a car was better than riding the roller coaster of Rusty's mood swings in a classic Mustang.

Of course, Rusty always said that normal was just the setting on a washing machine. John wondered what the last twenty-four years had been like for Rusty. He doubted that anyone could survive twenty-four years of uncontrolled cycles of mania and depression. He must have stayed on his medication for some of that time, maybe most of it. Maybe all of it. Maybe he had learned his lesson, but then something knocked him off the wagon into a manic episode, which led him back home. Maybe when they stabilized him, he would go back to Florida.

He smiled and pulled off the highway onto Horseshoe Road. It was late Saturday afternoon. He deserved a break. At the Inn he parked the Mustang out front among the half-dozen other cars, locked it, and walked in.

Kendall, hipster girl with a weakness for tattoos, hers and others, was behind the bar in a tank top and shorts. She worked the weekend day shifts and had a small following, which accounted for the crowd clustered on the end of the bar toward the door. It was the unlikely collection of twentysomethings that small towns produced—hipsters, goat ropers, jocks. On the TV above the bar, Pastor Jackson talked to a CNN reporter.

At the end of the bar, back by the jukebox and the door to the poker room, Battles and an older guy sat with three stools between them.

John walked past the kids and split the difference between Battles and the stranger, sitting with an empty stool on either side. The stranger looked him over. He nodded to the guy. The guy nodded back. John glanced at Battles. He was staring into a tumbler of scotch on the rocks, mostly rocks.

Kendall came down to the oldster section and spun a napkin in front of him. He looked at Battles. John preferred single malt, neat, but at the Inn they only had blends. A blend on the rocks was fine if you didn't have a chaser.

He nodded toward Battles. "Get me what he's having and another one for him."

Battles looked up at the sound of John's voice. He squinted his disapproval of John's presence within the same ZIP code as himself, but he didn't refuse the scotch when Kendall set it in front of him. He tossed back whatever was left in his glass and shoved the empty across the bar to her. Then he picked up the fresh scotch and gestured it in John's general direction.

"Mud in your eye."

John held his glass up. "May we get what we need, but never what we deserve."

Battles nearly choked on his whiskey. When his coughing fit subsided he turned to John. "I can't help thinking that somehow you're behind this . . . this . . ." He waved his hand, apparently too disgusted to bother with coming up with a word of sufficient power.

John didn't respond. He had taken the stool by Battles with the intention of asking him for advice about dealing with the media, but looking at the man—huge, overbearing, and utterly defeated—he didn't have the heart.

Battles drank deeply. "Gibson told me about this prison project last week. Said he heard about it from your daddy."

An image leapt into John's mind. Rusty in the Lone Star Grill, asking about Battles, giving him a good look after John pointed him out. Wanting to strategize about the election. That was . . . the first time he talked to Leonard, the day that Rusty wrecked things between Liz and him.

John shook his head. Rusty had been working on this thing for a week and a half. That might explain his absence over the weekend.

He must have gone back to Florida to get his business partner to play the part of Alonzo in his little sting. Or maybe he drove to Reno and got his actor buddy to come down and do it.

John glanced around, making sure Kendall was down with her fans. He and Battles sat with their elbows on the bar. He leaned toward Battles and lowered his voice.

"Right now, he's in the mental health center in Uvalde, drugged like a zombie and quoting Shakespeare." He straightened back up. "So I don't think he had anything to do with your . . . thing."

Battles studied him, seemed to accept the story, and shook his head like a bull trying to rid itself of a horsefly. He rattled the ice in his glass and held it toward Kendall. When she looked, he gestured to both their glasses. She came down with the bottle, Dewar's, and poured them each a double, her smile saying the extra was on the house, checked with the stranger, and walked away.

John and Battles clinked glasses and took a sip, John a small one, Battles a big one. Battles set his glass down and frowned.

"The thing is, it looked completely legit. Guy calls Gibson, says he's got a set of investors who targeted south Texas for a prison and want to talk turkey. Gibson says I should meet with the guys, says me bringing in jobs to Bolero would pretty much seal the election. I was all for it. And not just because of the election. I mean, this place could use a little stimulus package. Be good for the community. I like these people."

He looked around the bar. "Salt of the earth. Good folk."

He took another drink and leaned toward John until their shoulders touched, speaking confidentially.

"By the way, I hope you didn't take my ribbing personally the past few months. Just part of the game, you know, get in the other guy's head, psych him out. Like on an investigation. But you're an okay guy. Good people."

Battles held up his glass, which was mainly ice by now, to toast. John clicked his glass quickly and leaned away, forcing Battles to straighten up to keep from falling off his stool. Battles sucked the remaining liquid from the glass and slurped up an ice cube.

"So when Lindsey stepped up with his camera, I was surprised, but I didn't have anything to hide. I was talking business and I had a proposal to show for it." He smacked the bar with his palm. "And I did have a proposal. He pulled it out of the envelope, we went over it, he put it back in the envelope, he gave it to me."

Battles's face took on the same look of confusion as the photo in the *Bulletin*. Like a calf looking at a new gate.

"But it wasn't in there. Just the money."

"What did you do with the money?"

"Still have it," Battles said in a voice filled with wonder. "I'd give it back, but the guy disappeared. Who do I give it to?"

He didn't seem to expect an answer. He slipped off the stool in the direction of the bathroom, a bit unsteady. He grabbed John's shoulder for support.

"Whoa. I better sleep this off in the truck before I go home."

John nodded to the back room. "There's a couch back there you can use."

Battles nodded and wandered away. John watched him go, an unknowing casualty of the manic schemes of Rusty Lawson. Perhaps he should feel bad about that, but he didn't. He spun back around on the stool. Footage of the Easter fire at The Tabernacle showed on the TV above the bar. The shot cut back to Pastor Jackson obviously struggling to spin it. John held his glass up to Kendall.

She came down with the bottle. While she was there, the other guy got her attention for a refill, a vodka and tonic.

John had forgotten about him. He studied the guy in the mirror behind the bar. He had shaggy salt and pepper hair and a leather face like a topographical map, a tan line just below the hairline, like he spent a lot of time in the sun with a cap on. His hands were calloused, his nails jagged and dull, like they had been carved from a plastic milk jug by a clumsy kid. Older than John, but younger than Rusty.

Kendall came back with the drink. The stranger held out a twenty. She reached for it, but he held on. She looked up at him.

"I'm looking for a guy who's from around here. Name of Reggie Loftin."

Kendall shrugged one shoulder, the one with the Dia de los Muertos tattoo. "Never heard of him." She pulled the bill from his fingers and went to the register.

John shrugged off the shiver that ran through his body.

The guy looked up into the mirror and caught him. "You know him?"

John held his gaze. "Name sounds familiar. But I think he left a long time ago." He nodded to Kendall, who had returned with the change. "Before she was born."

The guy transferred his gaze to Kendall, watched her walk down the bar, and spun the stool to face John. He held out his hand.

"Brian Rogers."

John's reaction time was thrown off by the shock to his system. Rusty's business partner, the guy who didn't return his calls, sat three feet away. It wasn't the guy from the photos at the Surf and Turf. That guy had been younger, with black hair.

"John." He took Brian's hand and shook it. "This guy a friend of yours, a relative maybe?"

"Business partner. Not answering his phone and we got a matter that needs his attention."

"What kind of business are you in?"

"Charter fishing. Fort Lauderdale." Brian held out a card.

John took it, looked it over. "I've heard of you." He looked up at Brian. "I called a few weeks ago, left a message. Was wanting to set something up."

"You don't say?" Brian said, in a what-a-small-world kind of way, but then turned apologetic. "Reggie was supposed to be covering things for me. I had to go back to California, set up my mom in assisted care."

John made a sympathetic sound, nodded his head.

"But his girlfriend said he left town just a few days after I did."

"His girlfriend?" John said, a little too loudly. He dialed it down a few notches. "I mean, if it's the guy I'm thinking of, he's pretty old. Older than you."

"Yeah." Brian frowned at John's reaction. "He's old, but he's not dead. Not by a long shot. If you know what I mean."

"Okay. So why do you think he's back here?"

"He's not anywhere else. And he talks about this place all the time. Got a kid here. I figured maybe he came back to see him."

John looked over the card, noted the cell number, and slid it in his jacket pocket. "Tell you what, Brian. I'll ask around, see what I can find out, and give you a call if I get anything. Where are you staying?"

"Motel 6 in Uvalde."

"Okay. Good to meet you. Maybe I'll get out to Fort Lauderdale one day and look you up."

Brian nodded. "Sure thing. I'll take you out, on the house."

"I might take you up on that."

John slid off the stool and got Kendall's attention on his way out. "Another round for the gentleman, on my tab."

"Okay, Sheriff," she answered.

John didn't look back to see how Brian took it.

John drove slowly to his house on the back roads. Brian was obviously here for the money. What did Rusty do? Sell the business and split with the cash? Probably not. One partner would not be able to sell without the involvement of the other. So where did the money come from.

He made it all the way home without coming up with a satisfactory explanation.

It was getting on toward Saturday evening. He gave a cursory glance at the crumpled bag on the counter that held the muffin, got a beer out of the fridge, a cigar out of the humidor and went out on the deck to sort things out. The best thing was to get Rusty and Brian together in a jar, shake it, and see what happened. Would Rusty be lucid enough by tomorrow?

He sat back with his cigar and watched the sun set on Gibson's house.

DAY 13: SUNDAY

John caught up on his sleep Sunday morning. After lunch he called Brian, said he found Reggie. He arranged to meet at the motel. He took the Mustang.

On the drive down he realized he hadn't told Liz about Rusty. He thought about calling her, but decided against it. It wasn't a conversation he wanted to do over the phone. And he needed to stay focused on what was about to happen.

Brian was standing in front of the motel when John pulled up. He walked to a new Mercedes SL convertible and followed John the three miles through town to the mental health center. John's badge got them to the activity room.

An orderly buzzed them through the door. John walked in, scanned the room, and came to a stop in the doorway. Brian ran into him from behind.

Rusty sat in the same spot on the couch by the window. Mom sat next to him. Christopher sat in the same chair across the coffee table as yesterday. Christopher saw him first and stood up, gesturing to the other chair.

Mom and Rusty followed his gaze and saw John. Then Brian squeezed through the door and stopped next to John. Rusty stood, his eyes darting around the room as if looking for an escape route.

As John and Brian approached, Rusty slowly sat down. John snagged a folding chair, gestured Brian to the chair across from Rusty, and took a place at the end of the coffee table near Mom.

"This is Brian Rogers. He's one partner in a charter fishing business. The other partner is Reggie Loftin."

John expected Mom to ask who Reggie Loftin was, but she must have learned of the alias from Christopher when they checked in. She held out her hand to Brian. "Hello, Mr. Rogers. I'm Rusty's wife, Deborah."

It was Brian who became confused. He shook Mom's hand slowly. "Rusty?"

"You call him Reggie. We call him Rusty. Rusty Lawson."

Brian turned to John. "Lawson?"

Mom nodded. "This is our son, John, and his son, Christopher."

Brian turned to Rusty. "What about Mackinzie?"

Everyone looked at Rusty, waiting. The man who, as far back as John could remember, was always ready with a quote or clever comment, said nothing. His glance flitted between Mom and Brian, finally coming to rest on Brian in a mute plea.

"Who is Mackinzie?" Mom said.

Brian looked at Rusty, waiting for him to speak. His expression combined a complete lack of surprise with annoyance and weariness. John thought he knew how Brian felt, and also what he was going to say. He watched Mom to see how it would hit her.

When John walked in the door and saw her, he was surprised, but decided it was a good thing. She needed to hear the truth from someone besides him for a change. But now he wished he had turned around and pushed Brian back up the hall and waited until she was gone. He should have prevented this thing from happening this way.

"Mackinzie is his girlfriend in Fort Lauderdale," Brian said.

John felt as much as heard the sharp intake of breath as Mom's hand rose to her lips. He put a hand on her shoulder and her hand drifted slowly to come to rest on his.

"Was," Rusty said. "I'm back home, now." He patted Mom's leg in an apparent attempt to be comforting. If it had any effect, it was short-lived.

"What about the baby?" Brian asked.

"Baby!" Mom's hand clenched John's.

He squeezed her shoulder. As much as John suspected, even he had not expected this. Nor did he anticipate Rusty's response, the eyes squinting under a threatening frown, the hand that rose from Mom's leg to accuse Brian.

"I think we both know who the father is."

Brian flashed into a gesture of impatience. "Oh, come on, Reggie, not that again."

Rusty snorted and looked away, out the window.

John held back. For this to work, it couldn't come from him. It had to come from Brian, and ultimately, from Mom.

She dropped her hand back into her lap. "Rusty, did you father a child in Florida?"

Rusty pulled his gaze from the window. "Two months ago I come home after midnight, a week early from a business trip, and find him in my house, half dressed. Then last month Mackinzie says she's pregnant. You do the math."

Brian caught Mom's eye. "It's ridiculous and he knows it. They fumigated my house for termites. I slept on the couch at their place for one night. Then he shows up in the middle of the night in a rage and throws me out. In my boxers. I had to get Mackinzie to bring me my pants so I could check into a hotel."

"Rusty, why didn't you tell me about this?"

Rusty took Mom's hands. "That's in Florida. It's nothing to do with us. I'm back here, back home."

Mom pulled her hands away. "You're abandoning this girl and her baby?"

Rusty shot a glare at Brian. "The real father can take care of them."

Brian glared back. "Even if I wanted her back, which I don't, she wouldn't have me." He shook his head, leaned back in the armchair and sighed with a weariness that those who dealt with Rusty came to know very well. "But you know I can't be the father. I told you I had a vasectomy ten years ago."

Mom regarded Rusty with an expression that John didn't recall ever seeing on her face. He didn't know what to call it, but he was glad she didn't direct it at him.

John glanced at Christopher. He sat back in the other armchair, arms crossed, watching the action like it was a movie. All he lacked was the popcorn. Christopher looked at John, raised his eyebrows briefly, then turned back at Mom and Rusty.

Brian's voice shattered a silence as fragile as a mountain of Ping-Pong balls. "Look, folks, I don't want to impose on you any more that I already have. I just need to have a private conversation with Reggie, uh, Rusty. A short business conversation. We get that settled, I'm out of here."

Rusty started to stand, but John motioned him back onto the couch. "If it's about the cash, you might as well go ahead. We know about it."

Brian looked at John with alarm, then to Rusty. "So you do have it?"

Rusty looked at him for a while before answering. "Most of it."

"Where is it?"

"Where it's going to stay."

Brian shook his head forcefully. "No, it's got to go back. Before the fifteenth or—" He took in the crowd of people around him, especially John, before continuing. "Or bad things will happen."

"You bring that on my boat, behind my back, you bring it on yourself."

"Our boat, Reggie, our boat. And if I don't take it back, it won't stop with me. It will come to you. To Mackinzie." He looked from Mom to John to Christopher, where his gaze rested. "And maybe all the way to Bolero, Texas, if that's where it is."

Rusty contemplated the situation for a long moment. "Okay, but under one condition. You buy me out of the partnership. I don't want anything to do with that kind of business or that kind of people."

"I don't have that kind of cash."

"Then find it. Get a loan from your new partners. But no deal, no cash."

"You'd be insane to keep it."

Rusty spread his arms, gesturing to the room, and leaned his head forward and slightly to the side, looking at Brian from under his brows. "Feel free to call my bluff."

Brian looked around the room, as did everyone else. The usual tribe of zombies watched the Home Shopping Network on the TV bolted to the wall. One guy played Ping-Pong with himself, hitting it across the table, walking across the room to retrieve the ball from the floor, then hitting it from the other side, rise and repeat. The girl was back on the piano, now piecing together a one-fingered Coldplay melody.

He looked back at Rusty. "Okay."

"In writing."

Brian left the room to find writing materials. The four Lawsons sat around the coffee table.

Mom broke the silence. "Why did you come back, Rusty?"

Rusty was silent for a long time. "Because one day I realized I could."

Rusty got his letter of intent. John and Brian went out to the parking lot and transferred the suitcase from the Mustang to the Mercedes.

"Thanks, Mr. Lawson, or Sheriff, I guess I should say. I'm not proud of everything I've done, but I wouldn't want any harm to come to your family because of my mistakes. And because of Reggie's stubbornness. So I appreciate you kind of looking the other way on this."

"It's out of my jurisdiction, Brian."

Brian held out his hand. They shook on it. Brian looked at the Mustang.

"Nice car. You restore it yourself?"

"You like it?"

"Yes, I do."

"You paid for it. You could call it your down payment."

Brian eyed John, then the car. "I should have guessed. You look more like the Dodge Ram type."

Brian got into his SL and left.

John showed up unannounced sometime after six. Liz let him in. She was in sweats and a do-rag. Lesson plans and homework littered all available horizontal surfaces. John picked up a pile from a chair and sat down.

"Go get yourself fixed up. Some things have happened. We're going out for dinner and a long talk."

Liz had never left the door. She leaned against it and crossed her arms. "About what?"

"About all the stuff you said. About Rusty. About why I am like I am."

She didn't move, didn't respond, but her eyes changed a little, lost some of the hardness.

John held up the papers. "I'll grade these while I wait."

"Can you spell on a sixth-grade level?"

John flipped through the papers and searched the stacks nearby. "Don't you have an answer key?"

Liz closed the door, crossed the room, took the papers from his hand, and set them crossways on another pile. "Don't touch anything." She disappeared down the hall and soon John heard water running.

When she finally came out, John thought he'd never seen her so beautiful. He opened the door for her. When she stepped out, she saw the Mustang and stopped. "You're driving your dad's car?" She turned back to him. "Where is he?"

"That's one of the things we have to talk about."

He motioned to the car, opened the door for her, then got in and cranked the engine. Liz looked around the car.

"This is nice. Did he buy it in the sixties and keep it all this time, or did he restore it?"

John laughed. "He couldn't restore a book to a library shelf, much less a classic car to mint condition. You should have seen the interior when I picked it up."

John felt the temperature in the car lower by several degrees. He'd already started off wrong.

"There's something you need to know about this car. It was because of this car that he left twenty-four years ago. Well, because of this car and because of me."

Liz's expression mellowed slightly.

As he drove to Uvalde, he told her about his childhood, from the motocross bike he got for his eighth birthday to the day Rusty left. All the manic episodes and the consequences that ranged from amusing to enraging. The weeks of depression when John wouldn't see him for days at a time, or worse, when Rusty emerged from the bedroom looking like Caliban after a bad night with the goats.

He tried to tell it as dispassionately as possible, tried to be fair. As he talked, he saw and felt a change in Liz. She challenged some of the stories as too outrageous to be true. But they were true.

They arrived in Uvalde as John got to his sixteenth birthday. He pulled the car into the parking lot of The Fez and left the engine running with the AC on as he told Liz about coming home to see the Mustang in the drive and all that followed.

He had replayed the scene in his mind for almost a quarter century, each time reliving the righteous anger, each time feeling justified in what he had done, not only because the old man deserved it, but also because of what it accomplished, driving him away.

But this time as he told it to Liz and watched her face, he saw it through her eyes and the story turned into a confession. Nothing in the situation had changed. Rusty was still a self-absorbed manic, wreaking havoc upon all he left in his wake. Mom was still a bleeding-heart enabler who validated Rusty's antisocial behavior, perpetuated it.

But this time, for the first time, John also saw what he was. Not the victim of injustice, not the unwilling hostage of two well-meaning but fantastically dysfunctional parents. Just an ungrateful teenager, a cornered ego, lashing out to make sure the ones responsible for his misery felt the sting of it.

"Oh, John," she said and placed her hand on his arm.

They sat in silence for a long time, as if neither of them could bring themselves to speak. Liz was the first to break the silence.

"I can't imagine what I would do in that situation."

"Maybe I could have handled it better."

"You were only sixteen." Liz sat cross-legged in the bucket seat leaning against the passenger door. "Who else knows?"

John looked at her face illuminated in the soft glow of the reflection of the setting sun off the mosaic. He thought that if she asked right that second, he might agree to counseling. But only if she asked.

"Which part?"

"The last part. Your birthday."

"Nobody. Just me, Mom, Rusty." He shrugged. "And you."

"Not Jennifer?"

John shook his head.

"Not Christopher?"

"Just you."

Liz studied him for a while and then leaned over and kissed him.

John turned off the car, got out, and opened the door for Liz. Liz looked at the mosaic bathed in the warm tones of the last hour of sunlight.

"How did you find this place?"

"Jennifer and I used to come here. I haven't been here in . . . thirteen years."

"Why go back now?"

"Seemed like time to move on."

She must have liked the answer. She smiled, slid her arm in his, and nudged him toward the door.

Inside, the owner made the usual big fuss over John and insisted on being introduced to Liz. He found them a table that allowed John to sit with his back to a wall with a view of the front door.

John ordered a bottle of syrah and the sampler plate with hummus, baba ganoush, dolma, tabbouleh, and tzatziki. They studied the menu. John lobbied in favor of the lamb kebab but finally agreed to try the bamia bi banadoura—okra and garbanzo beans sautéed in a tomato stew. At least he liked okra. And there was always the sampler plate to fall back on.

The wine arrived. As the waiter poured, John saw Jennifer and Houston come in the door. He hoped it was dark enough that she wouldn't see him, but she must have seen the Mustang out front. Not many of those around. She threaded through the tables toward them as Houston watched impatiently from the hostess station.

Every eye in the room followed her progress, the men with appreciation, the women with appraisal. She wore a silky, shimmery cranberry blouse that was tight enough to display her charms but loose enough to avoid bragging, and a black skirt that wasn't quite as discrete. She came to a stop at their table.

"Hi, Liz, don't you look cute! I don't want to interrupt your dinner. I won't be a minute. John, I heard about your daddy and I just wanted to tell you I'm sorry."

She laid a highly manicured hand on his shoulder, squeezed it, and then left.

Liz looked at John in alarm. "What about your dad? Is he . . ."

"I was going to tell you. Just didn't get to that part of the story, yet." He took a sip of wine. "He's in the mental health center. Uvalde PD arrested him yesterday during a manic episode in Walmart."

"Full moon."

John nodded.

"We should go see him after dinner."

John shook his head. "After visiting hours."

"We should at least try."

John shrugged.

They had an excellent dinner. The bean and okra stew was pretty tasty, but John left wishing there had been some meat somewhere in the experience. They found a red Kia SUV where they had parked the Mustang. John checked and double checked, but Liz agreed this was where they had parked. They searched the parking lot. No Mustang.

Liz shook her head. "What kind of idiot would steal a car from a sheriff?"

John didn't bother to point out the thief couldn't possibly know the car belonged to a sheriff. He had a terrible premonition as to which particular idiot had stolen the car. If it could really be called stealing.

He turned to Liz. "Call a cab."

"You're going to get a cab back to Bolero? That will cost a fortune."

"Or we can get a ride to the airport and get a rental a lot cheaper."

He used his cell to call the mental health center. It took some talking but they finally agreed to check Reggie Loftin's room. It was empty, as he had suspected. No one had seen him since dinner, over two hours ago.

He told Liz while they waited for the cab.

"But he had to know we were here and would need a ride home."

John nodded. "Welcome to the world of Rusty Lawson aka Reggie Loftin aka Shiva, destroyer of worlds."

The expression on Liz's face was the kind to make an eighth grader spontaneously combust in his desk. He was afraid he'd undone all that he had built on this evening until he heard her next statement.

"This time I'll help you run him out of town."

On the way back to Bolero in the rental, John told Liz the story of the great ruin and downfall of Battles, of the arrival of Brian Rogers, leaving out the detail of the suitcase full of cash.

Liz wanted to know how old Mackinzie was. John had assumed she was some young twentysomething bimbo, but she'd been Brian's girlfriend before Rusty stole her away, so who knew?

The real question was whether Rusty was on the run or returning to his plan to retire in Bolero. He doubted Mom would give him refuge, but one never knew about Mom. He called her to get his horoscope on the off chance she might say something about seeing Rusty, but she didn't mention it and he didn't bring it up.

Whatever else happened that evening, John concluded he must have done at least a few things right. He got back to his place very late, feeling the warm glow of love for his fellow man, and particularly for one specific fellow woman.

Day 14: Monday

John was awakened by the ding of the microwave and the smell of coffee and pastry. He opened his eyes. Light spilled down the hall from the kitchen. He rolled over and looked at the clock. Five fifteen a.m. What was Christopher doing up at this hour? He rolled out of bed, pulled on a t-shirt, and shuffled into the kitchen.

Rusty sat at the kitchen table, his back to the bedroom. John walked past him without comment, got a cup, and poured himself some coffee. He turned around and froze.

A crumpled evidence bag lay discarded on the table. On a saucer in front of Rusty, steam rose from a muffin. The muffin.

Rusty spread butter across the top. It softened and dripped down the sides.

John opened his mouth to protest, but stood speechless as Rusty sliced the muffin down the middle, picked up one half, and then shoved the saucer across the table. The muffin didn't even whimper.

John watched as Rusty lifted the muffin to his mouth, took a large bite and a sip of coffee.

"A bit of wisdom for you to treasure in your old age, son. Muffins aren't meant to be cherished as a family heirloom. It is their nature to be eaten. A muffin uneaten is a dream deferred, a pile of leaves yearning for the flame, a word waiting for a breath to give it life." He took another bite.

John couldn't take his eyes off Rusty's jaw as he chewed, couldn't stop himself from following the invisible path of the muffin as he swallowed, imagining its slow progress down the esophagus to the stomach, hastened in its journey with generous gulps of hot coffee.

The muffin didn't say a word.

"You going to eat that?"

John pulled out a chair and sat as if in a trance. He regarded the half-muffin on the saucer in the middle of the table. The source of random nonsense that had somehow guided his steps the last two weeks, now sliced open, its innermost parts laid bare to reveal nothing but the innards of an ordinary muffin, brown and crumbly.

Rusty pushed his chair back impatiently and went to the counter to warm up his coffee.

John reached out tentatively, grasped the edge of the saucer, and drew the muffin slowly to him.

"*hollow the dart,*" it whispered to him.

He broke off a corner, placed it on his tongue, closed his mouth, and let it dissolve. He swallowed.

He raised the coffee cup to his lips with both hands, closed his eyes, and took a small sip, allowing the coffee to roll across his tongue, to gather up the remains of the muffin and wash it down his throat.

John sat with his eyes closed, seeing the bold, rich coffee flow into the spicy moist flesh of the muffin, and remembered.

He remembered the litany of childhood experiences he had recited to Liz the night before. He broke off another fragment, took another sip, and remembered some more. But this time the memories were not bits of evidence gathered to convict and banish the accused. They were the chronicle of the erratic efforts of a man reaching across the chasm toward his son in impractical grandiose gestures.

He opened his eyes. Dad sat across from him, looking at him.

"Late night?"

John didn't answer. Dad sipped his coffee.

"Can you grant me a favor, son?"

John grunted.

"Could you get my medication, maybe my clothes?"

"From Mom?"

Dad nodded.

"You going back to Florida?"

Dad looked into his coffee, swished it around. "Maybe I can do it right this time. Not screw everything up."

"You didn't screw up everything. Just a lot of things."

Dad looked up.

John smiled, a bleary morning smile. "But the meds, that could make a big difference."

Dad nodded.

"I'll see what I can do," John said.

John got a shower, got dressed, and headed out. He left Dad behind to crash, maybe get to know his grandson a little.

He went in the office and went through the motions, working with Lovejoy to tie up the loose ends of the arson investigation now that the feds had taken it over. Around eleven he called Mom's cell.

"Oh, honey, I haven't had a chance to get your horoscope, yet."

"You at the shop?"

"Yes."

"I wanted to get Dad's stuff so he'll have it when he gets out." Silence filled the air between them. "He's going back to Florida. It's the best thing for everybody."

"That's what he should do. He can't leave that boy without a father."

"How do you know it's a boy?"

"It's a boy. You should know better than to ask."

John smiled. "Tell you what, how about I come by around one and take you to lunch?"

"I appreciate it, honey, but my day is full. But I can do dinner. I'll even cook."

"It's a date."

John let himself into Mom's house and got Dad's stuff together. On the way out, the photos on the mantle caught his eye. He always saw the photos as revisionist history, as a polite little fiction, freeze-frame mementoes of the good times, the bad times tastefully edited out. But now he reconsidered. Maybe they were evidence that it hadn't been all bad, that there was plenty of good mixed in.

He picked up a frame, a photo of the three of them at South Padre Island sitting on the hood of the car on the beach, the causeway bridge in the background. John was ten, Mom and Dad in their thirties, young, smiling. It was the look he had seen that night on the porch as Mom worked out a chart. He didn't put it back on the mantle. Instead, he dropped it in Dad's suitcase.

When he got to the house, Dad and Christopher were in the driveway looking under the hood of the Mustang. John pulled the suitcase from the truck and put it in the back seat of the Mustang.

"Look at this," Christopher said. "There's practically nothing in here. Look at all this empty space."

Dad leaned on the fender on his elbows. "Back on those days, you needed to work on a car, you just climbed in there with the engine and got to it."

John snorted. "When did you ever work on a car?"

Dad looked in the back seat. "Got everything?"

John nodded.

Dad glanced at Christopher, then back to John. "What did she say?"

"She thinks you're doing the right thing."

Dad nodded slowly. Then he pulled the suitcase out of the back and walked to the house. "Be right back."

John figured he was taking his meds right away. It was a good sign.

"He's going back to Florida?"

John turned back to the car. "Got a kid on the way."

Christopher considered it. "Maybe he'll take me out on the boat."

"Better do it on the way to Africa, before Brian buys him out."

Dad came back out, put the suitcase in the trunk, and turned back to them. "Guess I better be going, then."

Christopher didn't hesitate. He stepped right past John and hugged Dad. Dad hugged him back, tightly. Christopher stepped back. Dad turned to John, stepped toward him. John took a step and they hugged. John squeezed tight, Dad squeezed back, and it felt good. He couldn't remember the last time they had hugged. Certainly not on the day Dad drove away, and not for some time before that.

Just before he let go, Dad said, "Doubt thou the stars are fire. Doubt that the sun doth move. Doubt truth to be a liar." He turned away quickly, got in the car, cranked it up, and with a final wave he drove away.

John whispered the last line to himself as he watched Dad disappear down the ridge. "But never doubt I love."

At 1:32 p.m., Sheriff John Lawson sat down on a picnic table bench and looked at three beef ribs on a sheet of butcher paper. Stella's beef ribs. Three, the number of completeness.

He pulled a plastic bottle from his coat pocket, shook out a pill, put it on his tongue and washed it down with tea. Unsweetened. He put the bottle back in his pocket and surveyed the components of his lunch—coleslaw, okra, red onion slices, and the ribs, of course.

He reached out, swerving neither to the left nor to the right, and picked up a rib.

BRAD WHITTINGTON

ENDLESS VACATION

(A NOVEL)

Endless Vacations: Day 1

Chapter 1

In three days, life as Dave Fletcher knew it would end, and his biggest regret was that he had failed to equip the chair across from his desk with an ejection seat.

He would miss many things about life as a special agent for the Secret Service. Vanek was not one of those things.

Vanek sat in that chair, that lamentably underpowered chair, regarding Dave with the stare of a hyena standing just out of reach of a wounded lion, waiting for the moment it staggered to its knees. Waiting for the moment he could snatch the corner office from Dave, and the title of lead agent of the Austin regional headquarters.

A smile that was more like the baring of teeth flickered across Vanek's doughy face. "I envy you."

Dave stared back, declining to comment.

Vanek was barely fifty but looked well past the mandatory retirement age of fifty-seven. He worked hard, partied harder, and smoked like a beater with a broken head gasket.

"This time next week, you'll be chilling on your deck with a Mexican martini. I'll be stuck here, chasing leads like a rabid pit bull in a day-care center."

Dave almost smiled. The only way Vanek would chase anything was if it had a kolache tied to it. "Speaking of which, how about you just cut to the chase?" He glanced around the room. "Come to measure for curtains, maybe?"

Vanek's pained smile fractured into a grimace. "About the Rivera investigation." He rolled his chair closer to the desk. "Looks like we maybe caught a break."

Dave was annoyed to hear that Vanek had been working the one case he had held onto, but he remained impassive, refusing to give the satisfaction of a reaction. "How so?"

"Word has it Rivera's got a guy on the inside."

The suggestion was too absurd to deserve a response. Dave had scrubbed the case down to the bare metal. There was no agent in regular communication with Rivera—not Secret Service, not DEA, not FBI. In fact, the only agent to come in contact with Rivera was Dave himself, back when he bought the Jenny from him. Back before the counterfeit money surfaced.

"Every time we get close, the mole tips him off, and Rivera fades."

"A convenient theory." Especially convenient for one who preferred speculation to investigation. "Any evidence to back it up?"

"We have a bead on a guy with a past connection. Pretty solid."

Despite himself, Dave leaned forward, his elbows on the desk. "Who?"

Vanek leaned back in his chair, suddenly casual. "No need to worry. It'll take a few days to round him up. You'll be gone by then."

Dave leaned back in his own chair, echoing Vanek's posture. Best not to give the hyena even a hint of interest. Despite his incompetence as an agent, Vanek excelled at politics. Every conversation with him had to be treated with the care of a biological weapon.

The grin returned to Vanek's face. "But you might be surprised."

Me, Dave thought. He's saying I'm the inside guy. He suppressed the urge to punch Vanek out of daylight saving time and clear into the next time zone. Instead he leaned across the desk and planted his hands with a sudden intensity that threatened to topple the smug scavenger out of his chair.

"What?" Vanek barked in an unnaturally high octave.

"Careful. Don't do anything you'll regret."

Vanek returned Dave's glare with a calm stare. "Just giving you an update."

"It had better be a joke."

"Who's joking?"

Dave suddenly realized he no longer had to play this game. "Whatever it is you're doing, keep me out of it." He left Vanek sitting in the corner office he had lusted after for more than a decade.

"Hey, where you going?"

All Dave gave him was a wave of his hand over his shoulder as he strode past the cubicles and through the front door to the hallway.

The closing of the door mercifully cut off Vanek's reply. Too impatient to wait for the elevator, Dave took the stairs eight floors down in a controlled fall. In the parking garage, he put the top down on his Z-51 Corvette and escaped downtown as fast as traffic would allow.

Not content with finally taking the corner office, Vanek had evidently concocted some harebrained scheme to implicate Dave in a corruption charge. That wouldn't last long. Anybody with a brain would see through it.

Now that he had escaped Vanek's nauseating company, Dave looked for a destination and settled on an hour of aerial therapy in his restored WWI biplane, the Jenny.

As he wove through the pre-rush-hour traffic, his mind wandered to Stephanie. He wondered what she would say about his pending retirement. Probably something like, "It's not Friday, yet. We'll see."

If he'd left the service fifteen years ago, he wouldn't have lost her, wouldn't have taken the promotion to lead agent in the Austin field office to escape her memory. Unsuccessfully, as he would have known if he'd been thinking instead of reacting. He was still thinking about her fifteen years later.

He turned west onto Southwest Parkway and changed the subject—the security company he planned to open. As usual, the main hurdle was financial. Borrowing against his retirement account and pulling the equity from his house would get him, at most, three to six months of operating capital, not the three years Uncle Rex had suggested he accumulate before retiring.

Dave pushed that thought aside as well. He was taking the Jenny out to decompress, not to increase his stress. He'd resume worrying when he was back on the ground.

The last vestiges of Austin fell behind him and the road split a hill. As he topped the rise and the road curved left, the limestone walls dropped away, and Dave got a glimpse of the Hill Country. It was his favorite spot on the drive.

Layers of ridges coated with scrubby juniper and a few live oaks drew him toward the horizon, Spanish oak lining the watercourses in the ravines. Condos poked up between the trees like prairie dog mounds.

He caught a red light, and the stagnant air settled around him like a cocoon. A cloud drifted across the sun, cutting him a break of a few degrees. It was a mild day for the end of May, barely in the nineties.

At Lakeway Airpark, he drove past the Ercoupe perched on a pole by the entrance, idled up to the last T-hangar in the row, and saw something that spiked his pulse higher than a visit from Vanek. A candy-apple blue Lamborghini.

He had the car door open before the engine stopped. He strode to the access door, threw it open, and scanned the dim interior for Rivera, but something else commanded his attention. A Glock 26 pointed at his forehead.

CHAPTER 2

Dave stared down the barrel of the gun at Rivera.

"Oh, it's you." Rivera squinted at him and lowered the gun to his side.

"Who were you expecting?" Dave tended to resent it when someone pointed a gun at him. He set his foot on a toolbox, bent forward, and came up with his own Glock pointed at Rivera. "Now, how about you set that gun down on the floor and back away?"

Rivera's eyes narrowed and his body tensed, but his voice was as casual as a pair of flip-flops. "Dave, my friend, you wound me."

Dave nodded at Rivera's gun, keeping his aim steady. He wasn't in the mood for banter.

Rivera bent over, not easy given his size, and placed the gun on the concrete.

"Good. Now kick it here."

Rivera gave it a nudge.

"Back away."

Rivera took three steps back.

Dave stepped forward and kicked the gun into the corner by the door. "Now, let's talk about why you're here."

Rivera gaze drifted from the gun in the corner to the gun in Dave's hand to the expression on Dave's face. "You have not been returning my calls. It is not polite."

"No point. We both know it's not going to happen."

Rivera glanced at the Jenny. "Sell it back to me. Name your price." He stroked the fabric on the upper wing.

"It's not for sale."

"Of all people, my friend, you know that everything is for sale. It's just the finding of the right price. Fifty thousand."

Dave shook his head.

"A hundred. I can fix it so it's tax-free."

One hundred thousand dollars. Plenty to set up that office downtown. He shook his head again. Even if he wanted to sell, he couldn't do business with a suspect. "Go home, Rivera."

"Two hundred." When he didn't get an answer, Rivera's gaze wandered around the hangar. "I always felt free in the Jenny."

Dave watched him, ready for a sudden move, but Rivera seemed focused on nothing, or maybe something only he could see.

"Sometimes a man just needs to go." Rivera grabbed a polished wooden wing strut. "To turn his face forward and not look to what is behind." He turned a resentful gaze on Dave. "Selling the Jenny to you, that I regret the most."

Dave's phone vibrated. Without taking his eyes off Rivera, he dug it out of his pocket and held it so he could see both Rivera and the caller ID. The name surprised him. "Uncle Rex. Can I call you back? I'm in a meeting."

"How about joining me for dinner?"

"Give Mr. Stone my regards," Rivera said.

Dave took a step forward, gesturing with the gun for Rivera to move back. "Sure. How's next week sound?"

"I'm thinking seven o'clock."

Dave frowned, both at the phone and at Rivera, who hadn't moved. "I can't get to Philly by seven."

"Probably not, but you can make it to Bee Cave."

"You're in town?"

"The Emerald, seven o'clock."

The call disconnected before Dave could respond. Uncle Rex was not an impulsive man. If he made the trip down from Philadelphia, it had to be for something that couldn't be done on the phone. Most likely bad news.

Dave pocketed the phone and returned his attention to Rivera, his pale face easily visible in the gloom of the hangar. Here was another man whose sudden presence was disturbing and whose reason for coming was equally unclear. Not likely it had anything to do with the Jenny. After all, Dave himself didn't know he was coming here until thirty minutes ago.

"Why are you here? How did you get in?"

"Even trade, the Lamb for the Jenny. You can keep the Z-51. And the cash."

Did it have something to do with Vanek's absurd claims? "Why were you waiting here for me? With a gun?"

"I just wanted to see the Jenny again, make sure it was in good condition."

Dave shook his head. "That's not it. Try again."

"I want to fly it, once more. I will pay for the fuel." Rivera reached for his billfold.

Dave jerked his gun, gesturing Rivera's hand away from his pocket. "Are you wired? Is that it?"

Rivera responded with a scowl.

"Your shirt. Take it off."

Rivera studied Dave for a minute, then shook his head and unbuttoned his shirt.

"Set it on the wing and step away." Dave waited until Rivera was ten feet from the wing and then inspected the shirt. Nothing. "Drop your pants."

"My friend," Rivera said, shaking his head. "You go too far."

"Just do it."

Rivera reluctantly complied until he was standing in his boxers and cowboy boots.

"Kick them here."

Dave checked the pants for a bug of some kind, especially the oversized belt buckle, but found nothing. He stepped back toward the door and gestured with the gun for Rivera to get dressed.

He debated what to do with the pathetic figure. Arrest him for breaking and entering? That would waste everyone's time, and he'd miss his dinner date with Uncle Rex.

Instead, Dave cleared the path to the door. "Get out of here."

Rivera buttoned his shirt as he left, but stopped at the doorway. "Maybe one short flight, my friend?"

Dave raised the gun. "I'm not your friend. I'm just the guy who made the mistake of buying a plane from you."

Rivera shrugged and bent toward his gun.

"Leave it."

Bent halfway over, Rivera frowned at Dave. "I have a CHL."

"You can pick it up at the office tomorrow." When Rivera hesitated, Dave said, "It's a lot cheaper than bail for burglary and assault with a deadly weapon."

Based on the glare Rivera focused on Dave as he straightened up, Dave doubted he would get a Christmas card from the man this year. As he watched Rivera's bulk fill the doorframe on the way out, he reflected that instead of *Güero*, Rivera's nickname should have been *Gordo*. Or maybe *Oso*.

Dave kept his gun trained on the doorway until he heard the Lamborghini drive away. Then he checked his watch and turned to the fully restored 1917 Curtiss JN-4D biplane.

He'd flown a lot of planes, but nothing gave him the open-cockpit experience of the Jenny. Even the cargo plane in Angola that had infected him with the flying bug as a kid couldn't compare. Buzzing low and slow to feel the rush of the terrain as it whipped past. Teasing the bottom of the clouds as you hit the inversion layer with a ride like a bucking bronco in the sky. Hovering above the earth close to stall speed, barely moving, like a hawk searching for dinner. Falling through the air and pulling out into powered flight, nothing between you and the sky but your clothes and a dose of adrenaline. Try that in a Learjet.

Dave still had enough time for a short flight before dinner, but the conversation with Vanek and the visit from Rivera seemed too much for coincidence. He scanned the hangar to see if anything was missing or disturbed, but all seemed as it should be.

Rivera didn't take anything away. Did he leave something behind? Perhaps Dave had been right about being bugged, but the room, not the body. He made a more thorough search with equally unsatisfying results. When he checked his watch again, he realized he was going to be late for dinner.

Figuring out the mystery of Vanek and Rivera would have to wait until tomorrow. Right now he had to figure out the mystery of Uncle Rex.

CHAPTER 3

Dave pulled off Highway 71 into the gravel parking lot of The Emerald, a small outpost of Irish culture established by the Kinsella family in 1984. In the intervening decades, civilization in the form of country clubs, subdivisions, and upscale shopping malls had gradually encroached on the little cottage nestled among the oaks, but it had stood its ground.

Near the door, Dave spotted the Mercedes that Rex kept at his Tarrytown house. He parked next to an SUV big enough to have its own ZIP code. As he entered through the vestibule of the rock cottage, a young woman with long, dark hair approached.

"Rex Stone," Dave said.

She directed him to the back room, where he found Uncle Rex, martini in hand. Rex set the glass down and stood, his arms outstretched.

Dave grabbed a hand to shake it, but Uncle Rex pulled it free and embraced him in a hug, one with plenty of bone and muscle behind it. Dave hesitated, then hugged him back.

Something was definitely up. He couldn't recall a single hug from Uncle Rex, not even the day Rex came to the boarding school to tell Dave his father was dead. The East Coast side of the family went for the polite handshake or the air kiss to the cheek. Mom had been the only exception, but Dave assumed she had picked it up from the Texas relatives, Dad's side.

Before Dave was fully seated, the woman placed a matching martini on the table and disappeared. Dave held his martini aloft. "You're not over the hill until the hill is over you."

Uncle Rex lifted his glass. "To life without regret."

Regret? Uncle Rex?

"Dave, good of you to meet me for dinner."

"Nonsense." Dave wouldn't miss a dinner with Uncle Rex if he had to break out of jail to attend. "But what brings you here in May?"

The Kinsella woman returned with flambéed onion soup.

Rex sampled it. "Bridget would have loved this."

Dave nodded. "Mom knew how to enjoy the finer things, even on a nurse's salary."

"You remember this?" Rex pulled a slender silver chain from the breast pocket of his jacket, a familiar pendant hanging from it.

Dave reached for it. A chip from the Rock of Gibraltar, fashioned from the mountain itself, the limestone edges smooth after four decades of service. He flipped it and read the inscription.

I SHALL NOT BE MOVED

The Stone family motto, a weapon that Bridget Stone had turned against the family itself.

Rex returned his attention to the soup. "We could all take a lesson from your mother in living without regret."

Twice was two times too many to ignore. "What's all this about regret? Think of all you've accomplished."

"Exactly! I've done quite well." Rex leaned over his bowl. "For myself."

"And others."

"But think of what I could have done."

The familiar intensity of Rex's gaze was mixed with a new element, something Dave couldn't quite place. Something that wasn't Uncle Rex.

"If it weren't for you, I would be living in a shack in Angola and giving inoculations to squirming babies." The life Dad and Mom had planned for Dave, the life he had escaped when they sent him to the States for his schooling.

Rex took the necklace from Dave's hand and rubbed the worn ridges with his thumb. Dave waited for an explanation. Rex resumed in a more relaxed tone.

"When Bridget turned twenty-five, took control of her trust fund, and ran off to Africa with Reggie, the family was outraged.

Married to a nobody? Yes, he was a doctor, but no connections, no money, and worst of all, an idealist. Oh, the shame!"

Dave never tired of this story, but Rex didn't finish it. Instead, he returned the necklace to his pocket and finished his soup.

"I won't deny that your father had his faults—perhaps overzealous at times, completely inept at managing investments, prone to rash decisions and extremes. Especially at the end. But he recognized what was really important. And Bridget believed in him. Few people achieved that honor." His voice dropped to a whisper. "I sometimes wonder if she didn't make the better choice."

All this second guessing didn't sit well with Dave. As his early retirement approached, he'd done enough of it for both of them. "Uncle Rex, it's not like your life is over. And even if it were, you have nothing to regret. Or apologize for."

With his own disappointing financial situation, Dave felt like he had more reason to complain of wasted time than Uncle Rex, who had a long list of accomplishments.

The next course arrived before Rex responded. Dave sampled the Dublin Lawyer Special: lobster tail in a flaky puff pastry, simmered in heavy cream and Irish whiskey. Dave wondered why anyone ever prepared lobster another way.

Rex savored a bite with his eyes closed, and then went for another. "When was the last time you saw Hensley?" he asked without looking up.

"Same time you did. Mom's funeral."

"Do you know where he is?"

"I know as much about Hensley's whereabouts as he cares to tell me. Which, as you know, is nothing."

"Track him down."

"He knows how to find me."

Rex started to reply, but stopped himself.

Dave speared a bit of lobster and considered this new line of conversation. Did this mystery have something to do with Hensley?

They were nearly through with dinner, and Dave still had no more idea of why Rex was here than he did of why Rivera was in his hangar or why Vanek was playing games.

They were silent as the dishes were cleared away and the dessert delivered: fresh oranges and orange marmalade in a chocolate-covered pastry puff accompanied by Irish coffee.

Uncle Rex took a slow, appreciative sip. "Angola wasn't easy on Hensley."

Dave snorted. "I made it through okay."

Rex studied him. "After a fashion." He took a bite of the dessert. "It's not a one-size-fits-all world, Davison. Some of us are more broken than others."

"Hensley's world is every man for himself and the devil take the hindmost."

As much as Rex had done for Dave, for the family, he wasn't there when Hensley handed Dave his coin collection like a consolation prize and disappeared forever. When he made a token appearance at Dad's funeral and disappeared immediately after. And the same at Mom's funeral.

The dance had gone on long enough. Since Rex had already breached the line of reticence behind which the two of them typically kept personal matters, Dave decided on a little plain speaking. "Uncle Rex, pardon me for saying, but you don't seem to be yourself. What's going on?"

Rex cleared his throat. Dave watched him, but Rex focused on his coffee cup.

"Davison, I did my best as I saw it at the time, but . . . I thought Reggie was misguided. Sincere, but naïve. I . . ." He finally met Dave's stare, eyes misting. "I hope you know how much I treasure the years we've had, but I didn't do right by you. I'm sorry."

Dave's confusion prevented him from speaking. This was the reason for the evening? An apology for doing the right thing? He studied Rex, really saw him for the first time tonight. Rex was changed from the dynamo of industry Dave had always known. He seemed frail, diminished, defeated. Dave wanted to avert his eyes from the unwonted apologies. The making of excuses for Hensley, who had betrayed the family.

"You did more for me than my own parents did, or could do." Dave struggled to keep his voice steady, not sure that he had succeeded.

Rex held his gaze, his eyes moist. He seemed on the verge of speaking, but instead retreated behind his coffee.

Dave waited, both desiring and dreading an explanation. There had to be something else, but if it was more comments in the vein of apologies and suggestions that he hunt down his prodigal brother, Dave wasn't sure he wanted to hear it.

But Rex seemed to be done. He stirred his coffee and stared at the Irish crème swirling around the vortex.

What had happened to the Uncle Rex who had built a commercial empire with business interests on practically every continent? Where was the man who preferred results to excuses, who didn't take no for an answer, who had eliminated the word "failure" from his vocabulary?

Neither side of Dave's family, the Stones or the Fletchers, talked much about feelings. But in the past five minutes, Uncle Rex had exposed more emotion than in the past thirty-six years combined. It left Dave unsure of how to respond. He felt like he should offer something to restore Rex to some kind of balance. The words were out before he realized he had said them.

"Maybe I'll hunt down Hensley."

Rex's expression as he glanced up from his coffee was an improbable mixture of doubt and hope.

CHAPTER 4

Dave and Uncle Rex parted in the Emerald parking lot with another uncharacteristic hug, and Dave pointed the Z-51 toward downtown. He was in need of serious decompression. Twenty minutes of cathartic driving later, he valeted the 'vette in front of Amicus Curiae, a bar on Colorado Street near the capitol. Inside, he took a seat at the end of the bar facing the door. The place was packed with judges, attorneys, clerks, and other nefarious types associated with the law.

He decided to start at the top and work his way down. He ordered the Talisker 25-year-old. As the bartender slid the stool over to reach the bottle, Dave texted Angela Martini, an assistant district attorney, inviting her to join him for drinks and possibilities. She lived ten blocks away in the 360 Condominiums.

The bartender set the scotch in front of Dave without a word. Dave used a straw as a pipette to transfer a few drops of water to the tumbler, inhaled the peaty aroma, and took his first taste. A memory rushed in with the vapors, a vision of the night Uncle Rex introduced him to scotch. The old Uncle Rex, the one who had never second-guessed anything in his life.

The stories Mom had told him around a fire in Angola of the family that she had left behind had seemed more like fairy tales than history. Stories of her younger brother, Rex, who was only ten when she married Dad, and how thirteen years later he took on the management of the Stone estate and reversed its decades-old decline.

Or her own story, the trust-fund baby who met an idealistic medical student working his way through school, who hid their marriage from her parents until she had control of her trust fund, who refused Stone charity when the clinic and poor investments drained their capital.

Even after Dad died, when Rex tried to rescue them, Mom had refused both the cash and the trust fund he had proposed as a compromise. She relaxed her stance of independence only once, to allow Rex to sponsor Dave at Warfield Hall, the family prep school alma mater.

In the following years, she must have regretted that concession. It had placed Dave in the heart of Stone territory at an impressionable age. The transition from uncle to mentor was as gradual and inevitable as a glacier transforming the landscape. Dave never returned to Angola.

He thought back through the conversation at dinner. Rex had greeted him as Dave but at the end had called him Davison. Rex hadn't called him that since Dad died thirty years ago. What did it mean? Again, he wondered what Rex had left unsaid in those long silences.

The promise to track down Hensley loomed before Dave like a panhandler with a "Will Work for Food" sign. He didn't know where to start or even want to start, for that matter, but he'd made the promise. Surely it could wait until he got his business started.

A hand on Dave's shoulder interrupted his thoughts. Angela slipped onto the stool next to him and caught the bartender's eye, but Dave spun her stool away from the bar and kissed her. It had been a long, frustrating day, and the one person in his life who could change that had arrived.

Angela laughed and pulled away. "Hey, I was ordering."

"We need to do something about your priorities."

She ordered a glass of pinot noir. "Speaking of priorities, have you found office space yet?"

After the scene with Rivera and the dinner with Rex, he'd forgotten about his financial inadequacies. He took another sip of whiskey and turned to the woman next to him.

Like his ex-wife, Angela was tall, almost as tall as his six feet, but with red hair styled to look all business in the courtroom and all woman after hours. Unlike Stephanie, Angela preferred older men.

She'd had a few bad experiences with men her age. Well, maybe that was something else she had in common with Stephanie.

"Time to start looking for change under the cushions."

She ran her fingernails through the short hair above his ear and around to his neck. "What are your options?"

Dave interlaced his fingers with hers and brought them back down to the bar. "Aside from the previously mentioned cushions? Recycling copper."

"What about your uncle? You want me to ask him for you? I can be very persuasive."

"I have no doubt, but that's not an option." The possibility hadn't even occurred to him. Obviously Rex would give him the cash in a nanosecond, and just as obviously, Dave wouldn't take it. Wouldn't even ask. Fletchers made it on their own, or they didn't make it.

Angela pulled her hand from his and turned back to her wine.

They had an on-and-off relationship. On when they first met, off when he discovered she was married. Yes, her husband was a philandering Neanderthal, but Dave would not stoop to poaching, regardless of how despicable her husband might be. Things had become somewhat serious, and it had cost Dave a few months of recovery when he called it off.

"I had a gun pointed at me today," Dave said.

"Dave!" She squeezed his arm. "How can you be so calm about it?"

Dave shrugged.

"Okay, be cavalier if you want, but I'm glad you only have a few more days." She sipped her wine, and then teased him with a sideways glance. "Did you cuff and book him?"

Dave shook his head. "I let him go. But I kept his gun."

"So you still have the handcuffs." She raised an eyebrow.

A smile slipped past his stoic nonchalance. A few years ago, Angela had appeared next to him at some fund-raiser, holding her drink in her left hand, her bare ring finger pointed at him like a sniper's scope. He had always appreciated her direct, no-games approach.

Soon they were on again, and it didn't take long to regain the lost ground. They were as steady as Dave was comfortable with, the arrangement he preferred after Stephanie left. In his estimation, law enforcement and marriage made a volatile potion that could explode at the most inopportune moment.

Angela broke the silence. "There's a long weekend coming up. My friend offered her house on St. Croix."

Dave studied her profile in the mirror behind the bar. They'd never done more than an occasional overnight trip. A weekend trip was an escalation of the rules of engagement. Dave's threat-level advisory climbed two notches from green to orange.

Angela leaned toward him. "With a private beach," she whispered. "And a hot tub."

As Dave considered the offer, he realized the old rules no longer applied. He had more than just a long weekend coming up; he had the rest of his life. And he could do worse than make Angela a part of it. In fact, it occurred to him that maybe that was what he wanted. He'd created a buffer to avoid repeating the past, but now that he was retiring, perhaps that was no longer necessary. The relief that seeped into his muscles surprised him.

But without a second career, it would be a life of eking it out on his retirement check. He wasn't willing to make the transition on those terms, to trade career tension for financial tension. "Can't," he said. "I have to find some capital to open the agency."

She met his eyes in the mirror. "Do it next week."

With considerable effort he shook his head. He didn't have the luxury of time. "The office space might not be available next week."

"This town is full of empty office space."

"Not like this one. All glass and steel and granite and fountains. Two blocks from the capitol, owner desperate for a tenant. He's going to cut somebody a deal, and I want it to be me."

A cold front crept across the bar. "Finding office space is more appealing to you than a weekend in the tropics with me?"

"Of course not. It's just a matter of timing." Dave mirrored her earlier gesture, brushing her hair behind her ear with his fingertips.

She picked up her wine glass. "You realize this is a one-time offer."

Dave took a deep breath. There would be other long weekends, like Independence Day or Labor Day. And after he got the agency running, they could take any weekend they wanted. Right now he had a lot on his plate. Getting financing, closing on the office space, setting up phones, computers, and networks, advertising, building a client roster.

But Dave knew better than to get into all that. "It's only Tuesday. Maybe I can get something going before the weekend."

Angela responded with a doubtful expression.

Dave nudged her. "Maybe we should go somewhere private and you can try to talk me into it."

She smiled.

"Plus, I've never been to the Virgin Islands. What should I pack?"

"Nothing," she whispered.

Dave took Angela's glass from her hand and finished off the wine. Then he leaned in toward her. "You want to come help me pack?"

CHAPTER 5

The gate opened as Dave approached his house in Lakeway. He whipped the 'vette into the two-car garage, leaving space for Angela to pull in her Lexus. She met him at the utility room door with a small overnight case.

Dave crossed the utility room, turned on the kitchen light, and held the door open. Angela entered and stopped, staring into the kitchen and blocking his path.

"Dave?" She stepped aside and he saw the room.

The kitchen was reduced to chaos, as if a sorcerer's apprentice had been called away suddenly in the midst of a particularly troublesome spell that had gone awry. He pushed past her and scanned the wreckage.

Dave held his finger to his lips and pulled Angela back into the utility room. Why hadn't the alarm system already brought the authorities? He glanced at the keypad by the door. No flashing lights.

As Dave attempted to decipher this new conundrum, a crashing noise came from beyond the kitchen.

"Stay here," he whispered.

Dave pulled the Glock 27 from his ankle holster, crept through the kitchen to the hallway, and peered to the left into the dining room. Nothing. He slipped noiselessly across the threshold and looked to the right into the den. Nothing.

He stepped to the left, intending to cross through the dining room toward the front entrance, when his feet tripped on something. He went down, sprawling on the floor. The gun clattered across the dining room, pinballing through chair legs.

He sat up and identified the cause of his fall, an olive-drab duffel bag. Dave got to his feet and inched his head around the corner. From behind the couch, backlit by the light above the wet bar, a head popped up. A large head with shaggy hair jutting out from under a tight-fitting cloth cap. Dave's pulse quickened. He scanned the room for something he could use as a weapon.

Then the head spoke. "Buckaroo! The hour produces the man!"

Only one person called Dave "buckaroo." From a long time ago. But it couldn't possibly be him.

The figure stood. It wore a long, white woolen shirt partially covered by a robe made of vertical strips of coarse brown-and-ochre cloth. The robe was secured with a long sash that trailed from the hip.

The figure held an ice bucket in one hand and a cocktail shaker in the other. "Fancy a martini?"

Dave approached cautiously, squinting. "Hensley?"

"In the flesh, as usual!"

A wave of relief and confusion coursed through Dave's limbic system. "What are you doing here?"

Hensley nodded. "Right, then, I'll just fetch some fresh ice." He skirted the couch, kicking aside stray ice cubes.

Seeing Hensley here, in his home, nonchalantly reducing it to a federal disaster area, affected Dave like the arrival of a dozen Vaneks. His right hand twitched into a fist. He longed to squeeze the ice bucket onto Hensley's head like a catcher's mask, but through the fading adrenaline rush he remembered Angela was present. "How did you get in?"

"Come on, Davison. Since when has a lock kept me out of anything?"

"The security system?"

Hensley snorted as he disappeared into the kitchen, then popped his head back out. "By the way, dinner's on you. Edamame salad, filet mignon, chicken Diane, lobster, butter sauce, grilled vegetable medley, bananas foster." He popped back into the kitchen. The sounds of ice rattling into the bucket flowed from ground zero.

The pan-European accent Dave remembered from Mom's funeral had intensified. Mainly British with flourishes of other accents tossed in to make it difficult to pinpoint a specific region. And what was with the gourmet chef impersonation? Dave retrieved his gun from under the dining room table and did a quick reconnaissance of the den. Hensley had set up camp. Clothes, dishes, blankets, pillows, TV on mute showing a Knight Rider rerun. He appeared to be here for the duration. But why?

What were the odds that he would agree to track down Hensley and a few hours later find his prodigal brother in his own house? Evidently, Rex had left out a great many things during his cryptic conversation.

Hensley's voice boomed from the kitchen. "Hullo! Fancy a martini, love?"

Angela's voice answered. "Only if you're having one."

Hensley returned with an overflowing ice bucket, sloughing cubes like bread crumbs on the trail to the wicked witch's house. Angela followed him and stopped at the doorway.

As Hensley passed, Dave studied his outfit. The shirt hung past his waist, the robe down to his knees. Underneath he wore loose-fitting woolen pants tucked into high woolen boots decorated in a maroon, red, and green pattern and secured with blue lashings.

"Don't mind the mess," Hensley said. "I'll attend to it directly." He set the bucket on the bar and began pouring ingredients into the cocktail shaker.

Dave converged on Hensley and whispered, "What are you doing here?"

Hensley answered in his usual stentorian voice. "Do I need an excuse to visit my kid brother?" He dropped ice cubes into the shaker.

Dave studied him. Hensley had a face of the high-mileage variety, craggy and weather-beaten. Not quite to Keith Richards levels but a respectable effort. "When was the last time you visited?"

Hensley shook the martini vigorously, his jowls waggling from the effort. He had no trouble talking over the noise. "Mother's funeral."

"Fifteen years ago. And before then?"

"Father's funeral."

"Thirty years ago. And this time?"

Hensley didn't respond. Dave glanced at Angela. She took in Hensley in Sherpa drag whipping the cocktail shaker around and raised an eyebrow.

Hensley set down the shaker, which was rimed with a frosty coating, and rubbed his hands on his robe to warm them. He dumped the ice water from two martini glasses into the sink, dropped a spear of olives into each, and decanted the liquid. It swirled in the glasses, cloudy with air bubbles and ice particles.

"I found myself between engagements and at liberty to explore other pursuits," he said while setting the shaker aside. He sampled the concoction.

"So, what you're saying is, you're broke."

Hensley breathed out a sigh of satisfaction and lowered the martini. "As always, Buckaroo, you apprehend my circumstance precisely." He held the other martini to Angela. "For you, my dear. May you wear it in good health."

He inclined his head toward Dave. "You're off the clock. Dial it down a few notches and join the party. We're well stocked. I can mix another."

Angela grasped the handle of her overnight case with both hands in front of her like a schoolgirl, an image that would stick in Dave's mind for a long time. Especially since he was powerless to stop the inevitable.

She regarded the martini Hensley held out and shook her head. "I should be going. You guys have a lot of catching up to do."

"You have cut me to the quick," Hensley said, "and laid waste my foundations." He bowed deeply without spilling a drop of either drink. Then he held out the martini to Dave. "It's all yours, Buckaroo."

Dave ignored him and followed Angela to the utility room. "Can I come with you?"

Angela laid a hand on his chest. "That's your brother in there."

"But I like you better."

"You haven't seen him for how long?"

"Not long enough."

"He's family. If that doesn't matter to you, it should."

She kissed him, a kiss that held all the things that could have been but now were not to be. From the darkness of the garage, she spoke.

"Don't forget about St. Croix."

Dave turned back to the devastation of the kitchen. He would have that martini to build up his strength. Then he would have Hensley's gizzard on a spit. Then he'd have another martini to celebrate.

ACKNOWLEDGEMENTS

Thanks to Ross, Blake, and Adrian at Lamb's Automotive for classic car expertise; Lanny Hall, Joel Ayala, Mark Mynheir, and Larry Lynch for law enforcement expertise; Norman McCallum for poker choreography; critique groups NIP and El Gee for invaluable feedback on matters great and small; Daniel for intensive story development efforts; Robert Lambert and Michael Brack for architectural and structural expertise; Dangerous Dan for manic episode source material; Jonathan Levine and Sean O'Toole for money-laundering ideas; first readers Mark Spyrison, Kelly Brewer, Daniel Whittington, Sherry Williams, Paul Mooney, Jeremy Grigg, and The Woman for refining the polish; Darla Hightower for an eagle eye and a deft touch; Merle Bobzien for a quick proofread; Amanda Cobb for translating my incoherent ramblings into an excellent cover design

— BRAD WHITTINGTON —

BradWhittington.com

ABOUT THE AUTHOR

Brad Whittington was born in Fort Worth, Texas, on James Taylor's eighth birthday and Jack Kerouac's thirty-fourth birthday and is old enough to know better. He lives in Austin, Texas with The Woman. Previously he has been known to inhabit Hawaii, Ohio, South Carolina, Arizona, and Colorado, annoying people as a janitor, math teacher, field hand, computer programmer, brickyard worker, editor, resident Gentile in a Conservative synagogue, IT director, weed-cutter, and in a number of influential positions in other less notable professions. He is greatly loved and admired by all right-thinking citizens and enjoys a complete absence of cats and dogs at home.

BradWhittington.com

CPSIA information can be obtained
at www.ICGtesting.com
Printed in the USA
LVOW12s1629080217

523625LV00005B/1003/P